MW00478967

# Anneville Road

SARAH BRIDGES

Anneville Road is a work of historical fiction. Apart from the well-known actual people, events, and locales that figure into the narrative, all names, characters, places, and incidents are the product of the author's imagination or are used fictitiously. Any resemblance to current events or locales, or to living persons, is entirely coincidental.

Copyright © 2010  Sarah Bridges
All rights reserved.

ISBN:  1453634975
ISBN-13:  9781453634974

For Mom,
because you gave me roots.


For Dad,
because you gave me wings.


All my love,
and honor always.

So many times I begin to tell a story, glamorous and grand, intoxicating, beautiful, and so artfully delusional, one may forget and lose oneself in it. But as I sit here tonight, my pen gliding across the paper, I tell a different story. Maybe it is not as one might hope it would be, but as it is, even more intoxicating, even more beautiful. The players represent us all, each and every one, complete with tragedy as well as triumph, learning to soar with broken wings. I tell it because it overflows from my soul, escaping onto the paper, longing to be heard, born of the deep desire to share the raw beauty of emotions and moments spent in this beautiful and amazing place we call life. For life and the living of it is precious, made up of experiences and people unique and intriguing in their own right. Each and every path crossed lends reason to stop and reflect, to appreciate the lessons learned and feelings felt. Life is beautiful, a gift. It should be savored with every breath. It is a light that burns out in an instant, leaving those who loved us in a world that will never be as bright as while we were in it. And now, my story...

## Anneville Road...

DUST WAS FLYING. As her foot pressed harder and harder on the gas, she sped faster and faster down the narrow dirt road. The few cars that she met pulled over into the ditch to let her pass. Could they sense the desperation with which she traveled, or did they merely see her as a careless young woman in a fancy car, with absolutely no rural Texas road etiquette? The thought flickered through her mind like a faint light and was gone. Darkness again, and hunger. Sheer desperation was back. She had to get home, the last house down Anneville Road. She had to get there as fast as she could.

As she drove past the house and pulled into the driveway, she barely slowed down. Only when she saw Gram did the beating of her heart slow and her palms stop sweating. She shot out of her car and convulsed into tears, sobbing uncontrollably as Gram gathered her into her strong arms. They stood like that in the driveway for some time, Reid drowning in the intoxicating sweet smell of her grandmother. "Everything's all right, child. You're home, now. You're home."

# Reid

November 2009...

Maureen Coleman didn't know what was bothering her grand-daughter but she knew it had to be pretty bad to bring her home. Reid had gone and never looked back. She had hated the small Texas town of Kilroy. While the others had made the best of it, even done well, Reid had dreamed of nothing but leaving since she was old enough to dream.

Maureen remembered how, as a child, Reid would tell amazing make-believe stories about places she had been and people she had met with a faraway look in her eye. Such tall tales about strange people in strange places doing strange things... Maureen had wondered where she came up with it all. Sometimes, it worried her. But soon Maureen, as well as the others, stopped wondering and worrying. It all became "Reid." How different she was. How wonderful she was. How much they all loved her.

Maureen Coleman got up from the kitchen table and began to tidy up the old farmhouse. She decided she would just have to tell Bob the truth, and the truth was that she knew nothing. She had no idea why Reid had finally come home. She would wait. Reid would eventually tell her. Until then, Maureen would act as if everything was fine. She would do the only thing she could, pray that everything was all right and enjoy her beloved granddaughter.

Bob Coleman came in through the back door and entered the kitchen, quiet as a mouse. He carefully closed the door behind him so as not to make a sound. The lights were out throughout the house and it took a moment for his eyes to adjust. He noticed the television was on in the den. His heart skipped a beat. Reid... She was always just right there, memories so precious. His heart always dared to hope, no matter how much time had passed.

He remembered how, over the years, she would wait up for him in the den until she could no longer keep her eyes open. He would come in and find the television on. At some point she would have stumbled down the hall to her bed, and the next morning she would not remember how she got there. But it was impossible. He hadn't seen Reid in years. She was in New York, of course. If he turned it to World News, he might be able to catch her. "That's the only way you'll see her tonight," he told himself.

Still, it wasn't like Maureen to leave the television on. Maybe one of the kids had come home. He thought for a moment, but could not remember Maureen mentioning anything about anyone coming to stay. He made his way through the old farmhouse to the front door. He opened the door and looked out across the huge front porch. The bright moonlight illuminated the night with a silvery glow.

There it was in the driveway. He could hardly believe his eyes. The little black Mercedes convertible caused him to chuckle at how

4

out of place it looked sitting in the driveway of the old farmhouse. The fancy car was a huge contrast to the simplicity of the landscape, just like Reid. The corners of his mouth turned up slightly. The child of his heart had come home.

He made his way to the refrigerator. The house looked a little different. He laughed aloud. It always looked different when Reid was there. He adjusted the lighting so that it would not be so bright. He didn't want to wake Maureen, if he could help it. She would only scold him for coming in so late, and pout.

He was exhausted. Bob Coleman just wanted to eat, shower, and slip into bed beside his wife. He never grew tired of holding her in his arms. After so many years, he still never took her for granted. She would argue that for sure, but in his heart he knew his feelings for her had only grown stronger as the years passed by.

Upon opening the fridge, he discovered what Maureen and Reid had eaten for dinner. Reid's favorite. Maureen had made her vegetable soup, the one with the cream broth. In summer, she used fresh vegetables she had grown in her garden. In winter, she used what she had put up in the deep freezer from the summer before. Bob considered the scene. Gram had made vegetable soup for her baby. He could see it, just as he had seen it so many times over the years. Maureen would work diligently on her soup, standing at the stove, cutting, stirring, and tasting, while Reid sat on the counter entertaining her with all that was going on in her life.

His mind began to wander. His girls, all of them had sat on this very counter, bright eyed, while Maureen patiently listened to their stories. No doubt there were secrets told as well, but never in his presence. They were reserved for Maureen, and he preferred it that way. First there was Frankie, then Elise, and of course, Reid. Where had the time gone?

The leftovers were in the refrigerator, with a note:

*Waited up for you.*
*Serves you right if you can't get*
*out of bed in the morning.*
*Will you ever come to terms with being an old fart?*
*Wake me when you get in.*
*Reid*

She was impossible. He began to chuckle to himself at the prospect of those fancy New York City news folks hearing her say "old fart" while she was on television. "She's a mess," he whispered to himself.

Bob had worked into the night trying to get the hay put up in the barn. He was so tired, but it had to be finished. He heard a door open somewhere in the house. Maureen... I'm gonna' get it now, he thought. He turned, expecting to see his wife coming down the hall.

... Reid. He smiled. His eyes lit up. She made her way into the kitchen. She sat down beside him at the old clawfoot kitchen table, rubbing her eyes just like she did when she was a child. Her red curls were all over the place. He took note that, as usual, she had snatched the top to his pajamas so that, as usual, he would have to search out another clean pair. Bob Coleman's heart was warm at the sight of his granddaughter. Thirty-three years meant nothing; she was still his baby

"I thought it was over," she said. "I thought you finally died out there."

Bob Coleman chuckled. "I'm not that damn old yet," he teased her.

But as the words fell upon her ears, Reid was noticing how much older he looked. It unnerved her. She threw her arms around his neck. "Papa, I've missed you so much."

The stoic Bob Coleman felt his eyes begin to burn, tears welling. He fought them back. "Well, I've been right here." He spoke softly as Reid smiled through her tears.

Bob Coleman held his granddaughter tight. All that he had not allowed himself to feel for so long was upon him, and it frightened him. Reid... Elusive, dangerous, dangerous to his heart. He could not ever bear to lose her. She was the light in his life. They all were, all his girls, but none burned in his heart brighter than Reid.

Standing in the kitchen with her in the middle of the night, he admitted it hadn't always been easy. She hadn't been an easy child to raise. Stubborn, willful, at times impossible, but she was the product of a strong, loving, hardworking family all taking part in her upbringing. Looking back, sharing this life with her had been a joy.

A painful memory threatened, tugging at the corners of his mind. Her beginning. He dismissed it. Instead he would think of what a blessing she was, how wonderful she was, how a room came alive when she was in it, how much he loved her. He would not think about how different she was. He would not think about how out of place she had always been with her strange ideas, the pain it had caused over the years.

He got up with his dish and put it in the sink. He kissed his grand-daughter on the forehead. "Come on, let's go to bed." She followed him down the hall. He went to his room. She went to hers. Him, glad she was home. Her, glad to be home. He knew better than to ask why she had come. She wouldn't tell him anyway. What a mess she was! Even as a child she gave nothing of herself away, and yet she gave so much, so very much.

Bob showered, and dressed in a clean pair of pajamas. Then he settled into bed with his wife. How warm she was. He held her close and kissed her softly. She settled herself into his arms. Maureen had always slept so sound. Soon Bob was fast asleep as well, his heart full.

Reid burrowed deep into her covers. The quilt caressed her body with its warm familiarity. She slept sound for the first time in a long, long while.

She woke late. The sun was beaming full force into her old bedroom and she could not believe it had not awakened her before now. She sat up and took note of her room. Everything was in its place. She saw the big antique iron bed, and touched the beautiful patchwork quilt that had been given to her when she was just a child.

Her great grandmother had made it from old dresses she had worn, some of them dating back to the twenties and thirties. Reid remembered kicking around in the attic with Nana that day. She had been about six or seven years old. She remembered being delighted when they came across the old trunk full of dresses. Nana never threw anything away. This was one of the many things that Reid loved about her.

She ran her fingers over the quilt and remembered each story Nana had told her. There was a marvelous story for each patch on the quilt. Her great grandmother had seen the world go through so many changes. Reid looked around at the beautiful furniture that she had always known. Beautiful mahogany pieces that had been in her family for years, she enjoyed them now as so many others had before her.

The smell of breakfast cooking filled the room. She threw on a pair of jeans and a loose cotton peasant blouse from Mexico that was beautifully embellished with bright colored embroidery. The blouse was perfect for keeping secrets. She began to dig through her closet for her favorite pair of boots. Finally, she found them. She pulled them on, smiling. They felt like old friends, so thankful she was that Gram had never pitched them. Next she washed her face, brushed her teeth, and braided her long red hair. Then she was done.

She made her way down the hall and into the kitchen, where she found Gram. Papa was nowhere around. They guessed he had gone to finish up with the hay and then to feed the livestock. Reid looked around the sunny kitchen. Red gingham was all over the place, and farm animals. In a homely, outrageously distasteful sort of way, it was attractive. Or was it that it was simply familiar, and that's why she found it so appealing? Reid shoved some food in her mouth, drank a glass of orange juice, and kissed Gram on the forehead. She mumbled something about riding over to Nana's. Then she was out the back door.

Maureen opened the screen door that had just slammed shut and called after her, "Everyone's coming to dinner at five!"

Reid called back over her shoulder, "Okay, I won't be late!"

Maureen laughed out loud. "We'll see."

Reid would be late. There wasn't a doubt in her mind. Reid was always late, not because she was scatterbrained or self-absorbed, like so many who didn't really know her assumed. But because she got lost, lost in whatever she was doing, lost in the heady sensation of life. The rest of the world was of no consequence. That was just Reid.

She made her way down to the barn, half walking, half running. She entered Pandora's stall with a bridle in her hand. The horse smelled the familiar smell and her ears perked up. The soft voice began to speak. "Hello, girl. I sure am glad to see you." Reid put her face next to the horse's and began to nuzzle with her. The horse nuzzled back.

Reid put the bridle on the horse and led her out of the stall. The barn smelled of sweet hay. The scent reminded her of all the naps she had taken over the years, all the dreaming she had done, all the plans she had made, safe and sound, right there in the beautiful old barn. It felt so good to be home. She led Pandora out into the sunshine and the cool November morning. She climbed onto the horse's bare back. Saddles are so overrated, she thought. She loved the feel of sitting on Pandora's bare back. Riding in the tall grass, with the warm sun on her face and the wind in her hair, she became one with the horse. She became an extension of Pandora's grace and beauty.

They rode alongside the fence, the fence that separated the land she loved, the land she grew up on, from Anneville Road and the rest of the world. After riding a couple of miles, she came over a familiar hill and saw Nana's house. The cottage moved her. It called to her. Built of stone, the red and brown stone native to the area, with ivy clinging to it in the most charming way, Reid thought it was the perfect place for Nana to call home.

At forty-seven, she had lost her husband. It was then that Ellen Adams found herself unable to live in the house that she had lived in for most of her life, the home that she had made with Lloyd, where they raised their children, the very house he had died in. So it was settled. The house in town was sold. Annalyn had been only ten years old then. She was overjoyed to leave the big house behind. It spooked her since her father was gone. So Ellen built the little cottage on a patch of land just down from the farmhouse, where she could be close to her aging Mama and Papa.

She had maintained her little house all alone until last year, when Maureen had suggested that they hire someone to come in a few days a week to help her keep it up. For years, Maureen had suggested this, but Ellen finally conceded last year. Her age was beginning to catch up with her. She was approaching one hundred. Even so, her mind was still as sharp as a tack and Reid preferred her company to just about anyone else's.

Maureen had put an ad in the Kilroy paper, advertising for domestic help three days a week for four hours a day. In less than a week the position had been filled by a woman named Janie Aarington. She and her husband had just moved to Kilroy a few months earlier. This was not what Maureen initially had in mind. She had hoped to fill the position with someone who was from Kilroy. That way, the person would be able to provide good conversation in the form of community updates for her elderly mother. However, it was not to be.

Maureen had instructed Janie Aarington to meet at her mother's house, discuss what was needed, and see if things might work out. She explained that her mother was not the least bit interested in any sort of help with her housekeeping, but she simply could not do it all any longer. Janie said that she understood and would meet them at the house later that afternoon.

Janie followed the directions that Maureen Coleman had given her. "I've never been out this way before," she said to herself. She had been given a description of the cottage and told that it was the next to last house on Anneville Road. "This is in the middle of nowhere," she grumbled. To find it, one had to take an old farm to market road five miles from the tiny town of Kilroy, turn onto Anneville Road, and then travel another four miles through the rural Texas countryside. It seemed so remote.

Finally, Janie Aarington drove into the driveway. She parked her car in front of the house, scurried up the steps, and rang the doorbell. The occupant that lives here definitely has a gift for gardening, she decided. Rose bushes grew along the iron fence, but there were no roses, for it was November. She imagined how beautiful they would be, come spring.

An older woman dressed in a mauve sweater and matching pants opened the door. She had grey hair, pulled back and secured with a jeweled barrette, and the most amazing pale blue eyes that Janie had ever seen. Her smile was warm and friendly. Janie decided she must have been quite beautiful when she was young, for even now, despite age, she was still very attractive. There was something warm about her. Janie liked her immediately.

She invited Janie in and introduced herself. "Hello, I'm Maureen. Come right in here."

The two women walked into the den, where Ellen was waiting. "Janie Aarington, this is my mother, Ellen Adams."

Janie could tell that the woman was not too thrilled about the prospect of anyone helping with her housework. Ellen got right to the point. "Where are you from and how long have you lived here?" Leave it to Mother to be direct, Maureen thought.

"Oh, I'm from Dallas. My husband is Edward Aarington. Do you know him? He says he remembers y'all. His mother passed on back in August and left us her place. We moved out here to retire and take over her place."

Ellen nodded her regal head and took note. Edward Aarington had been gone from Kilroy for over thirty years, and his wife was not originally from Kilroy. The "place" she referred to was the old Aarington farm across the river bridge. Ellen knew the land well. "The Aaringtons used to grow cotton. My father picked there awhile," she told Janie. Then she explained that she did not need help with the cooking. She was perfectly able to cook for herself and anyone else that might show up. She just needed help with things like the dusting and vacuuming, so that she would have more energy to do the things she enjoyed, like cooking and gardening. Janie said that she understood very well and that it all sounded perfect to her. She announced that she wasn't a very good cook anyway. Ellen and Maureen laughed. Ellen asked her if she would be able to start on Monday. She said that would be fine. Then she was gone.

Maureen stayed to visit with her mother a little while longer, to clear her breakfast dishes away and tidy up a bit. When she finished cleaning up the familiar kitchen, she joined her mother in the den. Ellen was sitting in her rocker with her dog curled up on her lap, a tiny Bichon Frise that had been a gift from Reid. Maureen studied her mother. She hadn't even noticed the beautiful pant suit that her mother was wearing. It was black, and she had gotten out her pearls. She watched her mother. Ellen was rocking, thinking.

"What's on your mind, Mother?" Maureen finally asked her.

"I think she'll do quite nicely, and it appeals to me that she's not from here. Her husband's been gone for over thirty years. I can't tell you how the thought of spending my morning surrounded by idle gossip repulsed me. I should like to know all about her family, you know, where she comes from, where she's been. Everyone has a story, some more colorful than others, but everyone somewhere inside has a glorious story to tell." She smiled at her daughter. "I should like to hear hers."

Maureen could not help but smile back. Once again, she had second guessed her mother and been wrong. She had never expected her mother to accept any domestic help. Ellen had always been a strong woman, fiercely independent, but she was willing to give Janie a chance.

Before anyone even realized it, a year had passed. Janie and Ellen had become "as thick as thieves," often getting themselves into precarious situations with their town excursions. But today Janie was at home. She had company coming, relations from Dallas. And Ellen was sitting in her chair, reading the newspaper, with a cup of hot coffee.

Reid tied Pandora to a large oak tree in the yard and clamored up the steps. She rang the doorbell. She was so excited. She could hardly keep still. Finally, after what seemed an eternity, she heard footsteps. Then she heard the familiar voice calling.

"Who is it?"

"Nana, it's Reid."

The door flew open. Ellen stood there in the doorway staring at her great granddaughter in disbelief. Reid flung open the screen door that separated them and threw her arms around her great grandmother. They stood there in the doorway with their arms around each other until they both began to laugh. Then together they walked into the house, arm in arm, not letting go, not even for a second.

They made their way through the house, Ellen chattering while Reid took it all in. Nothing had changed. Relief. This was what she needed, what she craved. The hardwood floors with soft worn rugs on them, beautiful family pictures on the walls... She felt warm inside. It was finally reality. She was home.

Ellen sat down in her rocker. Reid sat down on the floor at her great grandmother's feet and laid her head on the old woman's lap. Ellen began to stroke the soft red curls that escaped her long braid, and finally Reid began to speak, to really speak.

The whole story began to pour out along with a river of tears. Reid was in love. And it was serious, Ellen could tell. Reid had never been one to have many boyfriends. Growing up, she was not ever really interested in boys. There were always so many other things occupying her mind. She dreamed of traveling all over the world, places that never appealed to Ellen. In fact, places she had never even heard of were constantly finding their way into conversations that she had with Reid. She could only imagine what the child would do with herself when she came of age. She imagined her as some vaga-bond gypsy, with that wild red hair and those piercing grey eyes, constantly on the move.

But there had been another side to Reid. It was the unsure side, the side that was a product of her being spoiled, coddled, and pro-tected so fiercely by her family. That was the side that concerned Ellen. She was afraid it would hold her back.

She remembered when Reid was seven years old. Elise, her mother, had given her a little brown cocker spaniel. Reid named him Smooches because he was constantly kissing her on the mouth. The mere thought of this caused Ellen to clench her lips together. Reid had loved the dog beyond measure, as all children love their pets. But the dog had come up missing, and Reid was in a frenzy.

She would take the bus home from school every day, and Ellen would meet her at the road. It was a constant source of embarrassment for Reid. She was teased mercilessly by the older kids on the bus because her great grandmother waited for her every day. But she would not tell Nana; she would never tell Nana. Reid knew how much her great grandmother looked forward to seeing her get off the bus each day, and she just couldn't bear to take that away from her.

From the time she got off the bus until her mother came to pick her up in the evening, she would look for that dog. After four days, Ellen couldn't stand it any longer. She found Reid outside calling for Smooches, her voice hoarse from screaming his name. She came straight out with it, "Reid, he's dead. He was run over by a car. I'm sorry."

Tears began to fall from the little girl's eyes, streaking her dirty face. "How do you know?"

"Your grandfather found him on the road but didn't want to tell you because he didn't want to upset you."

Reid may have been only seven years old, but she understood. Nana never even had to explain. Reid knew she couldn't stand to see her search for something that she would never find, even if it hurt like hell. Her grandfather, on the other hand, was a different story. He would be content to watch her go through life wondering what had happened to her dog, never knowing the truth, if it meant that he could keep her from being hurt. Reid never mentioned the truth about the dog to anyone. She just merely stopped looking. She never even told Nana thank you. She didn't have to.

Now, Ellen looked at her great granddaughter. She was seven years old all over again.

"Nana, I'm so afraid of what he will say and do. I don't want to lose my family, but I cannot even bear the thought of a life without Reagan, and I cannot hide it any longer." Then it came, a whisper, "I'm pregnant."

Reid rested her head on her great grandmother's lap again. Ellen was silent. The longer she sat listening to Reid cry, the more rage she felt. The crime that had been committed against Reid was unfathomable, and Ellen had watched it for far too long.

She stroked her great granddaughter's hair, wishing that things were different. But they were not. The famous Reid Coleman, World News reporter that the entire world had fallen in love with, was crying her eyes out in her great grandmother's lap, right here, right now. And it was ridiculous, for she was a grown woman.

Reid had traveled all over the world in a desperate attempt to right some of the world's most horrifying wrongs, fearlessly. And yet in one fell swoop, she could lose their approval forever. Even though she had grown up, even though she had gone far, far away, she was still their Reid, and subject to their rules. She might as well have been seven years old all over again.

The seriousness of the situation was upon Ellen and she considered the effect it would have on her family. ...Her family, the one she had spent her entire life building, protecting, the very one she had devoted her whole life to. Ellen Adams had sacrificed much over the years in the name of family, and as a result it had grown strong and magnificent like the oaks that lined the driveway of the old farmhouse. She was not looking forward to this battle even though she had always known that it would come, somehow, someway. Even though she knew that in time they would emerge stronger, better, she was concerned about what would come to pass between now and then.

Nothing truly frightened her though. She was almost a century old and she had been through much in her lifetime. Born in 1910, she had seen the world go through so many changes. She held fast to her convictions. "One gets through life with family, and families must grow and become stronger if they are to survive, just like every other living thing," she said. She had learned that family was a precious gift from the Creator, a gift that offered a peek at how magnificent true love can really be. And after nearly a hundred years of walking in this world, Ellen had experienced profound joy as well as great sorrow, a direct result of both love and family. But nothing truly frightened her anymore, not even this.

She began to sort out the details of all that Reid had offered. Precious Reid, they all loved her so. But how would her choices affect that? Ellen felt a strong need to protect her. She would do everything she could to defend her. Ellen Adams could already feel her claws coming out. She considered the irony. She would have to protect her from the one that loved her more than anything. Perhaps that was the problem.

She took her great granddaughter's face in her hands and spoke to her in a deliberate manner, the strength and wisdom that had been acquired with years present in every syllable, "Does this man deserve you?" There were tears in her old eyes.

Reid nodded.

Ellen looked her straight in the eye. "With all that you have to offer, your most precious gifts, your heart, your body, your life, does he deserve that? Does he really?"

Reid looked back at her great grandmother. "Yes."

She felt Nana kiss her on the cheek and let her face go. "Then so be it."

They sat there for awhile. Nana stroked Reid's soft hair, considering her, loving her. "Reid, you know how your grandfather feels. I've never understood it. But you know he would rather never see you again than see you with a colored man." She continued as the

17

tears ran down Reid's face, "We will get through this. You know we will get through this. It may be a bumpy ride, but I'm telling you we will get through this. One thing you need to remember is that your grandfather loves you. Whatever happens, whatever is said to you, about you, or in front of you, is only in response to an intense love for you. Fear will come from this, all out of ignorance. It's the kind of fear that you and I don't even recognize, because we don't even know what it looks like. It may not seem like it for awhile, but don't forget that your grandfather loves you very much. We all do."

"I know."

"Then you must remember this, darling. I'm tough, and in almost a hundred years I've never backed down." They both began to laugh despite the seriousness of the situation.

Reid pulled herself together, and rose. They linked arm in arm and made their way out of the den, down the hallway, through the sunny kitchen, out the back door, and into the morning sunlight. Reid was so relieved that Nana knew her secret.

She gasped when she saw the backyard. It was amazing. Ellen explained that Janie had taken over much of the housework, leaving her with plenty of time to work in the yard.

Reid remembered seeing Nana garden all her life, and no matter how hot it was she always wore a wide brimmed straw hat and long sleeves. Reid looked at her great grandmother's face, at her beautiful skin. She decided it had paid off. Despite her age, Nana's skin was beautiful. Of course, it was wrinkled, but in a lovely way. And Reid had always loved her eyes. They were blue, so blue she had never seen anything like them. Except for Gram, Gram had those eyes. She remembered being a child and hearing Nana refer to her hair as "grey." She had asked her, "Nana, why do you call your hair grey? It's not grey. It's silvery white, like sparkling silver."

Just then Reid's attention was diverted to the sound of water. The little fountain that she had sent Nana from Spain looked so charming in the corner of the yard. Everywhere Reid went, whether she was on assignment or vacation, she always sent her something. Reid made her way over to it. She noticed the brightly colored goldfish swimming in the water at the base of the fountain. She clapped her hands and squealed with delight, "How smart you are, Nana. I never would have thought of that."

"I cannot take the credit," Ellen admitted with a shake of her head. "It was the plotting and scheming of those little cousins of yours."

"Aaron and Ryan?"

"Yes."

"Oh, I can't wait to see them. They won't even know me, but I'm going to smother them with hugs and kisses anyway."

"That's what you think," Ellen laughed. "They'll probably have you tied up before you can say hello. Your Uncle Bobby called last week and asked if they could spend the morning with me because he had some errands to run. Karen had something to do as well. I said I'd be delighted to have them. Janie was here to help me. What a day that was! They found a beehive, covered themselves with honey, got stung about six times each, let two cows out that made it all the way down to the highway, and carried these goldfish from your grandfather's pond over here to put them in my fountain, all before lunchtime."

"Did you paddle them?" Reid remembered all the times that Nana had threatened to paddle her over the years, but never had.

"Of course, not. It was great fun! I was exhausted by the time Bobby came to get those boys."

Reid could tell that Nana had enjoyed that day immensely. They sat in the garden for a few hours catching up on all that had been going on in each other's life. The age difference always seemed to pass away when they were together. They talked on without a moment of hesitation, darting back and forth between subjects. Finally their stomachs began to remind them that they had missed lunch. "I can't ignore it any longer," Reid told her. "I'm starving."

There was so much Ellen wanted to ask, so much she wanted to say. But not now. The time would come. It was obvious that Reid had come home for many reasons, some she probably didn't even recognize yet. Right now, one was obvious. She wanted to be a child again, for very soon she would be one no longer.

Ellen told Reid that she had left over roast beef and gravy in the fridge. Before she could tell her that it was cooked with carrots and potatoes Reid had taken off. By the time Ellen made her way into the kitchen, Reid was warming the food. Then she was on to pouring herself a big glass of sweet iced tea. Ellen sat down at the table in the sunny yellow kitchen and teased her great granddaughter. "Child, you are a savage!" Reid was glowing. Her heart was smiling, as was Ellen's, each woman lost in her own thoughts. ...It's so good to be home. ...I'm so glad she's home.

Ellen was always so interested to hear about Reid's assignments. As the face of the biggest news network on the planet, Reid had seen much. Her stories were fascinating, and the life that she lived in New York seemed so foreign. Ellen was so happy to be sharing stories with her beloved great granddaughter, so incredibly thankful to be sitting across the little table from her, eating left over roast beef and gravy. They hadn't seen each other in years. Of course, they spoke on the telephone often. But still, there was no comparison to sitting across from each other, being able to see each other, tasting the same food, smelling the same smells.

"Now, tell me all about Reagan."

Reid began to tell their story, how they had met at a dinner party hosted by a mutual friend. It had been a celebration in honor of wrapping up a big story for World magazine. They had featured the orphan crisis in Romania. Her mood suddenly became dark and serious. She educated Nana on the conditions there and explained what she had seen. Some of the children were naked because there were no clothes for them. Infants lay in cribs without mattresses, with blank stares on their faces. They had learned that, despite their cries, there was no one to pick them up. They didn't even notice anymore. And Reid told her that those were the more fortunate ones. She had seen hundreds of children living in the streets, scavenging in garbage cans for food. Ellen could not imagine how Reid could bear the scene, but that is what set her apart. She longed to experience life, all aspects of it, even if it hurt, in a desperate attempt to change it, to make it better. This, alone, was enough to keep her from fitting in, and it was precisely why Kilroy had not been kind to her.

Reid told Ellen about the party, about how she met Reagan. World boasted a global news network and magazine. He was the Editor-in-Chief for World magazine. Upon studying the information that she had gathered, and ultimately pouring over the story that she had pulled together in Romania, he decided he had to meet her. The passion in her story and the research she had done were amazing. She had searched out the families that had abandoned the children and presented their stories as well. It was amazing. She was brilliant. She had successfully done what few could do, what only the greats could do. "She makes you want to do something, to get up off your couch and do something," he had said.

They were introduced by Carson, the photographer that traveled with Reid and covered the story with her in Romania. They were drawn to each other immediately. They talked nonstop until dawn. (Ellen could not imagine a dinner party going on until the sun came up, but Reid assured her it happened all the time in New York.) Their conversations went back and forth between the different stories that they had both worked on. They had similar views on a lot of things. The issues that they disagreed on, they discussed for hours. Reagan was blown away by her. He held his own strong views. He was an educated man, well read. Reid was just as opinionated, but most of her views came from seeing the world. She had lived it.

They shared a cab home and discovered that they only lived a couple of blocks away from each other. They exchanged numbers. Reid eagerly accepted his invitation for dinner the very next weekend. That was the beginning.

She could hardly get through the week. The anticipation was driving her crazy. Work did not prove to be a diversion either. Since she had just successfully completed a huge assignment, she was in limbo, waiting for word on what would be next. Finally, on Thursday night, Reagan called to confirm. After discussing the possibilities for dinner, they settled on cooking at his apartment. He would be in charge of the main course. Reid would prepare the salad at his house and pick up a loaf of fresh bread on her way. It was settled. Neither one of them could wait until Saturday. So it was to be the very next evening, Friday, at seven o'clock.

Reid packed up all the salad fixings in a shopping bag. She had some fresh romaine lettuce, beautiful radishes, tomatoes, cucumbers, some wild field greens and mushrooms, as well as all the ingredients for a spicy vinaigrette dressing that she hoped he would like. She thought about hailing a cab. After all, she had to carry the bag. And at this time of year, early October, there was a piercing chill in the night air. She rarely used her car. She thought about Texas, how one could not function without a car. Everything was spread so far out, and in most places there was no form of public transportation. It was totally different in New York. She needed a car; she made frequent weekend trips to visit friends who did not live in the city. However, as far as the city was concerned, a car was a hindrance. There was no parking anywhere, in the whole silly city, so there was no sense in even getting her car out of the parking garage that she kept it in most of the time.

She decided to walk. She would stop by her favorite bakery on the way and pick up the bread. As she walked down Mac Dougal, she anticipated the evening. The cool night air made her feel alive. She drew it into her lungs. It was crisp. It felt good. Finally, she came to the address. She went inside the building, and up the stairs to find his apartment. Something smelled fantastic. She took a deep breath and knocked on the door. After a few seconds, she heard footsteps.

Reagan opened the door and saw her wrapped up in an old woolen scarf, wearing a black pea coat, looking like the most beautiful bag lady he had ever seen. They both smiled. He invited her in, and directed her to the kitchen. She put her bags on the counter, then proceeded to unwrap the scarlet scarf and take off the coat. Reagan took them from her and said he would hang them up. He disappeared for a moment while Reid studied his apartment.

His taste was impeccable. He, like her, had many books. They were all neatly displayed on heavy, intricately carved mahogany book cases. His furniture was simple, worn leather couches and a big oversized chair that looked so incredibly cozy that she thought she might try it. She plopped down in it and sat back. He had lots of pictures around. She wondered who was family, who was friend. It was a masculine apartment, with rustic iron candle holders and some amazing paintings on the walls. She felt comfortable. She felt at ease.

Soon Reagan returned from what she assumed was his bedroom. She watched him as he came down the hall. He was so handsome. He was wearing a camel colored turtleneck sweater with a worn pair of jeans and a comfy pair of hand stitched loafers. The contrast of the light colored sweater with his brown skin was incredible. He was clean shaven, and Reid thought his face was beautiful. His features were perfect. She looked at his eyes. They were so dark. She began to blush. He was staring at her.

Reagan looked at Reid. He thought she was gorgeous. She wore a dark grey cable knit sweater, faded Levis, and black cowboy boots. Wingtips. Her long curly red hair was pulled back in a loose pony tail at the base of her neck, making him more aware of her beautiful face. He noticed that her jewelry was very simple, but at the same time dazzling. Just earrings, diamonds. She did not wear a lot of makeup. She didn't need to.

Reagan broke the silence. "Did you have any problems finding the apartment?"

"No, and I can't believe how close you live to me."

"I know. It's a crazy coincidence, isn't it?" They both smiled.

"What are you making for dinner that smells so incredible?"

"My famous mushroom ravioli," he told her. "I hope you like mushrooms. I didn't even think to ask you."

Reid said she loved mushrooms. She announced that she needed to throw the salad together. Reagan showed her where to find everything in the kitchen. They talked, as she washed, chopped, and prepared the salad. Reagan was glad she was so comfortable in his apartment. She had a quiet confidence about her that he appreciated. He hoped she did not sense that he was a little nervous. She had that effect on him. Usually so sure of himself, he couldn't believe that she could make him feel this way. She finished the salad and placed it on the table.

He put the main course on the table and checked the bread in the oven. It was warm again, so he removed it. He opened a bottle of white wine and poured two glasses. They sat down at the table.

"This seems so formal and I feel so comfortable with you. Let's go into the den." He cleared off the coffee table and put some oversized cushions on the floor. He adjusted the volume of the music. Tracy Chapman, Fast Car... Reid hadn't heard the song in so long, and it was one of her favorites.

The conversation was good. It was easy. Both of them noticed that there was never an uncomfortable silence. Topics flowed from one to another. They learned much about each other. Their families were as different as night and day.

His family was well educated. His mother was a doctor, specializing in oncology. His father was a professor at Columbia University, teaching economics. Both of his parents were Haitian. This interested Reid more than anything else that he told her. She had been to Haiti in 2004, covering hurricane Jeanne. She had fallen in love with the country, with the people, and had longed to go back ever since then. She wanted to know how often he visited Haiti, how his family came to live in the United States, and what he thought about the political fiascos that had affected the country for so long.

He was slightly embarrassed. He had to admit that he knew very little about Haiti. "I've heard stories about the country for as long as I can remember, and you would think that since current events and world affairs are my business, how I make my living, that I would know more about it. But I've never really thought too much about Haiti. My sisters, my brother, and I never really identified with the country. My mother tried to teach us French and Creole when we were children, but we thought it sounded funny. And when she spoke it around our friends, it embarrassed us." He laughed at the memory of it. He told her that he had two sisters and one brother. He was the youngest.

Reid told him all about her family, about growing up in Texas. She told him about her decision to come to New York, to attend NYU, how it had upset her family so much.

Dinner passed quickly. They were finishing the second bottle of wine when Reid noticed the time. It was one o'clock in the morning. She felt embarrassed. What if Reagan was ready for her to go?

"I'm so sorry. I had no idea it was getting so late."

She stood up and was about to announce that she should go, but Reagan took her hand and pulled her to close to him. She could smell his skin. He smelled so good.

"Please, don't go. I cannot even begin to tell you how much I am enjoying this."

Reid looked him in the eye. Her gaze was startling, mesmerizing. "I know. I feel the same way, and I think that is the very reason I should leave."

She caught him off guard. She was so open, so honest. He liked this about her. He asked her to stay the night. He said he would act like a perfect gentleman. Anything, he would do anything. He just could not stand for her to leave.

"I can hear four generations of women telling me how incredibly inappropriate this is, but I can't bear the thought of leaving right now. I'm enjoying this way too much."

They sat down on the couch together and began discussing work, what they would each be doing for the next couple of weeks. Reid began to yawn. Reagan kissed her as soon as her mouth closed. She kissed him back. He got up and turned off all the lights. Only the dying candles illuminated the room. He lay down on the oversized couch. She settled into the crook of his arm. He held her until they both fell asleep. The bedroom was too dangerous. What they had was too special.

From that night on, they were inseparable. Days quickly ran into weeks, weeks into months. From quiet dinners to loud concerts, they wanted to experience everything together. Reagan couldn't wait to introduce her to his family. He knew they would love her.

He invited her to spend New Year's Eve with him, at his parent's house. They had a party every year. She agreed and was looking forward to it. But when the time actually came, she began to get nervous. This was important to her. It was important to her that Reagan's family like her. Approval was something that she had stopped searching for a long, long time ago. But this was different. She cared so much for Reagan. She wanted everything to go well.

Reid chose what she would wear very carefully. It had to be something simple. This would be their first impression of her, and she wanted it to be a good one. She chose a long sleeved vintage Dior gown of jet black velvet. It had a high neck that accentuated her own long graceful neck. It was fitted so that it showed off her slim figure, and flowed all the way down to her ankles. It was perfect. She piled her red mane on top of her head, and finished it all off with an antique pair of garnet chandelier earrings and matching garnet bracelet. Reagan could not believe his eyes. He also could not believe that she was ready. She was late everywhere they went. He thought about this and guessed she must be nervous. He kissed the back of her neck and told her that she looked beautiful. She grabbed her little black bag, and they made their way down to the car.

Reid was quiet. Seeing Reagan in his perfectly tailored black suit took her breath away. She ran her hand over his back, feeling the contours of his body under the suit jacket. He was such a handsome man and she loved him so very much. People on the street stopped to stare as he opened the passenger door to his Range Rover and gently helped her inside. They made a striking couple.

The hour long drive to his parent's house gave Reid time to relax. She wished they were making the drive in daylight, so that she could see outside. The New Jersey countryside sometimes reminded her of home. The large old homes and property were such a sharp contrast to the cramped spaces of the city.

They finally pulled into the driveway, and Reid fell in love with the house. It was an old two story red brick home, with two big white pillars in front. It was stately and elegant. They pulled into the circle driveway and parked. Reagan got out and went around to her side. He opened the door for her and helped her step out.

They made their way up the steps, and to the front door. Reagan rang the bell. Reid could hear voices growing louder, as figures seemed to grow closer through the beveled glass in the door. There were lights all over the house. It was beautiful. A pleasant man greeted them. Reagan did not know him. He introduced himself as Dr. Charles Worley, a friend of Reagan's parents. Reagan introduced himself, then Reid. They all shook hands. Dr. Worley recognized Reid from television. She blushed.

They made their way down the hall and into an old-fashioned parlor type room. It was filled with people. Someone was playing the baby grand piano, and singing a Nat King Cole song. There was a lot of laughter amid the tinkling of glasses, and interesting conversations were going on. Reagan saw his mother first. He took Reid by the hand and made his way through the room.

Reid looked in the direction they were heading and saw the woman that she knew had to be Reagan's mother. Her eyes were happy at the sight of her youngest son. She immediately withdrew from the conversation that she had been engaged in. "Excuse me, I see my son approaching." She opened her arms. She and Reagan shared a warm hug.

"You're late." She narrowed her eyes at him.

"Mom, this is Reid." He introduced the two of them. "Reid, this is the woman that made me miserable until I was eighteen, my mother, Margaret Jacques."

"My dear, I can say the feeling is quite mutual. However, you can be sure it was him that drove me completely crazy." She embraced

Reid and gave her a sweet kiss on the cheek. Reid was no longer nervous. Reagan was right. This would not be difficult.

Reid noticed that Reagan looked quite a bit like his mother. She was very attractive. Reid knew that she must be at least sixty, but she did not look it at all. She had the same perfect features that Reagan had, only hers were softer, more feminine. She was sophisticated and extremely well spoken, but sincere. Reid liked her immediately.

Margaret saw her husband across the room and led them away. Reagan gave his dad a big hug and introduced Reid. Pierre Jacques was a quiet man, but very sweet and likable. He was a little shorter than his wife, but they fit together well.

The party was amazing. There were all different kinds of people there, from starving artists to gallery owners. There were professors of music and drama, as well as poets that could not pay their rent. There were medical directors of prestigious hospitals, as well as foreign doctors that traded their services for a meal. The Jacques family was beloved by all. Reid could see why. She was having a great time.

As it got closer to midnight, Reagan pulled her away to the bar, where he got them two glasses of champagne. "Why aren't your sisters and brother here?" Reid asked him.

"This has been going on for as long as I can remember. We all do our own thing on New Year's Eve, now. I only came this year because I wanted you to meet my parents."

"There is something I want to show you." Reagan took her hand and led her through the crowded room, pausing to greet people and make introductions. It seemed as if everyone wanted to meet the stunning couple. "Who are they?" they wanted to know. But Reid and Reagan didn't even notice. They only had eyes for each other.

Finally, they emerged from the crowd and the noise, and disappeared down a hallway. Reagan opened a heavy wooden door to an elegant room. Reid was fascinated. She walked around the room, looking at the titles of the literature that lined the walls on beautifully hand carved bookshelves. She felt Reagan's breath on her neck, and the heat of his body behind her. He pulled her close to him, and kissed the back of her neck. She felt weak as he unzipped her dress, trailing kisses down her back. He turned her to face him and kissed her all over, as the beautiful black gown fell to a heap at her feet. She began to undress him as he kissed her even more deeply.

They made love on the floor of the magnificent library. Reagan, usually so controlled, was unable to control himself when it came to her. He was in love. He was gone, could think of nothing else. He had found what he had long since given up on, and he never wanted to be without her as long as he lived.

In the dimly lit room, as they made love, he put a diamond band on the ring finger of her left hand. "This is what I wanted to show you. Please, say you'll marry me."

Reid pulled him down to her, and said all that he'd hoped to hear since the night that he met her. "Reagan, I would have no one else."

Reid's love and desire for him made her weak. The intensity of her passion made her feel as if she were occupying a dream. They lay on the floor of the library. Reagan took a soft woolen throw from the couch and covered them. Totally naked, dozing in Reagan's arms, Reid knew she never wanted to be without him. She never expected to find what she had found in him. She didn't even know it could exist.

Reid had been in love only once before. So very young, she had been frightened by the ferocity of her love back then. It had ruled her. She remembered him: his golden hair, his big blue eyes, his laughter, his beauty, his goodness. They were kids, overtaken by their feelings and desires. Even so it had been real, and Reid had missed it every single day of her life until the day she met Reagan. She had loved that golden boy so long ago, and he had loved her. But the world with all its wonders had called to them, and they had answered. And once they left the cocoon that was Kilroy, they barely recognized each other anymore.

She had loved him beyond reason, and his love had rivaled hers. But understood her? Most certainly not. How could he? They were little more than children. And whoever claimed to understand Reid was a liar, the well that was her heart deeper and darker than any ever known, the searching of her spirit so elusive to all that crossed her path.

She lay content in Reagan's arms. She was not a child anymore. She was a woman now, experiencing a man's love. She knew full well that Reagan would never understand her, nor did she expect it. Her gifts, her treasures, her life, she longed to share with Reagan. But understanding her utterly feminine heart, her wanderlust, her dreamy eyes, would never come. She knew that. It was enough that he recognized her, her soul so like his.

That boy that she had loved so long ago was gone forever. The world had turned him into someone else, just as she had turned into who she was meant to be. And she knew that she would never forget those days of youth and first love, that she would always love the boy that remained at that place in time. But she could finally go forward with Reagan. He was her perfect match.

She curled tighter around his body. She never expected to find such a fit. The fit could not have been any more perfect. She knew. She knew he was the one.

"Are you awake?" he whispered.

"Barely." She snuggled closer.

"Good, because I think my mother just discovered us."

Reid's eyes flew open, and she sat up. "What!" she gasped.

Reagan began to laugh. "Someone just opened the door and walked into the room. I pretended to be asleep," he explained.

Even in the dimly lit room, Reid could see his dark eyes dancing. "Please, tell me you're not serious." She had begun to put her
dress back on.

"I think it was Mother. I caught a glimpse as she closed the door.
She was probably looking for us."

Reid felt sick to her stomach. She tidied her hair and sat down
on the leather couch to wait for Reagan to finish dressing. She was
horrified. Reagan's mother had caught them. She did not know
if she would survive the shame. Reagan sat down beside her and
took her hands. "I did not intend for that to happen." Reid knew
that he was sincere. "It's just that when I got you alone, I had to
have you. You make me crazy, Reid. I can't explain it. I am so in
love with you."

"Reagan, I'm all right. I just cannot imagine what she must think."

"Mom's not as uptight as she looks, but I know what you mean."
He was quiet. Reid studied him. He was troubled, she could see.

"Let's just slip out and go home," she offered.

"We can't do that. We're spending the night, remember? And
everyone is coming for brunch in the morning to meet you."

Reid put her head in her hands. "Oh, Reagan, I don't know if
I'll survive it." They looked at each other and their smiles turned
to laughter.

Finally, they knew they had to rejoin the party. Reagan directed
her to the closest bathroom in the house and waited for her. She
eventually came out, looking much like she had when they left his
apartment at the beginning of their evening. They returned to the
huge room, where most of the party goers were still going strong,
and drank entirely too much champagne. At last, the countdown
started. "Ten, Nine, Eight, Seven, Six, Five, Four, Three, Two,
One!" Everyone cheered the New Year. Reagan and Reid shared a
kiss, wanting each other all over again.

There were people drinking and couples dancing until three o'clock in the morning. It was customary for the party to go on until then. At three o'clock, the bartenders turned into baristas, and rich strong coffee began to flow. It was all very interesting to Reid. She took note, once again. There were still the starving, struggling artists, as well as the prestigious gallery owners. There were young hopeful playwrights, as well as wealthy financiers looking for something new. There were doctors, lawyers, teachers, musicians, people from all walks of life. Reagan and Reid talked for hours with a couple who had spent most of their lives together in the Peace Corps. The woman was trying to recruit Margaret Jacques for Doctors Without Borders, an organization that worked to bring doctors to underdeveloped countries. Reagan and Reid exchanged information with them, and agreed to meet them for dinner the following week before they left the country.

Reid could not remember ever having a more wonderful night in her life. She had never felt so happy, so full of life. She and Reagan were head over heels in love. He had proposed to her. Proposed to her! This gorgeous, brilliant, wonderful man was in love with her. In love with her! She could not believe all that had transpired since Romania. She loved Reagan so much. Sometimes it made her physically sick just thinking about it. She giggled to herself, uninhibited from too much champagne.

"What is it? What's so funny?" Reagan was amused by her.

"What a night! I became engaged, and got caught butt-naked by my future mother-in-law in her library. What a beginning. I don't know if I'll survive it."

Reagan convulsed into a fit of laughter, feeling the effects of too much champagne. When they finally regained their composure, Reid said she was ready to call it a night. He knew that even though she was trying to make the best of it, to find humor in the most uncomfortable of circumstances, she was truly upset that his mother had discovered them.

"Reagan, this has been the most wonderful night of my life, but I think I should go and get some sleep now. Will you please get my bag and show me where I'm sleeping tonight. I need to be rested and prepared to face your mother in the morning."

"Yeah, she's probably already called the others." Reid was horrified. He began to laugh again. "I'm just teasing you, relax."

He left her at the bar and went to get her bag from the back seat. She was beginning to nod off, sitting at the bar. He watched her, loving her. He wished they were going home to his apartment. He didn't want to waste a single moment, didn't want to be separated from her for an instant. He was going to marry the most beautiful, intelligent, funniest woman he had ever known. Sometimes it did not even seem possible. Was it real?

He went to her and helped her get down from the bar stool. She was tipsy, and extremely tired. He led her to the room she was staying in and kissed her good night. Then he went to find his mother. Better now than in the morning, he thought.

Margaret Jacques was in the kitchen. She was writing a list of instructions on a chalkboard for the kitchen staff, still in her grey satin evening gown. She looked tired, but pleased with herself. It had been another successful party. Reagan walked into the room and sat down in one of the chairs at the big round table. She never looked up.

"Did you have a good time?" she asked.

"It was a great party, Mother."

"Yes, it was. Where's Reid?"

"She went to bed. She's exhausted," Reagan replied.

"Of course, she is."

If Reagan had any doubts as to who discovered them in the library, they were gone. It was his mother. She had just let him know. It was the most she would ever say about the matter.

"Mother, I've just come to tell you that I proposed to Reid tonight, and she accepted. I thought you should know before tomorrow. Of course, we'll tell everyone else at brunch, but I wanted you to know tonight."

She stopped writing and turned to look at her son. It always startled her how much he looked like her. "Reagan, are you sure?" She paused. "How do you know?" She was worried. This was her beloved son that she was so proud of, and she knew very little about Reid. He had waited so long. Why now? Why this one?

"Mother, I know. I'm sure it's shocking to you because you don't know Reid. But you'll see. Sometimes, I think I don't even deserve her." He laughed.

Margaret was processing all that he said. He had been making a joke, but she was not amused. This was serious. She went to her son and hugged him. "My darling boy, you deserve all the good that life has to offer, nothing but good."

He embraced his mother and kissed her cheek goodnight. As he strode happily from the room, he turned to say one last thing. "Mother, tomorrow..." he hesitated. "Be kind to Reid. She is extremely embarrassed already. I don't want her hurt in any way."

Margaret nodded. That was it. She had lost him. He wasn't even ashamed of the scene in the library. He was too far gone. This was real. This was the one.

Reagan made his way through the house, the house he grew up in. It looked different tonight. Reid said yes! She said she would be his wife. He considered his childhood home. It was beautiful. It was a historic home, impeccably decorated and furnished. He wondered what their home would be like, his and Reid's.

It was no secret that he had been a privileged child, born to educated and successful parents, people that knew who they were. He had known parents with substance, that would never forget where they came from, Haitian immigrants that had persevered, had survived.

Even after he grew up, he had stayed close to home, simply moved over to the city. It was a natural progression. He had never wanted to live anywhere else. And now there was Reid. It seemed that life could not get any better. He could not ask for more.

Reagan undressed in what had been his bedroom, not so long ago, but any trace of his adolescent life had been removed. Gone were his posters, trophies, medals, photographs. This was a guest room in his parent's house, now. He showered in the adjoining bathroom. The water was hot and felt good on his skin. Reid... What was she doing? He missed her. He wished she was with him.

He finished his shower, dressed in a clean pair of boxers, and retrieved his cell phone. Wondering if she was still awake, he pressed speed dial. It rang about five times.

"Hello, Sweetheart," she answered.

He smiled on his end. "What took you so long?"

"I was soaking in the tub."

"I just got out of the shower as well. I was thinking about you."

"I was thinking about you, too," she told him.

"What were you thinking?" he asked her, beginning to feel warm.

"That one night is too long to be without you."

"Want me to come over and see you?" he teased.

"I don't think so. I don't want to get thrown out of my future in-laws house tonight."

They both giggled.

"Goodnight, Sweetheart."

"Goodnight," he told her.

He put his phone on the night stand, turned out his light, and hit his knees beside the bed. He was humbled, for he had been given so much. He prayed for their future. He said thank you. Then Reagan got up off his knees and climbed into the big mahogany sleigh bed. He curled up beneath the cozy down comforter and the soft sweet smelling sheets, and slept like a baby.

Reid lay in bed for hours. She couldn't stop replaying the night. Whenever she got to the library scene, her pale cheeks burned bright red. Reagan would be her husband. She was still and quiet, contemplating all that it meant. There was much to look forward to, so much. But before that, she knew there would be much to go through.

Reagan slept through the night, peacefully. Reid tossed and turned. The moment she took her first breath, her family had unknowingly placed an unfair burden on her tiny shoulders, one she should not have to bear. She was so tired, tired of carrying the burden of being born.

She woke to her phone ringing. She sat up and took it from the nightstand. It was Reagan.

"Good morning. Are you awake?" she heard him say on the other end.

"I am now. What time is it?"

"It's 11:45. We're supposed to be downstairs in fifteen minutes."

"What!"

"I'll be knocking on your door in fifteen minutes, so you better be ready." With that, he was gone.

She jumped out of bed and dressed hastily. She threw on a pair of jeans, a pale pink cashmere sweater, and some gray leather driving moccasins that she bought in Italy last year. She tamed her red mane as best she could, and just left it down. She brushed her teeth and applied a little makeup. She was just finishing up when Reagan tapped on the door. She told him to come in. He took one look at her, and smiled. She didn't even need fifteen minutes. She could have crawled out of bed and walked downstairs, and still she would have stolen everyone's heart. He knew that.

She left the bed a mess, telling Reagan that she would make it up when brunch was over.

"What happened to it?" he asked, looking at the bed. "It looks like you jumped in it all night."

"I couldn't sleep," she admitted.

He couldn't help himself. He had to ask, "Did you change your mind?"

She threw her arms around him. "Of course, not. You're stuck with me now."

They made their way downstairs. They could hear the laughter coming from the kitchen. Without hesitation they walked into the room, hand in hand. Immediately, there was an eruption from the small crowd. It appeared that they had all been waiting for Reagan. The star of the show had entered the room. Someone, Reid guessed it was his older brother, hugged him. It was a warm, masculine hug. Both men were beaming, truly glad to see one another. Reagan addressed the room.

"Everybody, listen up. I'm not going around the room making personal introductions. I'm only doing this once. Everybody, this is Reid. Reid, this is everybody."

They were all smiling at her. Some nodded in acknowledgement. Some said hello.

"Hello, everybody," Reid said.

Reagan looked at Reid with so much love that everyone could see it. He went around the room pointing out to her who was who. There was Meredith with her husband Rick, and their two kids: Liz at eleven, and Ricky who was seven. Then there was Denise with her boyfriend of many years, Corey. Next was Pierre, named after their father, with his wife Rena, and their three kids: Hunter who was seven, Judith at four, and baby Aaron who was six months old.

Margaret Jacques moved toward Reid and gave her a warm hug. "Good morning. Did you sleep well?"

Reid was truthful. "Not really, my mind just wouldn't slow down."

Margaret was touched by her honesty. She noticed the shiny diamond band on her ring finger. Of course, she thought. She took Reid by the arm, and Reagan as well. "Aren't you forgetting something?"

Reagan didn't know what she was talking about, at first. Then it hit him. He called out to the room again. "One more thing," he waited until he had everyone's attention, "I asked Reid to be my wife last night, and she actually said yes."

Eruption again, only this time it was louder. Reid was swept away into the sea of his family. She visited with everyone in the room. Little Judith took up with her, with stars in her eyes. They ate brunch, talked, laughed, and genuinely enjoyed spending time together. Reid thought Reagan's family was wonderful, and it only seemed right that he was a product of it. She thought about her own family. It was so very different. There had never been many children. In fact, until Uncle Bobby's boys, there had not been any except for Reid. All they had to give, had been given to her. All they ever wanted, had been handed to her. So much hope had been placed upon her. It was a huge burden to bear.

Finally Reagan found her and told everyone that they would be leaving. His sisters, sisters-in-law, and even Margaret herself offered to help with the wedding. Reid thanked them. Then she and Reagan said their goodbyes. Reagan's father, the older Pierre, patted her on the back and told her goodbye. He was a quiet man, with warm eyes. Reid didn't know why, she had barely spoken to him, but she liked him very much.

They drove all the way back to the city, discussing what to get rid of and what to keep, as well as who should move where. They discussed the previous night's party and brunch with the family, talking nonstop until they were back in Reagan's apartment. Reagan thought it was a little peculiar that she kept dodging the subject of the actual ceremony. She was so close to her family. He was sure she would want to share it with them. He put it aside. They would get to that soon enough.

The weeks kept passing, just as they had before, only Reid had moved in with Reagan. They combined most of their things, which had gone well because they had similar taste. The result was nice. His utterly masculine bachelor pad seemed to welcome her bohemian style. Reid labeled it "gypsy chic," both comfortable and interesting. Her trinkets, souvenirs from all over the world, gave the apartment an eclectic flair that had been missing. It was perfect.

Reagan and Reid seemed to float through the days on a cloud, with concerts in Central Park, quiet dinners with friends, and art shows in the village. Their friends were genuinely happy for them. Everyone remarked on how well the two of them fit together. It seemed as if they had stepped right into a fairy tale, happily ever after right around the corner.

Then came July... Reid had not seen the sun in two weeks. She sat in her favorite chair next to the window, watching the rain fall on the silent street below, sipping her coffee. People had given up. They seemed to be waiting it out indoors. Perhaps it was this that affected her mood. Or was it that she was keeping something from Reagan, and couldn't hold it any longer? She decided she could not control the rain, but she would have to tell Reagan what she had been keeping. She heard his footsteps coming down the hall. He had just showered and was wearing only a towel around his waist. Little water droplets clung to his skin. He could tell she was deep in thought.

"What is on your mind? You look like you're trying to figure out a way to pay the national debt."

She smiled at him. It was a weak smile. "This rain is driving me crazy. It was nice at first, but it's starting to get to me. Let's get out of here for the day, throw on some parkas, do some shopping."

"Where?" Reagan asked, wondering what she had in mind.

"Let's just see where we end up." She jumped up, gave him a high five, and headed for the bedroom to get dressed. She returned in a pair of cargo pants and a t-shirt, sporting a New York Yankees baseball cap.

Reagan was finishing his coffee, thinking how glad he was that she had bought an espresso machine. He saw that she was ready so he went to get dressed. He returned in jeans and a t-shirt, with a matching cap on his head.

"How cute," she teased.

"Just grab your parka." He grinned at her. They took off.

They covered just about the whole city on foot. They took a walk in Central Park and enjoyed some shopping in the village. They pounded the pavement in their parkas, so tired of being held captive by the endless rain.

"You ready to go home?" Reagan finally asked, after hours of being out in the horrible weather.

"Not really, I was thinking we might do something we've never done before."

He saw the sparkle in her grey eyes. "Like what?" With Reid, there was no limit to outrageous adventure.

"You told me before that you were ashamed to say that you were born in Brooklyn, grew up in New Jersey, and have lived in New York for almost twenty years without seeing the Statue of Liberty. Well, I've been here for almost fifteen and have never seen her myself. So let's do it. Let's go see the lady today." She was smiling, pleased with herself, knowing full well how ridiculous it was to get on that boat in the rain.

41

"What the hell!" He grinned. "Let's go." Reagan hailed a cab, which was no easy task in the terrible weather.

They did not have to wait in line. They got right on a boat. "The last boat for the day," they were told. The weather had cleared up for the moment, but a storm was coming that would make it impossible to run any more tours. So Reid and Reagan sat out on the last boat of the day, with the handful of crazies that didn't mind the weather either.

They watched majestic Manhattan grow smaller and smaller, then walked to the front of the boat. The wind was blowing so hard that it blew Reid's ball cap off of her head and over the side of the boat. Her red mane blew free in the wind. She and Reagan leaned on the railing, watching the statue grow closer. She was lost in her own thoughts, dark thoughts. He was lost in her. He leaned in closer and lifted her chin, softly, gently, to kiss her. She kissed him back. It was a sweet kiss, filled with so much love. Reagan took her in his arms and kissed her even more deeply. She relaxed and kissed him back.

They stood there together, lost in each other, until something caught Reid's attention. A photographer was taking pictures. She could hear the open and close of the shutter taking frame after frame of their intimate moment. Reagan turned to see what she saw. He spoke to the little man behind the camera.

"No pictures, please," he commanded and waved him away. The man spoke to him in French. Reid did not understand, but Reagan did, so he replied in French. The man left them alone. Reid looked to Reagan for an explanation.

"He asked if we were anybody," Reagan began, but Reid looked even more confused. Reagan could see she that didn't understand, "… like celebrities, or something."

"What did you tell him?"

"I told him, 'no, just two regular people.' I think he lost interest."

"I could tell he was disappointed." Reid giggled.

Soon, the Frenchman with the camera was forgotten, and they were consumed with their adventure all over again. The boat landed, and they spent an hour exploring the little island. They did not climb up into the statue. Reid decided it would spoil her grandeur to see inside of her.

They returned to Manhattan in the wind and rain, and Reid was insistent that they have pizza before they returned to the apartment. She ate more than Reagan had ever seen her eat, and he was surprised by the pizza issue. She normally didn't care for it. Around four o'clock they stumbled through the door. They both fell into bed and took a three hour nap.

When Reagan woke, Reid was in the living room watching an old black and white movie. He walked up behind her as she sat on the couch. Her hair was twisted into a knot, leaving the back of her neck bare. He kissed the warm, soft area of her neck, just between her shoulder and her cheek. She was so beautiful sitting on the couch, wearing his t-shirt.

She could see the love in his eyes, how much he trusted her, this wonderful beautiful man. He was taking a chance on her, and she knew it. At thirty-seven, he had never even thought of marrying anyone before her. He had told her, and she knew it was the truth. She knew she had to tell him.

"Reagan, we have to talk. I've been keeping something from you and I'm ashamed of myself."

The tears were already falling. Reagan could not imagine what she could possibly be hiding that was so serious. He laughed it off, "Well, I know you're not a man."

She did not crack a smile, but turned her face away from him. He touched her cheek gently. "Go ahead, I'm listening."

"It's my family. They're... It's just that..." She stopped.

"Well… they're different from your family." She finally got the words out.

"I know, you've told me."

"No, I mean it's more than that. I'm just really not sure how they will react to the fact that you're… you know… darker than me."

"Is that all?" He stood up and threw his hands in the air. "Reid, you were making me nervous."

"Reagan, it's serious to me." Her voice fell to almost a whisper, "I'm afraid they won't accept you."

"Reid, this is not 1950. Come on, this is ridiculous."

"Reagan, it's not."

"Then why have you never discussed this with me before?"

"There was no need. We're here, so far away from all of that."

"I realize that, but it was bound to come up. And obviously, you're upset about all of this. Anyway, you must be blowing this whole thing out of proportion. I can't imagine you coming from people as backward as that. Do they know that the President is black? Has anyone told them?"

Reid sprung to their defense. "They're not backward. You don't understand. It's so different there."

"Well, I can't imagine you defending them if they are prejudiced."

"I'm not defending them!" she shouted.

"All right, all right, let's both just calm down," he told her.

"Reagan, I'm not blowing this out of proportion."

Her frustration was apparent. He could hear it in her voice. "So Reid, just when are you planning on filling them in?" He had no patience for the issue.

"Well, you don't just pick up the phone and say 'Hello, everyone. By the way, I'm dating an African-American.' It's not…" Her tongue dripped with sarcasm. He'd never seen her this way. He didn't wait for her to finish. He gave it right back.

"African-American! You can save that term for someone else. I've never been to Africa. You can call me black. I'm black, and I like it that way."

Reid bolted for the door. She had to get out. This was too much. She loved him way too much for this. Reagan lunged for the door and grabbed her. He was rough. He was angry. Not with her, but with the circumstances. She buried her face in his chest and began to sob uncontrollably. He kissed the top of her head, then took her face in his hands. He kissed each of her crying eyes, tasting the salty tears that continued to fall. He moved on to her neck, unbuttoning her shirt. He undressed her right there by the door, and kissed her all over. Then, he picked her up and carried her to the bedroom, both of them whispering back and forth, over and over, "It doesn't matter..."

It wasn't long before Reid found herself feeling terrible. For three days she had vomited, and was so weak she couldn't get out of bed. Reagan called his mother. She would be able to tell him if he should be worried or not. She asked to speak to Reid. She wanted to know exactly what she was feeling. Reid said she was so sick that she couldn't even brush her teeth without throwing up, and all she wanted to do was sleep.

"Any chance you could be pregnant?" Margaret asked her.

Reid was totally caught off guard. "No."

"Well, then wait it out for another day and see if it starts to get better. I can call in a prescription for the nausea, if you want. Just make sure you drink plenty of liquids, so that you don't get dehydrated."

Reid said thank you, and gave the phone back to Reagan. Margaret told her son what she had said, and rang off. Reagan looked at Reid. She seemed to grow increasingly pale.

"Sweetheart, you are the whitest white person I've ever seen."

She gave him a weak smile. "Your mother said something that concerns me."

"What?"

"She asked me if I might be pregnant."

Reagan looked at her hard. "Well, do you think that you are?"

"I am late." She looked up at him with wide eyes.

"I'll be back." He grabbed his wallet from the top of the dresser and left the room.

Reid heard the front door close. She dozed off until she heard him return. He walked into the bedroom with a bag. He handed her a home pregnancy test kit. She thought that's where he had gone.

"Come on, just do it," he told her.

"Later."

"No, right now." He was firm with her.

She got up and took the kit into the bathroom. She closed the door and locked it. It seemed as if she had been in there for hours. Finally, she opened the door with the thing in her hand. Her mouth was wide open. He crossed the room to stand beside her.

"It's positive," she said, disbelief all over her face.

A huge smile spread across Reagan's face. He gathered her in his arms and carried her back to the bed. She thought she would faint. He felt her body go limp in his arms. He got into bed beside her, and they talked until the sun came up.

It was Monday, and Reid was filled with happiness about the prospect of the baby. She was still sick, but knowing the reason helped strengthen her. There were so many different thoughts filling her head. She called in sick, which really didn't matter since she wasn't working on anything important anyway. Reagan wanted to stay home with her. He was so excited about sharing this with her. She was the love of his life, and it just kept getting better and better.

But she told him that she really just wanted to spend the day alone, if that was okay. She asked him to keep the news to himself, until she had been to the doctor, until they were sure everything was all right. He agreed.

So there she was, totally torn between feelings of her own happiness and feelings of apprehension. The engagement was enough for her family to swallow. Now, she was more nervous than ever. Issue kept piling on top of issue. She entertained thoughts of just never speaking to anyone again, but the mere thought of never being with her precious family again was simply more than she could bear. She would have to come out with it all. More than anything she wanted to confront them, "How dare you!" It angered her so much, that it gave her courage. If they turned their backs on her, she could live with it, because she was just so tired, so tired of it all. It seemed ridiculous as she looked out at the New York City street, at the diversity of the people living peacefully, side by side. And she loved Reagan, she was moved beyond words that she was carrying their child. It was such a precious gift. There was just a tiny tug on her heartstrings for her family. It caused her to send up a silent prayer, a sincere prayer that the Creator would come down and straighten the whole thing out, and that she would not have to deal with it. She just didn't think that she could.

Reid noticed over the next few months that her relationship with Reagan was different. She confronted him, and he admitted that he was upset with her. Since they had moved in together, he had spoken to each of her family members on the telephone often, and it bothered him that they did not know he was black. It would be one thing if they didn't know because it just didn't matter, but it was quite another because it did. She told him that she intended on telling them soon. She asked him to have patience with her. He told her that he couldn't take it anymore, and he was insisting that she tell them now. He erupted with so much anger. She could not believe the man before her was her Reagan.

"My problem is with you right now. I do not care if those people accept me. I intended on the two of us building a life together, you and the baby being my family. The fact that you haven't told them that I'm black has me questioning you. I have my doubts about you right now."

Without a word, Reid took her bag off the kitchen counter and walked out the front door. She did not know what she was doing. She did not know where she was going. She only knew that she could not look at the disappointment in Reagan's eyes for another second. She loved him so much. She had tried to keep him safely tucked away. She wanted so desperately to keep their love hidden, not because she was ashamed, or even afraid, but because their love was so intense. It was sincere. It was precious. She wanted to protect it. She did not want it to be tainted by anything foul.

Reid hailed a cab and got in. The cab driver asked where she was headed. She looked at him with a blank look on her face. She had never even thought about that. Where was she going? She rattled off an address, and he nodded. He asked her if everything was all right. She said that it was as she stared out the window of the moving cab.

The driver came to a stop in front of the Waldorf Astoria. She paid the fare, offered him a generous tip, and got out. Reid said thank you, as she always did. He nodded, and drove away. She entered the hotel and walked up the steps, oblivious to the historic beauty that surrounded her. She did not respond when greeted by the concierge. She did not even hear him. She walked to the main desk and checked herself in. An attractive woman, wearing a dark suit and too much makeup, tried to make conversation from behind the counter. It was obvious that she recognized Reid. After what seemed like an eternity,

Reid was given her room key. She went to her room. By this time, it was almost ten o'clock and she realized that she had no toiletries. She called for a few things to get her through until morning.

After a warm bath, she sat on the big bed and began to cry. She was angry, angry that people could be so cruel, angry that the world could be so unkind. But most of all, she was angry because after she did what she knew she had to do, things would never, ever be the same. Even so, it was time. Reagan hadn't told her anything she didn't already know. It was the way in which he told her that hurt her so. She never thought he would talk to her the way that he had. But as much as it hurt, she understood. He was a good man. His integrity and character were impeccable, and this lie was eating him up.

She undressed and climbed under the covers. The sheets were cool. They had a sterile smell. Reid could not decide whether it was pleasant or not. She made plans as she lay in bed. The morning would be a series of phone calls. Then she would go to the apartment, pack a bag, get her car, and begin her journey. It would take her three or four days to get there. It didn't matter. She wanted to drive. It just seemed right. She would drive each day until she couldn't drive any longer, and stay the night wherever she ended up. She would tell Reagan what she was doing. She hoped it would ease the tension between them.

At last sleep found her, but it was fitful. She dreamed the same dream over and over. Her dream was bizarre. It had frightened her. She dreamed it was dark, pitch dark. She couldn't see anything, but she knew that she was outside, and she knew that she was in Texas. She was barefoot on a dirt road. It was Anneville Road. She walked in the direction of the farmhouse. She walked, and she walked, and she walked, but no farmhouse. She thought that maybe she had been wrong, that she had misjudged the direction. But if that were the case, she should eventually come to the highway. She kept walking.

Nothing. Just darkness and dirt under her feet. She was afraid. She kept waking to realize it was just a dream, only to find herself right back there on that road each and every time she fell asleep.

She woke up, exhausted. She showered and brushed her teeth, then put on the clothes she had worn the day before. They were all she had. She sat down at the mahogany desk in her room, with paper and pen, both embossed with the Waldorf Astoria insignia. She wrote a letter to Reagan. She hoped he would be there when she went home to pack her bag. She wanted to talk to him before she left. She wanted to kiss him, to hold him. But if she was unable to see him, she wanted him to receive the letter, saying all that she had not said.

Next, it was time to contact Harvey Finn, her boss and best friend. She picked up the telephone in her room and dialed his cellular phone number. She knew that he would not be in the office yet. She was surprised when he picked up the phone on the first ring. His voice was loud, as he tried to be heard over the busy morning traffic.

"Harvey, here."

"Hey, it's me."

"Good morning, darling. Whatever do I owe the honor of this early morning greeting? Did you finally see the light of day and realize that you've loved me all along? Did you dump that pretty boy you've been fooling around with?"

She couldn't help but laugh out loud. His accent and his good natured teasing always had the same effect on her. He was a New Yorker, all the way, and she loved him. He had hired her for World, just over ten years ago. Their working relationship had been wonderful. She had received other offers, some within World and some with other networks, but she had no desire to leave Harvey. She had learned that people like Harvey Finn were rare in the big city. He genuinely cared for her, was truly concerned with her happiness.

Sometimes, it seemed to Reid, that people in the city were on auto pilot. And even though she had been in New York City for almost fifteen years, dressed like a New Yorker, ate like a New Yorker, and could even speak like a New Yorker, people were always saying things to her like, "You're not from here are you? Where are you visiting from?" Reid was too friendly. It was a dead giveaway. But Harvey reminded her of home, of herself, and it was comforting just being around him. He had become a treasure to her. He had become her very best friend.

"Yes, my sweet. I was calling to see if you would meet me at the airport, so we can run away together."

"Just let me stop and pick up my wife, and we'll be right there."

They laughed together. Reid told him that something had come up and she needed to go home, home to Texas. She would be gone for two, maybe three weeks. He told her that he hoped everything would be all right, and asked if she needed help with anything, arrangements of any kind. She said no. He told her to take all the time that she needed, but to stay in touch because he would be thinking of her.

"Harvey, thank you."

"No problem. Just don't bring me a cactus or spurs or anything, okay?"

Reid hesitated. For a second he thought he had lost the connection. Then he heard her voice on the other end, broken.

"Really, Harvey, thank you."

She need not say anymore. He could hear the sincerity in her voice. She was such a special soul. He recognized it the first time he met her.

"Reid, you take care of yourself. And I mean it, you better check in with me. Love you."

"Love you, too."

With that, they rang off. Reid gathered her things, such as they were, and left the room. She checked out and left the hotel. The doorman hailed a cab for her. Smiling, he held open the door of the waiting cab. She paused, looking up at the New York City sky, feeling the chill of the November day. "Here we go," she said to herself. She was filled with conflicting emotions. She was excited to be getting on with her life. She knew that this was the beginning of something wonderful, life, real life. But there was also apprehension, for she didn't know how her family would receive her, she could only imagine. She handed the doorman a folded bill as she climbed into the cab, and then she was gone.

She was back in the apartment. She knew that she had just missed Reagan. His morning smells were all too new. The scent of his favorite cologne was still in the air. She could also smell the faint soapy scent of his skin. She walked into the kitchen to see if, by some small miracle, there was a fresh pot of coffee for her. No chance, an empty coffee pot sat soaking in the sink, but the coffee maker was left on. Either Reagan had left in a hurry, or he was preoccupied with all that had gone on between them the night before. She guessed it was probably both. She knew how meticulous he was. In fact, she knew he was sometimes annoyed with her because she was so forgetful, even though he would never admit it.

She packed hastily. There was no need to put a lot of thought into it. She was going home, and home was so far away on so many different levels that she didn't need much. If she had forgotten anything, she would just buy it. She turned off all the lights, gathered up her things, and opened the door to leave. She hesitated in the doorway as she looked around the dimly lit apartment. She had been so happy here. She couldn't wait to return. But she had a foreboding feeling, as if it would be awhile. She shook it off. She was just nervous.

Reid hailed a cab and directed the driver to take her to the parking garage where she kept her car. He chatted with her. She thought about Reagan, and how he had been taken aback by the way people were drawn to her. She was used to it. It had been that way her whole life. She just attracted people and their stories. It seemed as if they always wanted to share their story with her. She thought about it now, as the cab driver told her about his newborn daughter.

She loved the look in his eye, as if he had never seen anything more beautiful, as if he never would again. He was a total stranger, and yet she was truly interested in what he had to say. She genuinely cared for him, for people. It helped make her a great journalist. It was something Nana had taught her, she thought, that everyone has a special story to tell. "Maybe so," Nana had told her, "but the feeling that you give them is something that cannot be learned." The love and compassion that could be felt, simply by being in her presence, was not a skill that she had honed to get a story. It was sincere, it came from somewhere deep inside, and it was a very special gift.

At last, she arrived to pick up her car. It was such a beautiful car, an extravagance that Reid was always embarrassed to admit that she owned. She had gone over and over all the reasons why she should not buy it. She kept telling herself that she could do something worthwhile with the money, that it was useless to waste it on such an expensive car, that there were so many people out there doing without that she could not possibly justify it. It was Harvey who had convinced her to buy it for herself. They had gone to the Mercedes dealership together. He insisted on seeing the car that she was dutifully not going to buy. When he saw the pleasure that it brought her, he knew he had to convince her to buy it. He started in on her, full force. He brought up all the organizations that she regularly volunteered for. He reminded her of all the times she had given huge amounts of money away, because she felt sorry for someone in some part of the world where she was on assignment. "You bought some family in Romania a house, Reid. A house!" He finally convinced her to buy it, by telling her that there would always be people that needed help, and that money did very little to help people anyway. He told her that her job was secure, she made "damn good money," and that she needed to do something for herself every once in awhile. She knew he would not let it go, so she bought it. Looking back, perhaps this was why she had taken him to the dealership with her in the first place.

Reid felt free and alive as she drove through New York City. "I'll be back," she said aloud. She stopped off at a mail drop and mailed Reagan's letter, hoping that he wouldn't be angry with her for leaving without telling him. She hoped he would understand.

She opened her bag and took out the compact disc that she had packed from home. It was the one that she and Reagan had listened to on their very first date, over dinner at the apartment. It had played all night long as they fell in love. She chose song number seven. Tracy Chapman, She's Got Her Ticket...

"Ever been to Texas, Tracy?" She spoke the words out loud as the song began to play. She turned up the volume and got lost in the infectious beat. Then Reid drove out of New York City, with the top down, the morning sun on her face, and the cold wind in her flaming red hair.

And so Nana listened to Reid tell of driving down the eastern seaboard home to Texas. She stayed the night in different little places along the way, walked a lot of beaches, and ate whatever she wanted to, whenever she felt like it.

She actually had a wonderful time. It was time that she needed, time to be alone, to think. As much as she missed Reagan, she knew her life would be changing dramatically within the next few months. She needed to sort all of that out, to discover how she felt about it, so caught up she had been in how everyone else might feel. She had seized the opportunity to hop in her car, drive around the country, and just be Reid. And she was better now. She knew she would be all right no matter what happened. She had spent some time alone with her own quiet strength, and was slowly remembering how to use it again. How long it had been since she had needed it.

It was only when Reid realized that she was approaching Kilroy that she began to get emotional. Just recognizing that she was getting closer brought back feelings that she had long since forgotten. Driving through her hometown, and seeing it after so long, had brought her to tears. By the time she turned onto Anneville Road, she was shaking all over. She had pretty much collapsed in Gram's arms, overcome with emotion at coming home again.

She and Nana talked on and on until Nana was startled by something. "Reid, darling, it's after five. I'm truly enjoying you, but Maureen will have my hide. You're already late."

"Already?" Reid was shocked.

"Yes. You'd better hurry."

Reid kissed her great grandmother and raced out the front door. Ellen walked out onto the front porch to watch her leave. As Reid climbed up onto Pandora's back, Ellen called out to her, "Send my love to everyone at dinner."

"What do you mean?" All at once, Reid was troubled.

"I've had such a full day. I just want to climb into bed. I'll see you tomorrow."

"Are you sure you're okay, Nana?"

"Yes, child. I'm fine. I'm just tired, but it's a happy tired. I'm glad you came home."

"So am I," Reid told her with a grin. "I'll see you tomorrow." And then she was gone.

As the sun was setting on the horizon, Reid flew across the land she loved on the back of her magnificent dark horse. Brilliant reds, violets, and indigo hues lit up the Texas sky. Her red mane flew out from behind her, glowing from the light of the setting sun, while she rode on the back of the sleek black creature, whose movements were so graceful they seemed to flow like dark liquid, painting the beautiful canvas that was the Texas sunset. It was wild beauty and innocence. The rest of the world was of no consequence. It was a whisper on the wind: a living, breathing, beautiful moment in time that passes far too quickly.

"Reid Coleman!"

Reid could hear her grandmother's voice thundering across the pasture. "It's after five!"

She rode straight to the barn. She fed Pandora and gave her fresh water, after removing the bridle, then raced up to the house. She went in through the back door and walked to her bedroom. On her way, she noticed everyone at the dining room table. Of course, they were waiting for her. But she didn't stop. She went to her bathroom, cleaned herself up, and tidied her braid. She didn't even bother to change clothes. It didn't matter anyway.

As she came down the hall, everyone laughed. There was her mother and step-father Ron, her Aunt Frankie with Uncle Clint, her Uncle Bobby with Karen. (She had never called Karen "Aunt Karen." She and Reid were way too close in age for it to make any sense.) And then there was Gram and Papa, of course.

"Mother!" Reid squealed. She was so excited to see her.

Elise got up to hug her. "I just missed you this morning. I entertained the idea of surprising you at Nana's, but I know how you two are. Ever since you were a child, it's as if the two of you have this secret club. Anyway, I'm so glad to see you."

They both sat down at the table. Time seemed to stand still as Reid took note of her family. They were good, hardworking people that had given everything they could, everything they had, to her. Her grandfather sat at the head of the table, visibly older, but still strong and handsome. His warm brown eyes glowed with the pride that he took in his family, with the love that he felt for them. Her grandmother sat on his left. Everyone talked and laughed, catching up. Reid had been gone a long time, and while there were phone calls and letters, and a even a visit from Aunt Frankie, Karen, and her mother, it still wasn't the same as being back in the farmhouse together, where they had all grown up.

It was getting late. Bobby and Karen were the first to leave. The boys were at a birthday party, and they needed to pick them up. They promised to bring them the next day so that Reid could see them. Next, Frankie and Clint left. They had to be up early for work the next day. Ron said goodbye to Elise with a kiss, and told her he would see her at home. Bob excused himself and retired, leaving Reid alone with her mother and grandmother.

They cleaned the kitchen. It was their favorite time. Everyone was gone, and now they could really talk. They sat in the cozy living room of the old farmhouse, with no television, only the ticking of the grandfather clock. They got out a box of old photos. They laughed and talked, and ate homemade blackberry cobbler until they thought they would explode. And just when they thought it couldn't get any better, Nana came through the back door. The three of them jumped in surprise.

"Mother, what are you doing out so late?" Maureen was shocked. It was almost ten o'clock, way too late for Ellen to be out driving.

"Is everything all right, Nana?" Elise asked.

"Oh, everything is fine," Ellen assured them, "I was in my bed wide awake, and decided to get my old bones up and get over here. At my age, you never know if you're going to wake up to the light of day. I knew exactly what you were doing, and I said to myself, 'Get up and get over there, you're missing all the fun.' So here I am." She joined them in the living room with her own heaping helping of black-berry cobbler, where they kept it up into the early morning hours.

Reid never took it for granted. She realized how blessed she was to know her mother, grandmother, and great grandmother the way that she did. She had even known her great-great grandmother for a time. She watched them now, considered them. Crazy women in all their flawed glory... They were real, they were beautiful, and they were hers.

They were "wealthy," for they lived simply, within their means, owned everything they had outright. They were "powerful," for one look from any one of them could silence even the most disrespectful of children on any given Sunday morning at the Kilroy Church of Christ. They were "famous" as well as "infamous," for anyone could see that just by walking down the street with any one of them in downtown Kilroy. Everyone wanted to speak to them, and be spoken to. Their illustrious pasts commanded attention.

Reid smiled. This was what had shaped her, and she was incred-ibly thankful. For as long as she could remember, Reid had seen the power of their relationships with others. She had learned that there is power in passion so deep, that it creates strength that transcends reason. Their lives were such a rich, lyrical melody. The time they had together was a living, breathing, beautiful moment in time, and it was passing far too quickly. Oh, life... The living, the doing, the loving, the winning, the losing, the hoping, the praying, the laughing, the crying, the never giving up until the very last breath... It was all of them, and she was so glad that she had come home.

She remembered now what she was made of, and any thoughts or fears of losing them were gone. Even so, she knew the future would not be without much heartache, for there was one that was not cut from the same cloth. He was made of something completely differ-ent, something that frightened her. She watched the three of them.

She considered their fragility as well as their strength, and she was sorry, so sorry for what she was about to put them through.

After they were completely stuffed, totally talked out, and utterly exhausted, they ended their little party. Gram went straight to bed. Her mother took Nana home. It was far too late for Ellen to be out driving. Even though Ellen Adams and her driving had become Kilroy legend, prompting all the locals to pull over when they saw the 1957 Thunderbird, they did not want to take any chances. Reid still could not believe that Nana was able to drive at ninety-nine years old. She fell asleep thinking about it.

It took her a few days to adjust to being in Texas. She figured it was the pregnancy. She remembered Australia, riding in the back of that old dusty jeep, deep into the outback. The heat and the flies had nearly driven her crazy. She had not slept for three days before she took the jeep back into civilization. She had been given three days with an aboriginal tribe, only three days to get her story. She remembered that time, the heat, the exhaustion, the dehydration. She had been so weak that it had made her acutely aware of her own mortality. She remembered that time well. And even though fall in Texas was nothing like the Australian outback, she felt that way now. The weight of all she carried had begun to drain the life out of her.

After a few days of going to bed early and waking up late, lazy afternoon naps after gardening, and walking down by the creek, she felt much stronger. This place was still her home. It held her in some unexplainable way. There was so much intensity that accompanied her feelings for these people, for this place.

She spent a few days on the farm, just being Reid, until she found her courage. Now, she would go and spend time with her mother. Reid had been avoiding her. She was afraid that her mother would see it all.

Reid woke early, feeling rested. She opened her window to let in some fresh air. It was beautiful outside. The warm sun shone, and there was a cool fall breeze. She dressed herself. She had been living in old jeans, ragged western shirts, and her worn boots. But not today. She felt feminine. She felt young. She put on a pale pink eyelet dress, with dainty straps and a little skirt that was soft and flirty. She felt alive. She put on her cowboy boots and looked at herself in the mirror. She decided that she looked ridiculous. Perfect! She grabbed her bag and left the room. Gram and Papa were reading the Fort Worth Star Telegram, over coffee. The farmhouse was cold. She had been sleeping so late that the warm sun had taken the chill out of the old drafty house. But not today, for there was still a chill inside.

"Good morning," Gram said, surprised to see her up so early. It was barely eight o'clock.

"Good morning," Reid grinned. "I'm going to have coffee with Mother this morning." Her grandfather gave her some tools to return to Ron. She kissed them both and ran out the front door.

She jumped in her car and started it up. The usually shiny black finish on the Mercedes was dull from the thin layer of dust that covered it. The convertible top came down as she drove away from the farmhouse. She drove out from under the canopy of old oaks, and into the sunshine, finally turning onto Anneville Road. She drove slowly down the narrow dirt road, watching the dust trail in her rearview mirror. She had watched that same dust trail, as a child, through the back window of her grandfather's pickup truck. She remembered being a little girl, how she would turn around in her seat and watch it trail behind her as she traveled over the rough road. She sat in the middle, between Papa and Gram. George Jones was singing in the background. Sometimes, it was Tammy Wynette. Once, it was Charley Pride. As the wheels went over the dirt road, the dust rose behind her and briefly stood suspended in the air, then disappeared. She felt the wind blowing her hair as she drove, just like it did when she was a child.

Reid had a feeling. It was strange. She was torn. She was so far away from Reagan here. There were no dirt roads in New York City. There was the feeling again. Whether she was coming or going, Anneville Road always caused something to stir way down deep inside of her. It had always been the same. That road led her out into the world, and it led her back home again. Home, a place she couldn't stand to stay and a place that she couldn't bear to leave, all at the same time... Today was no different.

She came to the highway and drove on through the beautiful Texas countryside, admiring the ancient oaks with their welcoming, outstretched branches. Land unspoiled, wild and free, was on all sides of her. With the sun on her face and the wind in her hair, she decided she would just be Reid. Just for one more day.

She drove into the little town of Kilroy, slowly. How could a town stir her this way? She could go anywhere in the world and be completely comfortable in her own skin, but not here, not even now. How could this little Texas town cause her to feel so much? There had been beautiful, innocent days here. But there were people that had treated her terribly. She had been a child, with no knowledge of anything that came before her, and yet they had made her painfully aware. They had taken every opportunity to tell her that she was different, that she wasn't welcome. They tried to crush her spirit by despising her. Sure, there had been happy times as well, but even then she felt she must always be ready, constantly prepared for someone to tell her in one way or another that she did not belong.

But Reid was a woman now. She had been to places that these people had never even heard of, experienced cultures that they could not even begin to comprehend, and lived in some of the most horrible conditions imaginable. She was always trying to tell an overlooked and underappreciated story, always trying to right a wrong. And driving into this tiny Texas town after so long, with its lovely old homes, little barber shops, beauty shops, and hometown cafés, she hated to admit the truth, for the truth was that she still felt a little afraid...

She stopped at the one stop light and waited for it to turn green. People stared. Who was the young woman in the fancy car? Who did she think she was? Finally, it was green. She turned off the main road, onto Agnes Street, then again onto Kilroy Avenue. There was her mother's house. Reid noticed immediately the changes it had gone through. Elise and Ron had completed major renovations on it. It looked fantastic. It was an old house, built around 1920, with a huge front porch, complete with front porch swing. They had painted it buttercup and put some pale green and white striped awnings on it. The new beveled glass front door was the final touch. Her mother's flowers were blooming all over the place, despite the change of season, and Reid felt happy and welcome taking it all in. Her mother saw her pulling into the driveway and walked out to meet her.

Elise always looked great, from her perfectly styled blond hair to her neatly pedicured toes. "Good morning," she called.

Reid got out of her car and greeted her mother with a hug. "Mother, I love the house! It looks so good!"

"I know. It turned out great." She showed Reid all of the renovations and restorations that she had completed with Ron. They had even built a little deck out back, under the hundred year old pecan tree.

Reid was talking to Ron about the house when Elise interrupted her, "Honey, I'm sorry. I looked in my pantry and all I have is regular coffee. I don't have any decaf and I know you only drink decaf, now."

Ron said he would run down to the grocery store and get some decaffeinated coffee for her. "It's all right. I don't feel like coffee right now anyway."

They sat and visited for awhile. Ron went back to his latest project, refinishing an antique table in his little shed out back. He was such a nice man. Reid had always liked him. Her mother had married him right after she left for NYU. They had only dated for a couple of months, even though they had known each other for years. She was glad her mother was not alone. Life had taken Reid far away from Kilroy, as far away as she could get. She looked around at the beautifully restored home. She was glad her mother had found someone to share her life with, someone that enjoyed the same things.

After smelling coffee brewing for awhile, Reid decided she had to have some. "I think I'll walk down to the grocery store and get some decaf coffee, now. Mother, do you need anything else?"

"No, I don't think so." Elise got up from the sofa that she had been sitting on. "I'll go with you."

"No. No, it's okay, Mom. I think I'll walk alone. I would like to walk alone, if you don't mind."

Elise sat down. "Okay, but don't take too long."

Reid went out the front door and walked down the street toward the grocery store, in her pink eyelet dress and cowboy boots. Her bright red hair was glowing in the morning sunshine. She was in Kilroy. It didn't seem real. It didn't seem possible. She never had any desire to return. Never. So why now? Why was she drawn to this place? Oh, of course she had come home to tell them she was pregnant, to tell them all about Reagan. But she still had not done that. All at once, she was aware that she had come for other reasons, painfully aware.

She considered the town as she walked. Perhaps, through a stranger's eye, it was a cute little town. It was definitely an old town. She heard a baby crying, somewhere. She saw a young woman, about her age, hanging clothes out on a line. She kept walking in the direction of the only little grocery store in town.

She crossed the street and there it was, Robinsons, the only grocery store in town. She went inside. She thought about New York, the little corner markets with their variety of food and flowers. There were exotic foods, yummy foods, but here at Robinsons it was just the basics. She went inside and found what she needed.

There was a young girl working the cash register. She had her brown hair pulled back in a ponytail. Reid noticed how greasy it was. She greeted Reid and revealed tobacco stained teeth. She wore an old Kilroy Hornets t-shirt, and jeans that were too tight. The shirt said "State Champs 1989." So long ago, Reid thought. Isn't there anything else? Isn't there anything else that has happened here since then? Don't they care what's going on in the world? She imagined driving over the Brooklyn Bridge with the girl, greasy hair, yellowed teeth, Kilroy High State Champs t-shirt, and all. Reid imagined talking to her, getting to know her, and showing her the world.

The girl stared at her. She had said something. "Yes, that will be all," Reid replied, startled out of her daydream. She paid for the coffee and told her that she did not need a bag. The girl handed her the coffee. Reid took it, and left the grocery store.

She was not unaffected by the experience. She had seen them in the store. She had seen the way that they looked at her. They had whispered to each other, trying to figure out if that was really her or not. She was even more beautiful in person than she was on television or in magazines, but they would never admit that. To them, she was simply a bitch. According to them, she had always thought she was better. She had ignored them, they would say, snubbed them. But Reid had handled it exactly the way she had always handled it, the way she had handled it when she was just a child. She had gone somewhere, somewhere deep inside, and hid.

She stepped back out into the morning sunshine. She walked a short distance from the grocery store and turned to look back. She could see the little downtown area, the heart of Kilroy. There was the old rock building that was the city hall, and the tiny little library, the neat little houses, the farmers market in the bank parking lot. It looked exactly the same, just as it had all those years ago. It hadn't changed at all, and it could have been a small town anywhere. It could have been anywhere, but it wasn't. It was here, now, and all that she had fought back for so long was upon her.

She had loved them, and this place, but they had hated her. She felt the anger rise up inside of her as she stood there in the middle of the street. How could she feel so much for a town? For a place? How can you hate a place so much, and yet be drawn to it in a way that is unimaginable? She wondered, but even as she did, she realized that she already knew the answer.

She hated it because it had taught her truths about life and people that she wished she never had to learn, and it was still teaching her. But she was drawn to it for a completely different reason. She had something for it, though she didn't even realize it yet. Life was so much bigger than Kilroy, Texas. And by coming back, by simply walking through the streets of town after all that she had seen, after all that she had done, she spoke this silent truth. Standing right there in the middle of the street, she was living, breathing, beautiful proof that life is so much bigger than Kilroy, Texas.

The weeks passed by as if she were in a dream. It was just her and her precious family. She worked the horses with Papa. She drove cattle from pasture to pasture with Uncle Bobby. She gardened with Nana. She cooked with Gram. She shopped the local flea markets with her mother. It was almost as if she had never left.

It was Aunt Frankie that finally cornered her though. They had just visited the Modern Art Museum of Fort Worth, and were sightseeing, enjoying the facelift that downtown Fort Worth had received. "So when are you going to tell me what's really going on?"

Reid was shocked.

"Don't look at me like that. You've been here for three weeks, with no explanation. Did that job finally get to you?"

Reid simply said no.

"So are you going to tell me today? Or are you going to keep it?"

Reid gave her an angelic smile and kissed her cheek. "I'm going to keep it."

"All right, you go on and keep it. But whatever it is, just do what's right. And I don't mean what everyone else says is right, from their perspective. I mean what's right for you, what's really right." Frankie shrugged. She and Reid had always been close.

Frances Coleman left Kilroy at eighteen to go to college, but she fell in love with her History professor and married him. They moved to Kilroy and opened a dry cleaner's. She had done nothing her parents wanted her to do. She lived life on her own terms. It had been a decent little scandal, Kilroy style. And because she had left the tiny town for awhile, been involved in a little scandal, subjected to a little ridicule and come out on the other side, she felt like she understood Reid a little better than anyone else.

Late December came. It was cold, but Reid had to get out. She decided to ride. It was almost time for her to return to New York and she wasn't ready. She hadn't been able to tell them why she had come home. She knew she held a secret that would drive them apart, and she just couldn't bring herself to do that. She knew that once she told, there would be no going back. Things would never be the same, for any of them. She felt guilty. She felt weak. Reagan would never understand. How could he? Kilroy was so far from all he had ever known. There were rules that you did not break. Loving him was definitely one of them; having his child was unforgivable. And then there was the matter of why she even cared, but that was another matter entirely. She could never explain it to him. He would never know what it was like, the circumstances of her conception, her birth.

Before she even entered the atmosphere, Reid was in debt. She had been loved beyond measure. Born in the face of scandal, her mother had suffered much for her sake, her grandparents also. She owed them much. They had taken a chance on her so long ago. Her entry into this world had been a source of pain and embarrassment. But once they saw her, once they held her, they fell in love with her. And so it began. The burden was always there, just on the edge of all that she knew, unspoken. It grew heavier and heavier every day that she lived. She had escaped it for a time, fleeing to New York. But she had come home to face it. They did not even realize what they did to her. They never even saw it, so blinded they were with the love they felt for her. The only one who did not give a damn was Nana. She never had. She was an old woman. She had seen much, and was afraid of no one.

Reid had never known her father. All she knew about him came from Nana, and that was very little. Reid could never explain it all to Reagan. Yes, she could give him the details. But she would never be able to translate what those details meant in Kilroy, Texas. He would never understand what she had lived, and the debt that she owed.

Reid rode Pandora down to the creek. She rode as hard as she could. She knew she should not be riding so hard. She was pregnant. But she couldn't stop herself. She had too. "I'm half crazy right now," she told herself.

She missed Reagan and wanted to go to him, but she could not face him because she had kept her secret. She could not bear to disappoint him. The sun was setting. She turned her thoughts to the only one that could make any sense of it all. She rode harder and harder. She felt as if she might take flight on the wind.

"Are you there?" she screamed out at the Creator, but there was nothing.

"Where are you?" she screamed. She did not even realize what was happening. She was falling... falling...

Elise was impatient. Reid was supposed to be meeting her for dinner. She was leaving tomorrow, and they had planned this night, just the two of them. They were going to Dallas, to a trendy new restaurant. Elise was dressed up. She had just had her pretty blond hair cut into a chin length bob. She thought she looked really chic. She knew what Reid would say. She could hear her now, "You look so metroplex." That's what she always told her. That was Reid's term for women from the Fort Worth, Dallas area. They were attractive women, with an accessory thing going on that she had seen nowhere else on the planet. Reid was far less made up. Her look was natural, effortless.

Elise picked up the phone and dialed. Maureen answered.

"Mother, where's Reid?"

"Oh, she's around here somewhere. Probably down at the barn with Pandora. She said she was going riding. But I suppose she's back by now. It's dark..."

"That girl! What's wrong with her? We were supposed to be going to dinner in town, tonight."

"Hold on, Elise. Let me call her." Maureen opened the back door and stepped outside. She called Reid, but there was no answer. She walked out a ways, and saw what appeared to be Pandora walking around outside the barn. It was Pandora. She was limping. She was spooked. She called Reid again. There was no answer. "Bob, something's wrong!" He was out the door and walking toward the barn. Maureen went back to the phone, to explain.

Elise cut her off, "Mother, I'm on my way."

Bob saddled up his horse and took off. He told Maureen to call Bobby and Clint. It was dark. She could be anywhere. "Pandora has mud on her. She either came from the tanks, the river, or the creek," he said.

Bob rode hard. He was betting on the creek. It was beautiful there right now. He rode up and down the bank, with only the moon for light. He saw tracks and followed them. Then he saw her. Pandora must have lost her footing. There was a drop off and it was rocky there. She was not moving. She looked dead, but she was breathing. He did not know what to do. He knew that he should not move her, but he did not know what else to do. He looked her over in the moonlight. She was limp and banged up, but she was breathing. He sat there for a little while. Then he saw headlights in the adjoining pasture. He left her and rode toward them.

It was Bobby. He was in his jeep. He saw his father riding toward him, and he was riding hard. Something was wrong. He got out. Bob was shouting at him to follow as far as he could in the jeep. "Looks like Reid's been thrown. We've got to get her in the jeep, and to the hospital." Bobby did as he was told.

The two men carried her to the jeep. Bob smacked his horse on the rump and said, "Go home." The horse took off, and he got into the jeep with his son. They did not even stop at the house. Bob called Maureen from his cell phone. He told her to get to the hospital. She said that she and Elise were right behind them.

They drove up to the emergency entrance. There was a huge commotion as Bob carried his beloved granddaughter in. Some nurses directed him to take her behind automatic double doors. He carefully placed her in a hospital bed. They made him leave. It was like a bad dream. Reid... He loved her so much. Yes, in the beginning she had been an embarrassment. Everyone had talked about them all over again. It had been a mess. He had been so embarrassed, but even so he had loved her. He couldn't help it. She was so precious. It was as if she had come from somewhere else. He lived through her. They all did. All of her stories, the places she had been, the things she had done. She was fearless. But not him, he had many fears, and many insecurities.

Elise drove the twelve miles to the rural county hospital, down dark country roads, like a bat out of hell. Over and over, she prayed, "Please, let her be okay, please, let her be okay." The rest of the car ride was silent. Maureen was terrified. She had heard the distress in her husband's voice.

When they entered the emergency room, they saw Bob sitting in a corner with his head in his hands. He heard them approaching. Elise could see that her father had been crying. She prepared herself for the worst.

"She's inside. No one has come out," Bob said.

Elise took a breath. Just then a nurse came out and asked for next of kin. Elise told her that she was her mother.

"Oh my gosh, Miss Coleman. It's me, Kristin Bell. Don't you remember? I went to school with Reid. We cheered together."

Elise recognized her. She smiled weakly and followed her through the double doors. The doctor was waiting for her there.

"You are?" he asked.

"Her mother."

"What is her name?"

"Reid Coleman."

"Where is her husband?"

"She's not married."

"Not married?"

"No."

The old doctor was puzzled. "I just assumed she was, since she's wearing what looks like a wedding band, and ..." He stopped.

Elise looked at Reid's hand. Where had that come from? She had never seen it before. She would have noticed it. It was beautiful. "She has a boyfriend back in New York, but they are not married."

It was apparent to Doctor Russell that this woman had no idea that her daughter was pregnant. "How can I get in touch with him?"

"I have the telephone number to their apartment." Elise did not understand, but she did not question him. Reid had not moved since she came in.

"Your daughter has sustained a head injury. We are going to send her down to imaging to get some pictures taken. We'll know more after that. Is she allergic to anything?"

"No." Elise was in shock. The doctor disappeared from the room. The nurse brought her a chair.

After leaving a message on the answering machine, Doctor Russell returned to his patient. He decided to keep her secret for now. It was too soon to tell it. It might not even be necessary, for many different reasons.

From the hospital waiting room, Maureen called her mother. Ellen was watching the news in her pajamas when the call came. Maureen told her what had happened. Ellen wasted no time. She called the apartment in New York. No answer. What should she do? She called information. There was a listing for a Pierre and Margaret Jacques. Bingo! She had listened well.

Reagan was swimming laps in his parent's indoor pool as the snow fell outside. It was eleven o'clock in New Jersey. He swam harder and harder, killing himself, trying to chase Reid from his mind. He had not heard her voice in over a month, not since they argued. He had only received a short note by mail. It simply said that she had gone to Texas to straighten things out. He had left their apartment and gone to stay with his parents. He was commuting every day to the city. It was a pain, but he just couldn't stay in the apartment without her.

He heard his mother calling him. She found him in the pool. She watched her son swimming his heart out, while the snow fell peacefully just beyond the glass. "It's Ellen Adams for you."

What could this be about? Was Nana calling to say that Reid wasn't coming back? Reagan hopped out of the pool and wrapped his towel around his waist. His heart stopped. He would go to Texas and get her. He would tell her how sorry he was that they had argued, and beg her to come back.

"Hello?"

"Hello, Reagan. I'm calling about Reid. She's been thrown from her horse."

"A horse!"

"Yes, she's in the hospital right now. I haven't seen her yet. She's unconscious. I called you first. This has just happened."

He turned to his mother, "Get me on the first flight to Dallas." Margaret went to get her cell phone, not waiting for an explanation.

"Nana, I'm going to pack a bag. I'll call you back."

"Honey, I won't be here. I'm heading up to the hospital. It's the County Regional Hospital. Call there."

They said goodbye. Reagan was frightened and he was furious, all at the same time. He packed a small bag and went to find his mother. She already had a set of keys in her hand. They left for the airport. She told him that his flight would be leaving in little more than an hour. He knew that it would take them at least thirty minutes to get there, maybe more depending on the weather. He hoped he would make it through security in time.

It was a mad dash, but he made it. He did not allow himself to think until he was in the air. What had she been thinking? Was she trying to kill herself, or this baby? He knew better than that, but he didn't know what else to think. He didn't know what he would find, what kind of reception he would receive. It didn't matter. All he wanted to do was get to Reid. He would never let her out of his sight again.

The flight was nonstop to DFW airport. He rented a car, bought a Texas map, and was on his way. He looked at his watch. It was almost four o'clock in the morning. No, it was almost three o'clock.

He had gained an hour. He drove to the hospital. He didn't even know how he got there.

Now, it was four o'clock in the morning. He walked into the small hospital. There were very few people inside. Even so, he looked out of place. Even if he had been white, he still would have looked out of place, with his expensive clothes and quiet confidence. Most people around there thought blacks should be poor, and should look it. Reagan was not aware of any of this. He didn't realize that he had broken the rules. He wouldn't have cared anyway.

He walked up to the triage nurse and waited for her to respond. She never did. She ignored him. Finally, he blurted it out, "I'm looking for a young woman, Reid Coleman. She was brought here earlier." The woman rolled her eyes at him and sauntered away to a computer. After what seemed like an eternity, she mumbled something about ICU on the second floor.

"ICU!"

The nurse did not even respond. She turned her back on him and walked away. She couldn't stand "them," especially not fake ones like that one, she thought. Reagan knew what was going on even though he had never seen it before, not up close and personal anyway, never in his life. But he recognized it immediately.

He took the rickety elevator to the second floor and looked for signs for the Intensive Care Unit. He bumped into a woman and apologized. She smiled. She had a nice smile. It was warm. He spoke to her. "I'm looking for ICU."

"That's where I'm headed. I'll show you." He walked with her. "You have someone in the hospital?"

"Yes, my fiancée."

Elise thought that the man looked worried to death. He seemed nice. She wondered where he had come from. He was obviously not from around there.

"She fell, or was thrown off a horse. I flew all night to get here."

Elise came to a dead stop in the middle of the hallway. She turned to look at him. This was Reagan. "Oh, God," she whispered to herself.

She immediately put on what Reid referred to as her 'I'm so uncomfortable but I'm going to act like I'm perfectly fine' routine. Reagan went for it, hook, line, and sinker. He had no idea that she was coming apart at the seams. "You must be Reagan. I'm Elise, Reid's mother."

Reagan was shocked. They looked nothing alike. Elise was short, but she was slim like Reid. She had cropped blond hair, and was really done up. Reid was never done up like that.

"So nice to finally meet you," he told her.

"Yes, yes, you too."

"How is she? What happened?"

"We honestly have no idea... about either."

Elise explained to Reagan that she and Reid had planned an evening out, it being their last night together before she headed back to New York City. She explained everything up to that very moment, but Reagan did not want to hear the medical details secondhand. He wanted to speak to the doctor. He had questions.

"I want to see her doctor."

"Yes, yes, of course. We'll see if we can find him."

Elise appeared calm, but inside she was raging. If Reid survives this I'm going to kill her, she was thinking. How in the hell could she do this to me? Daddy will never get over this. In spite of her anger, Elise adopted her classic nervous laugh. Reid always called it her 'I'm on the brink of disaster' laugh.

They found Doctor Russell in the waiting room. He was talking with Bob, Maureen, Bobby, and Nana. Everyone had arrived, Karen and the boys, Frankie and Clint, Annalyn and her girls. Everyone had come.

All thoughts of racism had flown from Reagan's mind. He wasn't used to thinking in those terms. Reid was the first thing on his mind, then the baby. He interrupted them, "Hello, Doctor. I'm Reagan Jacques, Reid's fiancée. What is going on? How is she?"

The shock was apparent. Bob's mouth flew open. Maureen just stared. Bobby had to look away. Ellen was the only one that seemed fine. "Reagan, you made it." She embraced him warmly, then introduced him to the others in the room. She acted as if they had known each other for ages, instead of meeting for the first time. She explained that she had called him before she left home. No one was listening. They were too busy processing the fact that Reagan, Reid's Reagan, was black.

The doctor saw the shocked faces. This was getting good. "Mr. Jacques, I'll take you back to see her."

Reagan followed the doctor into the ICU. As soon as he saw her, tears started to burn his eyes. She looked like she was just lying there sleeping. She was so peaceful. "I'm sorry, Doctor. I haven't seen her in awhile. Seeing her finally, like this, is wrecking me."

"Mr. Jacques, I'm just going to get right to the point. She's lucky to be alive. She has sustained a head injury that is partially affecting her brain. There is some swelling, and we do not have the capability here to assess her injuries any further. Not to mention, she needs to be seen by an obstetrician that specializes in high risk pregnancies. I just told the family about the pregnancy. They had no idea."

Reagan thought about what he said. "So the baby is still alive?"

"So far, but I'm not sure for how much longer, with what's going on inside her body."

"How soon can we move her?"

"We just need her mother to approve, and I can get that going."

Reagan nodded. He went to Reid and took her hand. He kissed the tips of her fingers. He kissed her forehead. He touched her hair.

She did not move. The tears began to run down his cheeks. He tried to pull himself together. He got close to her. "Everything is fine, Reid. I'm here, and I'm not going anywhere. Just sleep. Sleep and get better."

He sat there with her, just watching her sleep. He was wide awake. After some time, one of the nurses came in to tell him that some other family members wanted to see her. She asked him if he would come out, so that the others could have a chance to visit. Only two visitors were allowed in at a time. He agreed. The nurse was kind to him, not at all like the triage nurse he had first encountered. He thanked her for her kindness. She told him that she had gone to high school with Reid. They had been friends.

Kristin Bell saw how the man touched Reid. She saw his tears. It was obvious how much he loved Reid. Kristin could barely look at him. He was so attractive and graceful. He made her feel self-conscious. There was just something about him. So this was Reid's fiancée, she thought. Perfect... Of course, Kristin couldn't be sure, but it appeared that Reid had found someone that loved her as much as she deserved to be loved. She hoped that her old friend was happy. She hoped that she was truly happy. "That girl went through enough here to last a lifetime," she mumbled to herself. She told him that if he needed anything, anything at all, to find her. Then she watched him go to the waiting room.

Bob and Maureen got up to go in together. Ellen saw them and touched her daughter's hand. "I'll go in with Bob. You can go in with Elise, next," she told her. Ellen would go in with her son-in-law. Maureen was too vulnerable right now. Ellen could not imagine what was going through her daughter's mind. It had to be painful. Seeing Reagan had to remind her...

Bob Coleman walked into the room with his mother-in-law and sat down beside Reid's bed. Damn it, he loved her! But he was infuriated with her right now! And she was just sleeping away. He wanted to accuse her. He wanted to tell her that he never wanted to see her again. He wanted to slap her, to get some kind of response. He wanted an explanation. "She knows exactly how I feel about niggers." He actually spoke the words out loud. It was the one thing he could not forgive. Out of everything she could have possibly done, this was the one thing he could not stand for. She would have to choose. "Your family or that nigger," Ellen heard him say. He had made up his mind. He got up and stepped away from the bed. Ellen watched him. She could see it all over his face. There would be hell to pay.

He turned around and left the room. Ellen sat there for a moment watching Reid sleep. "I know you're there. Something like this happened to me once, a long time ago. When I was asleep, I saw angels. Wonder what you'll see." She stopped to brush a stray curl from her great granddaughter's forehead. "You just keep sleeping. Let the Lord work on this." She got up and went back to the waiting room. It was funny how life worked out, she thought. They were all having to deal with each other, while Reid slept on.

Elise went in next, with her mother. Maureen was silent, lost in her own thoughts. Elise was torn. On one hand, she was sick with worry. That was her daughter there, her only child. Her love was boundless. On the other hand, she was angry. She had given up her entire life for Reid. What else would she have to give up? Elise would have to choose. There was no question about that. Elise did not think that her father would ever accept them. She would choose Reid, but at what price? What was Ron going to say? She almost laughed out loud, so unreal was the situation, and Reid was sleeping peacefully while pandemonium ensued. Just like Reid... Tonight is no different.

Bob never went back to the ICU waiting room. He found Bobby in the cafeteria, having coffee. He told his son to take him home. Neither man spoke until Bobby pulled into the driveway. He let his father out in front of the farmhouse and told him that he was going home.

"Dad, give me a call if you hear anything about Reid."

It was as if his father never even heard him. He got out and shut the door to the jeep, walked up the steps, and disappeared into the farmhouse. Bobby knew better than to say anything. It wouldn't have done any good, anyway. It was best that he keep his mouth shut for now. His father was a good man, for the most part, but he had a bad temper. Bob Coleman could be volatile.

Bobby hoped that Reid would be all right. He remembered her as a child. He had always thought she was spoiled, thought she would never amount to anything. She was always in her own world. But even though she was a brat, he still loved her. He couldn't help but laugh. What the hell, he laughed out loud! He remembered when she was about three, and he was sixteen. She begged and begged to sleep in his bed with him. He finally gave in. She had been so cute, and she had loved him so much. He woke in the middle of the night to a warm feeling spreading all over him. "Damn it, she pissed all over me!" he had yelled. Elise came running into the room to get her. It was funny, now. He and Reid had grown up close, in the same house. Elise had come home right before Reid was born, and they had never left. Bobby knew that he shared a special bond with Reid, one that could never be broken or duplicated. They had been children together, and he loved his niece very much.

He remembered the night before she left for college. She was flying to New York the next morning. They had tried to convince her to stay in Texas. They tried everything. In the end, Elise had even told her that she could not pay the out of state tuition. That didn't work. Nana said she would pay it. He remembered his father, the next morning, while she was putting her bags in the back of his pickup. "You know you can always stay," he told her. "You don't have to go. You can stay at home and go to North Texas."

Reid had smiled, kissed his cheek, and then jumped into the passenger seat of his pickup. "Not a chance," she had told him.

Bobby remembered growing up with her. She wasn't like them. She didn't think like them. He always imagined that she was like her father, because she was nothing like any of them. He understood why she wanted to leave. He remembered all of that and more, as he drove home to Karen and the boys.

Inside, Bob paced. He could not sit down. He was too wound up. After everything he had done for her. They had always been there, all of them. "And this is how she repays it?" he asked the empty room. He could not even stomach it. "She's sleeping with a nigger," he ranted. She disgusted him. He wanted to vomit. And now she was pregnant. "She's a whore," he said. He couldn't stop talking to himself. He never wanted to see her again. He walked around the living room and closed all the blinds, then sat still and quiet in the darkness. That was how Maureen found him.

She came in through the back door. The house was dark, even though it was only four o'clock in the afternoon. All the blinds were drawn, and the house looked like a tomb. Her eyes finally adjusted. Then she saw him. He was sitting in his chair, staring at nothing, with a shotgun on his lap. He never even looked up. She opened the blinds in the kitchen and began to make some sandwiches. She wanted to keep busy. She could not bear to hear him rant about Reagan. She knew it was coming.

Finally, she could stand the silence no longer, "I made us some sandwiches. Would you like some sweet tea with yours, or just a glass of water?" She waited, but there was no answer. "Bob, I said I made some sandwiches. What do you want to drink?"

"I'm not hungry." That was all he said.

Maureen decided to let him be. She knew he had a battle raging inside of him, and it was nothing more than pride. She knew him better than anybody else. She knew that, right now, he was sitting in his chair trying to decide what he would do, if he would make Reid pay, or if he would let his hatred go. The gun was for show.

Oh, how the world turned! The child that he had fiercely protected since the day she was born, the child that he had loved in spite of her odd ways, the child that had taken his heart and never let it go, was now a woman living her own life. And she had fallen in love with a man, a good man, a man that loved her, a man with integrity, someone that he should have been overjoyed to welcome into the family. But in Bob's mind, the one that he loved more than anything had turned on him. Right now, he was hurt. Maureen knew he would finally have to face his fears. She felt sick inside, but still she had hope. She prayed for Reid. She prayed for Bob too, that he would finally be free, that they would all be free. They had been imprisoned by his insecurities for far too long.

"After everything we've done for her..." The words floated in the dimly lit room where Bob sat. Maureen sat at the kitchen table eating her sandwich, with the blinds open. She heard him, but she paid him no mind. She ate her sandwich as if she were starving and had not a care in the world. All the while, it tasted like a cardboard box.

The best I can do is keep my distance, there is nothing else I can do, she thought. "I have to let him be," the words escaped her. She finished her sandwich and put her plate in the sink. She decided she would rest. None of them had slept.

Maureen thought of Elise, her daughter, taking control, doing all that she could for Reid. Elise and Reid were as different as two people could possibly be. Maureen had always wondered how it could be, that two people as close as they were could be such complete opposites. Their relationship as mother and daughter had not been easy. It had been such that they had raised each other. They were only sixteen years apart, and that gap was made even closer by Elise's simplicity and Reid's complexity. Reid had seemed to float on each day of her childhood like a cloud, daydreaming, seeing things that they could not. Maureen thought it was a curious thing, how Reid never wanted to get too far away, but all she ever dreamed about was leaving. It was a dangerous spot, caught somewhere in the middle. Maureen saw herself in the dresser mirror. She looked terrible. "Why, you're an old woman," she said to herself. She smiled at her reflection, exhausted, beaten. She thought of Reid. "My precious girl," she whispered. Reid had to be okay. She just had to. What would they do without her? They lived through her.

After spending a night and the morning in the little county hospital, Reid was transported via ambulance to a private hospital in Fort Worth. There was a room waiting for her there. They spent the afternoon getting her settled in. She slept on. Elise and Reagan worked together. Circumstances had thrown them together. Their common goal was Reid. They were bonding under her very nose.

Elise approached Reagan. He sat in a lounge chair beside Reid's bed. "Reagan, you're going home with Nana. You're going to drive her home and get some sleep. As soon as you're rested, you'll come back and relieve me."

Reagan immediately began to protest. He was not going anywhere.

"Reagan, please. I know how Reid feels about you, and I know how you feel about her. I respect that. But the fact is, in case you haven't noticed, you and I are the youngest people around and we have no idea how long recovery is going to take. Both of us are going to have to be healthy to keep this up, and that requires sleep. You can't keep your eyes open right now. You go now, with Nana, and relieve me when you're rested."

He was still not convinced.

"You'll only be thirty to forty-five minutes away from the hospital. I'll call you if anything happens."

Reagan had no intention of leaving. He was not leaving Reid, not now, not when he'd finally found her again. But Nana took his hand and patted it, "Yes, Reagan, please. Why don't you come home with me?"

He started to say no, but could not get the word out. There was something in her eyes that pleaded with him. He agreed. He told Elise that he would get some sleep and be back first thing in the morning. She nodded, relieved that he was leaving.

Elise gave Nana a hug and a kiss goodbye. Nana's tough, she thought, as she smiled to herself. She had hung in there with them until now. But this was Reid. Of course, she had. Elise thought about their relationship. Why was it so different? She would never understand it. She settled herself into the lounge chair that Reagan had been in. It was warm. She could actually stretch herself completely out in it. She began to doze. Ron would be coming back later. Right now, she just wanted to sleep there beside Reid, her baby. She wanted to forget about the rest of the world for awhile. Reid would wake up. For now, Elise would accept no other outcome. She wasn't strong enough to entertain any other thoughts. She would doze.

Reagan drove the forty-five minutes to Kilroy, with Nana. They were both quiet. She pointed out landmarks as they drove. He remembered Reid describing the small town. Even still, this was not what he expected. It was like something right out of a movie. A man was driving down the main highway that ran through the tiny town, on a riding lawnmower. Reagan could not help but smile. The man looked like he did not have a care in the world.

He saw the grocery store. Nana pointed out the building. She talked about building it with her husband. She explained that Reid's grandparents had sold the business, but still owned the building. Reagan looked around. It was a cute little town that could have existed anywhere, but it didn't exist just anywhere. This was Reid's hometown. He drove through Kilroy, at Nana's instruction, then down some farm to market road until they reached a dirt road. She told him to turn there.

He read the sign. Anneville Road... Nana told him that the area was once an early settlement that had sprung up along the Trinity River. But it had long since disappeared, replaced with farmlands and families that had been there for as long as she could remember. The little settlement had simply vanished, swept away on the winds of time. Kilroy had come after. The only thing that remained was the road, Anneville Road.

They drove down to where the road ended, to the last house. It was an old farmhouse, white with black shutters. It had a huge welcoming front porch on it. There were sturdy oaks lining the driveway, and a couple of rocking chairs on the porch. It was built on the side of a hill, facing a picturesque creek. He could imagine someone sitting, rocking, just listening to the creek run. It was truly beautiful. It was simple, not elaborate in the least. Reagan appreciated it. It reminded him of Reid.

"This is the farmhouse. I grew up here. I gave it to Maureen and Bob. Too big for one little old lady. Annalyn said she didn't want it. She never liked the country very much, so I gave it to Maureen and Bob. They raised their family here. This is the house that Reid grew up in."

So this was the house that Reid grew up in. Reagan could imagine her running up the steps and slamming the screen door, with her red hair flying. "I just thought you might want to see where she grew up. Who knows when you'll be out this way again?"

She instructed him to turn around in the driveway. They headed back down Anneville Road in the direction they had just come. She told him to turn into the next driveway. He did so, and saw her little house. The stone cottage was charming, and looked just like someplace Nana would live. It was cozy, and it was actually quite beautiful. Reagan took his bag out of the trunk of the rented car and went inside with Nana. Her little dog greeted them. "Hello, Foo Foo," she crooned.

He remembered Reid buying that dog for her great grandmother while they were in Canada. She was covering a story about criminals crossing the Canadian border. Someone was selling the puppies at a little outdoor market. She bought one for Nana. She had taken it with her every day while she was working. Reagan shook his head. He remembered having to edit out the dog's whining when he pieced the story together for the television broadcast. She sent the dog straight to Texas when they wrapped. She usually did that, come to think of it. She would send something back to Texas, something outrageous, a glimpse of where she had been, what she had seen.

While Nana busied herself in her little kitchen, Reagan showered. He stood there under the water. "Is this real?" he asked himself. Reid is in the hospital. She's in a coma. And I'm here at her great grandmother's house, out in the middle of nowhere, wondering if I'm going to wake up to a burning cross or something. He had seen places like this only in the movies, and had wondered, even then, if it wasn't exaggerated for dramatic purposes. He just could not believe that racism existed to that degree anymore. But now that circumstances had brought him face to face with this tiny Texas town, he was beginning to wonder. Reid had told him about Kilroy. There was not one black person living there. She said that something terrible happened a long time ago, causing all of them to leave. To this day, none had settled there. Reagan had never asked for details. It hadn't affected him, then. He wished now that he had asked more questions.

It was five o'clock. The sun was dipping lower on the horizon. He smelled meat cooking and realized how hungry he was. It smelled so good. He followed his nose to the kitchen, and out the open French doors. Nana was turning some steaks on her grill. He still could not believe that she was almost a hundred years old. He startled her.

"For a second I forgot you were here," she told him.

He smiled. "Did Elise happen to call while I was in the shower?"

"No, but she'll call if Reid wakes up. Believe that."

Reagan told Ellen that she did not have to go to all the trouble of cooking a meal for him. She told him that she wanted to. "This will give me a chance to get to know you. You're going to be my great grandson." He thought about this. He had no grandparents left. They were all gone by the time he was ten. He knew he was there for Reid, and for the baby. But it felt good having Nana cook for him, seeing her joy. Even in the terrible circumstances that they had been faced with, she was glad to have him in her home. She was gracious to him. She was kind. She was such a dignified old lady.

When dinner was done, they ate together at a table in her backyard, next to a huge stone fireplace. It was peaceful, Reagan thought. He took the blanket off of his chair and wrapped it around him. He could hear the fountain trickling, that crazy fountain that Reid had hauled around Spain in pieces. In pieces! It had been such a pain, so heavy. He knew why now. All at once, he got it. Of course, it had been a huge pain in the ass. There was no doubt about it. But seeing it now in Nana's backyard, what that little piece of culture and beauty had given to the middle of nowhere landscape, he got it. Reid... She was tireless when it came to making things beautiful, when it came to making things better.

Reagan told Nana it was the best steak he had ever eaten. "The meat is so fresh. I'm surprised it's not protesting."

She grinned. "I always love feeding people fresh beef. They usually don't realize the difference between fresh beef and what they normally eat until they taste it. Then they never want anything else."

Reagan was starving. He had even eaten most of the skin from his baked potato. The potato was the best he had ever tasted. He drank glass after glass of sweet tea, while they watched the sun set in the beautiful Texas sky. They talked and they talked. They talked politics. They talked about New York. They talked religion. They talked about the baby. Then the conversation turned serious.

Nana told Reagan that she knew all about why Reid had come home. She knew that they had argued. Reid told her everything, the morning after she arrived. Nana told him how Reid never got the courage to tell anyone else.

"Why?" he asked. "I just don't understand why. I know Reid. I know she's not ashamed of me, of us. I know she's not a racist. I only accused her of it because I wanted to know why she was keeping secrets."

"She can't explain it, Reagan. She might not even realize it herself."

"So then why did she tell you? Why you?"

"That one's easy. It's because she knows that she doesn't owe me anything. All I've ever wanted for Reid is wings, the same I wanted for everyone else, and she knows it. But she's torn. She's still trying to pay back what she thinks she owes."

Reagan looked at Nana. "Well, what is it? Hell, whatever it is, I'll pay it. What could she possibly owe?"

Nana took a deep breath. She had to make him understand, all of them. He must understand. It was critical, critical for Bob, for

Maureen, for Elise. It was critical for Reid, for the baby, for the future…

"It's her life, Reagan. Her life. She thinks she owes her life…"

Reagan did not understand. He sat there in Nana's little garden, wrapped in a clean horse blanket. He heard the crackling of the fireplace and the trickling of the fountain in the fading Texas twilight, then he listened to the old woman speak. She began to tell him the story, all of it, in a desperate attempt to be free, to finally be free.

"Who we are begins long before our first breath…" she began. Then she took him back, way back.

# Ellen

November 1917...

The cool November breeze kissed Ellen's Wilson's seven year old face as she stood still and silent in front of her mother. Dressed in her Sunday best, she watched as the day's events took place around her. She felt at any moment that she might leave her body, the scene so surreal. The only thing that kept her still, her feet firmly rooted to the ground, was her mother's hold, her mother's arms.

Abigail Wilson stood behind her daughter, afraid to move, for fear she might fall to her knees. They could see it coming. The wagon was slowly making its way up the road toward them. Ellen watched as it creaked to a stop in front of them, and knew that she would never forget this moment as long as she lived. The details would be seared into her memory for the rest of her days.

The casket, a plain wooden box, was covered by a thick blanket of dust. It had come all the way from the state insane asylum in Terrell, on rural Texas roads. At once, the hair on the back of Ellen's small neck began to stand, as she heard a loud gasp escape from her mother. Abigail Wilson began to weep, the pain in her cry so undeniably lonesome. Ellen could not take her eyes off her mother, even though she could not stand the sight of her pain. She watched as Abby, dressed in black, gathered her skirts and climbed up into the wagon. She collapsed in a heap, hugging the dirty casket.

Ellen's own tears fell down her cheeks, as she stood there in the tiny cemetery, grieving. She would not take her eyes off her mother. Abby's flaming red hair had escaped the severe knot that she wore at the nape of her neck, and her beautiful red curls tumbled down her back giving her a wild look that Ellen was not at all used to. Her heart was breaking for her precious Mama.

Finally, John Wilson climbed into the wagon and took his tiny wife in his arms. He held her as she cried. Ellen whispered to herself, "Thank you. Thank you, Papa." It wasn't like him to be moved to show affection. Ellen wasn't sure if he was really moved, or if he just wanted to put a stop to the scene. Whatever the reason, she was thankful.

Abby pulled herself together. Her husband helped her get down out of the wagon. Ellen watched, as her Papa talked to the two men that had delivered the body. They proceeded to move the coffin to the gravesite, where Ellen stood with the rest of her family. She could not believe that her grandmother was in there. She wondered what she looked like. Everyone had always said that Ellen resembled her grandmother. She had long thick ebony hair. For this, she was set apart from the rest of the Wilson brood. Their hair consisted of shades of red, from deep dark auburn to light reddish blond. Ellen was the only one to have the beautiful thick dark braids that hung down her back.

Ellen knew that her grandmother was a Cherokee Indian. She had married Ellen's grandfather when she was only fifteen. He was just off the boat from Ireland, and they had come to Texas in a covered wagon, from Tennessee. Now, Ellen struggled to put together bits and pieces of stories she had heard all her life, to make some sense of what she was experiencing. She wished she had paid more attention. But one thing was for sure, Grandma Flynn had died in the state insane asylum at forty-five and her body had come home to be buried.

Ellen surveyed the landscape with her seven year old eyes. The little cemetery had never seemed so cold and sad. She looked on as Grandpa Flynn stood there at his wife's casket, with his old felt hat in his hand. He paused to pray and then walked away, his feeble little Irish legs unsteady. Ellen wanted to hug him, to feel his warmth, to take in his gentleness. She shivered.

Papa was next. He paid his respects then went to stand with Grandpa. Ellen stood still and quiet with the rest of the Wilson children, under the stern gaze of Aunt Evelyn, her Papa's oldest sister. She was shocked when Mama took her hand and led her away in the direction of the casket. She felt as if she were in a dream. She listened closely to the words her mother spoke, in a soft whisper, that only the two of them and the Creator could hear.

"Please, Father, give me strength." It was a plea. It was a confession.

"Thank you, Father, for my life." Abby spoke with sincerity and thankfulness that she had been rescued from the torment, not so long ago.

Strength? Ellen thought about what her mother had said. It worried her. Mama needing strength was something that she never suspected. No one was stronger than Mama, no one. And hearing her mother say thank you for her life made Ellen sad, for she realized by the way that her mother spoke the words that it must have been in danger at some point in time.

Abby bent down and kissed the casket goodbye. Then she led her daughter away. She took her sweet child by the shoulders and turned her around to face her. She looked down into her blue eyes and whispered with conviction.

"We're strong, Ellen. We're not like that."

Ellen stiffened.

"You hear me, don't you?"

Ellen nodded.

"Nothing can break us." And with that, Abigail Wilson took Ellen's small hand. They walked away without so much as a backward glance, hand in hand, heart to heart.

That's how it was, a single day, a moment, an instant when people are never the same. It was a living, breathing, beautiful moment in time, even though it hurt like hell. Time and all that they lived through was shaping them, molding them, so that what they would become was greater, even more alive. And all of it would ultimately affect so many others, others that would come after. Some they would know. Some they would never know. But still so many would be affected by the choices that they made, when the making of choices was of the utmost importance, when it concerned right and wrong, good and evil, love and hate.

Ellen and her mother drew strength from one another. Abigail confided in her daughter as she had never confided in anyone before, nor ever would again. She confessed the sadness of being raised by a mother so tormented by mental illness, without fear or anger, resentment or even sorrow, but with resolve. That was the way it had been, but not the way it had to be. She knew that she was blessed beyond measure. She had survived. She had raised her two siblings, protected them from her mother when she was merely a child herself. She never let them out of her sight until the day they came to take her mother away.

Abby saw it only one way. Evil had tormented her mother, and there was nothing she could do about that. But she would spend the rest of her lifetime keeping it away from her and all that was hers. And it was at this pivotal point that the groundwork was laid, the strong foundation that would support the women that would come after her, the women that would be touched by her. It was in this way that Ellen Wilson was fashioned, seeking all that is good, seeking all that is right, a deep, inexhaustible source of love and strength that would be tested time and time again.

The world continued to turn. It was the summer of 1928, and life was beautiful. The Wilsons were on their way to a hometown picnic in their tiny town of Kilroy. The warm afternoon wagon ride was filled with laughter. It was days like this, free from the exhausting daily farm life, that Ellen Wilson looked so forward to. It wasn't very often that the family left the farm and went into town for something like this. It was almost impossible. It took hard work, all day, every day, to survive. The entire family had to work together to put food on the table. From Ellen, the oldest, all the way down to Jack, the youngest, they each had specific duties that got them through each day. There was little time for fighting for the seven Wilson children. They were way too busy.

The picnic was taking place down by the river, shaded by a grove of ancient oaks. Brightly colored, handmade quilts covered the ground. Children waded in the river. Young people introduced and reintroduced each other, enjoying the rare opportunity to socialize. Their parents visited with neighbors and other family members. It was here that Ellen Wilson met the man that would be her husband. Introduced to him by her cousin, she was immediately drawn to Lloyd Adams. She spent the whole afternoon getting to know him. When Brother Willingham asked for everyone's attention, and said he thought they should all start heading for home, Ellen felt something she had never felt before. It was a tugging somewhere inside her. She wasn't ready to go, but a storm was gathering and there was no time to be wasted. She gave Lloyd a backward glance as she called goodbye. Papa was already calling her. He had everyone loaded in the wagon.

The sky was dark. Angry storm clouds had gathered just overhead, leaving the horizon silvery gold. Ellen had seen this sky so many times before, and she could feel the fear rising up in her gut, like she'd swallowed river rocks. The wagon rumbled on as she studied the faces of her brothers and sisters. They were blank, evaluating the sky. She wondered what they were thinking. Martin, her younger brother by fifteen months, winked at her. She winked back. Maybe it was because they were so close in age, or maybe it was because they looked so much alike, that they were like twins. Whatever the reason, Ellen and Martin had a special bond. Bell, Caroline, Jane, and Rose were huddled up together. Ellen blew them a kiss and smiled, speaking with her eyes, "Don't worry, we'll be fine."

At seventeen, Ellen was the oldest of the seven Wilson children. Then there was Martin, who was sixteen, Bell, who was twelve, Caroline at ten, Jane at seven, Rose at five, and little Jack, the baby, at two and a half. He sat wide eyed at the front of the wagon, in between Mama and Papa. Ellen cleared her throat in an effort to suppress the fear rising up in it. "Papa, we're almost home, aren't we?"

John Wilson's voice was gentle, for he knew that she knew the way. She knew exactly how far from home they were. He also knew that she did not ask the question for her benefit, but for the others. "Yes, we're almost home."

Ellen could see the tails dropping down across the horizon. She counted them. 1, 2, 3, 4, 5, 6, 7… Tornadoes. She knew their path could be devastating. It did not matter how many times she had seen them, they still caused her to be frightened and nervous, for this was something Mama and Papa could not protect her from. They were too big, their rage beyond anything anyone could comprehend.

As the soft rain began to fall, Ellen marveled at how the day had begun. It had been clear, bright, and happy. They had risen early. She and Martin had helped Papa feed the livestock, and then they had all gotten ready for church. Church was something they never missed. They would ride the ten miles into town every Sunday morning. It was an enjoyable part of family life. The day had been special, because of the picnic, and most of all Lloyd Adams. Ellen felt that tugging again.

The Wilson family rode on in silence, each member lost in thought. Finally the road turned sharply to the right, and they were truly almost home. Ellen's heart leapt. The wind was starting to blow harder, which reassured her and made her feel better. She knew that this was good. It was when the stillness came that a person should be concerned. Right now, while the winds were free, they were still safe. She could see the house, at last.

The little farmhouse had never looked so inviting. She couldn't wait to get inside and change her clothes. Papa pulled the wagon up to the front of the house and all of the girls piled out. Ellen first, then the others jumping into her arms, one by one. Abby climbed down from the wagon and raised her arms so that her husband could hand her their youngest child. She kissed the top of Jack's head and shouted to the girls, "Inside, and get those wet clothes off!" They all ran for the house.

Martin rode with his father to the barn, to get the wagon and the horses in. Ellen changed out of her wet clothes and into a dry cotton dress with blue cornflowers on it. She smiled, remembering when she and Mama had bought the fabric. They had gone into town, just the two of them, and bought it. Mama was amazing. Ellen watched as her mother produced dry clothes for the children, with absolutely no regard for herself. Ellen began to help the others change into the dry clothes, so that her mother could change herself. But Abby just kept going. Not until everyone was totally dry and calm did she disappear into her room.

Ellen watched her mother constantly. It was always the same. Abby never came first, never. Ellen loved her mother deeply. She and Mama were close. Ellen loved her stern Papa, too. She was the first child, had been their first baby. Even if it was only for a short time, she was glad she had been first. For some reason, the thought that she had Mama and Papa to herself for just a little while made her feel good, made her feel special.

Just then the door blew open. The wind and rain assaulted the little farmhouse. Ellen tried to get a glimpse of Papa and Martin. They still had not come in from putting the horses and wagon away. Mama looked out the kitchen window, but could see nothing. Everyone was silent, waiting for direction. She shouted at Ellen, "It's getting worse. Get Jack! Wrap him up and head for the cellar. I'll get the girls."

Ellen did as she was told. She wasted no time. She took the quilt off of her bed and swaddled her precious little brother. She kissed his red curls quickly before she covered his head. He was always glad to be in her arms. For the first year of his life, he thought Ellen was his mother.

Abby draped quilts over the girls, and they made their way to the front door. She told Ellen to make a run for it. She would be right behind her. "Papa and Martin are already there. I'm sure of it." Ellen took a deep breath, said a quick prayer, and took off.

She ran out of the safe little farmhouse and into the cold rain, across the porch and down the steps, headlong into the worst storm she had ever known. The wind almost knocked her to the ground. She was not expecting such force. She kept pushing on in the direction of the storm cellar. She could hardly see. It was just a door on the ground, opening to some steps that led to a small room eight feet under the earth. How would she ever see it? Fear had her in its steely grip. She started to panic. The wind was so strong. She began to think she would be blown away. She was holding Jack as tight as she could, but she felt like she was losing her grip, like she wasn't strong enough to hold on to him.

She felt the wind under her skirt. She felt her feet leave the ground as she began her ascension up into the air. Disbelief gripped her. This could not be happening. She still had not let go of Jack. She could hear him screaming in her arms, but it was a muffled scream, like he was far away from her. Ellen could see the storm all around her. Debris was flying through the air, and she thought at any moment they would be struck and killed. Then she noticed that she was suspended in the air. She was in some kind of safe circle, protected. She could barely hear, barely see. She pleaded for her life. Then darkness...

Mama made it to the cellar with the girls. Papa and Martin were waiting inside.

John Wilson forced the cellar door open when he heard them approaching. He could hear their cries. They were terrified. This is a bad one, he thought. They might lose everything, but they would all be safe in the cellar.

Martin watched them rush in and hurry down the steps, panic rising. He screamed at the chaos, "Ellen!" His beloved sister was not there. She was not with them.

Mama turned her head sharply to meet his gaze, and then frantically began to explain, "She left the house, first, with Jack."

There was a moment of silence, as the implications of what she spoke became understood. Martin shot up the stairs as fast as he could go and forced the door open. He was pulled out into the storm as Papa tried to stop him. He heard Mama scream in terror.

John let out a defeated cry. He was angry, he was afraid, and he was humbled in an instant. His children were out in that storm, and he knew that he could not go after them. It was too fierce. He would never make it. Of course, he hoped that Martin would find Ellen and Jack, and that they would be all right. But he doubted it. Abby began to cry. The tears flowed down her cheeks as she waited. She would not give up hope. Martin would be all right. He would find them.

The storm raged on. But finally, after what seemed like an eternity, the winds died down and the rain began to let up. John took Abby by the hand and gave her a quick kiss on the forehead. Life for them had been hard, yes, but they had always been all right as long as they had each other. And the family that they had built together was their most prized possession, second to nothing in the world. He feared that what they would find now might change them forever.

She spoke to him in a calm and deliberate tone. "Go and get the doctor."

He protested. "We have to find them. Abby, they're probably..."

She did not allow him to finish. She spoke to him in the same tone. "I will find them. You go get the doctor."

It was ridiculous, but he did not argue. There was something about her that commanded him. At the moment, he had nothing to lose. So he ran for the barn, grabbed a bridle, jumped on his horse, and took off. Abby began to run. She didn't know where she was running to, but she ran. The girls were still safely in the cellar. They had been told not to move until she returned. They were afraid. They would do as they were told.

Abby's mind was blank. She could see nothing, think of nothing, but finding her children. She searched the scene, looking for something that looked familiar. Their home was almost gone. The pretty little white farmhouse had no roof or porch. What was left of it stood on the hill, all of the windows broken. But the storm's wrath was beyond her right now. It would have to wait.

Straight in front of her, she could not believe her eyes. It was. It had to be. Jack was walking toward her, eyes wild, no emotion. He must be out of his head with fright, she thought.

She ran. She picked him up and cradled him in her arms. She felt something so strange, something so strong. Holding her precious child in her arms, Abby looked up at the angry sky, to where the sun was peeking from behind the dark storm clouds, for just a moment...

"Jack, you've got to be brave. Everything's all right, but I need you to tell me where Ellen is, and Martin. Have you seen Martin?" She waited, searching his face for something, anything.

The rain had gone, the wind had gone, but they were not forgotten. Whole trees were uprooted. Pieces of the house and barn were everywhere. Abby saw her wash basin lying on the ground right beside her. She could not imagine how Ellen and Martin could survive this, but she put her doubt away. She knew full well what a defining moment she was caught up in.

Just then Jack started sobbing, "She's by the pecan trees."

Abby told him that he must go to the cellar and wait for her there. She began to run again. The pecan trees? How did she get all the way out there?

Then Abby saw her. She was lying on the ground. Abby screamed at her, "Ellen!" There was nothing, no response. She ran harder to get to her daughter. She bent down beside her and studied her daughter's fine face. A thousand thoughts raced through her mind. Everyone had always thought Ellen plain, but not Abby. She had always known that Ellen would turn into this beautiful creature. She looked at her straight nose and high cheek bones. Abby always saw so much of her own mother in Ellen. Ellen looked Indian, except for her Irish blue eyes. Her long dark hair had become her trademark, and Abby looked at it now, spilling all over the ground. It was beautiful.

She was afraid to touch her. She didn't know if she was hurt or even alive. She bent closer and pressed her cheek to Ellen's. She began to cry uncontrollably, her pain so deep. Then she felt it. It was faint, but she felt it again. Then again. Ellen's breath. A faint memory of how she would put her own face next to Ellen's sleeping infant face surfaced and was gone. She sat there touching her daughter's face for a moment, trying to decide what she should do.

She saw someone riding up, on a horse. But it was not John. Who was it? She couldn't tell until the young man rode closer. Lloyd Adams... It was the boy that was with Ellen at the picnic earlier. Was that today? Abby couldn't even remember.

He jumped off his horse, and with a quiet voice, barely audible, he asked Abby if Ellen was dead. Abby smiled a broken smile and said no. She told him that she did not want to leave Ellen, but Martin was still missing. She started to explain, "Martin went to look for her. He's still out here somewhere." Lloyd took off on horseback.

Abby watched him go and hoped he would find her son. He just had too. She sat with Ellen and drifted somewhere between disbelief and panic, lost in thoughts of happier days, begging the Creator for mercy. She saw the doctor's car slowly approaching. It stopped at the roadside, and Abby watched as her husband and Doctor Aarington got out. They began to run when they realized that someone was down. John looked at Abby's face. It was tear stained and looked so much older than it ever had before. "She's alive," she told them.

Doctor Aarington felt Ellen's pulse and tried to speak to her, but there was no response. He told John that they had to put her in the car. "The house is barely standing. We can't take her home." They decided they would take her into town, to the doctor's office. She would be comfortable there.

Lloyd came riding up and said that he found Martin down by the tank. He tried to get him on the horse, but Martin was in too much pain. Something was broken, but other than that he seemed to be all right.

All three men picked Ellen up and moved her to the back seat of the doctor's car. "Boy, what are you doing here?" John had finally noticed Lloyd.

"I was following you home, sir. I wanted to ask you if I could see Ellen again. I got caught in the storm and waited it out under a cleft in the hill."

John looked bewildered. His daughter's life was not even a certainty right now. He considered the boy's words. "Son, if she lives, you can see her as much as you like."

Lloyd put his hand on John Wilson's back. "Sir, she's going to live. I know she is."

John pulled himself together. There was no time. His son was still out there, and he was hurt. The two went together. After Martin was safely in the front seat of Doctor Aarington's car, John turned to Lloyd, exhausted. "It doesn't look too good to me. It might be her time to go."

Lloyd would not even consider it. "Sir, I know she's going to live, because she's still got to be my wife." Words that never would have been spoken under normal circumstances offered hope and faith to John Wilson, where there was none. But John could not look him in the eye. He just wasn't sure.

Night came quickly. John took the children to his father-in-law's house. The tiny, one-room farmhouse was not the most comfortable choice, but it was by far the most popular. The children loved Grandpa Flynn, dearly. He was a sweet, kind man that showered them with affection. Abby could relax, knowing that they were with her father. She would not be able to rest had they gone to Grandpa and Grandma Wilson's house. They were far too stern for her liking, and she had to concentrate on Ellen. She knew the children would be happy and safe with Grandpa Flynn.

In the days that followed, members of the Wilson family took turns sitting with Ellen, talking to her, touching her, watching her. She made no contact. There was no movement. The soft sound of her breathing was the only indication that she was still there. Lloyd became a permanent fixture, one of the family. It occurred to John that his daughter might not be in love with the boy. As much as Lloyd loved Ellen, she might not love him back. It was obvious that Lloyd had fallen for her at the picnic that day, and since then he had gotten to know her by spending so much time with the family. They told story after story of her, to keep them all going, to keep hope alive. Lloyd felt as if he knew her, and John could tell he was in love with her already. But what if Ellen woke and felt nothing for the boy? John took a deep breath and smiled. That was a problem he would be thankful to have.

He decided to stop thinking so much and asked Doctor Aarington's nurse for some ice to rub on Ellen's lips. They were parched and cracking. She brought the ice, and he began to rub it on his daughter's lips. Ellen had not been awake for three days. She had been in a bed at Dr. Aarington's office for three whole days. The doctor said she should stay there so he could keep an eye on her. He really didn't think she would make it and thought it best for her to stay there in town, so that when she passed it would be easier on the family. They had been through so much. They had lost almost everything, cattle, crops, their home, and probably their first born. He told them that if Ellen was still alive tomorrow, she would need to be taken to Forth Worth, to a hospital. There was more that could be done there. John and Dr. Aarington would take her in the morning, in the doctor's car, the forty-five miles to Fort Worth.

John patted his daughter's hand. Tears stung his eyes. Life had been hard for Ellen, already. At seventeen, she could farm like a man. She had pretty much raised the youngest three Wilson children, up to now. Her father considered that he had never, ever, heard her complain. He thought about all the things she had asked of him over the years. He thought of all the times he had said no. Did she even know that he loved her, that at seventeen years old she had earned her father's respect, for her strength and heart? Did she know that the mere thought of losing her was more than he could bear? He doubted it. After all, how could she? He rarely showed affection. He couldn't recall ever telling her that he loved her.

He watched her sleeping, pale and lifeless. She didn't look anything like him. He remembered when she was born. She had a shock of black hair and big blue eyes. He'd never seen a baby quite like her before. She was so odd, so different from him. It was hard to get acquainted with her. It took him a long time to get used to the fact that she looked so different. He looked at her now, as if for the first time. She was beautiful, not showy-like, but striking. Her face was unforgettable, just like her.

He stayed through the night. Finally, he heard the door open and saw his wife come in. She was tired, worn. Her hair was pulled back and secured with ivory combs. It was clean and shiny, so red that it still caught his eye. Abby stood in front of him with a broken heart. She knew that Ellen would have to be moved. And while she knew that Ellen had to go, she was apprehensive for her to leave. She couldn't stand not knowing what was going on. Ellen didn't seem to be in any pain. She just slept on and on. Abby wanted to take her and shake her. She wanted to scream at her to wake up. As moment after moment passed, she felt her patience running out. She prayed for comfort. She prayed for strength. She prayed for a miracle.

John told his wife that he would leave her with Ellen, while he headed over to the lumber yard. He needed to get an idea how much it was going to cost to rebuild. They were staying with Grandpa Flynn, and it was cramped. It didn't bother Abby. After all, they were staying with her father and she rather liked spending time with him. He was such a kind soul. But for John, who was accustomed to being the man of the house, the situation did not seem as cozy.

He said goodbye to his wife and to the nurse, Maggie. He walked out into the morning light. It was already hot. He crossed the street. The small town of Kilroy was already awake. He could see people waiting outside the store. It wasn't open yet. He could smell bacon and fresh biscuits coming from the café. Mrs. Reynolds stopped to inquire about Ellen. He told her that there was no change. She told him that she was in town to get some groceries. She said she was cooking a big meal for them and would be bringing it over later that evening. He thanked her and explained that he had some business to tend to. As he walked away, he thought about all the people that had fed them and offered help since the storm.

John Wilson had never been one that needed people very much, until now. There was something humbling about losing everything that he had worked so hard for. He felt vulnerable for the first time ever. He had lost his farm, and he could lose his daughter. The circumstances caused him to take note of his person before the storm. He thought he might not be so overbearing now, might be kinder. He would definitely try. He might actually listen when Abby read her Bible to the kids. He decided that he would.

Just then, he saw Abby running toward him, clutching her long skirt so that she wouldn't fall. Something was wrong. His heart began to beat faster and faster. "She's awake! She's awake, I said!" John looked at his wife in disbelief. Finally, he took her by the hand and began to run. His strides were so much longer than hers. He felt as if he was dragging her across the street and up the steps, back into the doctor's office. They ran into the room, where Maggie was giving Ellen a sip of water.

Ellen looked at them as they entered the room and smiled at them. She looked weak and pale, but alive. Maggie rose and said she would get the doctor. Abby and John began asking her question after question. Ellen spoke softly, as if it were difficult to respond. Doctor Aarington came in and told the Wilsons to calm down and to please leave the room while he examined Ellen and spoke to her. They were way too excited, and he thought it too much for Ellen. Abby started to protest, but Ellen shook her head yes and dismissed her mother.

John and Abby Wilson waited outside the room, listening at the door. They did not know what had happened to her. The last time anyone had spoken to Ellen, she was taking little Jack to the cellar. They had as many questions for her as she had for them. Doctor Aarington came outside and closed the door. He spoke softly so that Ellen could not hear him. He told Abby and John that their daughter had been in serious danger, and it was a miracle that she was alive. He didn't know the extent of her injuries because they were internal, and he had no way of assessing damage without certain tests. He said that Ellen should rest and not get too excited until they had a clearer picture of what they were dealing with. Abby and John agreed to speak softly and not get her excited. Dr. Aarington was stern.

They entered the room, and both bent down to kiss her cheek, Abby first, and then John. She smiled weakly at them. Abby sat down on the bed with Ellen, while John moved a chair closer to the bed for himself. Abby wanted to be close to her. She took her daughter's hand and kissed it. Ellen looked up at her mother, searching her face. Abby spoke first. "What do you remember?"

It was silent as Ellen gathered her thoughts. She spoke softly, "I remember wrapping Jack up and going to the cellar, but I know we didn't make it because the storm picked us up. I think it was a tornado, Mama." The tears began to stream down her face. She could hardly bring herself to ask the question, but she had to know. It made her head pound. "Jack? Where is he?" She looked into her mother's grey eyes and braced herself for the answer.

"He's with the others at Grandpa Flynn's house."

Ellen closed her eyes and began to sob. "I never let go, Mama. I never let go."

Abby took her daughter in her arms and held her tight, stroking her soft black hair. "I know, darling. I know. You did good." Abby smiled through her tears. She held her daughter in her arms, breathing in the smell of her hair, pausing for a moment to give thanks for the sweetness of the moment.

Abby told her daughter all that had happened, from the moment that she didn't show up at the cellar to the moment that she woke up. Ellen's delight could not be concealed whenever Lloyd Adams came up. There was a light in her eyes at the mention of his name. She could not believe that he had been around throughout the ordeal, or that she had been asleep for three days.

After awhile, John Wilson decided he would go and give the good news to the family. It was almost as if he wasn't there anyway. Abby and Ellen were talking incessantly. As he opened the door to go, he stopped. He turned to his daughter. "Ellen, I love you."

Ellen stared at him blankly. Her eyes welled up. "I love you too, Papa." Then he was gone, as both women stared after him in disbelief.

Ellen began to speak to her mother, to really speak. "Oh, Mama, I have so much to tell you. I was dreaming. I was so tired, and I hurt so badly. I didn't want to die, but I was just so weak. I could just feel myself slipping away, so I asked the Creator to take me. I was too tired to stay. And then there was this light, and there were angels, and they were all around me. And before I knew what was happening, I woke up. But it was real, Mama. It was real."

"I believe you," Abby told her, "Sometimes, we don't have an explanation for things. They just are." They sat there for a long time holding each other, discussing the storm, talking about all that had been lost, thankful for all that had been saved.

"Now, Ellen," Abby started. "There is something we have to address right now, while it's just the two of us. This boy, Lloyd, he's interested in you. But I know that you are fond of Tommy Newton. What I'm trying to say is... be kind to him, because I think he's in love with you."

Ellen gasped. "Mama! Now, you don't know that."

Abby narrowed her eyes and looked sharply at Ellen. "It wasn't that long ago that your father and I fell in love. I know what I'm talking about. I'm just saying don't be cruel to the boy."

Ellen smiled at her mother. "I won't."

In fact, Ellen knew full well that it was Mama that was fond of Tommy Newton, not her. Of course, she had been gracious to him, because she knew how her mother hoped that they would marry. Abby and Elaine Newton were old friends, and Abby thought Ellen and Tommy would be a perfect match. But Ellen had never felt more than friendly toward him. She was not attracted to him in the least.

Ellen spent the next two days in the little room at Doctor Aarington's office. She had to admit, in spite of the circumstances, she enjoyed herself immensely. She had a lovely little room to herself, decorated with beautiful English antiques, and the most glorious of antique poster beds she had ever seen. It was high off the ground. She felt like a princess.

Friends and relatives stopped in to see her, bringing flowers and all kinds of homemade treats. She almost felt guilty that she was being showered with so much attention, but decided to enjoy it. She knew that it would all be over soon. She would be back to cooking, farming, washing, and looking after the little ones.

The morning began early for Ellen. Maggie came in to wake her at seven, with a bouquet of fresh flowers that she had picked that morning. Ellen smiled when she saw them. Roses, she thought they were beautiful and smelled so sweet. She thanked Maggie for taking such good care of her. Maggie protested, by saying she was just doing her job, but Ellen would not let her dismiss it.

"Maggie, I do not thank you now for changing my bed sheets, changing my gowns, or giving me water. I thank you for waking me with flowers. I thank you for putting me to sleep with kisses. I thank you for praying over me at night, when everyone was gone, and you thought I was sleeping."

There was a knock at the door. Ellen asked who was there. Lloyd Adams announced himself. "Just a minute," Ellen called. She was horrified. She had not dressed, or washed up, or anything. What was he doing here?

Maggie recognized panic when she saw it, and Ellen was about to do just that. Maggie could not help but smile. She was young once. "Ellen, get yourself dressed. I'll go get some water for the wash basin and tell him to wait a minute." Ellen nodded and began to dress hastily in the only clean skirt and blouse that she had. It was a yellow cotton skirt, and a white cotton blouse with a pretty little collar that Mama had made for her. She brushed her long dark hair and braided it into one braid that hung down her back.

Maggie returned with fresh water for the basin, and Ellen washed up. She took one quick look in the dresser mirror and decided that it would have to do. She opened the door to see Lloyd standing there. She smiled at him. He smiled back. He nervously began to explain that he was there to pick her up and take her home. He studied her reaction. He decided that she was surprised, but not disappointed. She invited him into the little room that she had been staying in, and he saw her bags on the bed. She explained that she was all packed and ready to go.

Ellen told Lloyd that she would quickly say her goodbyes to Doctor Aarington and Maggie. He nodded and told her that he would carry her bags to the wagon and meet her out front. Ellen took one last look at the little room, and made sure she was not leaving anything behind. She closed the door behind her, excited to be leaving with Lloyd. She found Doctor Aarington in his office, talking to Maggie. Their attention was on Ellen as she entered the room. "Well, I see you're leaving us today," the doctor said.

"Yes, sir. I'm anxious to get home and see the rest of my family. I miss my brothers and sisters." She paused and began to look directly at the doctor. "I just want to let you know how thankful I am for the care that you gave me while I was here, sir."

Doctor Aarington was quiet. The girl that stood before him was something, so much wiser than her seventeen years. She was kind and gracious. She had an air of dignity about her that caught him off guard. He accepted her thanks and walked her to the door. He told her that if she had any pain, or felt anything not quite right at any time, to come and see him. He explained to her the possibilities of her trauma, and advised her that it was not to be underestimated.

After one last hug from Maggie, Lloyd helped Ellen into her father's wagon. He took the reins and drove off. Ellen waved to the doctor and his nurse, as they waved goodbye to her. As the wagon made its way down the road and out of town, they watched her go, hoping for nothing but the best for the special girl.

Lloyd felt a little nervous at being alone with Ellen. He began to explain that he had gone to her house to wait for her return, but found everyone so busy trying to get last minute things done. He had volunteered to go and get her, so that they would not have to stop. She began to ask him the questions that she had not wanted to ask Mama and Papa. She did not want to upset them. "Lloyd, just how bad is it?"

He didn't answer immediately, so she continued, "I know that the farm was almost destroyed, so be honest with me. Do you think they'll be able to rebuild?"

He paused a moment and then answered her. "Your father and mother have already repaired a part of the house, and they're living in that part. They will be able to rebuild the rest, a little at a time. The farm is another story. The barn is gone. They will have to build a new barn. Most of the crops are gone, as well as the livestock. It's just going to take a lot of hard work."

Ellen listened to all that he said, not with her head but with her heart. She could tell that he was concerned. His words were one thing, but she tuned into the heaviness of his heart when he spoke, and that was another. They rode on, in silence. Lloyd was so enamored of her that he was speechless. Ellen was so deep in thought; she was lost in time and space.

They veered sharply to the right, and Ellen thought back to the day of the storm. On that day, she had been relieved to make that same turn. It signaled the last leg of the journey. It had always meant they were almost home. She considered that one never knew when disaster was right around the corner. Disaster... No home... No farm... Nothing...

She considered hope. She considered faith. She felt them stir within her. She knew that something wonderful would come again. After all, was it not a miracle that Jack was alive? Was it not a miracle that Martin was alive? Was it not a miracle that she, herself, was alive?

As the farm came into view, she caught her breath. Tears ran down her face, tears of thankfulness. The little white farmhouse was mostly gone. There was nothing left of the porch. The only thing still standing was a small part that her father had walled in to make a space for the family to stay in. He could not stay another day at Grandpa Flynn's house. He was not the type of man to stay, indefinitely, in someone else's home. But Ellen saw that the land was still there, the hills, the oaks, the creek, the river. And for this she was so thankful, so very thankful.

Lloyd was right. There was no barn in sight. She thought about the horses. She had been told they were found in a neighbor's pasture, grazing. It was a wonder that they survived. She figured that the tornado had picked up the barn, sparing the horses. They had one cow left, a couple of chickens, and a little bit of corn left in the fields. Ellen, lost in her own thoughts, said out loud, "We'll be all right."

She looked at the land once again. It was still beautiful. The shady oaks with their graceful branches welcomed her home. The view of the creek, from where the porch had been, was still so peaceful. She hoped her parents would rebuild the house exactly as it had been before. It had been so simple, and so pretty, sitting on the hillside at the end of Anneville Road.

Lloyd helped Ellen down out of the wagon. They walked to the door of what was left of her home. As they opened it, they were greeted with a loud chorus of, "Surprise!" Ellen could not believe how many people were in that small space. She noticed that it contained the original kitchen and living room, so it still looked so much like home. She saw her parents, Jack, Bell, Jane, Rose, and Caroline, all so excited to see her. Before she knew it, she was in Martin's arms being picked up and spun around the room. She smelled him. He smelled of soap and horses, and chewing tobacco. She had missed her brother so much. There was a flood of laughter, talking, and the sounds of forks hitting plates. She smelled the aroma of home cooked food, and the sweetness of fresh pound cake baking. This was a coming home party for her, and it was wonderful.

She watched Lloyd circle the room, shaking hands, all smiles. He seemed to know everyone there, most of which was her family. It seemed a little strange to her. She felt as if she had just met him at the picnic.

Morning spent over coffee quickly gave way to afternoon and a big meal. And too soon, it was time to go. Ellen's grand-parents, aunts, uncles, cousins, and friends bid her farewell. They left her with many heartfelt gifts, as well as countless hugs and kisses. At last, Lloyd announced he must also be going also. He had some work to do at home. His own parents were expecting him. He told John that he would be back in the morning to join in the rebuilding effort.

Ellen walked him out to his horse and asked him, point blank, why he was doing all that he was doing for her and her family. He was not prepared for the question. He spoke truthfully, from his heart, "Ellen, quite honestly, since I met you at that picnic, things haven't been the same for me. All I can think about is you. I want to be as close to you as possible, and I don't know what I'll do if you decide that you don't really like me."

Her answer was not what he expected at all. "You know, I felt the strangest thing that day as we drove away from the picnic. I felt kind of sick the further I got away from you. If that's what being in love is like, I don't think I shall like it very much." And with that, she called goodbye and walked away. Lloyd Adams was struck dumb. He could not decide if what she had said was good or bad. What he did know for sure, as he jumped on his horse and headed for home, was that he was more in love with her today than yesterday, and quite possibly would be more in love with her tomorrow than today.

Ellen spent the afternoon walking over the land she loved, survey-ing the damage with Martin. They talked of all that happened after the storm. Martin filled her in on all that had really gone on. They laughed uncontrollably when he told of Caroline and Rose putting honey all over Grandpa Flynn, as he dozed in his chair, only to be awakened by ants attacking him. Poor Grandpa Flynn, thought Ellen. How he never lost his temper, she would never know.

The conversation took a serious turn when Martin began to confide in her, all that he had learned. He painted a grim picture when it came to the state of affairs for the Wilson family. He told his sister how he had overheard Papa telling Mama that he didn't know how they were going to make it. One night, when he thought the kids were all sleeping, Papa told Mama that he had borrowed a little money from Grandpa and Grandma Wilson to get started, but did not know what they would do after that. It made Ellen so sad. Everyone worked so hard, from Mama and Papa right down to little Jack. They all worked so hard, just to get by. Ellen and Martin decided that they would not let Mama and Papa know that they were in on their secret. If their parents had not told them, or even spoken of the situation in front of them, that meant they didn't want anyone to know.

Days went by with the entire family busy, trying to get the farm functioning again. No word was ever spoken of hardship. In fact, it seemed they had more than before in the way of food and clothes, and the house was being built even bigger and lovelier than before. Lloyd Adams had become a fixture. Not a day went by without hearing his laughter or being a victim of his practical jokes. He and Ellen had become an item, and it was obvious to everyone that they were in love, even Tommy Newton. Ellen knew that Mama still held on to hopes of her marrying Tommy Newton. "But Mama doesn't have to be married to him, I do," she told Martin.

She loved Lloyd's free spirit and his amazing heart. She knew when she met him that there would be no one else. They became engaged on December 25th, 1929, when he told her that he loved her, wanted her for his wife, and placed a ring on her finger. They were married at the office of the Justice of the Peace, on December 31st, 1930. And so, life took a turn…

It was a cold day in December, 1932, when Lloyd Adams saw for the first time exactly what his wife was made of. The economy was at its worst. There was no work anywhere. Migrant workers rode the rails looking for any type of labor that would put food in their bellies. Ellen Adams set a table down by the train tracks, with a crisp white linen table cloth and hot home cooked food, complete with cakes and pies. Lloyd could not believe it. His wife was feeding the hobos down by the train tracks, in the middle of what had become known as the Great Depression. He watched her visit with them and serve them, as if she were hosting the most elaborate of tea parties. He marveled. To him, she was the most beautiful woman in the world. He could not help chuckling to himself as he watched her. This was the most serious of affairs.

He finally had the chance to whisper in her ear. "What in the world are you doing?"

She answered him matter-of-factly. "Why, I'm having a party," was her reply. And she went on hosting the most unlikely guests he believed he would ever see.

Later on that night, as she lay her tired body down, she spoke sleepily, her voice trailing off into the darkness, "I know it was strange, but I just couldn't stand it another minute. You understand, don't you? Knowing that I had the power to do something…"

She was asleep as soon as the words left her lips. Lloyd Adams lay in his bed, eyes wide open, listening to her breathe. "Thank You," he whispered. "Thank You."

She continued to surprise him over the years. Life with her was more beautiful than he ever could have imagined, and it was full with raising two daughters, Maureen and Annalyn, as well as running the family grocery store. They had their struggles. There was a time, when the girls were small, that Ellen had only two dresses. But those were some of the happiest days of her life. She filled hard times with hard work, a little laughter, and so, so much love. She faced the worst of times head on. She knew that they were the most important of times, the times that ultimately defined her. "Times when you see for yourself exactly what it is that you're made of, times when you know that you're truly alive," she said.

Then came January, 1958... Lloyd watched, late one night, as she brushed her dark hair. She was forty-seven, and still had not spied a grey hair. He, on the other hand, had long since lost his hair, and what was left of it was grey.

She sat at her cherry dressing table, smiling and talking to him as she brushed. She was filled with excitement. He had seen her this way so many times over the years.

Maureen, their oldest daughter, had given birth that day to their first grandchild. They were grandparents! Ellen recalled watching Annalyn hold the baby for the first time, early that morning. She had been so gentle, so loving. At a mere ten years old, she had become "Aunt Annalyn," overnight, and she was taking the title very seriously. She had called home a little while ago from the Simpson's, where she was sleeping over with her best friend Kate, and announced that she was going to teach the baby how to fish. Ellen laughed at the prospect, knowing full well that worms always made Annalyn squeamish. She told her that they would talk about it tomorrow afternoon, when she returned home.

Lloyd did not even hear what his wife was saying. He was lost in thoughts of life with her, how thankful he was that he had married her. She turned and went to sit beside him on the bed. He had not been feeling well lately, and she was worried about him. She had urged him to spend less time at the store and more time at home, relaxing, taking it easy. She kept telling him they weren't as young as they used to be. It worried her even more, since he had actually begun to take her advice.

Lloyd at rest was a reason for concern. It didn't happen often. He had a mind for making money, with his hand in all kinds of businesses around town that had begun to pay off. His instincts had succeeded in making him and his family quite comfortable. It was the reason they had come through the Depression unscathed, so many years ago. While he and Ellen read of countless tragedies in the newspapers, they remained unaffected by it all. In fact, Lloyd had turned it into opportunity for them. They opened up a successful grocery business. That was twenty-five years ago.

As he lay in bed, just about to drift off to sleep, Ellen thought of all that he meant to her, all that they had shared together. She cherished the gift of her husband and her family, never taking them for granted. Life had been so sweet for her and Lloyd, and the struggles had made it even sweeter. She got into bed beside him. She was wiser, this wife that was now a grandmother, this wife that truly recognized the gift that she had been given in him. She fell asleep talking to the Creator that night. She was so incredibly thankful.

The next morning she woke early and cooked a big breakfast, complete with bacon, eggs, and biscuits with gravy. It was just the two of them. Annalyn would not be home until after lunchtime. They sat down and ate together, laughing, excited about the birth of the baby. Maureen had named her Frances. They would call her Frankie, after Ellen's own dear Aunt Frankie. Lloyd told Ellen that he was going to look for a nice rocking chair for Maureen, something like the mahogany one he bought for Ellen when Annalyn was born. He would just wash up in the restroom and be gone. Ellen had begun to clear the breakfast dishes when she heard him fall. Time stood still.

It was like a dream. It was like a nightmare. Lloyd lay on the bathroom floor. Ellen screamed out his name, as she struggled to hold him in her arms. He did not move, but she could feel his breath on her face. She put her cheek to his cheek. She was panicking. She was crying, praying, and calling his name, all at once. She felt him go limp in her arms, and realized he was going. He was leaving her. She sat there rocking him in her arms, sobbing. She knew he was gone.

She sat on the bathroom floor, holding him. She was in another world. She was in a world of firsts: first love, first kisses, first home, first car, first baby, first grandbaby. She lost track of time...

The light came beaming into the bathroom, signaling the midmorning sun. Ellen calmly got up and called Lloyd's doctor. She told him simply that the love of her life had gone. The young Doctor Kenneth Aarington told her that he was on his way.

He did not even knock. He opened the screen door to the handsome old home of Lloyd and Ellen Adams, and went inside. He saw a broken Ellen, still in her apron, sitting at the kitchen table. She was in a state of something that looked to him like disbelief. He asked her what had happened, what was going on. She looked at him with empty blue eyes and said that Lloyd was in the bathroom.

Doctor Aarington crossed the kitchen, and made his way to the bathroom. He found Lloyd Adams lying there, with a quilt tucked around him, as if to keep him warm. There was a pillow under his head. As the young doctor examined him, he could not help but get choked up. The man that lay dead on the bathroom floor had always been so kind. Kenneth Aarington had experienced it firsthand when he and his own wife were starting out. Mr. Adams refused to let them pay for their groceries at his store. He said something about Kenneth paying it back one day when he became a doctor. But even after he had gotten out of medical school, and taken over his father's practice, Mr. Adams had always insisted on paying his medical bills at the time of service.

Young Doctor Kenneth Aarington wished that he could turn back time. He wished that he could fix Lloyd. He wished that he could thank him. Oh, of course, he had said thank you. But he wished now, that he could really thank Mr. Adams, really let him know what he had done for a struggling newlywed couple. The doctor could not help but cry.

Just then Ellen came to the doorway. He wiped his eyes with the back of his hand. He did not want her to see him cry. She asked him if he was okay. She could see the emotion, all over his face. "I was just thinking about his kindness. Anne and I had some hard times when we were first married. I was in medical school, and we barely had enough money to eat. He would not let us pay for our groceries. He said that I would pay it back someday. I never told him how much we needed that. Of course, I said thank you, but I never..."

Ellen cut him off, "Believe me, he knew. We started out at the beginning of the Great Depression. He knew all about struggle. He knew." They both smiled in spite of the circumstances.

The doctor took control. First, he called the coroner's office. Next, he called the funeral home. After that, his wife.

Ellen noticed the time. Very soon, Annalyn would be returning from her sleepover. She began to panic. She did not want her daughter coming home to such a scene. She thought about Annalyn... Right this very minute, she was still innocent, still sharing life with her father. She had no idea that he was gone. "Doctor Aarington, do you think you could drive over to the Simpson's and let them know what has happened? Maybe you could ask them if they could keep Annalyn for a little while longer, until someone comes for the body. I don't want anyone to tell her. I'll do that. I just don't want her to see him. I don't want this to be her last memory of her father."

The doctor drove straight to Tom and Edith Simpson's house.

Ellen watched, as a stranger from the county coroner's office drove away with her husband's body. She took a deep breath and picked up the phone. Ruth Johnson was her first call...

Maureen was so close to her father that Ellen dreaded to make the call, but time would not wait. The phone rang and rang. Finally, her son-in-law answered. She asked if she could speak to Maureen. He put Maureen on the phone. Normally, Bob would have chatted with his mother-in-law a bit, but not this morning. There was something in her tone that did not permit it.

Maureen was on the phone. Ellen could hear the baby crying. "Maureen, give the baby to Bob. I need to talk to you."

The reply came after a brief hesitation. "Okay, Mother. What's the matter?"

"It's your father," Ellen told her. "Honey, he's gone."

There was silence. Maureen was speechless. Her mother had only said he was gone, but she knew what the words meant. She knew exactly what they meant. Through her sobs, she asked her mother what had happened. Ellen told her all that happened that morning. Maureen had so many questions, but her mother told her they would have to wait. She still had not told Annalyn.

Maureen cried into the receiver. "Mother, I want to be with you."

Ellen spoke gently to her oldest daughter. She knew how she was hurting."You will be, tomorrow. You know that your father would not want you to put yourself, or that baby, at risk. Rest another day. They've taken his body to the coroner's office. The funeral home will not even get it until tomorrow afternoon. Just rest another day. I'll ask Doctor Aarington to give you something to help you sleep." Maureen reluctantly agreed.

Ellen spoke to her son-in-law, and told him to keep a close eye on Maureen. He said that he would. "Annalyn is at the Simpson's.

She still doesn't know. I'm going there to tell her, right now." Ellen hung up the phone.

She parked her Thunderbird in front of Tom and Edith Simpson's house. She walked to the door, still in her apron. She could hear Annalyn's sweet voice, just inside. Edith came to the door. Ellen did not even see her. She looked through her. Ellen was somewhere else.

Annalyn Adams had a keen sense of danger. She knew that she wasn't safe the moment she saw her mother. It was the look in Ellen's eye, the disheveled state of her appearance, and the fact that she was still wearing her apron. Annalyn did not know what her mother was about to say, but she knew that it was going to change her life forever.

"Oh, sweet girl… Where do I begin?"

"Just say it. I know that something is wrong, Mother." Annalyn was impatient. Her mother was making her nervous. She just wanted her to get it over with.

Ellen took one last look at her daughter. Annalyn sat there on Edith Simpson's tacky purple sofa, with her bouncy blond curls and her knee socks, preparing for what her mother was about to say. Ellen told her that her father was gone.

"I have to go now and tell Mama and Papa." Ellen explained that she wanted to go out and tell them in person. Annalyn would stay at the Simpson's.

Edith Simpson watched as Ellen got into her Thunderbird and drove away. "How much can one woman take?" she whispered. Then she shut the door.

Ellen went back home. She needed a moment. She needed a moment to get her bearings. She needed a moment to catch her breath. Just a moment…

She looked around at the quiet, empty kitchen. She did not want to leave the house. She finished clearing the breakfast dishes, washed them, and put them away. There was much to be done. There had been a death, and a death in a tiny Texas town meant that there would be food and company until all hours. Tragically, she was the star of this show. How she wished things were different. She fought back her tears, "Not now."

Ellen pulled herself together, dressed in a simple black dress, and styled her dark hair into a neat knot at the back of her neck. She paused to look at herself in the mirror of her dressing table. She saw someone else. Despite her strength, she was weak. Her heart was broken. He was gone. The love of her life was gone. She sat there for a moment on their bed, letting reality sink in. How would she go on? What would she do with herself? There was still so much ahead of them. They had just become grandparents, yesterday. They had planned to retire, enjoy life, take a trip with Annalyn, see the world. It was to be a special time for them; golden years, they were called.

All at once they seemed like dark years ahead, full of nothing, just the passing of time. But she would not cry. She couldn't allow herself the luxury of tears or self-pity. Not yet. She was a mother. She was a daughter. She was a grandmother. She was a widow. For now, she must be all things to all people. Later, when everything was said and done, she would face herself.

She put her lipstick, emery board, some tissues, and her wallet into a black leather handbag. She was going through the motions of "normal." Her handbag must match her shoes. She found her keys and left the house.

She got into the beautiful convertible Thunderbird that Lloyd had just bought for her. The car had been the talk of the town. It was sleek and shiny, but she did not even notice it anymore. She drove through sleepy little downtown Kilroy and wondered how many people had heard the shocking news already. She watched them going in and out of the little coffee shop, in a perfectly normal, almost innocent way. She was no longer innocent, not when it came to death.

It had finally knocked on her door. Her elderly parents were still alive and well, but not her precious husband. Not her precious husband, with his practical jokes, belly laugh, and kind heart, for he was gone.

Ellen slowed down and made a right onto Anneville Road. She drove down the narrow dirt road to the last house. As it came into view, it was welcoming, inviting. The oaks lined the drive, greeting her happily, in sharp contrast to the sadness that chased her beneath the branches, out of the car, up the steps, and to the front door.

Seeing the freshly painted farmhouse caused Ellen to stop for a moment. She and Lloyd just had it painted last month. Ellen's siblings had said that it didn't need to be painted, because they didn't want to spend the money. But Lloyd hired someone to paint it for Mama, because it made her so happy. He had always been so good to her parents. The thought of telling them that he was gone filled Ellen with dread.

From her rocker in the front window, Abigail Wilson saw her daughter's Thunderbird pull into the driveway. She watched as Ellen got out, taking note of her daughter's appearance. Ellen crossed the big front porch and opened the screen door. She was startled to see Mama sitting right there in her rocker.

Abby did not speak. She knew something was wrong just by looking at her daughter. She waited. Ellen came right out with it. "Mama, I drove out here to tell you that Lloyd passed away a few hours ago."

She waited for her words to register before she went on. "Doctor Aarington thinks he probably had a heart attack."

Abigail Wilson sat back in her chair and began to cry. "Go and get your father. He's outside." She watched as her daughter walked away, heels tapping across the hardwood floors, through the living room and the kitchen. Abby heard the screen door slam shut, as Ellen went out the back door to find her father.

She sat in her chair in a state of disbelief and profound grief. She could not have asked for a better son-in-law. He had been a wonderful husband and father, and had gone above and beyond whenever it came to doing for his mother-in-law and father-in-law. She was grieved that he was gone, grieved way down deep in her heart.

Just then she heard the familiar slam of the screen door, and heard Ellen and John deep in conversation. Ellen was telling her father all that had happened that morning. Abby listened quietly as Ellen spoke. She could not believe it.

John was equally as shocked. He never expected to lose his son-in-law. After listening to all that Ellen offered, he and Abby bustled off to dress and prepare for the day. They also knew that there was much to be done. There would be time for sorrow, later. There would be time to react, later. For now, there was a man that had to be buried, and a town that was sure to be waiting for them. As much as he hated to see his daughter thrust into the center of the tragedy that had become her life, John Wilson was powerless to stop it. The show must go on, and that was exactly what it was, what it had become for them. In the tiny Texas town of Kilroy, life was a show, with everyone watching and waiting for what they would do next.

Ellen walked to the barn. It was funny how many memories the old home place held for her. She thought back to the sweet times she and Lloyd had spent out there, before they were married. Time had flown. It seemed to speed up with each passing day. How she had loved each day with him. Yes, there had been quarrels. There were many times throughout their marriage that they had a difference of opinion, but it was all part of the growing that they did together. How wonderful it was. What a beautiful thing to have grown with a man as wonderful as Lloyd. How blessed she had been, how thankful she was.

Out of the corner of her eye, she saw the door of the old storm cellar raised slightly off the ground. She walked over to it and looked at it, contemplating the past, not being able to conceive of a future. Then she raised her face to the sky, eyes closed. "Thank You, in spite of the pain, thank You."

That was all she said. That was all she felt at the moment. In spite of the pain, and the pain was great, greater than anything she could imagine, so great that she could not believe she would ever truly be happy again, still she was thankful. She could have gone her whole life without knowing the love of such a man. How great that love had been. She knew that nothing even close to it would ever be realized again. Youth and its struggles were gone, and now so was Lloyd. How exciting it had been. How much she had learned. How sweet those days, when everything was so new. She saw the cellar door. She was rushing headlong into a storm of another kind now, this one bringing independence and solitude, neither of which she was ready for.

# Lloyd

It was only after his passing that Ellen would truly understand the kind of man that her husband was. The morning of the funeral dawned clear and bright, a cold January morning. The day was new. The year was new. The feeling of emptiness down deep in her gut was new.

She had asked to be alone with her husband's body last night. What a night that had proved to be. As was the custom, visitation of the body occurred at home. Lloyd's body lay in a casket in their home for three days and three nights. That meant people and food, coming and going, at all hours, for three days and three nights. The first night, Annalyn was at home with her mother. That night was spent discussing the facts, facing reality, where they would go, what they would do. The second night, Maureen stayed with her mother. That night was spent in the past, reliving special times with a wonderful husband and father. But last night was empty. Sitting

125

there alone, seeing his body so still, was more than Ellen could bear. The realization that he was gone was devastating. It was loneliness like she had never known before. It was frightening. It was final. It almost drove her crazy.

The days following Lloyd's death had been a blur of friends, family, food, and flowers. All the while she wanted to scream, to run, to disappear. But she couldn't. She smiled when she was supposed to smile. She nodded when she was supposed to nod. She shook hands when she was supposed to shake hands. Ellen got through all the drama that goes with an old-fashioned country funeral by withdrawing. Bits and pieces of mindless conversations would bring her back to the reality that she wanted nothing to do with. She couldn't believe how people could discuss the weather, vacation, and life. Life without Lloyd...

"Show time." She patted the closed casket. She watched as the big shiny black hearse arrived in front of her house to pick up her husband's body. She felt nothing. He wasn't in there. She realized that. She had watched him for three days, looking for movement, for the rise and fall of his chest, praying to turn back time. She had no desire to gaze at his corpse any longer. He was gone.

The hearse drove away, heading the few blocks to the funeral home in downtown Kilroy. Ellen followed alone in her Thunderbird. When she saw all the cars, she wished she had taken Maureen's advice and let the family car pick her up.

"Why, the whole town must be here."

The perfectly manicured lawn of the local funeral home was awash with black. There were black suits, black dresses, and black hats, everywhere. She drove her Thunderbird onto the grass, right up to the front door.

"I can do whatever I want today."

She sat on the front row with Maureen and Annalyn, and Ruth. Ellen was right there, and yet she was a million miles away. She didn't hear a single word of the service.

After the funeral she rode in the family car to the cemetery. She did not speak. No one did. She thought about how strange life can be, how utterly unpredictable.

As they stood at the gravesite, with the cold January wind blowing, Ellen looked at her elderly mother. Abby was almost seventy. Gone were those beautiful red tresses. Now her hair was cut short, and it was grey. Ellen remembered how beautiful her mother's eyes had been, her startling grey eyes. She didn't think about it much anymore. She rarely looked past her mother's glasses. We get so caught up in daily life that we forget the details, she thought. She vowed that when she got through this, she would pay more attention. She would look at her mother's eyes again.

Ellen watched her mother. She remembered when they buried Grandma Flynn. So much had happened since then. She looked at Maureen and Bob, and baby Frankie. She looked at Annalyn, her rock. Reality rose up to meet her. Life had happened. Life, with all of its beauty and wonder, with all of its blunders and heartaches… She and Lloyd had seen the world go through many changes together. They had lived through the Great Depression, desegregation, gone from wagons to cars, and from outhouses to indoor plumbing. Each day had been a precious gift. Of course, she could cash it all in now, if she chose. Just stop and wilt. But my girls need their mother, my parents need their daughter, and little Frankie needs a grandmother, she thought.

Ruth took her hand as the preacher droned on. Their eyes met, but Ellen was somewhere else… Aah Ruth, my best friend, my sister, only you know. Only you know what I am thinking. Only you know this road so well. The pain in Ruth Johnson's eyes answered her.

Ellen looked at each member of her family. There was still so much to love, still so much to live for. She realized that in spite of Lloyd's death, she wanted to go on. She wanted to live. She wanted to see more, to do more. It didn't mean she loved him any less. Never could, never would love anyone like that.

She felt her strength beginning to stir. And before the preacher was even finished with his gravesite sermon, she turned and walked away. She got in the family car and told the driver to take her somewhere. But not home, anywhere but home. There were too many memories of Lloyd. She wanted to go somewhere else, a place where she could just be Ellen, a place where she was not a widow. She longed to be somewhere safe, somewhere before Lloyd. The last house down Anneville Road...

Maureen and Annalyn watched her go. They were both worried sick. They were afraid that she would just give up. Her spirit seemed so weary. But it wasn't the first time in her life that Ellen had been underestimated, and it most assuredly would not be the last.

Ruth watched her go, seeing it all with wisdom. Ellen was tired. Ruth knew that she was tired. Ruth knew that the pain was too great for Ellen. Her friend would succumb to it, or let him go. That decision would shape life after Lloyd. Ruth knew all too well what that was like.

Abby felt her daughter's pain. She had watched the young couple make a life together. She watched their love grow, year after year, and the way that love affected everyone that crossed their path. Together, Lloyd and Ellen were a force to be reckoned with. Abby had never shared that with her own husband. They loved each other, of course, but what Ellen and Lloyd had was different. It's like something the Lord himself joined together, she thought. That was enough for Abby. She would not worry anymore. Ellen would be all right, even now, especially now. Ellen's always been in the palm of His hand, Abby thought. Why should today be any different?

After Lloyd was buried came the business of death. Ellen absorbed herself in ledgers, lock boxes, fireproof safes, bank statements, and pages of paperwork declaring rights to oil and gas wells. She had never dreamed the extent of their assets. It never occurred to her that she was a woman of such means. She had always lived so simply.

The lengths her husband had gone to, to protect his family in the event of his death, were shocking. He had thought of everything. Lloyd left his wife well off, with trusts set up for his children, and any grandchildren that he might have at the time of his death. The forethought required was disturbing to Ellen. It was just too much.

It didn't take long for the business of death to get to her, but it was a safety deposit box at the bank downtown that brought her to her knees. She had learned of its existence while sifting through the piles and piles of paperwork that were left. She did not have a key, had not been able to locate it. Even so, she had been led into a room full of locked boxes, by a bank teller, with no hassle over identification. One of the benefits of living in a small town.

The teller pointed out which box was Lloyd's, then proceeded to unlock it. She handed Ellen some papers. Ellen thanked her and tucked them safely inside her handbag, the black one that matched her shoes. She would not look at them until she was at home. She figured it was just more of the same.

At home, she sat down at her kitchen table and took the papers out of her bag. It was a description of some sort of property. She could not believe her eyes. It was a deed. It was for Mama and Papa's farm. It was from 1929, almost thirty years ago. She fell to her knees. "Lloyd!" She suddenly knew what she and Martin had always wondered, how Mama and Papa had rebuilt the farm after the storm and how they had held onto it through the Great Depression. "Lloyd!" She began to sob.

She was out the door. She drove straight to the last house down Anneville Road. Papa was walking to the barn. She slid her car to a stop right in front of him. Bewildered, he stared at his daughter. She got out of her car and screamed at him. "What is this Papa? I have to know! I have to know everything!"

John took the papers from her. He looked them over. He was not the least bit surprised. "Let's take a walk."

They walked toward the creek. He began to explain. "Ellen, after the storm we lost everything. We were doing all that we could and it still wasn't enough. We were about to lose the farm." John Wilson took a deep breath. "The day after you accepted Lloyd's proposal, he bought it. I didn't know he was going to do it. He came to me and handed me the deed, and a right smart amount of money to fix the place up. He said he took all the money that he'd saved to buy a place for y'all, and bought our farm. Said y'all were young and had plenty of time to buy your own place. Said he knew you would understand. I told him I would take the deed when I was able to buy it from him. That day never came. We only spoke about it one other time. He said he didn't want you to know." John could see the pain in her eyes. It hurt her, knowing that Lloyd had kept a secret from her. "Your husband was a smart man, and he loved you very much. He said it wasn't good for you to know that you owned your parent's place. He said it would be like you weren't a kid anymore. He didn't want to take that from you."

John paused to hand Ellen his handkerchief, and after she was done blowing her nose, he continued. "He said it was ours, to do whatever we wanted with it, and after our death it would be yours."

Ellen looked at her father. It all made sense now. She thought back to their first few years of married life, how they had struggled.

They were the best days of her life. She wouldn't have traded them for anything. She thought about what it meant for Lloyd to have bought that farm and then gone to live in a rented shack with her. He had made all the right choices. He was a selfless, kind, wonderful man. He had been all she ever wanted in a husband, and more. She knew there would never be anyone else. Welcome independence and solitude, she had already known passion and commitment. She had known a communion of hearts, the like of which she never expected to find again, a living, breathing, beautiful moment in time that was gone forever.

And before she knew it, 1958 was gone as well. Life took a turn. She was the mother of two grown girls. She was a grandmother. She was a volunteer for almost anything. She taught Sunday school. She went to Europe. She had a love for people that was incredible. At sixty-eight, she even decided that she would go to work for the Fort Worth Zoo. "What experience do you have?" they asked. "Of course, that of a cashier, from working many years in the family grocery store," she responded. The girls were appalled. "Mother," they said, "you don't need to do this. You don't have to work." Of course, she did not need the money. Lloyd had made sure of that. Her need was something else, something so simple and sweet. It was a need to continue living life to the fullest, experiencing new things, meeting new people that would shape her world.

Ellen's life was filled with wonder, but not without heartache. She would bury Papa, then Mama. She would say goodbye to many other precious lives along the way. Even so, every morning she would rejoice over a six o'clock breakfast that she cooked for herself and ate alone, thankful that she had lived to see another day, no matter what the circumstances.

Time continued to gain speed. She grew tired, and yet life kept revealing still so much to live for. Then it revealed something she never thought she would see again, a baby named Reid with flaming red hair and haunting grey eyes. Ellen took one look at her and fell head over heels in love with her. She couldn't put her finger on it but for some reason this child was different. And while she would never admit it, would never show favoritism, this baby had stolen her heart. Their relationship would prove to be that rare communion of hearts that she never expected to find again. That soul would be a gift for old age, a soul so similar to hers. The child was special, someone to share the last of her life with. Ellen knew from the moment that Reid entered the atmosphere that she needed the child just as much as the child needed her, and she would cherish every moment that they had together, every living, breathing, beautiful moment in time.

# Maureen

Maureen Adams wrote her name and the date on a piece of paper. Mrs. Harris, her eleventh grade teacher, had been delivering the Arithmetic lesson when the principal knocked on the classroom door and motioned for her to follow him into the hallway. To Maureen's dismay, Mrs. Harris instructed the students to sit quietly until she returned. Maureen wanted to get the lesson over with and get on with other things. Arithmetic was her least favorite subject.

It wasn't long before she began to daydream. As she stared out the classroom window, something caught her eye. Movement... A shiny yellow bus stopped outside her school yard. At that moment, Mrs. Harris entered the room and startled Maureen. Maureen knew, at once, that something was wrong just by looking at her teacher's face. Mrs. Harris approached the front of the classroom and asked for silence. No one dared to stir, let alone speak. Everyone was looking out the classroom window, astonished at what they were witnessing.

"They did it. They actually did it," Maureen whispered.

Colored children were coming off the bus and walking into the school. No one moved. They sat perfectly still in their seats and did not make a sound. Mrs. Harris addressed the room. "Class, I informed you last week that Kilroy High could potentially become integrated." She paused and swallowed hard. "It seems that integration is being realized today. Now, I cannot be sure how long it will last. We'll just have to wait and see. For now, do the best you can."

Maureen remembered the week before. The principal had gone to each classroom and explained to the students that they might very well have colored students attending their school very soon. He didn't seem very happy, Maureen had noticed. Later that day, at lunch, she had overheard some of the boys talking. She heard one of them say that the colored folks were trying to get their own bus so that their kids could get to school. Another one said that they could never do it, that they would never be able to get their own bus. Maureen couldn't contain her smile. She wondered what that boy was thinking right now. She hoped he was watching.

She had spoken to Mother and Daddy about it last week. "What is it going to be like?" She had asked them. Her father had been honest and told her that it might be very difficult for everyone. He said that a lot of people didn't want blacks and whites to be together, so it might make it hard for the new students. Her father told her that she must mind her own business and focus on school. He told her to pay no mind to what people were saying.

She thought now how difficult that would be. Being sixteen, still innocent, full of love, and tenderhearted, was not a recipe for minding your own business at this place in time. She was witnessing something very strange, ugliness in people, people she had known her whole life. She was seeing racism, arrogant and audacious, stirring up the evil that for so long lay quietly in the hearts of men.

She could not believe the things that people were saying. She even heard someone say that colored folks weren't really people. Maureen did not know a lot about colored folks. She never really met any. Of course, there were a few colored families that lived out in the country, but they didn't come into town very often, and when they did, it was just to conduct business of some kind. She had seen them in the grocery store. They kept to themselves, did their shopping, and disappeared again. While she knew very little about these people, she knew one thing for sure... They were people.

With the Supreme Court decision, things were heating up all over the place. In the tiny Texas town of Kilroy, where Maureen had never known racism, she was catching on. She learned quickly that as long as everything went the way of the racist, racism was quiet, infectious, successful. But as people began to rise up and things began to change, she saw the racist rise too, and saw the dark evil in his heart come to the light.

Mr. Smith had been in the grocery store last week, and had announced that he did not want his children going to school with animals. His insolence had angered Lloyd Adams at once. Maureen heard something in her father's voice that day that she could not pinpoint. It scared her. His tone was even, commanding. "Harold Smith, you will not stir up trouble in my store. Those colored children have enough problems without you causing more. They are so poor that most of them don't even have shoes. Do you remember what that's like? Because I do. I'm only one generation away from sharecropping myself. My father worked the cotton fields, right along with them. And if I'm not mistaken, so did yours. Now you should be thanking the Lord that we have been blessed with opportunities and the good health to see them through. Leave those people and their children alone."

Maureen watched her father open the door to the grocery store and motion Mr. Smith to leave. "Lloyd, you and I go back a long way.

We was boys together. You better think about what you say. Ain't nothin' good gonna' come of it."

But Lloyd did not even look at his old friend. Holding the door open, he said simply, "I'll take my chances, because I learned a long time ago that nothing good comes with doing wrong." The words stung his friend. Harold Smith visibly winced, as if in pain.

"Damn him." Harold muttered. Lloyd had used his mother's words. Vera Smith had told her children that every day of her life, and Lloyd knew it. "Nothin' good comes with doin' wrong," she had said. Sadly, everything she tried to teach her son went with her the day that she passed.

Maureen watched, as Mr. Smith left the store. Her father walked back inside and started stocking the shelves. Ellen said nothing. She had been cleaning the windows during the exchange.

Maureen wanted to hug her father. There had been something threatening in Mr. Smith's tone. Something was going on. Maureen didn't know what, but there was something. It was something that she could neither see, nor touch, something she would never understand. Mr. Smith had been spending a lot of time in the grocery store, and her father had been avoiding him more and more, to the point of actually being rude to him. It was unlike Lloyd Adams. He was never rude to anyone.

It was with this memory that Maureen watched from the window of her classroom, as four colored students walked through the front door of her school. She could hear the whispers. It made her uneasy. Mrs. Harris told the class to return to their seats, as they had all gathered around the window. She proceeded to give the Arithmetic lesson. Maureen thought of her father. "Mind your own business and focus on school," he had said. How difficult that was proving to be.

The class finished their lesson and passed their papers to the front of each row. As Mrs. Harris picked them up, there was a knock on the door. Mr. Wells, the principal, entered the room and called for silence.

"Class, this is Jeremiah Johnson. He is a new student here at Kilroy High School." Then, looking straight at Junior Smith, "I don't want any trouble today, understand?"

Junior nodded, with the biggest smirk on his face that Maureen had ever seen.

"Jeremiah will need some help getting acquainted with the school. Could I please get a volunteer?" Mr. Wells knew that he had to be very careful over the next few days. Even though he didn't really give a damn about the young man, he had a reputation to protect. Principal at Kilroy High was just a stepping stone for Edward Wells. He had bigger dreams. The institution of education was his ticket out of the podunk town. He didn't care what side he was on, as long as it was the winning one.

Junior Smith raised his hand immediately. Before she knew what she was doing, Maureen's hand shot up as well. She knew that Junior was up to no good. She remembered that scene at the store. And this boy standing at the front of the room, cautiously scanning their faces in his worn out jeans and t-shirt, had already claimed her heart.

Mr. Wells considered his options. He was not ready for the sort of trouble that he was sure Junior Smith would bring. His only other option was a girl, trouble as well. He opted for the girl, for no other reason than because the alternative, without a doubt, would be worse for him that day.

"I'm going to give this job to Maureen. Jeremiah has expressed interest in the Reading Club that Mrs. Harris is working on, and I know that Maureen is helping with that."

Maureen watched as the boy took a seat at the empty desk that had been brought in for him. She studied the back of his head. He was two seats in front of her. She was curious about him. No one else seemed to care. She noticed, as the day went on, that he did not turn his head. He faced forward, all the time. When there was a bathroom break, he did not go. And at lunch, he sat alone and ate the food he had brought from home. Maureen tried to see what he was eating. It interested her. It looked to be just a sandwich and an apple. He did not drink anything though. The end of the day finally came and she waved goodbye, as Jeremiah Johnson got into an old Dodge pickup truck with what must have been his father. She watched as it drove out of town.

She thought about the day as she walked the four blocks to the grocery store. "Mind your own business and focus on school," seemed like a world away. She had done neither. She thought about the boy and wondered what he thought about her. What did he think of the school? She opened the door to the grocery store and greeted her parents, who looked as if they were trying to fix the cash register. They heard her come in, and greeted her with smiles and laughter. Annalyn came running out of the back. She always made it to the store before Maureen. It was a tradition.

Seven-year-old Annalyn would rub it in every day that she had beaten Maureen, and Maureen would act as if she was distraught over losing. She would vow to win the next day, and so on, and so on, it went. Lloyd and Ellen were glad that the competition brought Annalyn straight home from school, without any distractions.

The girls sat at the table, in back of the store, and ate home-made biscuits with honey. The honey had been a gift from Mrs. Wiley, a nice little old widow lady from church. She was a bee-keeper, and quite eccentric. Ellen would check in on her from time to time. Mrs. Wiley sent her home with fresh honey, yesterday. It was a real treat.

Maureen and Annalyn finished their meal of biscuits and honey, washed it down with fresh lemonade, and went separate ways.

Annalyn went straight to her dollhouse and began to play with her dolls. The back of the store was a sort of home away from home for the girls. Maureen took out her Language book and began her homework assignment. It was rare that she had homework. She usually finished her work during the free period at the end of the school day, but today she had been unable to concentrate. She could not get Jeremiah Johnson out of her head. His silent and almost but not quite unfriendly demeanor was incredibly interesting to her. What was he thinking? She wondered. Maybe he didn't really want to be there. Maybe his parents were making him attend Kilroy High. Maybe he was unhappy. She felt sorry for him at once, and innocently decided she would become his friend. She did not care what anyone said or thought, for she had already convinced herself that he needed her.

Lost in thoughts of the excitement the day had brought, Maureen jumped when the back door to the store opened. Her grandmother came in. Abby, or "Mama" as they all called her, laughed. "Child, I didn't mean to scare you." Maureen got up and hugged her. She was already three inches taller than her tiny grandmother. At just under five feet tall, it didn't take much to tower over the tiny Abigail Wilson.

"Oh, Mama, I was just thinking about school today." Maureen giggled.

Abby sat down with her granddaughter, and listened to her tell all about her day. Abby was worried. She had heard the talk around town regarding the state of affairs at Kilroy High School, and recognized early on that no one was going to be permitted to sit on the fence this time. And it was this getting off of the fence that worried her. "Desegregation," they called it. It was yet another time in her life, when she was experiencing the best of people and the worst of people. But she was not afraid for herself. She had seen much. And true to the heart of a good woman, she was already preparing to fight for those that were too weak or too tired to fight for themselves. Although she sensed it, Abigail Wilson did not fully understand the evil that was upon them.

Ellen heard voices, and walked to the back of the store. "Mama, hello. I didn't know you were coming by."

"I just had my hair done, and thought I'd come by to see you. Maureen was just telling me all about her day. She had some excitement at school. The colored folks got themselves a bus."

"Oh?" Ellen studied her daughter's face.

"Yes." Maureen answered her mother, with a twinkle in her eye.

"You'll have to tell us all about it over dinner. I'm sure your father will want to hear about it as well. Mama, would you like to stay for dinner?"

"No, honey. Papa's waiting at home for me. I need to get going soon. Where's Annalyn?"

"She's at the Simpson's. She went to play with Kate. I think she's losing interest in her dolls. She needs conversation." Maureen laughed, telling her mother and grandmother how Annalyn had tried to talk dolls with her, but finally gave up and sought out a playmate with similar interests.

Just then the back door flew open and Annalyn ran in. She was crying and screaming. All anyone could make out was something about Junior Smith and her dolls. Lloyd heard the commotion and hurried to the back of the store. He picked Annalyn up and held her. She buried her face in his neck and sobbed. He could feel the warm wetness of her tears soaking through his undershirt. He consoled her and told her that she was all right. He told her to calm down and tell him what had happened.

Everyone listened, not at all prepared for what would come out of her mouth. Annalyn showed her father her favorite doll. She had been clutching it to her chest, wrapped up tight in an old baby blanket that she now used for her dolls. Lloyd Adams gasped, unable to contain himself at the stench that permeated the room. "Junior saw me playing in the yard, with Kate. He came over and said that I should not be playing with white kids or white baby dolls. He snatched my baby from me and rubbed it in dog poo." She began to sob uncontrollably. "Then he threw my doll at me." Lloyd looked his daughter over. Physically, she was fine. Otherwise, she was destroyed.

Lloyd handed his youngest daughter, with her bouncy yellow curls and her tearstained face, to his wife. Ellen cuddled her and spoke softly too her while she cried. Mama and Maureen watched as Lloyd slammed the back door. He went looking for Junior Smith.

He walked to the Simpson's. He asked Tom Simpson if he could speak with Kate. He asked her what had happened. The frightened seven year old girl confirmed Annalyn's story. When she got to the part about the boy throwing the filthy doll at his daughter, Lloyd became enraged all over again.

He walked back to the store, got in his truck, and drove out to the Smith's place. He marched up to the front door of the house and pounded on it. Harold Smith opened the door, astonished.

"What is the problem, Lloyd?"

"The problem is your boy, Harold. Where is he?"

"He's not here."

"Do you know what he did to my daughter today?"

Harold Smith said that he did not. Lloyd gave him the details of the exchange between their children. The man seemed indifferent. "Lloyd, because we go so far back, I will make damn sure that Junior does not bother your girls again. But you need to think about what side you're on, 'cuz I can't control the whole town."

"Harold, do you remember when you were a boy, and you ran away after your mother died? Everybody in town was looking for you. I knew where you were, down by the tank. But I didn't tell anybody because I knew if they found you, you'd get whipped. So I snuck down there and convinced you to go home, so you didn't get beat. I'm telling you again, right now, you're doing wrong. Back then you were afraid of life without your mama, because you didn't really know your daddy. He was such a strict man, and he'd never said more than a handful of words to you your whole life. This is the same thing. You're scared of something you don't know. Only now you're a grown man. You ended up having a good life with your daddy. He loved you just like your mama did. He took good care of you."

Harold Smith looked at his old friend. Lloyd thought for a moment that he had reached him. And then, in an instant, all the happy carefree days of youth that had passed between them were gone. The veil returned to those steely blue eyes.

"Yeah, and my daddy hated niggers just like I do."

As soon as the words were out of his mouth, the space between them was insurmountable. It was if they had never carried cane poles down to the river together. It was as if they had never camped out all night and cooked the fish that they caught. It was as if they were never innocent boys together, climbing live oaks and skipping rocks until the sun went down. It was all gone, and Lloyd realized that he was fighting a different kind of battle, one that he had never known.

He remembered Vera Smith, Harold's mother, how kind she had been, how gentle, how she had loved her son. There hadn't been a mean bone in her body. She would have been sick to see what had become of her son. What a tragedy her passing had proved to be, a tragedy indeed.

Lloyd looked at the man that was once his close friend. "Keep your boy away from my family, or I will." It sounded just like the threat that he meant it to be. He turned and walked back to his truck, got in, and drove away.

Lloyd returned to find the store locked up. He checked his watch and saw that it was 5:30. Ellen must have closed the store and gone home. He drove the few blocks to the house. He parked the truck next to Ellen's car. As he approached the screen door, he could smell something cooking. It made his stomach turn. Normally, he couldn't wait to sit down and have dinner with his family. It was the best part of his day, when they were all back together again, eating Ellen's cooking. But today he couldn't bear the thought of food or pleasant conversation. He felt like brooding. He had a lot on his mind.

Lloyd entered the house. Ellen jumped as she heard the screen door slam shut. As she watched her mother, from her seat at the kitchen table, Maureen thought there was a lot of jumping going on lately.

Lloyd kissed his wife. She was standing there in her sunny yellow kitchen, at the stove, with her apron on. He smiled at her. It struck him funny that no matter what was going on, the world could be in complete shambles, and yet she always looked perfect, turned out in a dress and heels. She was making dinner in the lavender empire waisted dress and lavender pumps that she had worn all day at the store. Her dark, newly cropped hair curled around her face, looking just like it had first thing this morning. She truly amazed him.

He looked at his daughter sitting there at the kitchen table. He hated knowing that she was experiencing so much right now. He knew that the whole desegregation situation would have the greatest impact on her, but he never dreamed how much. He kissed her on the top of the head and sat down at the kitchen table. With a booming voice that said everything's okay, he spoke. "What's for dinner? I'm starved." He wasn't the least bit hungry, but he did not want to give his precious girls any indication that he was troubled. Not yet. It was still too soon.

Ellen teased him. "Oh, we thought you ate already. We were about to have some chicken and dumplings. I wish I had known you were hungry." She feigned surprise.

Lloyd spoke in pretend disgust. "Can't a hard working man even get a meal around here anymore?"

Maureen joined in, "Is there a hard working man here somewhere?"

They all laughed. The dark cloud seemed to leave the kitchen. They bantered back and forth for a bit, lighthearted and silly. But something was missing.

"Where's Annalyn?"

Ellen looked at him. "She's in bed. She said she wasn't hungry."

There was the cloud again.

Ellen put the chicken and dumplings on the table and served them. She filled their glasses with iced tea and put the pitcher on the table. They bowed their heads and Lloyd said the blessing. Ellen told her husband the details of Maureen's day, as Maureen ate her food. Lloyd listened to the events. Then, as a family, they decided that Maureen's choice to befriend the new boy, in an attempt to protect him from whatever mischief Junior Smith had in mind, had been the best possible decision. However, they all agreed that it had resulted in that mischief being carried out on Annalyn.

'Mischief,' was far too mild a word for it, Ellen thought. But it was the word that her husband had chosen to refer to the episode. He didn't want to upset Maureen anymore than she was already upset. He tried to downplay the day's events, in an effort to comfort her. But at the same time, he had to let her know that these were serious times.

"Maureen, what you did today was right. I understand why you did it and I'm proud of you. That took heart. For now, I want you to tell us everything that goes on at that school. No matter how small you think it is, tell us. I want to make sure that nothing else happens like what happened to Annalyn. Understand?"

Maureen looked at her father. "Yes, sir."

Maureen helped her mother clean the kitchen after the evening meal. She dried the dishes as Ellen washed them. She could tell her mother was lost in thought, so she kept quiet. She was sorry about what had happened to her little sister, but right now she was thinking of Jeremiah. For some silly reason she couldn't wait to see him tomorrow. Did she like him as a boyfriend? She asked herself. The answer was no. It was nothing like that. She wanted to be his friend.

The next day dawned clear and bright. Maureen and Annalyn walked the four blocks to school. Lloyd went to the store early to unload a delivery truck, while Ellen stayed home to tidy the house after the morning rush. Maureen walked Annalyn to her second grade classroom as her father had instructed. She usually just walked her to school, and Annalyn would go to class by herself. "But these are different times," her father had said. "I want you making sure she gets in her classroom." Maureen said she would. Now, with Annalyn safely in her classroom, Maureen made her way down the hill to the high school.

Kilroy Elementary, Kilroy Middle School, and Kilroy High School were in separate buildings, but all were right there together. Maureen walked to her classroom. Jeremiah was sitting in his seat. She smiled at him. He smiled back. He smiled back! She convinced herself last night, as she lay in her bed thinking about him, that he was unhappy and starving somewhere. But here he was, smiling and ready to start the day.

As Mrs. Harris tried to teach her something about government, Maureen studied the back of Jeremiah's head. She looked at the way his short dark hair curled so closely to his scalp. She looked at his skin, the back of his neck. It was dark brown. Whenever he looked down at his book, she could see where the sun had tanned it. The lighter part was exposed just inside the collar of his t-shirt. She looked at how broad his shoulders were. He was skinny like the rest of the boys in her class, but his shoulders were wide. He looked strong. She decided he must work outside a lot, with his suntanned neck and broad shoulders.

Mrs. Harris dismissed the class for lunch. Maureen barely heard her. She had brought her lunch from home. She went outside and saw Jeremiah sitting by himself, underneath a tree. He had his back to her. She strolled across the schoolyard and sat down beside him. He almost choked on his food. "Are you okay?" she asked. He shook his head, yes. She started babbling about the Reading Club. He listened and answered her here and there, but he was uneasy because people were staring.

Jeremiah Johnson watched the pretty girl in her pretty clothes, with her bouncy blond curls and big blue eyes, act as if he were her honored guest. He was wondering if she was crazy. He lowered his voice and spoke to her.

"Excuse me, I don't mean any disrespect. But in case you haven't noticed, everyone in the school is staring at us."

She addressed him with nonchalance, in a flippant voice. "Oh, really, I didn't even notice."

Jeremiah took another bite of his sandwich, chewed it up, and then swallowed it. "Come on, even the lady that works in the cafeteria has come outside to look. And I don't know what she's looking at, we all know she can't see."

They both tried to contain their smiles. Jeremiah could not resist. He had Maureen's attention. "I don't know who was responsible for hiring a cook that can't see, but I know I don't want any part of it."

Maureen began to laugh. "Is that why you bring your lunch?" she asked.

"Maybe," he answered.

He watched as she began to eat her lunch. She acted as if everything was completely normal. He gobbled his food and got up to walk away.

"Wait," she whispered.

He bent down and whispered back. "For what?" His eyes challenged her.

"I just thought you might need a friend," she told him.

He looked into her eyes with a gaze so deep it touched her heart. "I'm trying to be one." Then he left her sitting there alone, eating her lunch.

Before she knew it, the day was over. She packed up her things and left the building. She watched as Jeremiah got into the same old pickup truck and disappeared out of town. She ran to catch up with her best friend, Peggy. Maureen called out to her, and Peggy stopped to wait. The two girls had been best friends since the second grade. Peggy smiled at Maureen and invited her over to listen to records. Maureen explained that she had to get Annalyn and walk her to the store. Then she would go straight to Peggy's house. Peggy said she was sure it would be all right with her parents. It was Friday, so there was no school the next day.

Maureen saw Annalyn waiting in front of the school, just like she was supposed to be. Annalyn saw her coming and ran to meet her, "Hi, Sister." Maureen gave her a hug, then listened to her school stories all the way to the store.

They saw their mother in front of the store. As usual, she was cleaning the windows. Ellen hopped off the step stool. She was clad in her standard uniform of a dress and pumps. This time, both were grey. She offered the girls something to eat. Maureen explained that she was invited to Peggy's, and if it was okay, she would eat something with her. Ellen said she supposed that would be fine, but to be home in time for dinner. Mama and Papa were coming to eat with them. Maureen agreed, and then walked the few blocks to her friend's house.

The two girls listened to records, painted their nails, and talked about school. They had been friends since the first day of second grade and had never argued or fought like most little girls do. They liked the same things and were altogether incredibly compatible. Over time, they had grown increasingly closer. Peggy was glad that Maureen had come. She wanted to talk to her about something.

"Maureen, I've been meanin' to talk to you about that new niggra' boy." Peggy got up to close the door to her bedroom.

Maureen was sitting in the window sill, painting her toenails. A stray blond curl had fallen over one eye. She brushed it aside, using the back of her hand. With the nail polish brush still in hand, her gaze met Peggy's. "Peggy, why does he have to be that new niggra' boy? Why can't he just be that new boy?"

Peggy answered sarcastically. "I don't know. I suppose because he's a niggra'."

"Yes, I understand," Maureen said, "But I would've known who you were talking about, even if you hadn't said niggra'. You know that. What I'm trying to say is, it's almost as if people use the term for meanness, as a reminder of something, as if it defines him. I don't like it."

Peggy apologized to Maureen. "Maureen, I didn't mean anything by it. I was just gonna' tell you somethin' about him." She was hurt.

"I know. But I've just been doing a lot of thinking about him, and I really feel sorry for him," Maureen told her. "I'm not mad at you."

"Good," Peggy said, "Because I wanted to tell you what I heard. Karen King said her mother knows his mother, somehow, and he is supposed to be real, real smart. He wrote somethin' and won some kind of contest. He went all the way to Chicago last year."

Maureen was all ears. She was hanging on every word that came out of Peggy's mouth. "Anyway, his mother didn't want him to go to Kilroy High. He gets schoolin' through the mail, somehow. His mother was afraid people would mess with him. But he wanted to go to school. His father told him it was his own decision."

Maureen thought about what Peggy said. That's why he had been interested in the Reading Club. He must like books. He had written something. It had been good enough to win a contest. Maureen was even more intrigued than ever.

"Peggy, do you think he's cute?"

"Cute?" Peggy gasped. "Are you kidding? I think he's ugly."

Maureen looked at her friend. "Peggy Myers, you think he's ugly because you listen to everybody else. Look at him, on Monday, I mean really look at him. He's got the prettiest eyes. They're so dark, so dark they shine. And he has the longest eye lashes I've ever seen. They almost don't look real. And when you look at his face, I mean really look at it, well it's... I don't know..."

"It's what?" Peggy asked her.

"It's beautiful." Maureen dared to say it.

Peggy looked at her best friend. She was worried about her. "Maureen, you need to stop talkin' like that. You're startin' to scare me. You seem to be way too interested in someone you have no business bein' interested in. People are already startin' to talk," she warned.

Maureen began to put a second coat of polish on her toenails. "Let them talk."

The weekend passed quickly. Maureen spent most of it helping in the store. The commotion about desegregation seemed to subside, or so she thought. She found out on Monday that it wasn't going to go over that easily.

The class was about to compete in an Arithmetic relay at the blackboard. Mrs. Harris explained the rules. She would copy exercises onto the board. The boys would race the girls to see who would finish first with the correct answer. Each winner would earn a point. The team with the most points at the end won the relay, and bragging rights. Maureen was nervous. She was not very good at Arithmetic and she was even worse when it came to racing. She felt her stomach knot up. Mrs. Harris asked if there were any questions. Junior Smith raised his hand.

"Whose team is he going to be on?" He pointed at Jeremiah.

Mrs. Harris glared at him. She was annoyed. "The boys team, of course."

But Junior wasn't stopping there. "He's not going to be on any team with me."

Mrs. Harris told Junior that he was disrupting her class, and if he was not going to cooperate he would have to leave.

He was arrogant and hateful as he drawled at her. "I think I'll do just that, cuz I ain't gonna' be on no team with a nigger."

The class was speechless. Of course, they had heard the word before. In fact, most of them probably heard it come out of the mouths of their parents every single day. They probably used it as well. But the way that it sounded coming out of Junior Smith's mouth was unlike anything they had ever heard. It was filthy. It was dangerous. And they all knew it.

No doubt, some of them felt the same as Junior, but he took it a step further than they were willing to go. He was openly defiant, and filled with something they could neither see, nor touch. It was something that made the hair on the back of Maureen's neck stand straight up. She was horrified for Jeremiah, and it kindled something inside of her that she did not know she had. She wanted to fight.

Mrs. Harris told Junior to go straight to the principal's office. He said he would, and out the door he went. Mrs. Harris told the class to sit quietly, and she went out the door right behind him.

Maureen scribbled something on a piece of paper. She folded it up and wrote Jeremiah's name on the outside. She passed it to the girl in front of her, who then passed it to him. She saw him open it and write something. He passed it back. She opened it and read it.

She had written, "Will you eat lunch with me today?"

He had written back in big block letters. It simply said, "No." Maureen felt her face burn. He obviously wanted nothing to do with her. She felt stupid and ashamed. She would leave him alone. He didn't want a friend, and she wouldn't push herself on him anymore. She couldn't blame him anyway. She crumpled the note up and took it to the waste basket.

Somehow, she got through the rest of the school day. She started to wonder what had happened to Junior. Mrs. Harris had come back to class, and they had enjoyed the Arithmetic relay, everyone except Maureen. She was crushed.

She tried to put any thoughts of Jeremiah Johnson and Junior Smith, desegregation and racism, out of her mind. She was experiencing emotion and heartache like she had never known before. She was overwhelmingly drawn to the boy that didn't want any part of her. She knew that if things were different he would want to be her friend also. She hated that she had spent all weekend looking forward to seeing him again and it had turned out this way.

Finally, the day was over and Maureen could go home and feel sorry for herself. She had experienced something that she had never known before, rejection. She grabbed her satchel and left the classroom. Jeremiah was standing just outside the door. She tried to act as if she didn't see him but he walked past her and bumped into her. He jabbed a piece of paper into her gut, and she took it.

"I'm so sorry, I must have tripped," he said.

"It's okay." She tucked the piece of paper in her bag and watched him go. Then she began to walk up the hill to get Annalyn.

After retrieving her sister, and delivering her safely to her parents at the grocery store, Maureen announced that she wasn't feeling well. She said she was going home to lie down. It was only after she was safely alone, in the quiet comfort of her bedroom, that she opened the note. Sitting there, cross-legged on her bed, she smoothed out the paper and began to read what he had written:

> Maureen,
>
> I want you to know how much your intentions mean to me. But I am concerned that in an effort to make things better, you will actually make them worse.
>
> There are many people who do not want to see us become friends. I only wish to protect myself, and you.
>
> Miah

...Miah. He had signed it Miah. That must be what he went by. She read the note over and over again. Each time, she looked for a hint of the funny boy that she had seen at lunch that day. And each time, she came away with the same feeling that she was reading a note from her father. His words were calm, sensible. They were old! She folded the note and put it in her little wooden jewelry box. She curled up on her cozy bed and fell asleep. She woke to Ellen's kiss on her forehead.

"It's time for supper, sweet girl." Her mother spoke softly in her ear.

Maureen stirred, and smiled sleepily. She got up and walked down the hallway to the kitchen, where her father and Annalyn were already seated. They enjoyed their evening meal together, as was the nightly custom. After dinner, the girls bathed and went to bed. That night, Maureen prayed for Jeremiah. She had before, but this time it was different. She had him in her heart. She wanted him in her life. She didn't understand it herself, but she just couldn't stop thinking about him.

The next day at school, he completely ignored her. He acted as if he didn't even know her name. She decided she would just focus on school and forget about everything else. The day went by slowly. Jeremiah spent it alone, as usual. Maureen ate lunch in the cafeteria with her girlfriends. From them, she learned that all of the other colored students were gone. Things had been so difficult for them that they had not come back to school. Maureen thought about Jeremiah. What if one day he didn't come back? She might not see him again. But why did she even care? She finished her lunch, returned her tray, and went back to class. Junior Smith still had not come back to school. She hoped he would disappear, his father too.

She left school just in time to see Jeremiah leaving with a woman. They drove away in the same old Dodge pickup. She guessed it was his mother. She met Annalyn, and as usual they walked to the store.

Something smelled great. Ellen was in the back of the store, waiting for them. "Mother, what did you bake? It smells so good." Maureen saw an old fashioned black berry cobbler sitting on the little table. It was beautiful. Her mother didn't usually do such a good job with cobblers.

"Someone brought that cobbler. I didn't make it."

"Oh, how nice," Maureen said. "Who?" she asked, as she cut into it and served some to her little sister.

"A woman came by, just a little while ago, and brought it. She said she wanted to say thank you for the way you had treated her son."

Maureen stopped. She looked at her mother. Ellen looked back at her. Maureen was dumbfounded. Jeremiah's mother had made the cobbler. She knew it immediately. And she had come to the store. Maureen smiled at her mother. Ellen smiled back.

"Oh, Mother, he has been awful to me," she whined, while Ellen looked concerned.

"Well, not really awful." She corrected herself. "I guess more like indifferent."

"What do you mean?"

Maureen sat down with her cobbler and told her mother about everything from start to finish, how she had tried to be his friend but he had rejected her.

"Darling, sometimes we don't understand what's going on. We see things a certain way, but that may not be how they really are. Jeremiah lives in a totally different world than you do. Think about it. It is unimaginable to be hated for something that you have no control over. There are people that hate him simply because he is different. And it's serious. The truth of the matter is that horrible things are happening to colored folks all over the country right now. He and his family are right to keep their distance. They are only doing it to protect themselves. I worry about you, also."

Maureen told her mother that there was nothing to worry about. He wouldn't even talk to her, now. She ate the warm yummy cobbler and decided it was the sweetest she had ever tasted. She thought about Jeremiah. He must have told his mother about her. She wondered what he said.

Ellen began reading a book to Annalyn. Maureen interrupted her without even thinking. "Mother, you were nice to her, weren't you?"

Ellen looked surprised. "Of course. Why wouldn't I be?"

"I don't know," Maureen answered. But she knew how intimidating her mother could be, not because she meant to, but because it was just her way. Her quiet ways could easily be misunderstood. Maureen had no idea that it was actually her mother that was uncomfortable upon meeting Ruth Johnson, so caught off guard she had been by her dark beauty and grace. Maureen settled down at the table and began to read a book, returning now and again to her thoughts of Jeremiah Johnson.

She couldn't wait to get to school the next day. She decided she would not mention the cobbler to Jeremiah. She did not want to give him the opportunity to ignore her again. But she did hope that the day would be different and that he would talk to her. Maureen soon learned that would not be the case. He was absent. She hoped he was okay. She hoped he would come back. She talked with Peggy and asked her if she had heard anything. Peggy said she had not.

Day after day passed, but still no Jeremiah. Nobody knew anything about him. Maureen finally asked Mrs. Harris if he was coming back. He had been gone for an entire week. Each day of that week Maureen hoped he would return, and each day she had been disappointed.

Mrs. Harris said his parents had come that very morning and spoken to her. They said he would not be back. Maureen was heartbroken. She asked why, but Mrs. Harris said they did not offer any explanation. Maureen was angry. She supposed Mrs. Harris didn't ask for one either. They were all glad he was gone, but she wasn't. She wasn't.

Maureen went straight to bed as soon as she got home. She told her mother and father that she was ill. The next day she did not go to school. She said she was too sick. Finally, her father told her he was taking her to the doctor. She had not eaten or gotten out of bed for three days. She broke down and wept. "Oh, Daddy, I don't need to see the doctor. I'm sick with worry. Jeremiah has not come back to school, and I'm worried." She sat there on the bed, telling her father how she could think of nothing else. She was afraid something had happened to him.

Lloyd talked with his oldest daughter and was, as always, amazed at how tender her heart was. She barely even knew this boy, and yet she had made herself sick over the thought of him being hurt, or even worse, intentionally harmed. Lloyd told her that he would find out where the Johnsons lived and drive out there to check on the boy. She sat straight up in bed. "Oh, Daddy, I have to go. I have to go with you. I have to see him with my own two eyes."

He looked at his daughter. How he cherished her. She was so like him. His wife was made of stronger stuff, but not him. And Maureen was like him, tenderhearted to a fault. He would take her. He understood. He knew she would not rest until she had answers. He told her to dress while he went to the school. He would find out where the boy lived and inform her teacher that she would be absent again that day. Maureen did as she was told. She bathed and dressed herself.

She waited on the front porch for her father. At last, he pulled up and she got into his pickup. She asked if he knew where to go. He said that the family lived pretty far out in the country, somewhere on the river. He said they would find it. They drove for a good fifteen minutes, winding through the country alongside the river. Finally, they came to a mailbox that said Johnson. Lloyd turned his pickup, and headed toward the house at the end of the narrow dirt road. Maureen saw the old Dodge and got excited. "That's it."

Lloyd drove up to the house. It was a cute little house, Maureen decided. It was a small frame house, painted pale yellow. It had pink rose bushes and a little garden off to the left. There was a little girl playing outside. She looked to be about Annalyn's age. But this little girl had cute little braids all over her head, with bright colored ribbons. Maureen saw a woman come out onto the front porch. She must have heard the truck coming.

"Cora Bell, come inside." The woman looked incredibly apprehensive, almost afraid, as she looked at the truck. Lloyd and Maureen got out, and Lloyd introduced himself to the woman. He could tell she was suspicious of him. Maureen studied her. She was gorgeous.

Just then, a man came out onto the porch. He was holding a shot gun. Maureen stopped in her tracks. This was not going at all how she had planned. The man was telling Lloyd to get back in the truck, but when he saw Maureen he looked confused.

Jeremiah came running from somewhere around the back of the house. "Daddy, no, it's all right. This is Maureen…" And then she heard him, sounding so sweet, words that had never meant more, nor ever would again. "…my friend."

The man looked at his son. He understood. He put the gun down and began to apologize to them, looking incredibly relieved and embarrassed at the same time. Then he jumped down from the porch and introduced himself. "I'm sorry, sir. I'm Joe Johnson, Jeremiah's father. And this is my wife, Ruth."

Lloyd Adams shook the man's hand. He began to explain that Maureen had been very concerned when Jeremiah had not returned to school. He said they had come to check on the boy, to make sure he was all right.

Mr. Johnson invited them in. They all sat down at the kitchen table. He began to tell Lloyd of the trouble they had been having. He sensed that Lloyd was uncomfortable and guessed that he didn't want his daughter to hear what they were discussing, so he asked his son to show her their farm. The two left through the back door.

Maureen followed Jeremiah. He led her to the barn. He did not say a word. Was he angry? She wondered. After an uncomfortable silence, he turned to her and smiled. That smile almost brought her to tears.

"You were worried about me?" he asked her.

She was honest, tears welling up in her eyes. "Yes."

He told her that his parents had gotten some threats, demands to take him out of school. He said that the day his mother had brought the cobbler to the store, someone had followed them home. "Two men in a truck, they wanted us to know they were following us. I couldn't go back. I wanted to, but I couldn't stand to see my mother cry. I can't do that to her."

Maureen was overwhelmed. She did not understand. This made no sense to her. They spent a long time in the barn, talking. They were doing something they had been unable to do, until then. They were being sixteen. They were being friends.

The two of them walked down to the river. Maureen was shocked at how beautiful it was. The old oaks welcomed her with their vast branches, and the grass was so green. It was incredible. They walked down to the bank, took off their shoes, and put their feet in the water. They talked more about school. They talked about their families. They laughed and teased, and it came to Maureen that this was what she knew was inside of him, this joy. She didn't know how or why, but she knew that their paths were meant to cross. She just knew.

"Why do you want to be my friend?" The words came out of nowhere. Jeremiah had stopped splashing her and was curiously looking at her, eye to eye. Maureen was uncomfortable. She shifted. He was too close to her. She stopped for a moment to think before she spoke. There was something about the way he asked her the question. He was serious.

"When I saw you that first day, I felt like you needed a friend."

"So, you felt sorry for me?"

"No, I ..."

"Yes, you did."

"No, no I didn't." He was making her uncomfortable.

"Maureen, you should always be honest with yourself."

He was making her more and more uncomfortable with each passing moment. Honest, he wanted honest. She would give it to him. "Well, actually, I needed one."

"What?" He looked puzzled.

"...a friend. I needed a friend."

"You?" He couldn't help but laugh. "You are the smartest girl in the school, not to mention the prettiest." She could feel her cheeks blazing with embarrassment. "Every boy at that school is in love with you, and you act like you don't even notice."

"I notice. It's just that I'm not interested."

"Why not?"

She smiled at him. "I can't answer that."

"Why not?"

"Because I really don't know."

Jeremiah nodded, acknowledging her answer. He watched her put her head down, and still, he could not figure her out.

It was her turn to catch him off guard. "I heard you're a writer."

"Where did you hear that?" He was surprised.

She smiled. "A little bird told me."

"Yes, I wrote a story and entered it in a contest through the mail. My aunt lives in Houston and works as a secretary at an all-black university there. She's the one who got me involved."

"I'd like to read it sometime."

"Why?" He was looking at her.

The whys were making Maureen uneasy. It was impossible to have small talk with Jeremiah. He wanted more.

"I'm interested," she told him.

"Finally, something you're interested in," he teased.

As they sat there on the bank of the Trinity River, with their feet in the water, Maureen thought about how nice it was. She loved talking to him, being with him.

"Jeremiah, you speak so well, almost like you're from someplace else. You don't sound at all like you're from Kilroy, or even Texas. Why is that?"

"I've been all over."

"What do you mean?"

"Books. They take me all over the place. I've been to England, France, Greece, New York, California. You name it, I've probably been there. I read all the time. My mother is afraid to let me out of her sight. I stay around here and read all the time. My aunt sends me books."

They sat for a long time discussing what they had read. They loved Shakespeare, didn't care for Poe, and hadn't read Lord Byron. Finally, Jeremiah asked Maureen a question that he had been wanting to ask for quite some time.

"How come you and your family aren't like all the other white folks?"

"Because we're from outer space," she answered matter-of-factly.

"No, really, you don't hate us."

"My daddy grew up with colored people. His father was a share-cropper and picked cotton." She touched his arm. "Jeremiah, not all white people hate black people."

He sat there for a minute thinking about what she said. "I guess it's the ones that do, that stick out."

Maureen nodded in agreement.

After awhile, they saw their fathers coming down the hill, to-ward the river. The two men were laughing. It was nice, Maureen thought. Lloyd told her it was time to go. She looked at Jeremiah. She put her shoes on and told him goodbye. She took her father's hand, and they walked back to the truck. Maureen told Mrs. Johnson that she had been delighted by the cobbler and that she hoped to see her again soon.

Ruth Johnson could hear the sincerity in her voice, but she didn't trust white folks. Even though she genuinely liked Maureen and Lloyd Adams, and was thankful that a kind soul was in that school that her son wanted to see so badly, she secretly wished they would disappear. For her, happiness was peace, pure and simple, without looking over her shoulder. She desired no one but her maker, her family, and a few close friends, least of all some white folks that she knew nothing about. But her children were another story. They were young and had been sheltered from so much of the evil in the world. She had seen it firsthand. But life was calling to them. They wanted to live, while she wanted nothing more than to protect them from all that she had seen. And to make matters worse, she had a bad feeling.

Maureen got into the truck with her father and they drove home. "Daddy, Jeremiah is my friend and I understand why he won't be returning to school, but I still want to be able to see him."

Her father was quiet for a moment, lost in thought. Finally, he spoke. "Maureen, I want you to listen to what I'm about to say to you. You may be thinking of yourself more than anyone else. I understand your concern for Jeremiah. I know that you think you're making things better for him. But I want you to consider for a moment that you could quite possibly be making things worse. I had a long talk with his father, and they never had any problems living here, until Jeremiah went to school. Now, they are walking around with shot guns. As for the boy's parents, they are more concerned now with his safety than his happiness, and rightly so. Right now, you don't understand because you're young, but when you're older you will. When you've been through some things in life, acquired a little wisdom, you'll understand. You won't care for money. You won't require the excitement that you need in your youth. It's peace that you'll seek. It's peace that you'll need. And that's where they are. They want peace. I wish there was something that we could do, but I don't think there is."

Maureen listened to what her father had to say. She felt an incredible sorrow for the Johnson family. She felt it for herself. She wished she could forget about Jeremiah, but she knew she could not.

Two weeks passed. Maureen and Jeremiah had begun writing to each other. The Johnsons did not have a telephone. She ran to the mail box every day after school to check the mail. She made it her job. She was excited to receive something that looked like an invitation of some sort. It was a little card. It had Jeremiah's return address, but it was not his handwriting. She read the card. She was being invited to a birthday dinner for him. Seventeen, it said. He would be seventeen. She was elated. It never occurred to her that she might not be able to go.

Ellen said no, and it was not open for discussion. Maureen was upset with her mother. "Why?" she pleaded.

Ellen explained to her that it didn't look good. She was going to dinner at a boy's house and they didn't even really know him.

"Mother, that's not why, and you know it."

But Ellen still said no. Maureen went to her room and shut herself up. She would not come out for anything. It was this scene that Lloyd Adams came home to, expecting to have a nice dinner with his family. Ellen explained what was going on. He went in to talk to his daughter.

She lay with her back to him and did not stir when he entered the room. He saw the invitation on her nightstand. He picked it up and looked at it. He put it back in its place and sat down on the bed beside her. "Maureen, your mother and I have decided that we will discuss this matter of a birthday invitation with you, in the kitchen, right now." He bent down and whispered in her ear, "Pull yourself together and use your head. It's your best chance." He then strolled out of her bedroom and closed the door behind him.

Was Daddy on her side? She wondered.

She smoothed her dress and hair, then checked her face in the mirror. She decided she looked as best she could, under the circumstances, and proceeded to the kitchen. Her mother was sitting at the kitchen table with her father. They told Annalyn to go play in her room. Her mother spoke, after Maureen sat down.

"Maureen, your father and I have discussed this matter and we feel you should not go. We also recognize the fact that you are sixteen years old, and that you are entitled to your own opinion." Ellen paused to take a breath. "We will allow you to bring your opinion to our attention, at this time. That does not mean you will change our minds. It simply means that we respect your feelings, and we will hear them out."

Maureen wanted to burst into tears, throw a tantrum, and demand to go, but she knew that would not work. She decided to appeal to her mother's sensibility and spirit of good will. "Mother, Daddy," she addressed them both, "I simply must go to dinner at the Johnson's house. You see, Jeremiah was treated terribly at school. Do you know that he never even went to the restroom at school? And I know why. He knew better than to go into the boy's bathroom. He would have been beaten up." The tears began to run down her face. She went on, "That's how bad he wanted to go to school."

Emotion overtook her. She forgot her plan and spoke her heart. "I don't know why I feel this way about him. But since the first day I saw him, my heart broke for him, and I could not bear to sit there and do nothing. I can't explain it to you. You could never understand..." She threw up her hands, turned her face, and fought back the sobs.

Ellen interrupted her daughter, with barely more than a whisper. "No, I do. I do understand. You may go."

Ellen told her to go on to bed. She wanted to talk with Lloyd. Maureen walked down the hall, to her bedroom, and got herself ready for bed. She never even had dinner. It didn't matter. She wasn't hungry anyway. Before she got into bed, she wrote a short note saying that she would be coming for dinner on Saturday. She would mail it tomorrow. She got into bed and fell fast asleep.

Ellen and Lloyd sat in the kitchen, discussing the situation. Maureen was sixteen. They knew full well what could come with her spending time with this boy. And while they knew the two of them were only friends, they also understood the delicate balance between friendship and more. At the same time, at sixteen, it was ridiculous to be told you could not go to someone's birthday dinner. Of course, Ellen had immediately said no because of the racial tension. She didn't want any trouble for her family, and she didn't want any trouble for the Johnsons. But she did understand what Maureen was feeling. And what would she be teaching Maureen if she denied her the evening? Perhaps that one should stop living in the name of fear. That was something that she never wanted any of her children to learn. Never...

Saturday came. Maureen was ready for the party, all day. Finally it was time to go. The whole family was driving her there. Ellen wanted to see for herself that the situation was acceptable, and reserved the right to change her mind if she didn't like what she saw. And so, they drove out to the Johnson's house.

Lloyd introduced Ellen to Mr. Johnson. She had already met Mrs. Johnson, the day she brought the cobbler to the store. Ellen liked them both. They were friendly and kind, with a warmth that reached her down deep, and penetrated her tough exterior. Ellen saw Roy King's boy there, his pale face easily recognizable in the sea of dark faces. Ruth Johnson explained that she and the boy's mother were friends. Their mothers had known each other. She and Dorothy Martin, now Dorothy King, had grown up together.

There was a lot of family there, and more than a few young people Maureen's age. It looked like a fine time. Ellen would allow her to stay. She had a feeling about these people. They were good people. And she felt more comfortable leaving her daughter at the Johnson's house than anywhere else. Even though it was completely outside the confines of all that Kilroy's social code endorsed, Ellen let her daughter stay.

She was just as taken with Ruth Johnson, as Maureen had been with Jeremiah. There was an instant connection between the two women. And Ellen Adams knew from the moment that Ruth Johnson walked into her store, that they would be friends. She could tell by the way Ruth carried herself, that she was a force to be reckoned with. She would soon learn that she had finally met a woman whose strength surpassed her own.

Ellen looked for her daughter. Maureen was talking to Jeremiah's oldest sister, Pauline. Lloyd announced that he would be back for Maureen in a couple of hours. Maureen watched, as her family got into the car and drove away.

Jeremiah spotted Maureen sitting with his sister, and went to steal her away. When their eyes met, his whole face lit up. He took Maureen around, introducing her to the rest of his family. There were so many family members. They had come from all around. Some had driven up from Houston. There were grandparents, aunts, uncles, and cousins. Maureen recognized Alfred King from school, and his younger sister Patricia. They were the only other whites there. Not that Maureen cared, it was just impossible not to notice. Jeremiah and his grandfather were talking and teasing each other, when they heard Ruth's voice.

"Jeremiah, get in this house before you wear your grandaddy out!"

"Yes, Mama." He kissed his grandfather on the forehead and raced to the house. As he reached the front porch steps, he smelled supper and realized how hungry he was. Jeremiah opened the screen door and flew into the kitchen.

His father chuckled. "Whoa, boy! Where's the fire?"

Jeremiah looked at his father. Joe Johnson couldn't help but smile as he watched his son enjoying himself at the party that was being given in his honor. "Git on in here and wash up. Mama's almost got supper cooked."

"Yes, sir."

"You help Mama fix the table up, son. And when you're done, you can call everyone in to eat."

"Yes, Daddy."

Maureen had come inside to look for Jeremiah. When she saw what he was doing, she asked if there was anything she could do to help. Ruth told her to wash up and she could pour lemonade in the glasses. Jeremiah helped his mother set the table. He took pleasure in this simple task. He had been helping her set the table for as long as he could remember. As his hands laid out the dishes, he began to hum a tune. Ruth recognized it and began to sing along.

"Amazing grace…" She sang from somewhere deep inside.

"How sweet the sound…" The sound was strong and so very beautiful, just like her.

"That saved a wretch like me…" Her voice filled the room with something timeless, too powerful for words.

"I once was lost…" Maureen could hear it. She could feel it.

"But now I'm found…" Mesmerizing.

"Twas blind…" The sound of sorrow, of pain.

"But now, I see…" Miah sang in little more than a whisper. His was the voice of hope. Not at all the strong sound of his mother's voice, instead his was gentle, almost fragile. He looked at his mother with tears in his eyes. He loved her. She was so strong, and so beautiful. He looked into her eyes. They were bright green. They changed, just like the leaves, from brown to green and back again. And her dark skin, matching his own…

Maureen watched, as something passed between mother and child. Ruth took him in her arms and whispered to him, "Boy, you're my heart." She held him tightly to her, his head on her shoulder, as if to take him inside and keep him there. She wanted to protect him, to keep the evil of the world far, far away. Maureen was taken in and lost, watching them and all that passed between them. It was as if time had stopped for a moment, as if mother and son were one again, for just an instant. Maureen witnessed, in that living, breathing, beautiful moment in time, the strange and intricate relationship that exists between a mother and her son. She watched them with appreciation and the utmost respect, sensing something deeper that she could not possibly comprehend.

Mothers have a way, some primal instinct perhaps. They can sense when their children are in danger. They feel it way down deep in their gut. It gnaws, and gnaws, and gnaws at them. Ruth Johnson felt it. Each and every time she watched Miah, she felt it. He was different, special. He was young and strong. He was smart, and he wasn't afraid of anything. For this, she was proud, so very proud of her beautiful boy. But he was also black, and growing up in rural Texas in 1955. And for that, she was frightened. She was terrified.

Lost in thoughts of her son, Ruth was startled when everyone clamored in for dinner. There was Joe leading them in. They all sang to Jeremiah, and ate wherever they could find a spot. The food was good. There was barbecued brisket, greens, and potatoes. It was delicious. They had cake and homemade ice cream. Jeremiah's grandfather got out his fiddle. They danced and sang, and had a wonderful time. Maureen was sorry to see the night end. Lloyd came to get her, and Mrs. Johnson sent some birthday cake home with them. Maureen was quiet as they drove home.

"Did you have a good time?" her father asked.

"Yes, it was wonderful. But Daddy, I thought they would be..." She paused, searching for the words.

"What?" he asked.

"I don't know... different."

"How so?" Lloyd was intrigued.

"With all the talk around town of them being dirty and stupid and such, I just didn't expect it to be like that."

"Like what?"

"Well, like that. They are incredibly well mannered. They're truly wonderful. And Jeremiah is the smartest person I've ever known. And their house is way cleaner than ours. And they play the most wonderful music."

Lloyd Adams could not help but smile at his daughter. "Maureen Adams, are you telling me that you believe all the mess you hear? Haven't I told you not to listen to it?"

"Daddy, I don't listen to it, but I can't help but hear it sometimes."

"And it plants an ugly seed, doesn't it?"

"It sure does."

Ellen was waiting for them at home. She wanted to hear the details, but Maureen said she would tell her all about it in the morning. She said she was exhausted and wanted nothing more than to go to bed. Ellen said she understood.

But Maureen really just wanted to be alone, to replay the night in her mind. She had such a wonderful time. She changed into a white cotton nightgown and climbed into bed. She burrowed deep into her covers and closed her eyes.

She began to replay the evening in her mind. She remembered his face when he saw her get out of the car. He couldn't help but grin. She was wearing a new pale yellow dress, the same color as her hair. It brought out the blue in her eyes. He told her that she looked beautiful, while they were sitting down watching Ruth and Joe dance to the fiddle. Her intentions with her appearance were innocent. She hadn't meant to entice him in any way. That wasn't Maureen. She remembered he had said that she was the prettiest girl in the school. She didn't want to disappoint him. She wanted to please him.

What a night it had been, unlike anything she had ever known. The food was great. And the music... It had been amazing. She never realized how beautiful a fiddle could be. She had only ever heard it whistle Dixie. But tonight she heard it play something lovely and sad, all at the same time. It was a haunting instrument. Jeremiah stood beside her, listening to it sing as the sun was going down. He looked so handsome in the new blue shirt that had been a gift from his parents. He had been so close to her that she could smell him. He smelled soapy and sweet.

Maureen didn't go to a lot of parties, not since she was a child. They just didn't interest her. The kids her age were all dating. This one liked that one, but that one didn't like this one, and so on, and so forth. It just did not appeal to her at all. But learning about Jeremiah did. He intrigued her.

Maureen woke to her mother opening the pale pink curtains in her room, urging her to hurry, saying something about being late for church. Maureen looked at the clock. It was almost ten o'clock. She couldn't believe she had slept so late. Ellen told her to hurry once again, and then was gone. Maureen groomed herself then hurried out of the house. She heard the slam of the screen door as she ran to the waiting car. On the way to church, she told her mother about the party. She tried not to talk about Jeremiah too much. She didn't want her mother to worry.

Days turned into months, with Maureen and Jeremiah living for the moments that they could be together. The rest of the world was of no consequence. It was just the two of them learning from each other. They lived for weekends and holidays. Their time together didn't come often enough and always ended too soon. Inevitably Maureen would find herself back in school on Monday, counting the days until they could be together again.

She found herself daydreaming more and more, always about Jeremiah. His letter came on a Wednesday. He told Maureen that he had been accepted to a school. He would be attending Texas Southern University in Houston, in the fall. "Mama is still apprehensive about it, but everyone there is colored so that makes it a little more appealing to her," he had written.

She remembered that he had gone to Houston in order to take a test, to see if he could attend the school. Obviously, he had done well. "I am coming to the store with Mama to get some things, on Friday," he went on to say. "I'm not leaving for another five months, but she says there is a lot to be done. Please, be there. I want to see you. I miss you." She felt his words swell inside of her, warming her entire body.

She was so happy for him. He would finally be able to attend school, and he would be safe. Maureen didn't know anything about Houston, but judging from conversations that she had with Miah before, it sounded like a nice place. He said that the colored folks had their own area. And since they owned their own businesses, they didn't have to deal with whites very much. While Maureen was truly glad that he would finally get to leave Kilroy, she was incredibly sad at the same time. His entrance into her life had awakened her to the world around her, and she couldn't bear for that door to close again.

Friday came. Maureen practically ran home from school. Annalyn complained the whole way home that Maureen was walking too fast. She saw the car that belonged to Mama and Papa and figured they were inside. She went in and said hello to everyone. As they sat there at the little table in the back, catching up, she heard the front door. When she saw who was coming through the door, she felt sick. It was Mr. Smith, and in case that wasn't bad enough he had Junior with him. Ellen got up to greet them, but Lloyd touched her shoulder. "Let me deal with them." He walked to the front of the store and asked if he could help them find anything. Maureen prayed that they would get what they needed and get out of the store, before Jeremiah and Ruth arrived.

Instead, just as they were cashing out, the door opened up so wide that it almost knocked Harold Smith over. It was Jeremiah. He was smiling and rushing in to find Maureen.

"What the hell is wrong with you, nigger?"

Miah's smile faded. He turned to face Mr. Smith. He was shocked.

Maureen looked at Miah. She saw the realization of what he had done, all over his face. He began to apologize to Mr. Smith for hitting him with the door. "I'm sorry, sir. I didn't know that you were standing back there."

To Maureen's horror, Mr. Smith started cussing him up one side and down the other. The whole scene was spinning out of control. Ruth Johnson entered the store and stood in the doorway, in sheer disbelief. Junior Smith bowed up to Jeremiah and looked as if at any moment he would attack him.

It was Ellen that claimed order. Lloyd tried to calm them down, but it was Ellen that commanded Harold Smith's attention. Her poise and manner of speaking always reminded him so much of his own mother. "Harold Smith, this child did not intend to hit you with the door and you know it." She was angry, and he could hear the disgust in her voice. "He has apologized for it. Now, you will calm down and apologize, in turn, to every soul in this store for that disgusting language you subjected us to. If not, you will leave my store and not return again." She narrowed her eyes at him. He made her sick to her stomach, with the smell of alcohol and stale cigarettes.

Maureen had never seen her mother so angry. It was something that was inconceivable to her. But Ellen did not stop there, "And Junior, you will step away from that boy right now. He is a guest in my store, while you are not. And if you do not move quickly, I will have you arrested for whatever you put in the front left pocket of that jacket that you think I'm too stupid to notice." Junior's mouth fell open, but he did not move.

"Now!" she screamed through clenched teeth.

Junior stepped away while his father addressed Lloyd. The disgust on Ellen's face was not lost on Harold Smith. It was almost more than he could bear. His hatred was kindled. He turned to Lloyd. "I tried to tell you about these niggers. You're the only one in town that's holdin' out. We'd have 'em run out by now, but everybody's waitin' to see what you're gonna' do."

With an ugly twisted smile, he turned to Jeremiah. "Better be careful, boy." Then he was gone.

As he went out the front door with his son, he spat chewing tobacco at Ruth Johnson. She stepped back just in time to have it land on her shoe. At once, Maureen grabbed a towel and bent down to clean it off. When she was done, Ruth told her thank you. The tears in Mrs. Johnson's eyes broke Maureen's heart. The air in the room was so thick Maureen could hardly breathe. It was like a bad dream that she could neither control, nor escape. No one said a word. No one knew what to say. It was Mama that broke the silence.

"Vera Smith was my friend. She would roll over in her grave if she could see her son right now." Then she spoke to Jeremiah, words that Maureen would never forget as long as she lived, "It's a good thing you're leaving this place, son. The bad knows how good you are."

Maureen shivered. She felt a chill. Ellen invited Ruth and Jeremiah to the back of the store for iced tea and sandwiches. They followed her to the back, but neither was hungry. Everyone chatted casually about the building going on at the edge of town and Miah's acceptance to the university. But no one could overcome the scene that had shaken them so.

Finally, Ruth gave Lloyd a list of things that Jeremiah would need for school. He told her that he would get it all together and deliver it to them. She told him that she would pay for his gas and explained that she really just wanted to return home at this point. He said that payment for his gas would not be necessary and that he understood. He insisted on following them home.

She told Lloyd that Joe was waiting for them at home and they would be fine. But Lloyd already had his keys in his hand. He would not hear of it. Jeremiah told everyone goodbye. Maureen could not help but cry. She could not control it. The day that she had so looked forward to had been disastrous. Her heart broke for Ruth and Jeremiah. She considered how vulnerable they must feel, how threatening the Smiths had been. She never worried for herself, only for Jeremiah. For she was safe, or so she thought...

Lloyd followed behind the Dodge pickup. He considered the Johnsons. Every emotion, from sorrow to rage, flooded his consciousness. Something changed inside of him. He became convicted.

Up until that moment, he thought he would be able to mind his own business and continue doing the right thing. He saw now that was impossible. Minding his own business had been the wrong thing. They had tried to get him to join in their sick little game, the game of scaring the "uppity niggers," as they called them. He had ignored them. He realized now that he should have done more from the beginning. His fear for his own held him back. But this thing was not going to go away. He had to face it.

Lloyd drove all the way out to the Johnson's place to make sure they made it safely home, but he did not stop there. He went in to talk to Joe. He wanted to make sure he understood the seriousness of the situation. And there was something else, something else that this man should know. Lloyd would tell him all that he knew. Joe was a kind, hardworking, family man. Lloyd would give him what he himself would want if the tables were turned, the truth.

Joe Johnson was not expecting his wife and son back so soon. He was fishing down by the river with Cora Bell, when he heard the truck in the distance. He heard the sound of another vehicle and ran to the top of the hill. There was a pickup pulling in behind them. He relaxed when he realized it was Lloyd Adams. He reeled in his line, gathered Cora Bell, and walked up the hill to meet them. He could see immediately that something was wrong. Ruth's skin looked grey. She thought she might vomit at any moment.

"Is everything all right?" Joe asked, as he searched his wife's eyes. They said no.

He turned to Lloyd for some kind of answer. His wife turned away. She could not meet his gaze. Lloyd wasted no time telling Joe Johnson about the altercation at the store. He was straightforward. Joe asked his wife and his son to leave them alone. Ruth and Jeremiah took Cora Bell back to the house with them, while the two men stayed behind to talk.

"Joe, I feel like your family may be in danger."

Lloyd told him how there were at least ten men that were up to something. He told him how, for months, they had been trying to get him to come and play poker with them. He told Joe how he had refused any dealings with them. Lloyd did not know exactly what they were planning because he had been avoiding them and whatever their intentions were.

Joe listened to all that Lloyd offered. He was speechless. He could not believe that things were coming to this.

"I never thought this would happen."

"Neither did I."

"What do you think they'll do?"

"They want you gone, so I guess whatever it takes."

"Lloyd, this is my home. I grew up here. My wife is from the city. I met her in Houston. But me... this is my home."

Lloyd couldn't bear to see this man struggle with all that he had put before him. He watched Joe look around at the land he loved. His land, his home...

"You know my daddy bought this land from the man. He was a sharecropper, and he bought all this."

It was ripping Lloyd's heart out to hear him. "How did he buy it?"

It was no small accomplishment for a sharecropper to purchase land. Lloyd Adams knew all too well that sharecropping was indentured servitude, and it was his opinion that it was far worse than slavery had ever been. Slavery broke the body, with year after year of back breaking work, no end in sight. Sharecropping was different. It broke the spirit, with year after year of back breaking work, knowing you were free, but unable to do a damn thing with that freedom.

"He never told us how. But I know he bought it. The man would bring my daddy tobacco too, ever' so often. I can still smell his pipe." He hesitated, unable to go on.

Finally, Joe smiled through his tears. "Sure would like to know how he bought it."

Lloyd smiled back. "Now, I'll bet that is a story." Both men laughed out loud.

"Maybe you could just leave for a little while and let things cool. They're all riled up right now. Maybe if you disappear for a while it'll blow over."

Joe sat there for a moment considering what Lloyd said. He looked at the man who had become his friend and challenged him. "You know as well as I do, if we do that, it's gonna' be even worse when we get back."

Lloyd Adams looked away. He was ashamed. These people had done nothing wrong. They were good people. He did not know why, but he felt ashamed.

"Lloyd, I respect you. You have been good to my family, and I know what you all have risked for our sake. Furthermore, I trust your judgement. If you were me, what would you do?"

Lloyd sat there for a moment, considering it. He looked at Joe Johnson and said but one word, with incredible sadness. "Leave."

Joe turned his head. He felt tears start to sting his eyes again. The answer told him the depth of what was going on. He shook his head. He understood.

They talked for awhile about the town and the people involved, and leaving. Joe said they would pack tonight and leave in the morning. They would go to Houston and visit family, and decide what to do from there. Joe told Lloyd he would be in touch, and Lloyd agreed to help him in any way he could. He offered anything from the store that they might need. He even went so far as to tell Joe that he would put up a business loan if they decided to stay. Joe thanked him and said he would be in touch. They would pack and leave first thing in the morning. Lloyd shook his hand and started to walk to the truck. He turned back and hugged the man that he had only recently come to know and respect. And all because his daughter couldn't mind her own business. How much she was like him, he thought. He got in his truck and headed for home.

They were all waiting for him: Ellen, Maureen, Mama, and Papa. Annalyn was in her room, but the others were sitting at the kitchen table when he got home. Ellen asked what happened. He told her he had gone in to talk to Joe. "That's what took so long," he said.

They all sat around the table talking about what was going on in Kilroy. Papa said, "It's not a spark anymore, it's a fire." Mama said that it couldn't go on like this. Something had to change. They discussed and rediscussed, and still they came up with nothing. The bottom line was that they didn't know what to do. Everyone else in Kilroy felt just like the Smiths, and if they didn't, they were too scared to say so. It was the reality of the world at the time, and nobody that could do anything about it would. Maureen listened. She felt sick to her stomach. She was filled with worry. She had been awakened to something that she wished she never had to learn.

Maureen wondered if evil had taken hold of Mr. Smith and Junior. She had known the Smiths her whole life. Their family went back as far as hers. They had always been around, and Junior had always had a mean streak, as far back as she could remember. The more she thought about it, the more she had to admit that evil had probably always been there. But then there was Kitty Smith and Toby Smith, and they were nice. They were kind. Maureen had fallen out of a tree a couple of summers ago, and Kitty Smith had patched her knee up. Maureen wondered if she would have done the same had it been Cora Bell. Something told Maureen that she would have. She remembered the way Kitty had touched her leg and smiled at her. She was a gentle soul, with a kind heart.

No, Maureen thought. She just couldn't dismiss the entire family like that. It wasn't that simple. It was just old Harold Smith and

Junior that were the rotten ones of the bunch. But the rest of the town just didn't seem to see it. Or was it that they just didn't care because it wasn't happening to them? They went right along with it, the cowards.

Maureen had learned that she and her family were the exception. The others were the rule. It made her angry. It made her sad. Why? She looked up at the sky, appealing to the greatest power of all. "Please, do something," she pleaded. She was beginning to absorb the truth, and the truth was that she was just a teenage girl growing up in a tiny Texas town in 1956, and that she had no more control over what was going on than the man in the moon.

Lloyd could see how upset his daughter was. She had passed crying. Her cheeks were bright red, flushed with fear and anger. He thought of sending her to her room many times as the conversation got more and more serious, but he knew she would not be able to stand it. Finally, Mama and Papa said that they must be going. Maureen kissed and hugged them goodbye then went to her room.

She took out the little wooden box that held all of her letters from Miah. She got them out and looked at them. She looked at his handwriting. She wondered what he was doing. She would have to convince her father to take her to see him tomorrow. She looked at the clock in her room. It was nine o'clock. She decided to go on to bed, knowing she would not sleep, hoping the night would pass quickly. Her prayer was simple. "Please, please..." she whispered in the darkness.

Maureen woke with a start. She heard something. What time was it? It was late. She heard it again. Someone was in her room. She could barely see but she knew someone was in her room. She felt it. She lay still and did not breathe. Her heart began to race. She saw something move in the shadows. It was Annalyn. She grabbed her and pulled her into the bed. "What are you doing?" she whispered. Annalyn sat up in the bed and began to explain.

"I got up to go to the bathroom and I heard Mother and Daddy in the kitchen. They were talking about Jeremiah and his family. They are leaving in the morning. I heard Daddy say that they have to get out of town if they want to be safe. Mother and Daddy went to bed, but I can't go back to sleep. I'm scared."

Maureen hugged her sister in the darkness. She rubbed her cheek on the top of Annalyn's soft curls. She felt the tears well up in her eyes and fought them back. He was leaving. She was horrified and yet she was relieved. He would be safe. He would also be gone from her. She had to say goodbye. She told Annalyn that there was nothing to be afraid of. She told her that she could sleep in the bed with her. Maureen lay in the bed with her little sister until she heard her snores. She knew that once Annalyn began to snore, it was over. She would not wake up until morning.

Maureen, still in her nightgown, did not even bother to get shoes. She found her father's keys. She had never driven alone before. Daddy had let her drive with him a few times. She knew she could do it. She slowly opened the door to the pickup. Its squeak was deafening in the quiet of the night. She climbed in and put the key in the ignition. For a moment, she thought of abandoning her plan, but it occurred to her that she might never see Jeremiah again. She started the pickup and was gone.

Her mind raced as she drove further and further out of town. If Mother and Daddy woke before she got back, she would be in so much trouble. What did it matter? She asked herself. There is nothing they could possibly do to her that could be worse than what was already happening. He was leaving.

She parked the truck on the main road, next to the mailbox. She left the keys in the ignition and walked down the narrow dirt road to the little house. She went to Jeremiah's window at the side of the house and tapped softly.

"It's Maureen," she whispered. She did not want to get shot.

He pulled back the curtains almost instantly. He had been lying in bed, wide awake. "What are you doing?" He could not believe his eyes.

She could see him smiling in the moonlight. She couldn't help but smile back. She started to explain but he stopped her and climbed out the window. Standing there beside her, he did something she never expected. He took her in his arms and kissed her. She kissed him back. It was a sweet kiss and Maureen felt warm from the inside out. "I came to say goodbye." He took her hand and they began to walk down to the river.

They stood together on the side of the bank in silence, except for the sound of the running water. Jeremiah began to laugh. She was in her nightgown. She knew what he was thinking and began to explain. "I didn't want to wake anyone. I was afraid that I wouldn't get to see you if I…"

He moved closer and put his finger on her lips to hush her. He kissed her again. Something was happening. They knew they did not have much time.

Miah was powerless. She looked so beautiful. Her white cotton nightgown had become transparent in the moonlight and he could see the perfect silhouette of her body. Her long blond curls hung loose and free down her back. He kissed her even more deeply, and she kissed him back. He stood there before her, bathed in the moonlight. He had only a pair of blue jeans on. She rubbed her hands over his strong shoulders and looked at his beautiful face kissing her in the moonlight. His eyes were closed. Hers were open, watching him, as she got lost in his kiss.

It was Miah that finally pulled away. He had to stop this. Of course, he was in love with her. He had been since she showed up at his house that day.

"I love you," he whispered.

"I love you too," she whispered back.

He sat down on the bank and pulled her down beside him. They began to talk. Maureen began to cry. "I won't be able to stand it when you go," she said.

"Yes, you will. We'll write."

He could tell her heart was breaking, as was his. He touched her face. "Maureen, be realistic. We don't have a chance, here."

She nodded in agreement. There was nothing she could say. She knew he spoke the truth. She couldn't even look at him. It hurt too badly. He took her face in his gentle hands and turned it up to meet his gaze. "Meeting you is the best thing that ever happened to me. It's as if the moment you raised your hand in school that day, I started living. My mama kept me hidden out here, so scared something would happen to me. Yes, she kept me safe, but it was you that made me feel alive..."

She interrupted him. "I know how she feels. I love you so much. I want you to be safe too."

He pulled her face up to his and kissed her softly. Then, he looked into her eyes. She felt as if she could see the depths of his soul. "Safety is overrated if it makes you a prisoner." And with those words, he turned his back and stripped off his blue jeans.

She was shocked and speechless upon seeing the beauty of his body in the moonlight, as he ran and jumped in the river. Maureen followed. He turned his head while she stripped off her nightgown. They swam in the cool night with nothing but the moon, the stars, the water, their love for the Creator, and their love for each other. There was no hatred, no fear, no anger, just peace, youth, hope, and love.

Maureen was the first to walk out of the river. She picked up her abandoned nightgown and pulled it on over her head. Jeremiah came right behind her and pulled his blue jeans back on. They were both wet. He took her in his arms and told her everything would be fine. He told her he would write first and then she would have his address. She told him to hold her one last time, and then she would go. He took her in his arms and held her tight. They began to walk back to the house. But just before the two of them got to the top of the hill, there they were.

"Well, what do we have here?" Harold Smith asked, with a twelve gauge shotgun in his hands.

Junior's voice answered, "A nigger and his bitch."

Maureen took Miah's hand and started to walk past them. "You don't scare me."

As she walked past Junior, he hit her over the head with the butt of his gun. She fell to the ground. Jeremiah gathered her in his arms, to shield her, to protect her. He began to call for help as the blood poured from her head. It never even crossed his mind to run, to leave her.

Ruth Johnson woke to the sound of a shot being fired. She sat straight up in bed. Joe heard it too. He was instantly up and grabbing his gun. He looked out the back door, in the direction the shot had come. He saw nothing. He ran to the front of the house and saw nothing.

Just then Ruth started screaming. He ran to her. "Jeremiah is gone!" she screamed. He was out the back door, running in the direction of the sound of gunfire. He never knew what hit him. He was running, only thinking of his son, when the second shot took his life.

Ruth heard the shot and fear gripped her. She and Pauline took Cora Bell to the storm cellar to hide. The panic was rising inside of her. She knew they were in danger. But was that Joe's gun, or had it been someone else's? Thoughts rushed in and out of her mind as fear took hold. They sat in the cellar for what seemed like an eternity, but she would not come out. She would not come out until Joe came for her. He knew where they would be. And if he did not come...

Well, that meant it wasn't safe. She tried to keep her wits about her. Cora Bell was looking up at her, wide-eyed. Pauline was shaking all over. They waited.

Lloyd Adams woke to the sun streaming through the part in the pale blue drapes. His sleep had been restless. Most of it was spent thinking, waiting for morning. He got up and dressed in a clean shirt and pants. He washed his face, cleaned his teeth, and decided to shave. But Annalyn's voice stopped him. Faintly, he heard her calling him outside the bedroom door. She woke Ellen, who sat up and told her to come in.

"Where's Maureen?" she asked.

"What do you mean?" Ellen got out of bed and took her matching silk robe from the antique dressing table. She put it on and tied it around her, as she followed Annalyn out of the bedroom. Lloyd was right behind them.

"Maureen is gone. I went and got in bed with her last night, right after you went to bed. I was scared because I heard you talking about the Johnsons. She said I could sleep with her, but when I woke up she was gone. I thought she went somewhere with Daddy because the truck is gone." Lloyd flew to the window. She was right. The truck was gone.

He knew exactly where Maureen had gone. He told Ellen to give him her keys. As he put his shoes on, he asked Annalyn if she had told Maureen that the Johnsons were leaving. She said she had. He began to think. They had gone to bed around midnight. It was now six thirty. ...Six and a half hours. He took the keys from Ellen. He slammed the front door. The next thing Ellen heard was the wheels of her car spinning, uncontrolled, as it shot out of the driveway. She wanted to go with him but he had said no. He told her to stay with Annalyn.

He drove as fast as he could through the country. He tried to remain calm but he had a bad feeling. Lloyd saw his pickup on the main road. He guessed Maureen had parked it there. He drove up to the little yellow house and got out of the car. Where was everyone? He knocked and called for someone, but no one came. His knocks soon turned to pounding, and his calls to screams. Something was wrong. Joe's pickup was still there. Lloyd knew that the Johnsons must have been there when Maureen arrived. They had probably been in bed.

He saw an open window at the left side of the house. He climbed through it and entered a bedroom. The bed was unmade. He saw that all of the beds were unmade. Everyone was gone. He went out the back door and ran to the barn. He went in through the open door. Then he saw them.

He ran to them. Joe and Jeremiah were hanging from the beams in the ceiling. He started screaming. He grabbed the boy's legs. He tried to get him down. He felt and saw blood all over the place. He knew they were dead. Lloyd Adams screamed. He screamed, he cried, and he panicked. A lone thought reached him on the brink of insanity... Maureen. He began to call her name. She was nowhere. Ruth... Pauline... Cora Bell... Where were they?

He thought to jump in the car and go get help, but he ran down to the river instead. Then he saw her, lying in the green grass. She was still wearing her night gown, the morning sun on her sweet face. She lay still and motionless in the blood soaked grass. He laid his head on her chest and listened for her heart. It was still beating. She was still breathing. She was alive!

He picked her up and began to run. He ran to the car, lay her carefully in the back seat, and drove like a maniac the fifteen miles to the new county hospital. He almost ran over an elderly couple in the parking lot. He pulled up to the emergency entrance and was yelling and screaming for help. Hospital employees, dressed in white, came out and took Maureen from his arms. They put her on a stretcher and rushed her away. He called after them through his tears and madness. "Save her, please."

He ran to the nurse's station. He was still yelling that he needed the sheriff when a nurse and a county officer came to calm him. He told them the story. He was crying and screaming. They thought he was mad... He was.

They dispatched more county officers to the hospital. One recognized him.

"Mr. Adams, it's me, Casey Miller. Do you remember? We used to live next door to you?"

Lloyd nodded his head. He tried to calm down.

"Mr. Adams, tell me what happened. We want to help, but right now we don't understand."

Lloyd told them where the Johnsons lived. He told them what he saw. He also told them what had been going on. It was then that Ellen arrived. A nurse had contacted her and she called Mama to come and get her immediately. The scene was spinning out of control and Lloyd was at the center, shocked and frantic. She saw her husband sitting there on the little sofa with a deputy. She went to him. He saw her walking toward him. She stretched out her arms and he sank into them, sobbing. She felt herself stiffen. She prepared herself. Maureen must be dead.

She did not utter a single word. She turned her thoughts toward the only one that could help her at the moment, and she spoke from her heart. "I know You can do anything. Anything." She closed her eyes and prayed, while she held her husband. "Please make this go away. Whatever it is, I know You can change it." She did not even know exactly what was going on, but she did know that the Creator could do anything. She begged the Creator to step in and fix it all before she had to live through the nightmare. "You can do anything," she whispered. Lloyd pulled away.

"Where's Maureen?" Ellen asked him.

"They took her. I don't know if she's all right or not."

Ellen collected herself and walked to the nurse's station. She calmly inquired about her daughter. One of the nurses told her that her daughter was still alive and that the doctor would be out shortly to talk to the both of them. One thing at a time, she told herself. Maureen was alive, now to find out what had happened.

She joined her husband on the couch just as the deputy was telling him that they would be leaving to investigate. "Ruth Johnson and the two girls may still be alive," Lloyd told the officers. "I did not find them." Ellen listened. Someone must be dead, she thought. The county officers left them, after calling for still more officers.

Lloyd began to tell Ellen all that had happened since he left her at the house. She was calm and cool, on the outside. But inside, her quiet strength was quickly leaving her. The only evidence was her tears. They ran down her face, soaking the matching blue handbag that lay on her lap. It was truly a sight to see, for Ellen never cried.

The doctor interrupted them. He told them that Maureen was barely alive. He asked what had happened to her. Lloyd told him that they did not know right now. The doctor was worried that she may not wake up. "She may not survive," he said. "We'll know more in a couple of hours." They wanted to see her. The doctor conceded. He did not want to deny them the opportunity to be with her, since it was a possibility that she might not make it.

Ellen took a deep breath when she saw her daughter. Her white nightgown lay in a heap on the floor, blood soaked. It had been cut off of her by the nurses. She was in a hospital gown.

"Oh, Lloyd..." It was all that Ellen had the strength to say.

Lloyd looked at his daughter lying there. Ellen saw his face change. He told her he would be back. He told her to stay with

Maureen. She did not try to stop him. She just sat there holding Maureen's hand as Lloyd left the room.

Lloyd Adams left with purpose. He got in Ellen's car and headed back to the Johnson's place. Ruth, Pauline, and Cora Bell were still missing. He knew his daughter might not survive, but there was nothing he could do about that right now. So he left. All he could see were images of Joe hanging there in the barn, husband, father, friend. Maureen's fate would be the same whether he sat in that hospital or not. So Lloyd chose to go back to the place that he never wanted to see again, for he himself was a husband, father, and friend. His friend's wife and two daughters were still missing. They could be dead, or even still in danger. He had to find them.

As he approached the house, he saw the cars. There were about seven or eight of them, all county cars. He approached the house and an officer told him that he would have to leave. "This property's a crime scene, sir," he said.

"What about the woman and the two girls?" Lloyd asked. "Have they been found?"

The officer started to answer, but then they heard another officer yelling, "Over here! There's someone here!"

Lloyd and the officer that he had been speaking with took off. The officer was so consumed with what was going on, he did not even notice Lloyd following him. They ran to the storm cellar. It seemed to Lloyd like the officers were trying to convince someone to come out. He walked closer.

"Ma'am, we need you to come out. There's been some trouble here and we need to talk to you."

Lloyd heard no reply. The officer kept coaxing, but to no avail. Lloyd walked over to the cellar. He could see Ruth and the girls sitting there at the bottom. He walked right past the officer and took three steps down into the cellar. He saw Ruth's face. She was terrified.

He went to her and held out his hand. She took it. He led her out of the cellar, with the girls right behind her.

They climbed out into the sun. Ruth was blinded after being in the cellar for so long. She held on to Lloyd's hand. She wanted to stop time. She knew. When Joe didn't come for her, she knew.

They went into the house and sat down at the kitchen table, while an officer explained what was going on. He told Ruth that her son and her husband had been killed. Lloyd would not leave her side. He sat there with her at the kitchen table. She never let go of his hand. Pauline and Cora Bell were sitting on the front porch. They had no idea. Lloyd told her all that he knew. The county officers told her all that they knew. She was dead inside. There was nothing left. She looked at Lloyd. He could barely hear her.

"And where is Harold Smith, and his son?" she wanted to know.

The officer explained that they had already sent someone to the Smith's place, based on all that Lloyd had told them. Ruth nodded. It didn't even matter. Her heart was gone. The moment that she understood Jeremiah was gone, nothing mattered to her. Hope was dead. She wanted to leave this world. She didn't want to stay another minute. And Joe, he had always protected them. He gave his life trying to keep them safe. And for what? So that she could be left here with the very ones that had robbed her of the thing that mattered most in the world to her, the only one that gave her hope, her precious son.

She spoke only to Lloyd. "I want to see them."

Lloyd looked at the officer. The officer addressed her. "Mrs. Johnson, if you want to see them I won't stop you. But I wish that you wouldn't."

"Please take me to them, Lloyd."

He took her by the arm and led her to the barn. It was unreal. He felt as if he were in a nightmare. He walked with her into the barn. Jeremiah and Joe lay on the hay covered floor. They had been taken down from the rafters and covered with some dark colored blankets. Lloyd pulled the blankets back for Ruth. She seemed to be unaffected. She bent down over her son and spoke to him as if he were still living. "Did they come for you? I would have stopped them. I would have killed them." She kissed his cheek and whispered softly, "You're my heart, son. You are my heart. I'll see you again someday."

Lloyd Adams almost sobbed out loud, so powerful was the scene that he watched. Ruth faced it all, as if it was expected. He considered her. She had expected this. That's why she was not shocked. Lloyd considered what that meant. The strong, beautiful, smart woman that loved her family beyond measure had lived her life expecting this. There was so much that he took for granted. Every day, he walked out his door and never once questioned the safety of his family. The Johnsons were no different than own his family, and yet they had been hunted. Their family had been destroyed. And it was not about the color of their skin. It wasn't about that at all, never had been. It was something much deeper than that. And for the first time, he recognized what he was dealing with, what he had been dealing with all along. It went back to man's desire to rule, to be God.

The Johnsons had been hunted because Jeremiah dared to live, because he would not be ruled. Lloyd was shaken to his core. He broke. Right there in the barn, the strong woman that had just lost her husband and her son held him in her arms and comforted him. For now, she had put it aside. She would come back to it when she was stronger.

Lloyd finally pulled himself together. He was embarrassed. He was ashamed that he was so weak. This was her own family, and yet she was so strong. He stepped back so that she could do what she needed to do. She came around to where her husband lay and whispered in his ear. Lloyd couldn't control it. His tears began to fall again. "Rest, darling. Rest now," she said. She kissed Joe on the forehead and walked out of the barn, back into the light of day. Lloyd followed her.

She did not slow down or wait. She walked quickly back to the house. She sat in the front porch swing with Pauline and Cora Bell and told them that Jeremiah and Daddy had gone. She never shed a tear. She couldn't. She was dead.

Lloyd insisted that she and the girls go to his house until they knew what to do. Ruth said she would get some things together and be there shortly. He told her he would not leave her until she was safely in his home. She packed some things for herself and the girls, and followed him in the old Dodge pickup. He took them in, showed them the house, and told Ruth to make herself at home. He gave her a loaded shotgun, then left her and went back to the hospital.

Ruth sat down at the table in the sunny yellow kitchen. She fought back the anger that was rising up in her. She had too much to think about right now. She had to get in touch with family, she had to decide what to do, and she had to find out who killed her husband and her son, even though she was sure she already knew. She was glad that she was alone with her girls. There was a lot to think about.

She thought back to the days after her father's death. She remembered what her mother had said, when people asked how she was getting through such a difficult time. Her mother had said that she could feel her husband giving her strength. Ruth laughed out loud. It was a dark laugh, for she felt no such thing. They were gone, gone from this world. Her strength would have to come from somewhere else, because she knew it would not come from them.

Lloyd returned to the hospital to find Maureen still unconscious. Ellen had thrown herself into caring for her daughter. Ellen did not talk. She was quiet. He knew she was praying. She was in a constant state of prayer.

Days turned into weeks. Maureen finally came home, but still she did not speak. Harold and Junior Smith were found dead in their beds. Kilroy said that the Smiths must have thought Maureen would eventually talk, and as soon as she was able to speak the truth would be discovered. Everyone thought that the Smiths had taken their own lives, everyone except one particular deputy that happened to hate colored folks even worse than he hated the Smiths. He didn't think those two would take their own lives. He didn't believe it for a second. He had a feeling.

He questioned Lloyd, late one night over a bottle of whiskey. Then, the dangerous accusation came, "I think it's that nigger bitch." Lloyd had to fight back the urge to come out of his seat and kill him with his bare hands. He fought to control himself. As much as he hated it, this man was the law, and Ruth's fate was in his hands. There was no hesitation. Lloyd knew what he had to do. With all the self control he could muster, he leaned in and asked him a single question. "What would you do if your daughter was knocked in the head and left for dead?"

The deputy had cocked one eyebrow, then slapped him on the back. "Case closed," he roared with laughter.

Lloyd suspected all along that it had been Ruth, but Ellen was the only living soul besides Ruth that knew for sure. Ellen had not been able to sleep since Joe and Jeremiah were murdered. She couldn't rest as long as she knew that the Smiths were still out there. It was the middle of the night, and she had gone to kitchen for a drink of water. She saw Ruth sitting there at the table, shaking all over. Ellen noticed that she was fully dressed and had black smudges on her face. She asked her what was wrong. Ruth looked up at her with empty eyes. She seemed to be out of her head.

"He'll never touch anything of mine again."

"Shhhh... You'll wake everyone. I know. I understand. Now keep quiet and go on to bed." Ruth nodded her head, and walked down the hall to the room that she had been sleeping in.

The next morning, bright and early, the deputy came knocking on the door to notify the Adams household that the Smiths were dead. He told them that he had gone out to see why they hadn't shown up for more questioning. That's when he found them. Both Harold and Junior were dead. It appeared that they had killed themselves, although he couldn't be certain.

Ruth was shocked. "The boy, the boy is dead?" she kept asking. Ellen absorbed it all. Lloyd thanked him for coming to tell them. Ruth did not understand. She did not harm the boy. She knew that he wasn't a threat. He was a coward, and with Harold dead, he would simply fade away. She would never know exactly what happened to him. Perhaps he realized the depth of what he had perpetrated. In any case, she was relieved. She could go now. She could leave Kilroy and never look back. She would take the girls to Houston and start over with her family's help.

She wasted no time. It was over. Jeremiah and Joe had been buried in the colored cemetery, and she didn't have to be afraid of the Smiths anymore. There were others, of course, but it seemed that they had disappeared back into the woodwork that they had come out of. Over the next few weeks, Lloyd and Ellen helped Ruth pack and put the farm up for sale. Lloyd would look after it until it sold, and then he would forward the funds to her. He gave her a sizeable loan to get on her feet.

The day she left was gut wrenching. Maureen watched silently as Ruth secured the rope that held everything together in back of the old pickup. She was dressed in a simple black dress and black heels, with her hair in a knot. She was striking, and strong. She was determined. She may be dead inside, but she would find her way. She just kept right on going. She had sent the girls ahead on the train, in case there was any trouble. They had already arrived. They were safe in Houston with her family.

Ellen could not take her eyes off of Ruth. They had all come out onto the porch to say goodbye. Maureen stood there, still not speaking, watching the events. Annalyn waved goodbye. Lloyd was quiet as he watched her go. Ellen heard the crunch of the wheels turning on the gravel and something inside her gave way.

She began to run. The truck began to move a little faster as it pulled out of the driveway and onto the street. Ellen ran faster. Everyone in town stopped to watch. Graceful, dignified Ellen Adams ran after the old pickup truck with the colored woman driving it. She chased it into the street. She ran as if her life depended on it. They thought she'd surely gone crazy. But not Lloyd, he watched as she ran after the truck. She was yelling, arms flailing, "Wait! Wait!"

Finally the truck came to a screeching halt. Ruth jumped out and Ellen ran to her, breathless. She stopped right in front of her. They stood so close that Ruth could feel Ellen's breath on her face. Before Ruth could ask what was the matter, Ellen spoke, winded from chasing her.

"I want..." She had to stop to catch her breath. "I want to go."

"What?" Ruth asked in disbelief. She didn't understand.

Ellen said it again. "I want to go with you."

Ruth was confused. "Why?" she asked, as she searched Ellen's face trying to understand.

"I just can't stay here and do nothing."

"Ellen, you've done so much..." Ruth's voice trailed off. She turned away. She couldn't look at her friend. She didn't want Ellen to see the fear and uncertainty that she held inside

"Ruth, please, I have to go with you. Please, for me."

Ruth did not know what to say. "But the girls, who will look after them?"

"Lloyd. And Mama can stay at the house to help him."

Ruth looked as if she might be considering it. Ellen begged.

"No. I can never repay what you have already given. I will accept no more from you." Her eyes spoke truths that existed between the two of them, truths that no other living soul would ever know. "You can't go. Maureen needs you. Ellen, she's mute."

Ellen looked back at Maureen standing on the porch. No doubt she would bear scars, but she had seen her daughter's eyes. They were still alive. She knew that Maureen would be fine.

"Before all this happened, Maureen tried to tell me something..." Ellen paused. She could barely speak for choking on her tears so.

"...something that I had forgotten."

Ellen closed her eyes. She saw hobos and train tracks and the woman that she used to be, the one she wanted to be again. She pulled herself together. "I'm going." She was defiant. "I'll take the train back after you're all settled with the girls. Maureen will understand."

She left Ruth standing in the street. She walked to the passenger side of the old Dodge pickup, opened the rusty door, and got in. Ruth hesitated, not sure what she should do next.

"Well, get in," Ellen said. "Let's go tell Lloyd."

Ruth got in, turned the truck around, and drove back to the house.

Ellen got out and slammed the door. He knew before she uttered a sound. He knew what she would say.

"Darling, I have to go. I can't ..."

He finished her sentence, "... just do nothing."

She smiled at him. "I'll be back in a few days after she's settled safely with the girls."

He nodded. "Do you have plenty of money?"

She turned to her youngest daughter. "Annalyn, go and get my handbag from the kitchen table."

"Yes ma'am." Annalyn ran off to retrieve it.

"Don't you need to pack your overnight case?" Lloyd was surprised. She never traveled without it.

She smiled up at him. "I don't want to take the time to pack anything." She reached up to hug him, then kissed his ear. She whispered so that only he could hear her, "I'm afraid if I walk into the house I'll lose my nerve."

He smiled. Lloyd was worried, but he knew he could not change her mind. Of course, if he said no, absolutely not, she would never cross him. But he would never do that to her.

Ellen took Maureen by the shoulders. Maureen looked into her mother's face. "Darling, I'm going with Ruth to help her get settled. I'll be back in a few days on the train. You'll be fine with Daddy. Do you understand?"

Maureen nodded. She understood. She understood very well indeed. Her mother hugged her tight, then waved goodbye with only her little handbag. Maureen watched her go. And for the first time since that horrible night, she felt something that she thought she would never feel again. The corners of her mouth turned up slightly into the remnant of a smile, but still she would not speak. And as she watched her mother disappear out of town in that old Dodge pickup that she had watched for so long, her heart screamed. It cried out with all the strength that was left in it, beating fast and furiously. "Go, Mother! Go!"

# Ruth

APRIL 1956...

There are moments when there are souls so attracted to one another that everything seems to stop while that attraction is realized. Once they find each other, nothing matters. It is as if there is no space, no time, nor anything existing outside of the pair. It is as if they have spent their entire lives looking for each other, without realizing it, living for the moment when they would come together. Somehow they recognize each other, the attraction so tangible, feeling as if they had been torn apart. The world keeps turning, but for them time stands still. It seems to stop while they discover each other, while they learn whatever it is that they have to learn from one another. It was so with Maureen and Jeremiah. And so it was with Ruth and Ellen.

They rode out of town in silence, afraid to speak. It went on for hours. Passing through tiny towns, getting further and further from Kilroy, neither uttered a sound as they headed for Houston.

Finally, Ruth spoke. It took Ellen a while to respond. She was unsure if that was really Ruth's voice that she had heard, since she never took her eyes from the road. Then she heard it again.

"Why'd you come?" Ruth asked her.

"Because I wanted to."

Ruth looked at her friend for a brief moment then returned her gaze to the road that stretched out ahead of them. Ellen pushed her hair out of her face. The wind from the open windows caused it to fall down in her eyes, but she did not care. The breeze felt so good.

"I could sit here and tell you I wanted to make sure your girls were okay and to see you safely to Houston. I could say it's because I'm worried about you and didn't want you to drive alone. But the truth is, I wanted to come, Ruth. I just wanted to come."

Ruth nodded. "You hungry?" she asked.

"Starving." Ellen wished she'd thought to grab some food.

"I was planning on stoppin' just outside of Corsicana to get something to eat. Joe's cousin has a little cook shack there. Just a little shack where colored folks can find a bite to eat. Plays music too. You'll be all right with that?"

"Of course."

"Won't be whites there."

"I understand."

They drove on in silence until Ruth spoke again. "He lives just a couple miles out of town. Elizabeth, his wife, cooks. Good home cookin'."

Ellen nodded.

"Even better than yours." Ruth was not able to resist teasing her. Cooking was serious business to Ellen. She had been cooking since she was a child. She was the best cook that she knew and she didn't mind letting everyone know that she thought so. She wasn't conceited. It was just a fact. Ruth thought she wasn't listening. Then she heard her.

"I doubt it." Ellen wrinkled her nose while Ruth giggled.

They drove through Corsicana and turned off on a dirt road. They were heading to the tiny little town of Raymond.

At last, there it was. Ruth pulled the truck into the grass and they got out. Cook shack is right, thought Ellen. It was definitely a shack. The roof was in desperate need of repair. It was just a little old clapboard building with two tables outside and a few tables inside. There appeared to be a small makeshift stage at the back of the little shack. There was no kitchen, but every table was filled.

People were eating and talking. Some had stopped to stare at them. Ellen tried to pay no attention, but it wasn't easy. The folks there were trying to figure the two women out. Both were well dressed, both attractive, one black, one white. Or was she? They couldn't tell. Maybe mulatto? Probably Indian, they decided. Ellen heard Ruth ask an old man, "Where's Rascal?" Ellen guessed that Rascal was Joe's cousin.

The man pointed to the back of the shack. Ellen followed Ruth inside. It took a moment for their eyes to adjust from being outside in the sunshine. Ruth scanned the room looking for Rascal or some other familiar face. Finally, she saw Ruben. Ruben was Rascal and Elizabeth's oldest son. He looked so much like Jeremiah that Ruth's heart leapt, then was dead again. Ellen noticed the resemblance at once.

"Cousin Ruth!" he called out as soon as he saw her. "What you doin' here?" He hugged her.

"I stopped off to fill my stomach with your mama's cookin' on my way to Houston. Where's your Mama and Daddy?"

"Daddy walked up to the house to bring some more food down. We're real busy tonight. Ya'll go on up to the house. Mama will want ya'll to go to the house." He stared at Ellen from the top of her dark hair to the bottom of her stylish shoes. She didn't look like anybody he had ever seen before.

"Ruben, this is my friend Ellen."

Ellen held out her hand. He took it shyly. "Nice to meet you, Ruben."

"Nice to meet you too, ma'am."

He was shocked. They all knew what had happened to Joe and Jeremiah. He could not imagine Ruth being with a white anybody after that. There must be something to it.

They turned to leave the little shack and heard Ruben call out. "Cousin Ruth, we're gonna' have music tonight. Ya'll make sure and come have a listen after you eat."

"Maybe we will, Ruben."

The two women walked through the tall spring grass to the house. Ellen thought it was a cute little house. It looked a lot like Ruth's house had, only it was painted white. It had honeysuckle clinging to the picket fence around it. Ruth and Ellen walked up the steps and rapped on the door. They could hear a lot of commotion coming from the kitchen.

"Rascal! Elizabeth!" Ruth called them.

They saw what appeared to be a man coming down the little hallway toward the screen door, where they waited. And then the tall dark man dressed in overalls answered the door. He was ready to send them on their way. It was getting to be more often that white folks would show up inquiring about their little business. Some of them were looking for cooks. Some of them were looking for trouble. He wanted no part of either.

He took one look at the darker woman and grabbed her so tight that her feet left the ground. "Ruth!" he shouted.

It felt so good to Ruth, strong arms, family. "I'm on my way to Houston. The girls are already there. Thought I'd stop here for a bite to eat and have a quick visit on my way. Don't know when I'll make it back this way again."

Ellen had been completely forgotten, until Elizabeth's voice came booming down the hallway. She was a big woman, with her hair wrapped in a yellow turban. She wore a matching yellow apron over her dress. She was approaching the woman in the doorway.

"I ain't gonna' be no cook."

Ellen was speechless. The woman was talking to her! Ruth was at her side, at once. "Lizbeth, it's me, Ruth. This is my friend, Ellen."

Elizabeth was immediately embarrassed. She wiped her hands on her apron and shook Ellen's hand. "I 'pologize. It's just that white folks come out from town to try to hire me." She was visibly very embarrassed.

"It's all right. I understand. You must be a very good cook." Ellen responded graciously.

Elizabeth smiled at her. "I reckon I am," she said.

After Ruth and Ellen helped Rascal and Elizabeth deliver the rest of the food down to the cook shack and collect everyone's money, they all sat down at a table and ate together. Ellen found it very interesting. They cooked the food at home, carried it down to their "cook shack," and served their paying guests there. No sooner had one table full of people finished, than another group was waiting to take their place. They had a good little business. Ellen imagined what they could do if they had a bigger place. The possibilities were endless.

She considered them. It did not matter to her what color they were, but it did to a lot of people. She imagined how their business could grow with a little startup money. She also imagined the trouble that could grow right along with it out there. As long as they stayed small, they were safe. But if they took off, there could be trouble. Ellen was noticing a pattern. A few months ago she realized none of this, but she was learning quickly. She had never realized the extent of the oppression. She had never realized that they lived in two different worlds. She was still trying to figure out what to do about it. She had already seen, in the worst way imaginable, that the line between helping and hurting beyond repair was sometimes one and the same.

Rascal and Elizabeth had questions. They had been unable to believe the news about Joe and Jeremiah. That was precisely why Ruben did not attend school at all. While he was receiving absolutely no education, at least he was safe. He was alive. Sometimes, that was the most they had to offer him. Ruth could not discuss it. She endured and answered some of their questions for a time, but then no more.

"Please, no more about this." Her voice was quiet. "Some days I don't know how I'm still breathin'. If it weren't for the girls... I'm just not strong enough to talk about it right now. Someday, but not now."

"Ruthie, we're sorry. We just can't believe it. That's all." Elizabeth apologized.

Ellen considered Ruth, what she had been through. Her husband and her son were gone. They had been murdered, and she had no time to grieve. It was a luxury not permitted for a colored woman. She had to pick herself up, dust herself off, and take care of what was left of her family. Ellen respected her more than she had ever respected any living soul in all her life, for Ruth was strength. Ruth was beauty.

She was survival, right there in the flesh. She had looked evil in the eye. Harold Smith would not have stopped until they were all dead, and Ruth Johnson knew that. He would have killed them all. But Ruth would not allow it. She knew full well that justice would never come her way. No one would protect them from the monster. Not in Kilroy, Texas. Not in 1956. So she looked that evil straight in the eye, and then she blew it away.

Ellen watched her. Her delicate hand guided her fork from her plate to her mouth and back again. She saw the graceful tilt of her head, the strong resolve of her posture, and she was moved beyond words to even be in her presence.

And so they ate the delicious meal that Elizabeth had prepared. It was smothered steak in cream gravy, turnip greens, corn on the cob, and fried potatoes. Conversation was light, about weather, crops, that sort of thing. Ruth was right. Elizabeth was an excellent cook, Ellen thought. She could see how the white folks in town would want to hire her to cook their meals. The food was delicious.

They were finishing up their meal when the music started. It was a little band made up of local men. Ellen recognized Ruben on the piano. The little place began to really come alive. The shack swelled with still more people. Ellen and Ruth sat with Rascal and Elizabeth at the table right in front of the stage. Ellen was really enjoying the music. She had never heard live music like it before. She was fascinated with the whine of the saxophone.

Then a woman hopped up on the stage and started to sing. Ellen continued to be fascinated. She had never seen or heard anything like it. It was so much fun. It was soon standing room only in the little cook shack. The band started an upbeat jazzy number with Ruben banging out the melody on the little piano. Elizabeth grabbed Ruth's hand, and then Ellen's. She pulled them out of their chairs and to the front of the stage. Ellen protested at first, but it was no use. No one could hear her. So they danced, she and Ruth. They danced for hours. They laughed until their faces hurt. They knew everyone in the whole place before they left. They hated for it all to end, but they still had a long way to go.

They said their goodbyes to Rascal and Elizabeth. Ellen told Elizabeth if they were ever around Kilroy to please stop by. She told her where they lived and where the store was. She told her they were welcome in her home anytime. She thanked them for the wonderful meal and the hospitality. "Not to mention the dancing." She grinned.

Ruth hugged them all goodbye. "Ruben, if you have any trouble, you come to me. You hear? I'm gettin' out of all this. I'm stayin' in the city. You understand me?"

"Yes, ma'am," he told her.

They climbed up into the battered old Dodge pickup and headed back to the main road. It would be late into the night when they reached Houston. Ruth wondered if they should have stayed the night back there, but it was too late now. Ellen rode quietly, thinking about their evening. It had been unexpected. For a brief moment, all the evil that they had endured seemed far, far away.

For Ruth, it felt strange to have enjoyed herself. Her beloved husband and her precious child had been brutally murdered, with absolutely no regard for their lives. They were gone from her. She had put the pain away, found a place for it. She had to. It was the only way she could get up in the morning. It was the only way she could put one foot in front of the other. She still had to make a life for her girls.

She had told Joe so many times that she wanted to leave. Why didn't he listen sooner? For so long, she wanted to go back to Houston where she had grown up, where she felt safe. He would not go. He loved his little farm, and he owned it, free and clear. He knew he could always feed his family there. It was all he had ever known, and he was afraid to leave. His own people were there. But Ruth had always known they weren't safe. Somehow, she had always known what was coming. She wished she had taken her son and fled. The agony, the feeling of her heart being ripped from her chest, the wild rage just under the surface threatened to take over again. What she loved most in the world had been taken from her in the most horrifying way imaginable. She cleared her head. She put it away yet again, knowing that she would not be able to do that forever. She drove on.

Ruth Johnson was a beautiful woman by any standards. She had dark hair that was curly and thick. She wore it knotted at the back of her head most of the time, in an effort to draw no attention to herself. She could not hide her eyes, however. They were haunting, hazel, the contrast of her brown skin making them even more noticeable. She had been her father's darling little girl, his only little girl.

She had left Houston when she was very young, newly married to Joe, with her whole life ahead of her. She was about to return older, a widow, tormented by all that she had endured. She wondered what life had in store for her now. She had plans. She would open her own little store. She would build a little business for herself right there in her old neighborhood, where her girls would be safe. In the crowded, all-black area of Houston, they would be safe. They would grow up among colored folks that were educating themselves, people that were making changes. She had plenty of money to get started. When the farm sold, she would repay Lloyd and Ellen.

Lloyd and Ellen... Maureen... Sometimes she did not know how to feel about them. She was caught somewhere between the intensity of her rage and her love for them. Would her precious family still be here if it weren't for Maureen? She wondered. She teetered on the brink of rage, and even violence, thinking of that girl. But when she was around her, when she watched her, she felt nothing but love for her.

Maureen and Miah, for reasons still unclear to Ruth, had loved each other. For that brief beautiful moment in time there had been light. Just watching them together had been beautiful and bright. Just seeing her son live and love had been a gift. Recognizing it, does not mean she understood it. She did not understand at all. They had not known each other for very long. They were not courting each other. It was nothing like that. That was impossible. That did not happen. It couldn't happen. Even so, they were drawn together. All regard for danger had been cast aside.

Ruth thought about Jeremiah, how he had lived. She thought about his smile, his ways, his laughter, his hope. She thought about how most people lived. She could not help but cry, flooded with thankfulness that she had been the privileged one to bring him into the world, to know him, to love him, and to be loved by him. She would carry it with her to her grave. He would be just beyond consciousness, every second, every day of her life.

She thought about the way things were going. It seemed that for every step her people fought to take, they were pushed back ten. There had been such a small window of opportunity for Jeremiah to attend that school, for now it was segregated again. And because he was not content to live in the shadows, her son had been killed. Then there was Maureen, damaged by all that she had lived through. She did not even speak anymore.

Ruth was sure she was in there. She had gone somewhere inside herself to survive. Perhaps that is what softened her toward the young girl. The pain, the fear. They would put it away for now, both of them. But not forever. They would have to face it someday. And whether they liked it or not, Ruth and Maureen would forever be joined. For one had spent the first few beautiful moments of life with Jeremiah's special soul, had been there when he took his first breath, had looked him in the eye the moment he was born. The other had been with him at the end, the last few moments before he left, and only she knew what had happened. Maureen remained unable, or was it unwilling, to speak. Ruth couldn't be sure yet. But one thing was certain, there would be much that passed between them over the years, much indeed.

Ellen slept, while Ruth drove on. They finally entered Houston around two thirty in the morning. The old Dodge pickup had delivered them safely. Ellen woke, as they pulled up in front of a little brick house in a crowded neighborhood. She and Ruth went to the door and knocked. Ruth's mother answered the door. She was a darker version of her own Mama, Ellen thought.

"What took you so long? I'm panickin'. Panickin', I tell you." She saw a woman standing there, just behind her daughter. She looked at Ruth questioningly.

"Oh, Mama, I'm so glad to see you." Ruth hugged the aged woman in the doorway. "This is Ellen Adams. You know, I told you about her." Ruth's mother nodded her head and held the door open as they entered the house. "She didn't want me to come alone. She's taking the train home, day after tomorrow."

"I see. Thank you for coming with her, Mrs. Adams."

"I wanted to," Ellen said.

Ruth explained to her mother how they stopped off just outside of Raymond and ate supper with Joe's kinfolks. Etta Brown studied her daughter's face at the mention of Joe's name. She saw nothing. Ruth gave nothing away.

More than anything, Ruth wanted to see her girls. She went into the spare bedroom and saw her precious girls sleeping peacefully in the cozy double bed. She got into the bed with them. She had survived the business of death. She had gotten her girls, and now herself, out of that town and safely to Houston. Still in her clothes, Ruth collapsed in the bed with her daughters, all she had left. They were her everything and she would spend the rest of her life loving them, protecting them. She would not take a single day for granted. She kissed little Cora Bell's warm forehead, stroked her little braids. She snuggled up against Pauline's back, and felt her warmth. She dozed. In spite of all she had lost, in that instant she felt victorious. She had survived. They had survived. Of course, there would be days when her pain was so great that she wasn't sure why she wanted to. But not tonight. Tonight, she tasted victory. She felt her spirit stir, then she was gone. Ruth Johnson was fast asleep, safe, broken, and victorious.

Ellen helped Etta make up a rickety cot at the foot of the double bed where Ruth slept with her girls. She reminded Ellen so much of her own mother, the way she moved, the care she took with the business of putting the clean bedding on the cot for her unexpected houseguest. Ruth's mother was so very much like her own.

Ellen thought about her own family. They were all fast asleep by now; she was sure. What about Maureen? Was she dreaming? Were they sweet dreams, or were they terrible? She missed them. She was rarely away from them. But it was Maureen that she missed most of all. Her feelings were so strong for her oldest daughter right now. What was going on inside of her? Ellen loved her so much.

She lay on the little cot, cozy and comfortable but unable to sleep. She started to pray, but her mind began to wander. She just let it wander, mumbling to her maker, seeking guidance, protection, and direction. It was 1956. Innocence was gone, shattered by all that life had brought. Why? She wondered. There was a time when life had been easy. Life had been simple. Not anymore. Ellen was aware now, aware of what was going on around her, what was going on in the world. She had been oblivious. Oh, sure, she had known how colored folks were treated. They all knew. But it didn't affect them. They had never actually seen it until now.

And what had Maureen done? Had she cost the child his life? Why Lord? What do we do next? "I feel so much for Ruth," she prayed, "and for Pauline and Cora Bell. They have lost so much. What next? For them? For all of us...?" Finally sleep found her, deep and dark, as she lay there wondering. She dreamed of Lloyd, his love so real and so strong she could almost touch it.

Ruth had no dreams that night, or if she did, she slept too sound to remember them. Pauline and Cora Bell woke her with hugs and kisses, laughter, and even a few tears. They were so glad to see her. She looked at her oldest daughter. Pauline looked older to Ruth, as she sat there in the bed, dressed in her violet night gown with a silk scarf around her head to protect her big city hairstyle. She had only been in Houston for a couple of weeks, but already she had gone from a country girl to a city girl. Her grandmother had taken her to a beauty shop. She had her hair cut and styled the way "everyone is wearing it" in the city. Ruth decided she did not like it. She wasn't used to it. But if it pleased Pauline, she would take her to get her hair done as often as she could afford it. It warmed her heart to see her daughter pleased about anything. After all that they had endured, finding a little pleasure was no simple task.

Pauline talked about being enrolled in school. She loved her school. Ruth couldn't help but smile. Cora Bell climbed into her mother's lap. Their talking woke Ellen. She went to the bed and got in it with them. There they sat: Pauline in her nightgown with her scarf on her head, Cora Bell with her cute little braids, in her mother's lap, Ruth still in her clothes from the day before, and Ellen in a borrowed pair of Etta's pajamas. The girls had questions. Ruth told them she would answer them later. For now, she wanted to show Ellen the city of Houston. "She's leaving tomorrow. I'm gonna' show her the big city today." The girls giggled. They were going to a party in the neighborhood with their grandmother.

Ruth helped her mother get the girls ready for the party. They would eat lunch there. Everyone had slept through breakfast, so exhausted from the night before. Etta had waited up entirely too late for Ruth to arrive, and the girls had stayed up way past their bedtime as well, in anticipation of their mother's arrival.

After the girls left with their grandmother to attend someone's fiftieth wedding anniversary party, Ruth and Ellen were alone in the little house together. Ellen made her travel arrangements first. She then phoned Lloyd to tell him when she would be arriving.

"Adams Residence," he answered.

"Lloyd, hello." She was so glad to hear his voice.

"I've been worried. I thought you would call last night. I was just deciding whether I should come looking for you."

"Darling, I'm sorry. We didn't get in until real late. I should have called."

"Yes, you should have." Ellen could tell he was annoyed. He must have been really worried.

"I'll be returning on the first train tomorrow. I should be arriving at around two o'clock."

"I'll be there," he told her. He was about to hang up when he heard her speak.

"Lloyd... Lloyd, are you there?"

"I'm here."

"Please, don't waste any time being angry with me for not calling sooner. I'm safe, and I'm sorry for not calling last night. We've seen so much lately. Let's don't waste any time being angry with each other."

There was a pause on the other end. "You're right, as usual. I'll see you tomorrow. I love you."

"I love you too." They rang off.

Ruth drank her coffee with Ellen, in her mother's kitchen. They sat comfortably at the little oak table with the light green and yellow plaid seat cushions. It is a pleasant little kitchen, Ellen thought. They talked about the first steps Ruth would take to open her store.

"You know Lloyd and I will help you in whatever way we possibly can."

Ruth studied Ellen's face. She recognized what she saw there, grief, guilt. She took a moment to gather her thoughts. What she had to say was important.

"Ellen, you are not responsible for what happened to my husband, or my son." She said the words and looked her friend square in the eye. Ellen could not meet her gaze. She had to turn away.

"How can you be so sure? We still don't even know what happened. The only person that does is Maureen. We may never know. If she hadn't been there..." her voice trailed off.

"If she hadn't been there, we may have all been killed. The Smiths went to my house for a reason that night. They never expected to find Maureen there. Hell, none of us did. I want to blame Maureen, but I can't. Besides all that, you're right. We may never know what happened that night. But I know what didn't. I know what you're wonderin' about, and I know my son. I know that nothing dishonorable happened."

Ellen looked back at her friend. She was right. Ellen kept replaying the whole nightmare in her head ever since it had occurred. It always ended the same way, with her asking the same question. What happened to them? She felt guilty that Ruth had lost almost everything, while she had lost nothing. She felt guilty that Ruth and all that was hers had been so despised and so hunted, while she and all that was hers had been spared.

"Ruth, you're right. I know Maureen. She just wanted to say goodbye. I'm sure of it. She had no idea the danger..." Ellen turned away.

Ruth nodded. They sat there for awhile, each woman lost in her own thoughts. Finally, they got dressed. Ruth wanted to show Ellen her hometown. They set out walking. Ruth was dressed in another simple black dress, black shoes, and carrying her matching black handbag. Her hair was neatly coiled in its trademark knot. Ellen was dressed in the same blue dress. She had ironed it and put it back on. Back on went her stockings and blue pumps. She carried her blue handbag. They sat out at midday, walking through the streets of Ruth's old Houston neighborhood, just glad to be together. They could have been sisters spending the day together, their relationship so close, so precious, and so bright. They had been brought together by the love their children had for one another, bound by all that had become of it.

The first stop was lunch. Their growling stomachs led them to a little café called "Charlie's." Charlie turned out to be a ninety year old woman with a mean pot roast. After they filled their stomachs, they walked around the neighborhood. They happened upon a little junk dealer and began to explore what he was selling. Ellen found a cute little doll. She would take it home to Annalyn. She found a pretty pin for Maureen. It was a flower. She thought it might make her smile. But it was the conversation with the old man that sold it to her that was the greatest prize of all.

He asked her where she was from. She told him. He asked her how she made her living there. She told him that she and her husband were in the grocery business. "Just like me," he said with pride. "Eat or starve, I'm responsible for my own affairs. Don't work for nobody. Nobody. Answer to myself," he had said, patting his own chest. She shook his hand and told him goodbye.

She and Ruth headed back to the house. Ellen was quiet as she walked with Ruth. She could see why Ruth loved it here. The people were just living, loving life. And "eat or starve," as the old man had put it, the fact of the matter was, they were not afraid. They were going to college, running for public office. They were teaching school, and opening businesses. Ruth was right to come here. She will do well here, Ellen thought, but most importantly she would not be afraid.

The evening was spent with Ruth, Etta, and the girls. They had nice conversation about the neighborhood and its goings on. It was soon time for bed. Ellen was to be at the train station by seven the next morning.

They set out at six. It was still dark. They climbed into the old Dodge and drove to the station. Ellen laughed out loud.

"What is it?" Ruth took her eyes off the road to see what was so funny.

"Day three for the blue dress. I've had this dress on for three days. Lloyd may leave me at the train station. There's Elizabeth's cobbler right here and Charlie's pot roast here." She pointed to the spots on her dress.

Ruth laughed at her. "You did wash your drawers though, didn't you?"

Ellen convulsed into a fit of laughter. "No!" She sputtered through her giggles. Ruth was overtaken as well. They laughed until they both had tears in their eyes.

"I'm gonna' miss you." Ruth looked at her friend.

"I know, me too." Ellen answered.

"Ellen, I can never ..."

Ellen stopped her. "Don't. Nothing too serious right now. It hurts too bad." Ruth nodded in agreement. They drove on to the train station.

Ruth put her friend on the train. "Goodbye, Miss Dirty Drawers," she whispered in her ear. Then she smiled through her tears, all the way back to her mother's house.

# Robert

APRIL 1956...

Ellen stared out the little window of the passenger train, barely seeing the rural Texas countryside pass by. She had so much on her mind. Ruth... She would be all right. She was surrounded by her people now, good people. As for herself, she was going home. Home... She thought of Lloyd, her beloved husband. She had dreamed of him in Houston. She missed his strength, his love. She had not planned to travel to Houston with Ruth. It had been a wild impulse, but that wild impulse had changed her life. She smiled, remembering Ruth's face when she told her that she was going with her. There had been confusion there, but also relief.

She thought about how impulses could change lives so. She thought of Maureen. She wondered if she had spoken yet. Part of her hoped that Maureen had told Lloyd everything, all the terrible details while she was away, so that she did not have to know them. He would filter them for her. He would tell her only what she could live with, what Ruth could live with. Ellen straightened in her seat a bit. All that was discovered about that night was Ruth's by right. The child had been her son. The man had been her husband. Every detail that ever saw daylight, no matter how terrible, belonged to Ruth. Ellen would see to it that she got the truth. She would hold nothing back. As a woman, as a wife, and as a mother herself, she knew how Ruth must feel. The need to know was more compelling than anything else. There would be pain in knowing what had happened in those last few moments, great pain. But Ellen knew full well that not knowing would eat her up slowly, from the inside out.

She spent the rest of the train ride dozing. She stirred only when the train reached its stops. Finally, she heard the short little man announce her stop. "Next stop, Fort Worth," he called. She saw a few other passengers gather their belongings about them, but not her. She had no belongings.

She clutched her hand bag and watched through the small window, as the train pulled into the depot at last. She could not help but smile when she saw them. Her family... Lloyd had them dress in their good clothes to come and get her. She would have to remember to tell him that she approved. He couldn't care less if they were dressed in rags, so long as they were covered. But he knew that his wife did, so he had tried. There was Maureen, looking so grown up, and so detached. There was sweet little Annalyn. Ellen could see Lloyd's attempt to style her hair, the big pink bow crooked and crumpled. She waited as the train came to a complete stop, watching them. They did not see her. She sat there for a moment, still watching them from her seat on the train. They watched the front of the train, looking for her. Ellen was overcome with emotion. She loved them so much, so very much.

She thought about Ruth. Ruth was starting over with her girls. She had lost her family. That special unit was gone. Ellen couldn't

216

imagine it. She could not stop herself, she began to sob, so overtaken with the emotions she felt. Ellen never cried. But there they stood, just beyond the glass. They would never know how the mere sight of them could move her so. She watched Lloyd in his freshly pressed pants and shirt, sleeves unbuttoned and rolled up to his elbows, suspenders, hat, looking for her. She saw Maureen with the sun bouncing on the top of her blond hair, a million miles away. Little Annalyn, looking so cute and so excited, was waiting for her mother. They were her gift. She would consider every moment with them. She would not waste a single day. They had so little time together. No matter how long they lived, it would never be enough. She took a deep breath and stole one last look at them before she departed the train.

They saw her. They smiled and waved. Lloyd was relieved. She stepped off the train, right into her husband's arms. For a moment she just breathed him in. Annalyn hugged wherever she could reach. She was wrapped around her mother's waist. Maureen put her arm around her mother, and laid her head on her shoulder. For a moment, they were one silent, grateful, mound of flesh, with a love so strong you could almost touch it. People stared, wondering what their story was, watching the family embrace like there was no tomorrow.

Lloyd led as they walked to where Ellen's car was parked. Ellen walked with her girls, holding hands, Maureen on her left and Annalyn on her right. They got in and drove home. She told them all about Houston.

It was sunset when they drove into town. Ellen saw her hometown. Kilroy was glowing, lit by the last few rays of sun before they disappeared beyond the horizon. There was no Charlie's café. There was no charming, eccentric junk dealer. There was no college with all the wonderful things that go with education. Of course, there were no Johnsons. They were gone. But not just them. All the colored people had gone. They had gone from Kilroy without looking back, walked

217

away from their homes and their farms after what had happened there. Ellen felt depressed and ashamed to be returning to Kilroy, to the town that was responsible for so much darkness. She had grown up there. It was the only place she had ever lived. She wondered what was next for her, for them.

Lloyd drove through the little town of Kilroy and turned onto Oak Street, their street. There was the house. He parked Ellen's car underneath the carport. Ellen got out of the car and saw her home. It did feel good to be home. She remembered when she and Lloyd bought the house. They had lived so long together in a rented shack that when they finally bought the huge old house they did not know what to do with all the space. For the first year, they lived in only four rooms. They had been so used to living on top of each other, they didn't know any other way. She remembered their neighbors helping them paint the house and fix the old warped floors. So many people had helped them get started. It almost seemed like it had happened somewhere else, not here, where there was so much meanness.

The entire world was in a state of confusion, it seemed. She wondered what would happen to it. What would the outcome be? Would they ever be able to live together, work together, eat together? It had been so nice in Houston with Ruth. For that brief moment they had been free, free to enjoy an afternoon together without ugly looks or hateful words, with no fear for their safety.

They all clamored up the steps to the house. There was someone sitting in the porch swing. By then, the sun was sinking in the sky and it was hard to make out whom it was.

"Mr. Adams, it's me. Robert Coleman, sir."

Lloyd could barely see the young man. He spoke so softly, Lloyd could hardly hear him. Ellen sensed danger. She pulled Maureen and Annalyn closer to her, standing there on the front porch. Lloyd moved to stand in front of them, to shield them. For the both of them, it was instinctual.

"Yes. Yes, I see. Is everything all right, son?"

"Yes, sir. I just wanted to see if you had a job for me at the store, sir."

Lloyd could tell he was embarrassed. There was no danger, not tonight. Instead, something was wrong, wrong with the boy. He sent Ellen and the girls inside so that he could talk to him.

Lloyd sat down in the swing beside young Robert Coleman. He just sat there for a moment, quietly catching his breath. The entire day had consisted of bringing Ellen home, and he was tired. He sat there for a moment with the boy, just rocking in the porch swing. Finally, he spoke.

"What kind of work is it that you're looking for?" he asked him.

"Whatever you got."

Lloyd thought about the boy's answer, before he spoke. He hadn't given Lloyd an example of a job that he would like to do. He had said, "whatever." Whatever meant need. Lloyd considered him for a moment. He was sure that finding the boy waiting in the porch swing after dark meant desperation.

Lloyd chose his words very carefully. "Robert, I may have some work around the store, but I would never want it to interfere with your schooling. Do your parents know that you are looking for work?"

"Yes, sir. Well, my mother does anyway, but not my daddy. He's sick, sir. I don't want him to know."

"I see." Lloyd tried not to look too surprised. "Well, son, if I hire you, you've got to tell your father. Can't be keeping secrets like that. Besides, wanting to work is an honorable thing. Maybe he'll surprise you. If he says it's all right, then stop by the store tomorrow after school and we'll talk some more about it."

"Yes, sir. Thank you, sir."

Lloyd watched as the young man got up to leave. He thanked him again and walked down the steps. Lloyd called out to him. "Son, did you walk here?"

"Yes, sir." The boy called back. "My daddy's old truck won't start." He made excuses.

"Come back. I'll give you a ride home."

Robert Coleman called back to him through the darkening night. "No, sir. I'll walk. My father doesn't know I've come. He's got a lot on his mind right now, being sick and all."

Lloyd let him go. He sat there rocking in his front porch swing, listening to Ellen's voice drifting through open windows. It was coming from the kitchen. She was talking to Annalyn and Maureen. Maureen did not answer. Ellen just kept on talking as if she had. It was beautiful, the sound of her voice. How precious were the familiar sounds of her taking charge of her household. He was so thankful that she was home again. It would be so nice to lean on her again. He thought about the Coleman boy walking home. The Colemans lived about four miles out of town. He heaved his tired body up out of the swing and opened the screen door.

"I'm taking the Coleman boy home. I'll be right back"

Ellen told him to hurry. She searched his face for signs of danger. "Everything is fine," he told her. The screen door slammed shut and he was gone.

Lloyd was surprised to see how far the boy had gotten. "Clear down to the feed store," he muttered to himself. The boy must be walking fast, he thought. He slowed the pickup down as he came up behind him.

By that time it was dark, and the headlights nearly blinded Robert Coleman. He turned to see who was behind him but could not tell. He thought it was Mr. Adams. He heard a man telling him to get in. It was Mr. Adams. Lloyd stopped the pickup so that he could get in.

"Mr. Adams, you don't have to take me home." He hesitated inside the open door of the pickup truck, but Lloyd could tell he was glad to see him.

"Son, I would not be able to sleep tonight knowing that I let you walk home in the dark."

"Sir, I do it all the time." He answered with mock surprise that Lloyd would be concerned for his safety. He tried to seem tough, but Lloyd wasn't falling for it. He knew the boy's mother. She kept him pretty well under her thumb so that nothing would happen to him. Robert Coleman got into the pickup with Lloyd and they drove out of town.

The Colemans had a little farm north of town. They were poor. The boy's mother came into town often to sell her vegetables. Lloyd always bought whatever she had to sell, whether he needed it or not. He liked her. She was a very meek, soft spoken woman. She was honest, and judging from the vegetables that she sold to him for his store, she was a hard worker. She also happened to be married to the town drunk.

Everyone in Kilroy knew that Clyde Coleman would eventually drink himself to death, and leave his wife and eight kids to fend for themselves. The Colemans were a huge source of gossip, with Clyde constantly giving the locals something new to talk about. Lloyd Adams stayed out of the gossip, but he could not help but draw his own conclusions. It was obvious to him that Clyde Coleman had already left his wife and children to fend for themselves, a long time ago. It was the dying he had yet to do. Not a day went by that didn't end with him passed out drunk somewhere. Tonight, Lloyd had his only son in the pickup with him seeing that he got safely home. There was no telling where the boy's father was.

"Is Maureen all right?"

Lloyd wasn't expecting the boy's question. In fact, he didn't even know how to answer it. Was Maureen all right? He didn't even know, himself. No one did. How could they? She wasn't speaking. While Ellen was gone, he asked her what had happened that night at the Johnsons, but there was no response. He found himself demanding that she tell him. He had even raised his voice at his daughter, which he had never done before, in a desperate attempt to reach her. Still, there was no response. In fact, not only did she act like she didn't hear him, she acted like she didn't even see him. He had not discussed it with Ellen yet, and could not decide if he should. It had upset him deeply. He wondered if Maureen had lost her mind.

"Maureen's been through a lot. I don't know if she'll ever be herself again. You understand?"

"Yes, sir."

Lloyd drove the rest of the way to the boy's house.

"That's our mailbox right there. You can let me out there. I'll walk the rest of the way."

Lloyd stopped and let the boy out. "Son, you come by the store tomorrow if your mother and your daddy say it's okay."

"Yes, sir." He started to slam the door to the pickup. "And thank you, sir," he added just as the door slammed shut. Lloyd watched him until he could not see him any longer, then he drove home.

Robert Coleman walked into the tiny house where he lived with his seven sisters, his mother, and occasionally his father when he wasn't so drunk that he couldn't find his way home. The only person he saw tonight was his mother. She was sitting in her chair, sewing a button on one of his shirts. He only had two shirts that she referred to as "acceptable" for school, and one of them had lost a button. She was startled when he came through the front door.

"Robert, where have you been? It's after dark." She was obviously worried.

"Mr. Adams wants to hire me. He was talking to me about a job."

"Hire you? To do what?" She was surprised.

"Just to help him out in his store."

"Robert, you can't quit school," she said softly, as she turned back to her sewing. Martha Coleman was in no way prepared to go to war with her son over quitting school to go to work. "Please, not tonight. I've got a lot on my mind."

Robert could see how tired she was, and he hated it. He hated seeing her work herself to death, on the farm, to feed them. He hated to see her cook, clean, wash, and make the living, while his father drank himself to death. It was no secret he hated school and wanted to go to work. He wanted to help her.

He heard the familiar sounds that signaled his sisters were getting ready for bed, the splashing of the wash basin. They had no indoor plumbing. School tomorrow, he said no more about it.

He never wanted to be the source of any pain when it came to his mother. He loved her more than he dared to admit. He was the only boy, her only son, and the bond between them was strong and unspoken, for they were the most affected by Clyde Coleman's life-style. The girls were less affected by their father. Their mother had always successfully overcompensated for their father's absence and behavior. Where Clyde was unreliable, you could set your watch by Martha. Where Clyde couldn't be bothered to pay their debts, Martha would show up a day early to make sure all was paid in full, and on time. She would leave the debt collector wondering how in the hell she managed. The family was poor, yes, but Martha Coleman was a proud woman. She would not be pathetic. The girls identified with her and were less affected. Robert, on the other hand, was still trying to find himself. At seventeen, he was still trying to decide who he was going to be. And that was no easy task with no decent man to identify with, unable to identify with a woman.

"Yes, ma'am," he said. He kissed her cheek and was gone.

She stopped sewing for a moment and watched him walk down the narrow hallway of the tiny house to his bedroom. He had his own room while the others had to share. The joy that she felt just watching him was immeasurable. While she loved her daughters so very much and enjoyed watching them grow, day after day, into beautiful young women, it was her son that brought her joy. The girls were oblivious to so much. They were fiercely protected from reality and gossip. It was Martha's son that tried to take care of her, that tried to protect her. She was always so moved by how he tried to help her. But as much as he helped her on the farm, with the girls, with his father, as much as he touched her by his fierce love for her, she would not allow him to do the one thing he begged of her. She refused to allow him to quit school, refused to let the mess that had become of her life hold him back, ever.

She was an intelligent woman, had done well in school, and was not unattractive. She had wanted to be a teacher. But she had fallen in love with the boy that was always the life of every party, and had married him despite her parent's objections. "He has nothing to offer you," they told her. But she had not listened. All she needed was his love, until the first baby came, and then the next, and so on, until it became more and more difficult to feed them. Love was not enough anymore. And instead of busting his ass to take care of his family, Clyde Coleman sunk deeper and deeper into a bottle of booze until his wife didn't even know him anymore.

Gone was the funny, handsome, young man that made everybody smile. In his place, was a snot slobbering drunk that didn't know whether he was coming or going. The only reason that Martha could even continue to live with him was because he owned the farm, free and clear. As long as she stayed, she could take care of her family. And one day, when he finally drank himself to death, it would be hers. Besides that, he was not a violent drunk or an abusive drunk. He was a sloppy, disgusting, whoring drunk. She could live with sloppy and disgusting. She could even overlook the whores, for the sake of her children. But violence or abuse she would not tolerate. As long as he was neither, she would continue to live with him. Still, she knew it was not without consequences. She was not a fool. She did not expect her children to be completely unaffected by him. She just tried to get through one day at a time, minimizing the effects however she could, working herself into the ground to feed and clothe them.

Robert got ready for bed. He would go see Mr. Adams tomorrow after school. He had told his mother, not exactly the way the story had actually gone, but he had told her just the same. As long as he stayed in school, she would be all right with him working. He knew that. His plan was to learn everything he could from Mr. Adams. He may be only seventeen, but he was smart enough to realize that Mr. Adams knew how to make money, and he was sick and tired of being poor. He was tired of seeing his mother look like she had tonight, like she might drop dead from exhaustion. He planned to help her with the money he earned, while saving some for himself so that he could make his own way. He wanted to be something. He wanted to be somebody.

It was no secret that Robert Coleman had a huge chip on his shoulder. Most of the time, he walked around with his head down, looking at his worn out shoes, never meeting anyone's gaze. He knew they watched him, all of Kilroy. His father, they called "sorry and worthless." His mother, they said was "pitiful." The family, worst of all, was dismissed by one word. Trash... He moved through life just trying to blend in, never wanting to do anything to draw attention to himself. It was a sad existence. He loved his mother so much. How could he not? He watched her, day after day, try to make a life for them. All the while, his father slipped further and further away.

At only seventeen, he was already being destroyed by all that raged inside of him. He still loved his father. At the same time, he harbored an intense hatred for him. Unconditional love and red hot anger were at war within him, taking him prisoner, holding him captive. He was laughed at, talked about, even sometimes beat up. And he had never done anything to anyone! There was much to endure for being his father's son, and he blamed his father for all of it.

Robert Coleman was smart. He understood his schoolwork. He just couldn't ever seem to get it completed. He was always helping his mother on the farm. They had to eat. He was not unattractive, in fact he was quite handsome. He couldn't help it that his clothes were too small, his shoes were falling apart, and his hair was uncut. It was his father that was always drunk, causing a scene, and running around town with filthy women, not him.

His father had come to the school last year upon receiving a note addressed, "To the Parents of Robert Coleman." He was drunk and had pissed all over himself, leaving Robert to clean it up. The note had been notification that because he had missed so much school, he might have to be held back. Robert remembered it like it was yesterday, the pain still so fresh. Mrs. Tolliver had been sorry she sent it, so sorry that she had passed him on through to the next grade. She thought she was helping him.

The looks on people's faces were the worst. Some of them felt sorry for him. Some of them were disgusted by him. That was how he moved through life, either being pitied or being despised. It was a wonder there was anything good left in him at all. But he would show everybody. He would make a way for himself. He was tired of going to school and hearing the other boys talk about the things his father had done. It was embarrassing. He was tired of going to school and being made fun of because he always wore the same clothes. He did without so much, so that his sisters could have more. He chose to.

He loved them and he was well aware that he was the only thinking, functioning male in the house. And in 1956, there were still so many limitations for women. But he was convinced that he would pull them out. And for the first time in a very long time, Robert Adams fell asleep thinking about himself, not feeling sorry for his mother or worried about his father. He went to sleep excited, in anticipation of learning the business and making a dollar. Mr. Adams was giving him a chance. He intended to run with it.

Tuesday, April 17, 1956, was the longest day of his seventeen year old life. He didn't hear a thing Mrs. Harris said. He spent the entire day waiting for two o'clock so that he could get out of there. Just when he thought it would never come, the bell rang, signaling the end of the school day. Robert was the first one out the door. He eagerly walked the few blocks to the grocery store while Mrs. Harris made herself a note to talk to his mother about his grades. They were getting worse and she could see he was slipping further and further behind in her class. Of course, she had heard all the gossip regarding his father. She knew all about the incident with Mrs. Tolliver, Robert's teacher last year. Disgusting, all of it. It only caused her to have even more respect for his mother, for what she was trying to do. Mrs. Harris would let her know as soon as possible that he would end up having to be held back, if he didn't start taking his studies more seriously. Most teachers would just pass him on through so that he could go on to work, to make a living. But not Mrs. Harris. She believed in education. And after the horrible murder of that colored boy, she started taking a little more interest in her students. She would talk to his mother and make sure everything was all right at home.

The store was only a few blocks away from the school. Robert reached it in no time. He ran up the steps and flung the door open, excited to see Mr. Adams. Lloyd smiled at him. He had wondered if the boy would show up. Here he is, he thought. Now, what am I going to do with him?

"How was school?" Lloyd asked.

"Boring," the boy answered.

Lloyd was shocked by his honesty. "Schooling is only boring when you don't appreciate it," he told him.

Robert did not answer, so Lloyd continued. "I wanted to go to work just like you. Didn't want to sit in a school listening to somebody talk. I knew it all. Was going to be a farmer just like my daddy. Only he didn't see things my way. He said I was going to finish school. Of course, he had to bust my butt a few times to keep me there, but eventually I gave up the fight and ended up learning a few things. Got interested in economics when we learned the concept of supply and demand. Now here I am running my own business, all because my butt was sore the day we studied supply and demand."

Robert laughed with him. Maureen walked in. She had come from the back of the store where she had been working on her lessons. She would not be returning to school. She would complete all of her coursework from home, and receive her diploma at the end of the school year. Her father had made sure that she would not have to see the inside of that school again. He kept a close eye on her, so did her mother. She was so fragile now. Some days she forgot to eat. Lloyd and Ellen, both, were constantly trying to feed her. She was quickly becoming emaciated. She made her way down one of the aisles, picked up a notebook, and began to return to the back of the store.

"Good afternoon, Maureen." Robert spoke to her. She acted as if she did not hear him. She disappeared again, into the back of the store.

"Robert, it's not you." Lloyd felt the need to explain. "She doesn't speak to anyone. She hasn't spoken since the Johnsons were murdered that night. I'm sure you heard. She was there."

Normally, Lloyd would not have entered into this conversation with anyone, but he felt sorry for the boy. There were enough people mistreating him already. He did not want him to think Maureen was being rude to him exclusively, personally. And besides that, he liked the boy. For some reason, he even trusted him.

"Yes, sir. I heard. No telling what she saw. I didn't expect her to speak sir, but I know she can hear me. Maybe someday she'll answer back, but if we stop talking to her altogether, we may never hear her voice again."

Lloyd Adams put his arm around Robert Coleman. "You're right about that, son. You're right about that."

Lloyd began by showing him the stockroom, where everything was located. He showed him how to check in a delivery. He showed him where to record damages. He taught him everything there was to know about receiving and stocking merchandise that first day.

Just before time to go home, a truck rolled up at the back of the store, carrying fabric. Lloyd greeted the driver and supervised as Robert checked in his first shipment, recorded damages, and stocked the merchandise. It was interesting watching the boy's unsure hands handling the delicate fabrics that he stocked in his store. Lloyd instructed him that there was a special order for Mrs. Betty Clayton, to call her and let her know it had arrived. He pointed to the clipboard that was mounted to the wall by the telephone. It was labeled, "Special Orders." It had names, telephone numbers, and addresses, as well as a description of what they were waiting for. After Robert finished with Mrs. Clayton, Lloyd told him to get his things together. Ellen would drive him home. The boy started to protest. He did not want to be a burden. If he became a burden, they might not keep him, he thought. Ellen quickly shushed him.

"Robert, if you won't allow me to drive you home, I won't allow you to work in my store." She told him matter-of-factly. "I will not have you walking that far every day. It's just not right."

She and Lloyd had talked it over. Robert Coleman had been sitting in their front porch swing at precisely the right time. Most of the time, opportunity was all about timing. And he had timed it just right, unbeknownst to him. Ellen wanted to spend more time with her girls and less time at the store. With all that they had been through, she felt like she must. Robert Coleman would learn the grocery business, and she would spend more time with her daughters. She had to minimize their scars, especially Maureen's.

And so it went, five days a week, Monday through Friday. Lloyd was closed on Saturday, and insisted that the boy not work on Sunday so that he could prepare for the week, catch up on his studies. Robert began to pay attention in class. He had actually begun to learn some things. He began to change.

As long as his father stayed gone, Martha Coleman thought her son would be fine. For so long he had gotten by without him, made the best of living in a house with eight females, made the best of being poor, had even learned to overlook the fact that his father was a constant source of embarrassment. The more time he spent with Lloyd at the store, the more his mother saw him smile, and that was a beautiful sight.

June came to Kilroy, with plenty of warm sunshine. The small town was buzzing. It was the week before graduation. High school graduation in Kilroy was a town affair, and Adams Grocery was the only place in town to get groceries, as well as invitations and party goods. It was a very busy time for the store. Business was booming. Lloyd had come to depend on Robert Coleman like he had never depended on any hired help. He and Ellen had always handled their own business, but not anymore. He needed the boy. Maureen was still lost somewhere. Still, she had not spoken. Lloyd was afraid it was becoming normal. He felt as if she was getting further and further away from them.

Lloyd trusted Robert with absolutely all of the store's business. He gave Robert more and more responsibility every time he went to Houston, and he went there often to consult with Ruth about her business. Lloyd had dedicated himself to her. Whenever there was a problem he would jump in the car and head to Houston to help her work it out. She was tough. She could do most everything on her own, but there were times when she began to doubt herself, and he would go. Ellen insisted.

It had been a rough start for Johnsons Grocery. There were so many times he thought that Ruth should just close the doors, cut her losses, and do something else before she lost everything she had. But Ellen wouldn't hear of it. She was prepared to go bankrupt herself before she would let Ruth fail. Every time Lloyd approached her with a profit and loss statement, Ellen would wave him away and simply say, "Freedom." He knew what she meant. He knew how important success was for Ruth, but for awhile he had been nervous. He was a good business man, and he could not get Johnsons to stop operating in the red. Finally, after construction was completed in the area of town that Johnsons operated in, people began to move in and Ruth's store began to take off. In fact, now it was doing quite well. Lloyd had even been able to maximize both of their profit making abilities by trading goods. If Ruth was unable to sell something, he would bring it to his store. If he couldn't move a good, he would send it to her. Between the two of them, there was a market for just about anything, making business good for the both of them.

It was five o'clock on Friday. Robert was leaving. Normally, he stayed to help Lloyd close the store, since he would not be returning until Monday afternoon. However, today was special. He was leaving early for graduation practice. The Kilroy High School Class of 1956 was going through the motions of the graduation ceremony that would officially take place Saturday afternoon.

Robert walked to the back of the store and found Lloyd. "It's five, time for me to go."

"Of course, graduation practice." Lloyd was proud of Robert. He had worked hard to bring his grades up so that he could graduate. Lloyd recognized how hard he tried, all the way around. He tried his best at the store. He tried his best at school. He tried his best at home. Lloyd knew what he was feeling. He had figured him out. To Robert, everyone that believed in him was taking a chance on him. He did not want to disappoint them. Because he was Clyde Coleman's son, Kilroy thought nothing good could come of him. It was no secret. The whole town watched him, expecting him to turn out just like his father, waiting for something new to talk about.

But watching Lloyd, Robert decided who he would be. He would give everyone nothing to talk about. He would be perfect. He would prove that he was worthy of his mother. He would prove that he was worthy of Mr. Adams. Lloyd and Robert developed a relationship that looked more like father and son than employer and employee. Lloyd had seen him go from right on the edge of out of control, to strong and steady, always trying to do the right thing. It was amazing to see what had become of him since someone had taken an interest in him.

His mother had tried. She had done all she could. But there was a limit to what she could accomplish with him. She had seven other children and Clyde Coleman to contend with. As far as Robert was concerned, the best thing that ever happened to him was going to work for Lloyd Adams. Lloyd's example had rescued him from his father's fate. And sometimes, when Clyde stayed gone long enough, Robert could almost forget that he was his son.

"We'll see you tomorrow," Lloyd told him.

Robert looked shocked. "I thought Maureen was not going to be a part of the ceremony."

"She's not. We're coming to see you."

Robert could not contain his grin. "Really?"

"Really. And I've got something for you, too. I'll give it to you then."

Robert could not contain his excitement. He was overwhelmed that Mr. Adams was coming to see him graduate. He was graduating from high school! He never thought he would. He had struggled to get through school, but when he finally found himself working for Lloyd, he began to care about everything. It was all because he had started to feel like he was worth something. He wanted to own a store someday. He thought he would be able to. He actually believed he would be able to. He had already saved up some money, and was still saving as much as he could, after he helped his mother, of course. Life had become a little sweeter for Robert, and for Martha and the girls. The money helped. Adams Grocery had been a blessing all the way around.

Robert Coleman walked the few blocks to the school. He was happy. He was actually smiling. Smiling wasn't something he did very often. The ceremony would take place on the football field.

The class listened as instruction was given as to how the ceremony would go. They were instructed how to properly receive their diploma. There were no chairs yet. They would be set up tomorrow before the ceremony. They were given a pre-printed program that outlined the ceremony, so that they could go over it. Robert went through the motions as he was instructed. He began to daydream. He would enjoy every minute of the day tomorrow. He had earned it. His mother was proud of him. His sisters were excited for him. He had done it. He had actually done it. He had gotten through school, and tomorrow after they threw their hats in the air, he would be free. Free...

He walked home that day. He couldn't even remember the last time he had walked home. He was usually in the pickup with Lloyd, or in the car with Ellen. He didn't mind walking today at all. He had a lot on his mind. He walked through the downtown area, looking at Kilroy. He imagined that one day he would own one of the small buildings. He imagined that he would wear an expensive suit, that he would be respected. Respect felt good. He walked the rest of the way home daydreaming of all that he might do, all of it right there in Kilroy, never even considering leaving, never even realizing that he could.

Because it was June, the days were getting longer. Even though it was almost seven o'clock, it was still daylight when his father pulled up beside him in his old truck, so drunk he nearly hit him.

"Get in," he said smiling, with eyes not quite seeing his son.

Clyde had been surprised to see his son walking down the road. He hadn't seen him in almost a month. He'd been taking it easy with Wanda Parker, at her place down close to the river bottom. Her old man, as she called him, had left her some money when he died. She was the latest woman to take up with Clyde. She may be ugly as hell, Clyde thought, but he liked her. She bought him all the booze he needed and took good care of him, all because she was afraid to be alone. Her old man had been mean to her, turned her into a drunk just like Clyde. The two of them were perfect for each other, living down close to the river bottom, drinking life away.

But that day, she had sobered up long enough to go see her mother in Fort Worth. The old lady was sick. Her absence left Clyde restless, looking for something to do.

"No thanks, I'll walk." Robert walked away from the battered truck. Clyde drove away, weaving so close to his son he almost hit him. Robert didn't care. He'd rather risk getting run over by his father than get in the car with him. He just couldn't stomach him anymore.

Clyde drove the rest of the way home. "Ungrateful!" he said out loud. "Ever since he went to work for that nigger lovin' Lloyd Adams, he thinks he's better than me," Clyde told himself. He'd deal with him later, right after he saw his wife and girls.

He weaved up the road to the little house and parked his old truck close to the shed in the back. Martha saw him coming and wondered what he wanted. He stayed gone longer and longer recently, and she preferred it that way. She busied herself with finishing dinner. They were eating late this evening. She had been preoccupied altering a pair of pants that she had bought for Robert. It was a surprise. She had bought him new clothes for graduation. Even though he had put back a decent amount of money, she knew he would never buy anything like that for himself. For his sisters or her, yes, but never for himself. Clyde staggered in the back door and cursed the screen door as it slammed shut on him.

"Hello, Martha," he said, as he kissed her cheek. The kiss was wet and warm, and as he came closer to her she fought the urge to shrink away from him in disgust. He stunk, and yet again she wondered how her husband could have turned into this filthy man. She wanted to hate him, but she could not. Instead, she was sickened by him, so repulsed with what he had done with his life.

"Hello, Clyde. What brings you here?" she asked, not once stopping to look at him.

"I live here, remember? In fact, it's my house," he told her.

Martha was not about to get into any sort of discussion on that subject with him. There was too much to do. Robert was graduating tomorrow. Maybe, just maybe, if she could control herself, he would eat a hot meal with them and be on his way again.

"Of course, it is, darling. Won't you stay for dinner?" She asked him in the kindest, most humble voice she could summon.

"I'd love to." He smiled at his wife.

"Girls!" he called.

All seven of his daughters came looking for the sound of his voice in the kitchen. They had been following their mother's instruction to make sure their best clothes were clean for tomorrow's graduation ceremony, while she finished cooking their dinner. For the most part, the Coleman girls were glad to see their father. He loved them. There was no doubt about it. And because Martha and Robert protected them so fiercely, the girls knew very little about his antics. They were able to love him back.

There were hugs and kisses. They were used to the way he looked and smelled. They did not remember him any other way. They were glad to see him. Robert came through the back door, and into the kitchen. All of the excitement he had allowed himself to feel about graduation was gone. Just seeing his father drove it far from him.

"Welcome home, son. Did you have a nice walk?" Clyde jeered at his son.

"Yes, sir. Thank you for asking," he answered through clenched teeth. He had unknowingly formulated the same plan as his mother: be cordial and wait for him to leave. He prayed that no one mentioned graduation. He did not want his father to know anything about it, for fear he might actually decide to show up.

The younger girls set the table quickly, but meticulously, as they did every night. They all sat down at the big maple kitchen table to eat. Martha had taken great care with dinner. She had slow cooked a ham and prepared some of her fresh garden vegetables. There were homemade biscuits too. Clyde ate like he hadn't eaten in days. He talked and laughed with the girls. It was Martha and Robert that remained silent.

Robert studied his father. He appeared to be wearing new clothes, but they were wrinkled and dirty like they hadn't been changed for days. He was even thinner than usual. Robert had never seen a man so thin. His hair had been cut, but it was uncombed and slightly disheveled. He felt something strange creep up, something foreign, as he watched his father eat the dinner that his mother had prepared. It took awhile for him to figure it out.

It was power. He saw them all eating the ham that he had bought with his own paycheck, sitting at the table in the house that he had just paid the taxes on. He saw his sisters and his mother dressed in new clothes made with fabric that he had bought. His sisters had even been spared the burden of belonging to Clyde Coleman, because he carried it for everyone. And sitting there watching them all eat together at the dinner table, he was able to put his anger aside. He felt his power, and he liked it. It was at that moment something in him changed. He would never forget how it felt... To have power, to have control. He never wanted to be without that feeling again.

He loved them all, even his sorry father. Of course, he did. He felt himself smile watching him. Robert didn't need booze. It would never touch his lips. It was this new feeling, power, that he would seek. It was intoxicating, and furthermore it was the only thing that had ever even come close to knocking that nagging chip off his tired shoulder.

The evening passed rather quickly. Robert and Martha, both, even laughed a couple of times. The longer Clyde stayed, the less drunk he became. Robert thought he caught a glimpse of the father he remembered. Being the oldest, he had a few early memories of his father that were sweet. He tried to keep them far from his mind, though. They hurt too much.

It was time for Clyde to go. He knew that Wanda would be home soon, and if she knew he was visiting his family, there would be hell to pay. He had a good thing going. He didn't want to spoil it. He tucked his girls in bed, sitting with each one as they said their prayers. All seven of them included him. They prayed for him just as they did every night. Their sweet prayers brought tears to his eyes. Martha stood in the doorway, listening. The four older girls were old enough to realize it might be best to change the way that they usually phrased their prayer for him, but not the youngest three. Their honesty caught him off guard, and his sobriety did little to assuage his guilt.

"Please, be with Daddy while he's sick from the drink," Joy said.

"Please, get Daddy well so that he'll come home." That was Helen.

Clyde fought back his tears. His head was beginning to ache. He needed a drink.

And then there was Theresa, the youngest. She came the closest to reaching him that night. "God, please, let Daddy be here when I wake up in the morning, and please don't let him die tonight. Amen." That was all she said.

He kissed them and walked into the tiny hallway. He looked his wife in the eye. The drunken fog that he normally functioned in had lifted. For a split second she thought she saw her Clyde. "Will you pray for me tonight too, Martha?"

She could not look at him any longer. She turned away. "I have never stopped," he heard her say.

She left him standing there. He crossed the little hallway and entered his son's room. Robert was getting ready for bed. He was not wearing a shirt and Clyde was speechless, seeing for the first time what he had been too drunk to recognize for so long. His son had grown up, and he had grown up without him. Lifting the heavy boxes at the store had built substantial muscles in his arms and chest. The muscles in his back flexed as he turned around. He was a man.

Clyde was pretty close to completely sober by this time. He stood there just inside his son's small cramped bedroom, embarrassed, unable to open his mouth to speak. His son was no longer a child. For Clyde, this was devastating. It meant that, as a man, his son must be able to see his father, truly see his father through a man's eyes. Clyde couldn't find words. He just stood there, unable to look at his son.

"Everything all right, sir?"

"Yes, son. Fine, just fine." He just wanted to leave, to run out of the house. He needed a bottle. It would make him forget.

"I better be going."

"Yes, sir." Robert finished dressing for bed.

"Listen, son, I know you're working for Lloyd Adams at his store right now. Pretty sure you like making that money. But you watch out for them. Spend too much time with nigger lovers and people will start to think you are one. 'Specially that daughter. Stay away from her. If I was her father, I'd have killed her. She was gonna' run off with that nigger boy but the Smiths got to 'em first."

Robert Coleman was struck dumb as he processed all that his father had just said. He was furious, but he did not want to cause a scene. His sisters were in the next room. He bowed up to his father, his face so close Clyde could feel his son's hot breath, and Robert could smell his filthy father.

"Get out," he told him. Clyde didn't understand. Robert felt rage. How dare his father say anything about them, anything at all. He fought back the urge to jump on him and strangle him. Clyde Coleman was not about to let his son order him out of his own house. He squared up to his son, ready for a fight. But something in his son's eyes stopped him.

"Listen to me, you bastard. Your daughters are in the next room so I'm going to make this short and sweet. It is because that man gave me a job that you had a house to come to tonight. It is because that man gave me a job that you had food to eat tonight. Don't you ever talk like that about them again. If you do, I swear it, I'll kill you. I'll find you, you sorry worthless piece of trash. And the last thing you'll ever see on this earth is your own son spit on you right before you walk through the gates of hell. I wish to God you weren't my father. I wish to God you were dead."

Clyde was speechless. Who was it that spoke to him this way? It couldn't be his Robert. The Robert he remembered adored him. But that Robert had gone a long time ago. Clyde was torn. He didn't know whether he should beat his son within an inch of his life, or if he should walk out of the house and never come back. He didn't have to think about it for very long. He heard the shotgun cock behind him and saw sweet Martha standing there. She had heard the whole thing.

"Go, Clyde."

Clyde said nothing. He walked out the back door, started up his old pickup, and drove away. Robert began to shake. His mother held him as best she could. He was so much bigger than her now.

She whispered into his sweet smelling hair. "You've suffered most of all, Robert. I know that. God bless your heart, sweet boy. God bless your heart."

It took awhile for him to regain his composure. He would not cry. It would take more than that to break him, much more than that.

After lying in bed for hours, he finally fell asleep. He woke to a beautiful spring day, graduation day, only it did not possess the same feeling as it had the day before. After all that had happened between him and his father last night, he had a hard time feeling happy about anything. He thought he would probably never see him or speak to him again. He remembered the look in his father's eye. Robert had reached him. He had gotten through to him. Clyde had been sober enough to hear his son and sober enough to remember what he said.

Clyde would leave his son alone. Robert was sure of that. He had left him alone up to now for far less than that.

He dressed and headed for the kitchen. He found his mother sitting there at the table. "Good morning," she said, her warm eyes searching his face. He forced a smile and told her good morning. "I have a surprise for you," she told him, pleased with herself. She hoped the gift would cheer him. Robert's eyes followed her to the kitchen cabinet. She produced a wrapped package. He took it from her. He could not imagine what it could be. There were nine people living in a little farm shack. How could she possibly keep anything a surprise?

He unwrapped the package. Folded neatly, were the most beautiful shirt and pair of pants he had ever seen. It took a moment for him to realize that they were for him. He didn't know anyone that owned anything as fine as this. He picked up the pieces and studied them, very careful not to soil or wrinkle them. They were so well made. He had never seen anything like them. The shirt was white, but it was not just any white shirt. The fabric felt good and the sewing was impeccable. He had never owned anything before that wasn't made by his mother.

"Mother, these are beautiful," he told her.

"Robert, I spared no expense. This is a big day. I wanted to show you how proud I am of you."

"Where did you get them? I've never seen anything like this before."

"Lloyd ordered them for me from a tailor he knows in Houston. He picked them up last time he was there. I altered them yesterday, so they should fit perfectly."

"I was just planning on wearing my best clothes today. Didn't even think about getting anything new."

"Go try them on right now," his mother told him, "that way, if I need to alter anything else, I can."

He carefully folded the pants and disappeared into his bedroom. A few moments later he appeared, looking like someone else. Martha could not take her eyes off of him. He looked so handsome. The pants and shirt fit perfectly. She was amazed. He couldn't help but laugh out loud at his mother.

"Are you all right?" he teased her.

"I'm fine. I just can't believe how handsome you look," she told him. "I wanted you to have something today that you could see and touch. You've turned into a good man, son. I could not have asked for anything more."

"Have I?" he asked her with regret.

Martha took a moment. She had to find the right words. "Robert, I believe you're questioning it because of all that happened between you and your father last night. Now I have never allowed any of you to be disrespectful to your father. Never. You know I will not tolerate it. But last night, the things he said to you made my skin crawl. Would I have liked for you to have controlled yourself and said nothing? Yes, of course. But son, you are human. And we both know how hard life has been for us because of all that he has chosen. You are a good man, son. I call you good because you have been nothing but good as far as I am concerned. I call you a man because you have proven that you are one."

Robert thought about all his mother said. She was right. He tried to be good. He tried to do what was right. He never wanted to hurt anybody, anybody at all. He had been hurt so much in his short life. He never wanted to cause anyone any pain at all, even his father. But because he had endured so much, at the hands of so many, for so long, he had learned how to inflict it right back in the worst possible way, in an effort to protect himself. This was something he never wanted to learn. Even so, it was too late.

He gave his mother a hug and disappeared, looking for his sisters. He wanted to show off his new clothes. She went back to cleaning the kitchen, what she had been doing when he found her.

One o'clock came quickly. They all walked into town together. Robert, his mother, and all seven of his sisters were dressed up and excited about attending his graduation. It was a nice walk, but inside he yearned to own a pickup truck.

Martha and the girls were seated in the bleachers, now. Robert could see them from where he sat on the football field. They were all there. His eyes scanned the crowd. Lloyd and Ellen sat at the back. Lloyd had his hat on. Ellen was, as always, dressed impeccably. He considered his two families. There was his first family, his mother and his sisters. For them, he felt fiercely protective, unconditionally loyal. But they felt heavy. They made him sad. For this new family that had touched him so, he felt proud. Just being with them made him feel important. He felt good. He felt free.

The preacher from the First Baptist Church had come to stand at the podium while the graduating class sat behind him. He faced the crowd and began the invocation. Robert bowed his head. He didn't even hear the prayer. He was lost in his own thoughts. Something his father had said... He couldn't get it out of his mind. Clyde had said people would start to think he was a "nigger lover." The prayer went on in the background. Robert didn't hear it though. He was too busy thinking about what his father had said. Robert didn't know it yet, but his father was on a downward spiral as a result of the tongue lashing he received from his son. Even so, it would never compare to the damage done to Robert, with the threat of all that his father's words implied.

There were no colored people in Kilroy anymore, anyway, he thought. They had all gone. Robert had always been told to stay away

243

from them. He had never even questioned it. He didn't know any colored folks anyhow. He was glad he didn't. The last thing he wanted was to give anyone anything new to hate him for. He could not begin to imagine defending himself in Kilroy for that. Lloyd and his family were different. They could do whatever they wanted. They could stand up for anything they chose. They weren't poor. Standing up for anything didn't even occur to Robert. Going against the grain was inconceivable. He was out to prove he was just as good as everyone else. So far, his life had been spent on the outside looking in. He wanted to be on the inside with everyone else, safe and accepted. For Robert Coleman, being known as a "nigger lover" could be terrible. It could be devastating. It could even be deadly.

And so his father's words began to work on him as he drifted in and out of the graduation ceremony. His vision of his successful future became murky, when he considered his father's threat. He was not sorry for what he said to his father. He meant it. How dare Clyde speak one word against the people that had rescued him? He was so thankful for the chance they had given him, for the opportunities they had given him, for all they had taught him. But his father had appealed to something inside of him that would not be quiet, the pain of not being accepted. If he ever wanted to make it, he would have to distance himself from Lloyd and his family, he thought. He was just starting out. They had already made it a long time ago. He didn't necessarily hate colored people, but he did believe that nothing good could come from associating with them.

Look at Maureen, she'd gone crazy, he thought. He had heard talk about what happened out there. Some people said that she was in love with that kid. Some people said that she was going to run off with him. All Robert knew was that if something like that had happened to any of his sisters, they would be dead. "That's a line that you just don't cross out here," he had heard so many times.

And as far as Kilroy was concerned, the Coleman girls were trash. They were dispensable. But no one dared to bother Maureen. Robert thought he knew why. All of them, be they Adams or Wilson, had an air of dignity about them. The very air that swirled around them screamed untouchable. Because Robert grew up dirt poor, he naturally assumed it was because they had money. It would be a long, long time before he realized how wrong he was. They were untouchable for one reason and one reason only, and all of Kilroy knew it. They would never back down when it came to doing what was right. They'd have to kill them all. And Kilroy, Texas had no intention of doing any such thing. No matter how different they were, no matter how much they all hated them, Kilroy would never turn on them. For they were from Kilroy, born and bred. They had a place there. They belonged. And besides all that, there was one simple truth that was plainer than the nose on all their faces. They made life in the sleepy boring little town far more interesting.

Robert listened as they began to announce the graduating seniors. One by one, they filed past the podium and received their diplomas. No sooner had he gotten his in his hand than he saw a man in a cowboy hat leaving the bleachers with his mother. It was Tuck Riley, the County Sheriff. He felt sick to his stomach. What had his father done this time? At least this time Wanda Parker could bail him out. Robert would do no such thing, not anymore. He worked hard to save his money and he would not keep using it to get his father out of jail. Surely, the sheriff could have waited for the graduation to be over. Did he have to come and embarrass him? People were probably already talking.

Robert knew immediately something was wrong when he saw his mother clutch Tuck. He didn't know if he should go to her or if he should keep still. He returned to his seat with his diploma in his hand. It was time for the benediction. The Trinity Baptist preacher got up and walked to the podium. Robert bowed his head and fiddled with the diploma. The prayer seemed to go on forever.

Finally, the words that signaled the end, "Friends, family, faculty, I now present to you the Kilroy High School Class of 1956." The crowd cheered. The graduating class threw their caps high into the air. It was a tradition. But not Robert Coleman, he walked as fast as he could toward his mother with his graduation cap in his hand. Gone was any bit of excitement he had about the day. Forgotten was his joy. He did not throw his cap into the air. Instead, he crumpled it in his hand. He would not be tossing it in the air today, for he still was not free.

Tuck Riley saw Clyde's boy approaching. He hated having to tell the boy that his father was dead, and at his graduation too. It was terrible. But he couldn't waste any time. The body was still down at Wanda Parker's house, and it was a hot day. Nobody knew what to do with it. Would his wife bury him? Or would Wanda? Tuck thought about Wanda. It was the first time he had seen her sober in years. Clyde Coleman had died in her bed. That had sobered her up real quick. Tuck thought about his dead, naked body lying there in Wanda's bed. He'd never seen anyone that skinny.

Tuck knew the Colemans well. He was the same age as Clyde and Martha. He had gone to school with them. It always amazed him how Clyde had turned out exactly like Old Man Coleman, his father. Old Man Coleman had died young too. He had driven off into the river one night. "Drunk as a skunk," everybody said. Clyde's mother had died a few years ago. She had a heart attack. She left Clyde the farm.

Clyde had been fun loving with a free spirit, while Martha had been strong and steady as an oak. He couldn't believe the two had married. Hell, the whole town was shocked. The two were as different as night and day. Tuck had been in love with Martha then. He got drunk the day she married Clyde Coleman, then he moved on. That was a long, long time ago. Right now their boy was walking toward him, and he hated to give him the news. He hated telling Martha too, but he had to. Besides the fact that they all went way back and he didn't want them hearing it from one of his young deputies, he had to know what they wanted to be done with the body.

Robert came to stand beside his mother. His eyes searched the sheriff's face for an indication of how bad it was. What had his father done this time? "Everything all right, sir?" he asked.

Tuck Riley was surprised each and every time he had to deal with Clyde Coleman's boy. In his line of work, it was his experience that the apple didn't fall too far from the tree, but this one did. Robert was soft spoken and kind, not drunk and crazy like Clyde. He was always polite and respectful, but for Tuck it did not go unnoticed that the boy couldn't looked him in the eye. Usually, people that couldn't meet his gaze had something to hide. Shifty, he called them. But this boy wasn't shifty. He was ashamed, ashamed of his father.

"Robert, I'm sorry," he struggled to get the words out. "Your father's dead."

His mother took his hand. Robert knew Tuck well. He had been dealing with Tuck for as long as he could remember, trying to keep his father out of jail. For the first time in his life, he looked Tuck Riley in the eye, searching his eyes, searching for answers. What he saw there was more than he could bear, pity and finality.

He ran. He ran out of the gates of the small football stadium. He ran down the road, away from the school. He ran past the little houses. The town was deserted. Everyone was at the graduation. He didn't know where he was going. He just ran. He was still wearing his graduation gown, running through the streets of Kilroy. Tears were streaming down his face. He gasped. He hadn't planned to go to the store. He didn't know where he would go. He just ran. But when he saw it, he knew. It was the only place he could go where there was

247

no Clyde. He always felt safe there. He was weak, so weak. He felt like he was breaking.

He ran to the back door. He didn't have his key. He panicked. He tried the door. The knob turned. It opened. He went inside, closed the door behind him, and locked it. He rested with his back against the door for a moment, catching his breath. Then he began to sob, gut wrenching sobs that wracked his whole body. He slid down to the floor of the storeroom and sat there with his back against the door, his head in his hands, crying his heart out. His father had left him a long time ago. Now, what remained of the man was gone, and with it, any hope of seeing his father ever again.

Maureen stood back in the shadows of the storeroom, listening. Ellen and Lloyd were at the graduation. Mama and Papa were at the house. They had come to stay with her and Annalyn while her parents were gone. She had taken the keys and gone to the store to get some sugar for Mama. She and Annalyn were making a cake for the Colemans, for Robert's graduation, when they discovered that they did not have enough sugar. None of the neighbors were home to even borrow some. Of course, they were all at the graduation. So Mama had given Maureen the keys to the store and told her to go and get some sugar. Maureen took the keys and walked across the street toward the store, without a word.

She was getting the sugar when she heard someone at the back door. It wasn't Mama or Papa. She could hear someone crying just beyond the door. It scared her. Everything scared her now. She was hiding in the shadows of the dark stockroom when she saw someone opening the door. It was Robert. He was upset. Something terrible had happened. She hid, waiting and listening.

"Oh, my God," he kept saying. "Oh, my God!" he cried.

He began to cry harder and harder. "It's my fault. It's all my fault," Maureen heard him say. She was afraid to come out. She didn't want him to know she was there. His pain was reaching her though, like nothing else had. She heard him scream. It sent chills up her spine.

"I killed him," he said, "I killed my father!"

Maureen began to shake. She did not know what to make of what she heard. He killed his father?

Then he started talking to himself. She listened, shaking all over in the shadows. "Lord, I didn't mean it. What I said, I didn't mean it. Please..." He was in agony. "I don't really wish he was dead. I didn't mean it. I just wanted him to change, to come home. If you heard what I said, I didn't mean it. Fix it back. Please, fix it back," he cried.

Maureen pulled herself together. Clyde Coleman must be dead, but Robert didn't kill him. In the shadows of the storeroom she had unwittingly been a witness to the depths of his pain, his guilt, his feelings. He must have said some terrible things, must have even wished his father was dead, because now he was blaming himself. She stood there listening to him, the pain in his cry, the sorrow, the regret. But it was the guilt that reached her, like nothing else could. It matched her own. She walked out of the shadows and went to him.

Robert jumped when he saw her. He thought he was alone. She sat down beside him on the storeroom floor without saying a word. His eyes found hers. He saw it, the pain, the sorrow, the deep dark regret. Nothing needed to be said. She took him in her arms, cradling his head on her chest. She rocked him gently back and forth. Then softly, he heard her in his ear.

"It's all right, I'm here. I'm here, Robert, and I understand."

They sat there like that for some time, long after Robert Coleman's tears had ceased. He was in her arms. He held on tight.

That was the way Lloyd and Ellen found them. They had learned about Clyde at the graduation. Martha and Tuck Riley found them and told them. They said Robert had taken off somewhere and they were worried. Lloyd and Ellen had gone straight home. They decided Ellen would stay there in case he came to the house, while Lloyd would leave and go looking for him. But upon returning to the house, they discovered Maureen had gone to the store. When she did not return, they got worried and went to look for her.

They entered the store through the front door and found them sitting there together, holding each other in the storeroom like there was no one else in the world. Ellen watched her daughter hold him. She saw Robert holding on for dear life. She considered the two of them. At only seventeen, they had already lived through more than she and Lloyd had lived through in their whole lives. She ached for them, but there was nothing she could do. She could not turn back the clock. There was no going back.

Ellen watched her daughter. It was so utterly female, so like a woman, what Maureen had done. For herself, she would not fight. She would disappear. She would not face or speak of what had happened at the Johnsons. She would simply disappear, because for herself there was no fight in her. But for someone else, someone being hurt, someone in pain, she would go to war against anything. Her own fears, her own pain, were forgotten. She became consumed with protecting someone else. It was nature. And while Ellen was wise enough to appreciate a woman's protective nature as an exclusive gift, when it came to her daughter, she wished that things were different.

Ellen realized, as she watched Maureen holding Robert, that she had made a very grave mistake. She wished that she had taken the time to teach her daughter a very important truth. A woman cannot truly protect anyone or anything, unless she can fight like hell for herself. Ellen knew, in that instant, that she had done a great disservice to her daughter, one that would have far reaching consequences. But it had never occurred to her before now, because life had been so kind, and she had been blessed with so much. There had never been anyone or anything to protect herself from, and now her daughter didn't even know how. Ellen could only hope that in the end her example would be enough. She prayed that in the end it would be enough.

Lloyd broke the silence. "Robert, we heard. Are you all right, son? You're mother is looking for you. She's worried."

"He's all right, Daddy. He just needs a minute."

Lloyd and Ellen almost fell on the floor. They hadn't heard Maureen's voice in so long; they had forgotten what it sounded like. For a moment Robert was completely forgotten. They looked at each other in disbelief. Then they heard someone rapping on the front window of the store. Lloyd went to see who it was. It was Tuck and Martha. He let them in.

"He's here. He's in the back." Lloyd told them.

Martha felt her whole body relax. She figured he needed to be alone, to grieve. She remembered the scene from the night before, at the house. She was still a little worried that he might harm himself. She had always feared that. But now, seeing him sitting safely in Maureen's arms, she could breathe again. He was all right. Now she could focus on something else. Clyde was dead, and she was so angry right now she couldn't even see straight.

If she could bring him back, she would kill him herself. How dare he go and die after that scene with Robert! Why couldn't he have died before, or even some time after? So that Robert's last memory of his father wasn't the argument that they had. She could forgive anything. In fact, she had forgiven everything, but not this. She would never forgive him for this. And she couldn't even yell at him. She couldn't even hit him. He was dead. He was gone.

"Son," she addressed him gently, carefully. "I have to go with Tuck. I had them take the body to the county coroner's office. I want an investigation done because he didn't die at home. You understand?" Robert nodded.

"I'm going with Tuck to Wanda Parker's house," she told him.

He looked at his mother and got to his feet. "I'm going with you."

She started to tell him no, but she couldn't. She knew he would want answers too. If they waited, they may never get them. It was better to go now, while Wanda was shocked and sober. Robert took Maureen's hand. She walked out the door and got into the back seat of the sheriff's car with him. Martha got in the front. They drove away, heading to Wanda Parker's house down by the river bottom. Lloyd stood on the front steps of the store with Ellen and watched them go, wondering what in the hell had just happened to his daughter.

No one said a word as they drove out of town. Robert braced himself as they came to a stop in front of the Parker place. The house was in desperate need of repair. Nothing had been done to it since Wanda's old man had died. It was falling apart.

They walked up the creaking steps. Robert's skin felt warm and clammy. It was an area referred to as "the river bottom." The house was built under a cloak of trees, so densely shaded there wasn't much light or air. Something was bothering him. He realized that he still had his graduation gown on. He hadn't even realized it until now.

"I must look ridiculous," he said. He let go of Maureen's hand just long enough to fumble with taking the gown off. She helped him get it off quickly, sensing his vulnerability, taking his hand when he touched hers again. Tuck knocked hard on the door.

"Open the door, Wanda."

After what seemed like an eternity, Wanda Parker came to the door. She looked Martha in the eye. She was so ugly. Her wild hair was all over the place. "I don't want no trouble," she told them.

Martha, always a lady, didn't flinch. "I've not come to bring any. I've brought my boy. We just want to know what happened to Clyde. That's all."

No one would ever know what Martha Coleman was feeling that day. No one would ever know that she wanted to knock Wanda Parker to the ground, jump on top of her, and pull her hair out of her head. She wanted to unleash all the pain of the last fifteen years upon her, upon this woman that had been living with her husband. Instead, she was kind. She was composed. Martha was no fool. Right now, Wanda had power. She had answers. Martha would control herself for her son. He would need to know what happened to his father, for closure. She knew that. She had no intention of stealing that from him.

Wanda told them to come in. Robert looked at the house. It was filthy. There was stuff everywhere, dirty clothes, bottles of booze, some empty, some half full. He could see the kitchen. There were dirty pots and dishes everywhere. The trash can was overflowing. Trash spilled onto the floor. It was a disgusting scene. Robert thought about his own house. They were poor. There was no doubt about that. But his mother had made a decent home for them, a good home. Their house was clean. Yes, it was dreadfully small and they didn't have much, but it was happy, and there was love and goodness. There was no goodness here. As he looked around the house, seeing cigarette butts where cigarettes had been put out on the floor, and mouse droppings in a corner, he couldn't help but think about his father. This is what he lived in, he thought. This is where he spent his last moments. It was devastating. Robert hadn't known what his father's life was like, but he never guessed it was quite like this.

It was then, sitting on the sofa in Wanda Parker's filthy house, that he told himself he would never live like that. For some reason, his father had been drawn to filthy living, like a moth to a flame. But not Robert. He would live a clean life, doing right. He never wanted to turn out like his father, to have an end like that. He didn't need to hear a thing that Wanda Parker had to say anymore. He held Maureen's hand tightly in his own. He had seen all he needed to. He made up his mind right then and there. He would live right. He would do right. So that he would have a good life. And he was sincere. For the rest of his life, he would try. The only problem was, with Clyde Coleman for a father, right and wrong weren't always so clear.

# Elise

NOVEMBER 1965…

…John 3:16. She didn't actually hear the words but they were there, heavy, solid, creeping into the corners of her mind. She lay outstretched in the handmade wooden pew, her ruffled eyelet ankle socks and black patent Mary Janes resting comfortably on the hard wood of the pew, while her head lay on her mother's lap. Maureen sat stroking the curly blond tendrils at her daughter's temple, tucking them behind her ear. Every now and again, Elise felt the cool breeze of her mother's paper fan, as it lulled her into a still deeper sleep.

And so it went on Sunday mornings for Elise Coleman, five years old, sweet and soft, blond curls and big blue eyes, bathed in light and love and goodness. In and out of consciousness, she was serene and secure, eventually awakened by an invitation for sinners to repent and save their souls from the fiery depths of hell accompanied by congregational singing. Still half asleep, she stood for the closing prayer, along with her parents and her big sister, Frances. Frankie winked at her. They were both glad it was almost over.

As far as the Coleman girls were concerned, the best thing about Sunday was lunch. Church services were usually followed by a big meal. Elise loved fried chicken, banana pudding, and sweet iced tea.

Frankie couldn't wait to get out of there. She was starving. She never understood how her sister could sleep through church. The preacher was so loud. She wished she could sleep through it too, so that it would go by faster.

Frankie and Elise had not developed the attention span for the hellfire and brimstone sermons that their parents appeared to love listening to. In fact, the preacher's sermons would have been enough to scare the living daylights out of the two little girls had they been remotely interested, and if they weren't so used to hearing them.

As soon as old Jack Ramsey, with his blue suit smelling like mothballs and his gray hair growing out of his ears, said "Amen," Frankie and Elise Coleman took off. They weren't unlike the other children at the little church, waiting and listening for that one word that meant freedom. It was "Amen" after the closing prayer. They raced out of the church with all the other children to play outside on the green church lawn, while their parents visited. Elise almost ran over Mrs. Vera Jeanne Rollins.

"Elise Coleman, how old are you now?" Elise stopped in her tracks. She knew better than to keep going.

"Five, ma'am," she said with her eyes downcast, afraid she was about to get it.

"You're getting a little too old to be running out the door," the old lady told her, visibly disgusted with her.

"Yes, ma'am. Sorry, ma'am." Elise looked like she might burst into tears at any moment. She did not mean to almost knock the old lady over.

Maureen came up behind her daughter and put her hand on her shoulder. It was a gesture of reassurance. It was a gesture of protection. "Hello, Mrs. Rollins. How are you today?" Maureen Coleman flashed her beautiful smile at the cranky old lady.

It only resulted in making her more cranky, seeing Maureen looking so pretty and so obviously well to do. Vera Jeanne Rollins did not care too much for Maureen. "Too high and mighty," she always said.

"I'm well, thank you. But I was just telling your Elise that she's getting too old to be running out the door after church. She needs to learn to control herself."

Maureen looked at the old lady that was poured into her navy Sunday dress looking like a stuffed sausage. Mrs. Rollins wore a permanent scowl. Maureen imagined telling her all that she really wanted to, like how her grandson had thrown a rock at the window of the store last week, after being told several times to stop throwing rocks, and had broken it. Bob told the boy's father about it but had not made a big stink. They knew that Tate Rollins could not afford to fix it. It was enough that he was truly sorry and would talk to the boy.

Maureen wanted to speak her mind. She wanted to tell Mrs. Rollins that she wasn't fooling anyone, that this was not about a five year old little girl running her over on her way out of the church building. It was much deeper than that. It had begun long before Elise. It was the green-eyed monster with a dose of self-righteousness, plain and simple, that try as she might Maureen could not escape.

Instead, she smiled sweetly at the old lady and dismissed her. "Elise is just overflowing with love for the Lord this morning, ma'am, rejoicing in his grace."

"Let the old bat argue with that one," Maureen muttered to herself.

She took Elise's hand. And with all the dignity she could muster she walked away, leaving Vera Jeanne Rollins staring at her back.

She waited until they were out of earshot to address her daughter. Maureen saw her little girl put on her brave face and prepare for a talking to, but Maureen did not feel like reprimanding her this morning. She recognized how difficult it was for the girls to sit still for that long sermon, just listening to the preacher drone on. And besides, Maureen felt good this morning. It was a beautiful November day. The sun was shining, but there was just enough of a cool breeze to make the warm sunshine welcome. She loved this time of year, before winter came. Just when she thought she could not stand another minute of the suffocating Texas heat, she would find herself on a day like today, her skin touched by the coolness of fall, the blazing Texas sun forgotten for a time.

"Next time, why don't you run over Mrs. Spears?" Maureen giggled.

Elise looked up at her mother. She was confused. "Run over Mrs. Spears? Why?"

"She likes you," Maureen stated matter-of-factly.

Elise grinned. That explained everything. "Mrs. Spears does like me." She nodded to her mother.

"Now, go have fun. We'll be leaving soon."

The little girl turned to run off. "Wait." She stopped and called out to her mother. She wrinkled her cute little nose, squinting at the sun. "Can I ride home with Nana?"

"Yes, but y'all have to come straight home for lunch."

Frankie heard the exchange. "Can I ride with Nana too?" She pleaded.

"Yes, you both can, but hurry home so that we can eat."

The girls took off. They went to play tag with the other children, underneath a grove of oaks to the left of the church building.

Maureen went to find her mother. Ellen Adams was visiting with the church ladies. More and more often, it seemed that this was the highlight of her week. She would stay outside on the front lawn of the church, visiting. Some days they were still there long after the preacher locked the front door.

Ellen had always attended church, but since she had become a widow about eight years ago, she had gotten more involved in it. It seemed that there was always something that the church ladies were involved in. Ellen had always known that church ladies in a small Texas town were a force to be reckoned with. They could feed a whole town, after a funeral, on a moment's notice. They could mobilize in seconds, in the midst of a crisis, with a strategy, a chain of command, and a thirst for victory that rivaled any army in the world. Ellen had found her calling.

After Lloyd passed, she became the most effective, the most unconventional, and the most popular of all the church ladies. She decided that they needed her. They needed some new ideas, some new goals, a new attitude. So it became her mission to revolutionize the church ladies. Sure, there were a few like Mrs. Rollins that fought tooth and nail to make her feel unwelcome, to try and scare her away. Sometimes it worked. But it was the people who needed her, that loved her, that genuinely appreciated her, that strengthened her resolve. The busy bodies would always try to make her feel unwelcome. That was nothing new. But Ellen did what she wanted to, and she had decided that she wanted to be a church lady. There weren't enough self-righteous busy bodies in Kilroy that could keep her from it.

Ellen saw her daughter approaching. She thought Maureen looked especially lovely this morning. Maureen always wore her clothes well, because she was so slim, only today it looked like she was beginning to show a little. She was pregnant with her third child.

Ellen thought about her two precious granddaughters and wondered where they had gotten to. She had seen her son-in-law. Bob had been talking to the preacher about donating some goods to some of the families that were having tough times. Ellen had gone in search of her friends, not wanting to get into his business. Since Lloyd's death eight years ago, she had removed herself from that business. She helped Bob if she could, when he asked. But she had enough sense to stay out of things unless he asked for her opinion. It was his business now, and Maureen's.

She had run the store herself for a while after Lloyd died, with Bob's help. But in the end, she had Adams Grocery appraised, then gave it to Bob and Maureen. That very same day, she went to the bank and withdrew the exact value of the store from her own account, took it to another bank, and deposited it into an account for Annalyn. Cash money. Independence. Done. Fair and square. She still had more money than she could ever spend, with investments that generated a handsome monthly income. Annalyn could go into business for herself when she came of age. The store belonged to Bob and Maureen. Ellen wanted to travel, see the world, meet new people. She wanted to make the most of the time she had left. Whether she had two days or two decades left, she wanted to live it to the fullest.

Ellen spotted the girls. Her heart warmed at the sight of them playing in their pale green Sunday dresses on the church lawn. Frances was growing up. She watched her talk and giggle with the other little girls her age. For so long, she couldn't even look at that child without thinking about losing Lloyd. He passed away in her arms the day after she was born. It took some time, but eventually when the gurgling baby turned into a little person, with a voice and an opinion and a personality, Ellen stopped looking at her in terms of losing Lloyd. She ceased gauging life without him in terms of her growth, and started seeing Frances, her granddaughter, that jumped into her arms when she saw her, the very same little Frances that begged to ride in the car with her and clapped her hands when the top was down. The 1957 Thunderbird... Lloyd's last gift to her. She smiled, remembering. He had bought it for her right before he passed. How happy he had been when he gave it to her. The beautiful car, with the convertible top, the chrome, the whitewalls... She turned her gaze back to her girls. She would drive that Thunderbird 'til the wheels fell off.

Just as she was about to call Frankie, she saw Thomas Aaron ball up his six year old fist and punch her precious Elise right in the stomach. She ran to the child. She watched Elise sputter for breath. She watched her struggle to keep standing. She saw the tears blur her granddaughter's pretty blue eyes, and saw the pleading in them for her to stay where she was. Ellen Adams stopped just short of snatching that kid baldheaded.

With wobbly five year old dignity and her voice shaking, Elise told the boy, "It's true and you know it." Then she walked toward Nana and took her hand. It was only when she felt her hand in Nana's, and knew he could not see her, that she let the tears slide down her sweet little face. Ellen's heart was breaking for her little granddaughter, and yet she knew already that Elise's mouth had once again caused her some serious heartache. The smart little thing had a mouth on her and a wit that matched it, and at five years old hadn't the slightest idea how to control either one. Ellen knew before she even heard the child's story that Elise had once again become the victim of her very own mouth.

The little girls climbed into the convertible Thunderbird. The usual pleasure at riding with Nana in her car was gone for Elise. Ellen pulled the car out of the church parking lot and began the drive home. She looked down at the top of Elise's head. The child's head was down so that Ellen could not see her face. She saw her little ankles with their white ruffled socks and black patent shoes sticking straight out. They were still too little to reach the floorboard. Frankie kept quiet.

She didn't want to set her little sister off. She hated to hear her cry. Elise didn't cry very often, but when she did it was a loud wail that made everyone wince in agony to even have to hear it.

They rode in silence until they turned onto Anneville road. The dust began to trail behind them and Ellen spoke. "All right, now tell Nana what happened."

Elise looked up at her grandmother. Fresh tears began to well in her eyes. "Well, Tommy kept pulling my hair and calling me a pickaninny."

Ellen was calm and stared straight ahead at Anneville Road. "And what is a pickaninny?"

Elise thought about it, puzzled. She thought this would explain everything. Surely, Nana knew what a pickaninny was, even if she herself did not. "Well, I don't know," she said.

"And I'm quite sure Thomas doesn't either," Ellen replied.

Elise never heard the "but I bet his parents do" that was spoken under her grandmother's breath. Ellen knew full well that this insult was meant for Elise for one reason, and one reason only, and that was because that kid had heard his parents talking. Racial slurs, spoken just out of earshot, were something they had all learned to live with.

"But that does not explain why you got punched in the stomach, my darling."

Elise did not want to recount the rest to her grandmother, but she was too exhausted to protest or make something up, so she blurted out the truth. "I told him that I'd rather be a pickaninny any day than him that's too dumb to 'member his mem'ry verses in Sunday school."

"Ouch," Ellen returned.

Elise, at a mere five years old, had added insult to injury with that comment. If the boy had not been able to memorize his verses, then he would have been reprimanded in front of the whole Sunday school class by their contrary Sunday school teacher. Elise had poured salt in his little wound. But as far as Ellen was concerned, it was nothing compared to the venom that he spewed at her granddaughter. Kilroy had not forgotten all that came before little Elise. And while Elise had no idea why, they intended to make her pay for it every day of her life, in one way or another.

"Elise," Ellen stopped, searching for the right words for her granddaughter. "You have to learn to ignore people when they aggravate you. Don't let them get to you." She looked down at the little girl, with her big blue eyes looking up at her. Ellen couldn't help but smile. For heaven's sake, she thought, she's only five years old. How can I ever make her understand? She looked at Frankie, next to Elise in the front seat. Frankie waited for what Nana would say next. Ellen could tell that Frankie was following her, but then she was almost eight. Maybe Elise would understand when she was almost eight. Ellen hoped.

"I don't care if Thomas calls you a booger monster from the depths of the devil's nose, you do not speak back to him. Don't ever honor a dummy with a response. Do you understand me?" The two little girls erupted into peals of laughter. Could their Nana have just said booger monster?

With that, the convertible turned and they continued on to the house. The girls stood up in the front seat of the Thunderbird as they always did, and rode the rest of the way up the oak lined drive. The sun streamed through the beautiful canopy of oaks and Ellen basked in its warmth the way she always had. These were precious days, all of them, she thought. The good and the bad...

Maureen was putting the Sunday meal on the formal dining table when she heard the front door open. She heard her girls running to their bedrooms, stripping off their church clothes along the way. Her mother appeared. She began to tell Maureen about the incident with Thomas Aaron, then decided against it. Maureen was in her first stages of pregnancy. Ellen decided to keep it to herself.

"Anything I can do to help?" she asked her daughter.

"No, not really. Everything is already done."

Ellen looked around at the beloved farmhouse, the house she had grown up in. Now her daughter was raising her family in it. Ellen loved watching them make a life on the farm that she had loved so much as a child, the very place where she had been a child. She enjoyed watching her grandchildren grow up on the land that she had loved so much. She and Lloyd had raised Maureen and Annalyn in town, close to the store. But even so, family life had always revolved around the farmhouse. Mama and Papa had lived in it up until they couldn't really take care of it anymore, at which point they had bought a little house in town, close to the grocery store and church, so that it was easier for them to get around. Ellen had sold her house in town after Lloyd died, and built herself a little cottage on a few acres of land, just down the road from the farm. But it was the farmhouse, the last house down Anneville Road, that still held her heart. The spot at the end of the road called to her, flooding her with memories, making her laugh, and making her cry. She loved the sound of the creek. She could always hear it from the front porch. It spoke to her soul in a way that was familiar, in a way that was alive.

Bob entered the room and caught her off guard. "Hello there, mother-in-law." He patted her on the back and bent down to kiss her cheek. She smiled and told him that he was about to have a new foal in a few days. He grinned at her. "You saw Lila?" He asked her.

"Yes, she'll be delivering any day now."

"After lunch I'm going to put her in the barn and keep her there 'til she has her baby."

Ellen nodded. They talked about all that was going on around the farm, and a little about what was going on at the store. Elise came running in. Her father scooped her up and kissed her all over her little face. She giggled and squealed. "Daddy, stop. Stop!"

He told her that he heard that she had been picking fights at church with Tommy Aaron. She looked at Nana accusingly. Nana's eyes said no. She had not told about what happened. "Who said that?" she asked her father.

"Never mind. How many times do I have to tell you that you have to get along with everyone? You want to have friends don't you?"

"No, because they are mean to me."

Bob studied his daughter. Then he spoke firmly to her. "Elise, you have to be nice to those kids. If you don't, you are going to be all alone with no friends and no one to play with, and everyone will talk about you and make fun of you. Is that what you want? Is it?" Her father's grip on her arm was a little too tight. It hurt. It brought tears to her eyes.

Ellen had to fight back her tongue from ripping him to shreds. Didn't he realize what he was doing to Elise, what he was doing to them all? But he didn't, he had no idea what he was doing.

In his desperate attempt to protect his children, he was ruining them. He was distorting their perception of life, every day making them more concerned with what others thought of them and less concerned with the things that really mattered. And while Ellen loved her son-in-law, had loved him even when he was just a young boy working in the store, she spent every day of her life trying to undo the damage that he was doing to his family, to her family. She was getting tired.

It was Elise that she worried the most about. Frankie was a quiet child who loved her books and her toys. Even at seven years old, she always thought before she spoke, and was very mindful of what was going on around her. She was also a little rebel, but she knew how to control herself. It was as if she had already learned how to get by in Kilroy. She knew how to avoid trouble. Elise was a different story. She was a train wreck. She was a wild child, with a heart bigger than any Ellen had ever seen. She had a love for practical jokes that she most assuredly had inherited from Lloyd, and a mouth and a wit quicker than any child should. She was so strong willed that she scared Ellen. Ellen was afraid for her.

Whenever she looked at Elise, she missed Lloyd so much it made her sick. She wished he had been here to see this one. He would have loved her so much and he would have been so good with her. Instead, in his absence, Ellen picked up the slack. Elise became her sidekick. Ellen would keep her very close, very closely indeed. She would watch after her, protect her, spend the last of her life desperately trying to breathe life into the spirit that her parents tried, unknowingly, to smother. For Bob and Maureen were afraid for her, as well. They knew full well the price of being different in a place where different was unwelcome. Her parents only wanted to protect her. Instead, all they did was wind up making her a prisoner.

They were just finishing Sunday lunch when Elise saw the sleek black Cadillac pull into the driveway. A smile touched her face and lit up her eyes. She recognized the car at once. Ellen walked out the front door to meet it, with Elise right behind her. It was Ruth, and she was smiling too.

"What are you doing here today?" Ellen called to her in surprise. "You didn't tell me that you were coming."

The two women embraced and walked up the steps of the farmhouse together, a little older, a little greyer, but just as glad to see each other as ever.

"I told you that I thought I might drive up this weekend to tend the graves."

"Yes, but I told you that I had already done it. I put fresh flowers out so that you didn't have to."

"I know, but I came anyway." Ruth grinned at her old friend.

Elise flew into Ruth's arms. Maureen greeted her with a kiss on the cheek and downcast eyes. Even after so long, she still could not

look Ruth in the eye. Bob exchanged pleasantries while Maureen set
an extra place at the table. They talked store business and got caught
up on the goings on of their families, until Ruth said she was ready
to go to the cemetery.

Maureen found Elise's sweater. She helped her daughter get her
little arms into it and buttoned it up. She kissed her on the cheek.
"Now you be good with Nana and Ruth. Don't run off."

"Okay, Mama," Elise said. The little girl hated to see her mother's
eyes. They were so sad when Ruth was around, so very sad.

Maureen watched her daughter run down the steps of the farmhouse and climb into the front seat of the Cadillac. She climbed over
Nana and sat between her and Ruth, satisfied to be in their company.

They drove through the gates of the colored cemetery and parked
the car. They walked the familiar path to the graves. Ellen and Ruth
sat down on the little wooden bench that Lloyd had built nearly a
decade ago, and as usual the two women got lost in conversation
while little Elise explored the old colored cemetery.

She thought about her sister. Frankie didn't like to go to the
cemetery. It gave her the creeps. But Elise, being Ellen's sidekick,
was used to it. She didn't think about death when she was there.
She thought about life. Each grave represented a life, a life that was
lived. Death never occurred to her. She would explore and play, and
was always just within ear shot of Ruth and Nana, and their stories.

She was a witness as they laughed, cried, and laughed some
more, first at the colored cemetery and then at the white cemetery. Then they would drive back to Ellen's house for the night.
Elise loved spending time with them. They made her feel safe.
They made her feel special. And they gave her a sense of history
that made her feel strong. She just wished that her mother was
not so sad when Ruth came to visit. And she hated it when her
father stopped speaking to them. He wouldn't even look at them.

Elise would always see her mother crying after Ruth left, even though she thought nobody noticed. It would take years and years of sifting through hateful words for Elise to understand why, and it would take nearly a lifetime to break the chains that bound her as a result of all that came before.

It wasn't her fault. She didn't even understand it. But for as long as she could remember, there was something there, something that hung over her, over them all. They must always be aware of what everyone thought if they wanted to be safe in Kilroy, if they wanted to be accepted. They must always be dressed impeccably. They must never get in trouble. Elise must be the smartest in her class, the best at her sport, the most popular, the prettiest. It was expected. She must never question anything. She must do all that was expected of her. It was understood. And each day that passed, this lesson was learned over and over again.

But then he came, the boy that would steal her heart, and he caused something to stir inside of her, the fire that her parents tried to put out. He awakened her spirit, made her believe that anything was possible, and she had to go. She just had to.

It was October, 1976, Homecoming Night, and Isaac Ingram pulled his 1973 Chevy Chevelle up to the visitor's gate of the football field. The game was just about over. He turned the motor off, turned the lights off, and waited. What if she didn't come? Would he go without her? He knew that he would not. He could not leave her to face everyone by herself.

He was just about to give up when he saw her. Still wearing her blue and white cheerleading uniform, she made her way to the car. Her long blond hair was parted down the middle and hung in two braids down her back. She began to run when she got outside the gate. He leaned across the seat and opened the passenger door. She got in and he drove away, steering with one hand, holding on to her with the other. It was only after they were safely out of town that they spoke.

"You sure?" he asked. She nodded and gave him a weak smile.

"You sure don't act like it." He was worried. He held her hand even tighter.

She studied his face. He was so handsome that he made her blush. She touched a lock of the sandy hair that fell over his ear. She disappeared into his green eyes for a moment, and then came back again. "I'm sure. I can't stay here. I just feel so bad for Mother and Daddy, and Nana. I'll miss them."

"Elise, you'll see them again. It's not like we're leaving the country. We're going to California. They can drive out and see us. We'll get a big house. They can stay as long as they want."

Elise nodded. "What do you think they'll do when they realize we're gone?" she asked him.

"Probably nothing. I'm seventeen. You're sixteen. And besides all that, your note explained everything, didn't it? Once they know, they won't come after you."

She reached up and kissed his cheek. He grinned at her. She didn't want to tell him that she hadn't been able to put her real reasons for leaving in her note. She just couldn't do that to them. She couldn't bear it. Even hundreds of miles away she just couldn't bear it.

It was about ten o'clock, Homecoming Night. Her parents would not know for a few more hours. They would be at the dance until midnight. They expected her to be home at eleven. When they came in to kiss her goodnight, they would see the note that she had pinned to her pillow. The thought was enough to make her sick. She decided to think about something else, something happy. She giggled.

"What is so funny?" Isaac asked her.

"I was just thinking about school, what everyone is going to think." She smiled up at him.

"They are all going to wish it was them."

"Of course, they will." She grinned.

He put his hand on her belly. It was firm, just barely beginning to round, revealing the secret that they had been keeping. It had been so difficult for her to tell him that she was pregnant. She had been so distant. He thought that she was getting ready to break up with him. If she did, he didn't know what he would do. He was so in love with her, couldn't imagine anything without her.

If it wasn't for Elise, he would have been long gone. When she told him that she thought she was pregnant, he began to develop a plan. He had to get them both out. He knew full well what Kilroy would do to her, and to his child. It had been bad enough for him. They had hated him since the day he moved there. He was an outsider. He could only imagine what they would do to Elise. She was one of them, but she had broken the rules. It was unforgivable. She was sixteen and pregnant, and Isaac Ingram was the father. The combination was inconceivable. They would make her pay, one way or another.

Elise did not want to leave her family this way. She would never have done it were it not for the baby. She could not bear facing her parents. She could not bear their disappointment. Of course, she feared her father's wrath. He would probably try to kill Isaac. He would be so angry. But more importantly she was afraid what her parents would do to her. She was only sixteen. What if they tried to take her baby? She would not take any chances. She would go with Isaac. No one was going to take that gift from her, ever.

Isaac Ingram was a free spirit. He was also a damn good musician. And from the moment he stepped foot in Kilroy, he was the talk of the town. He didn't talk like everyone, he didn't dress like anyone, and he didn't think like absolutely anybody in town. The first time Elise ever saw him she thought he was strange. Even so, she was drawn to him. Her parents thought that they had long since stifled any bit of creativity and rebellion left in her sixteen year old body, but in reality it was still there, just under the surface, at war with the fear of being different that they had instilled in her. Isaac made her question everything. He made her remember who she used to be, the light that her parents had tried to put out. She felt brave with him, and she hadn't felt that in so very long.

As she rode through the Texas night, she thought about the first time she saw him. It was the first day of the ninth grade, first day of school at Kilroy High. Everyone was talking about the new boy, how cute he was, how weird he dressed. He had moved to Kilroy from California, and he was an instant celebrity. His mother was a school teacher. His father was a writer, and a Jew. That was enough to get them run out of town.

The code of belonging in Kilroy was such that if you hadn't been born there, there was no chance you would ever be accepted. And if you had the misfortune of being born there, then you were held to their standard of belonging, that stripped you of every critical thought or independent idea that ever entered your mind. It took generations, lifetimes, to create such an atmosphere. No one ever really knew how the Ingrams ended up in Kilroy, but everyone knew that they didn't belong there.

Elise remembered sitting in English class. The teacher was quoting the Bible to them, making a claim about something the Scriptures said. Isaac asked, "Does it?"

The teacher did not know what to make of his comment. "Excuse me, Isaac, did you say something?"

"Yes. I said, does it? Does it really say that?"

Mrs. White's face had turned bright red and she had been angry with him. Elise was able to read her in an instant. She was angry at him for questioning her, but she was even angrier because she wasn't sure, and she knew that he knew that.

Elise had fallen in love with him that minute. He was larger than life. And to a powerless girl in a small Texas town, stripped of everything that makes her special, Isaac Ingram was like a drug. And before she knew it, she would not be able to get enough of him.

They had been drawn to each other, and before anyone even realized what was happening, they were inseparable. They had made plans for when they graduated, where they would go, the things they would do. The world was calling them. And for the first time in her life, Elise could see herself existing far, far away from Kilroy.

"So your friends know we're coming?" she asked.

"Yes, they're expecting us. Stop worrying." He grinned at her. He knew she was nervous, but he had thought of everything. He had made arrangements for them to stay with some friends until they could find a place of their own. He had enough money that they should not have to worry for awhile. He must remember to call his parents when he got to California. He told them that he would, in the note.

Elise snuggled close to him, rested her head on his shoulder, and fell asleep. He kissed the top of her head. There was absolutely no doubt about the choices he had made. He had to get her out of there. He swore he would never go back there for as long as he lived. He hated Kilroy.

They drove all night, only stopping to get gas. At daylight they finally rested. They got a motel in Albuquerque, slept all day, and headed back out, bound for Los Angeles.

As they drove into the city, Elise was speechless. It was early morning. The enormity of it overtook her. She looked at Isaac. He was ecstatic. He was home. She tried to look happy, but she was terrified. Elise studied everything outside her window. The people looked like they came from another planet. Their style of dress was unlike anything she had ever seen before. She looked down at herself, still wearing her cheerleading uniform. She looked like she was dressed for Halloween. Isaac watched her face. He did not like what he saw there. "Yes, don't worry. Our first priority after we get to the apartment is to get you some clothes."

She nodded, and watched while he parallel parked the Chevy Chevelle on the busy street. There was nothing but buildings everywhere. Elise had absolutely no idea where she was. He took her hand. They climbed several flights of stairs before he knocked on the door to an apartment, number 504. Elise felt sick. The door finally opened. A guy around her age, maybe a little older, stood there in jeans with no shirt on. It was obvious that they woke him. His dark hair was disheveled and he was barely coherent. Isaac hugged him and introduced Elise. The guy was Isaac's friend, Ross.

Ross was the lead singer of a band that played the local clubs in LA. He and Isaac had grown up together and had played music together all of their lives. He had been so excited to hear that his friend was blowing that Texas town and coming back. They needed a good guitar player. The only problem was that he wanted to bring his girlfriend. Ross was afraid that would cause some problems.

Elise was overwhelmed. Ross and Isaac began talking loud, faster and faster. Four other guys came out to see what was going on, with two girls. They were all yelling and hugging. Elise was forgotten. Finally, Isaac introduced her to the rest of the band. He explained to Elise that they had just gotten in from a local gig, and had just gone to bed when they heard the door. His friends took one look at her in her cheerleading uniform and could not contain their laughter. She was crushed. "I suppose I do need to get some different clothes," she said. Then she laughed it off and acted like it didn't bother her, a skill she had honed from growing up in Kilroy. She was far too overwhelmed to say or do anything else.

Isaac began to make breakfast with his friends. He kept checking on her, making sure she was all right. She told him that she was fine.

Little did he know, she was busy convincing herself that she had made the right decision, the only decision for the baby.

After they ate, everyone found a place and bedded down. Elise and Isaac made a bed of blankets on the living room floor. She settled into the crook of his arm and fell asleep, wondering what was going on at home, missing everyone there desperately.

She was the first one to wake up. She roused Isaac and told him that she couldn't sleep anymore. They went and bought some clothes for her and a few groceries. He told her he had to practice with the band. They had a gig that night. He told her that it wasn't far away. She could stay at the apartment and rest if she wanted to. She was terrified. She would go with him.

She dressed and got ready for the evening in the new blue dress they had bought. It had an empire waist. She thought it would go a long way in covering her growing belly. As soon as she walked into the club where the band was playing, she wished that she had stayed behind. She had never felt so out of place in her whole life. Their clothes, their shoes, she had never seen anything like it in Kilroy. The bell bottoms and collars were bigger than any she had ever seen. It wasn't long before everything about L.A. made her homesick. All she could think about was Texas, home.

Even though Isaac had spoken to his parents, and she was sure he knew what was going on, she had not asked. She didn't want to know. They had finally saved up enough money to get their own apartment, but life was still miserable for Elise. She was completely dependent on Isaac. It wasn't his fault. In fact, he really didn't know what to do with her. She was afraid of everything.

She was terrified on the evenings when he had to leave her alone. She would stare at the clock until she heard his key in the door. She could not go to the clubs with him anymore. She was getting close to delivering the baby. The doctor's guess was that she had about three weeks to go.

It was around eleven o'clock on Saturday night when Elise heard a knock at the door. She had been gone from home for four months. She was too scared to move. She knew it wasn't Isaac. He would not be home until much later. The knock persisted. She sat in her nightgown, just on the other side of the door, listening.

"If you're in there, you better open the door before I break it down."

It was her father. She didn't know what to do. Bob Coleman began to pound on the door. At last he heard the sound of the chain. Slowly the door opened. His heart leapt at the sight of his daughter, and then the light in his eyes went out at once. She was pregnant, very pregnant. He had no idea.

He felt like he had been kicked in the stomach. He was going to kill Isaac when he found him. Elise saw the realization in her father's eyes and wanted to disappear. She wished she could disappear.

"Where is he?"

"He's gone." She couldn't even look at her father.

"He left you here alone?" Bob was horrified.

"He plays in a band. They're playing at a club, not too far from here."

"Get dressed. I'm taking you home."

Elise stood there searching his face. "Daddy, I can't go home."

"Yes, you can. Everyone's gonna' talk, but you're coming home anyway."

"Get dressed, Elise." The tears began to stream down her face.

"I'll take you to tell him goodbye, but you're coming home with me."

Elise got herself dressed. Her father couldn't even look at her. He looked through her. She wanted Isaac. She wanted him to rescue her. She locked up the apartment and left with her father. She got into his pickup. As she rode through the streets of L.A., life felt like a dream. None of it seemed real. They parked outside Onyx night-club and walked to the door. The doorman waved them away. Elise explained to him that she needed to talk with Isaac Ingram in the band. He took one look at her belly and told her to hold on.

He finally came back and told her that the band was on a twenty minute break and that they were in the corner by the bar. She followed his direction, with her father close behind her. It was dark and smoky. The music was loud, and people stared at her. Her eyes surveyed the bar for Isaac. She saw Ross and the others. Then finally, there he was. He was sitting with a woman. They were deep in conversation, and a little too close for Elise's comfort. She walked over to him. He finally noticed her approaching and got up to meet her. The look in her eyes ripped his heart out. Her heart was broken, beyond repair. He would explain it. It wasn't what she thought. Then he saw him, her father, right behind her.

Elise stood before him with empty eyes and told him that she had come to say goodbye. Her long curly blond hair was all over the place. The long ivory dress that she wore accentuated her belly, brought attention to the baby, his baby. Isaac watched her. She was so self-conscious standing there in the nightclub. She had no idea how beautiful she was. She had no idea that he didn't even see other women anymore, didn't even notice them. She was gone before he even realized it, and he never got to tell her that she looked just like an angel.

Bob Coleman took a step toward him and whispered in his ear. "I've got a gun in my pocket, and if you make one move to stop her I'll blow you away. You kidnapped my daughter."

Isaac nodded. He understood. He had lost this one. He searched Elise's eyes. What he saw in them scared him. She was gone. "I'll come for you. We're married. He can't keep you there forever. You're almost seventeen, and it's my baby. He can't keep you away from me."

Elise looked at him with dead eyes. She nodded and then she reached up and kissed his lips. It was a kiss that would haunt him for the rest of his life. And then she was gone.

She wouldn't remember any of it, nothing of her time in L.A. She would not remember the silent journey back to Kilroy, the child's birth, or anything else about those days. She became a prisoner at the house, the last house down Anneville Road.

It was only when the child began to recognize her that Elise came back to her senses. She was a mother, and everything in her world revolved around her child. She named her Reid. No one else would ever know why, but Isaac would. He would recognize it. He would remember the night the two of them sat up for hours, reading the Scriptures together, how he had translated Hebrew for her, and she had learned that the Red Sea was actually the Sea of Reeds, what it had meant to her. She had learned so much from Isaac. She had learned that there was so much life outside of Kilroy. She had learned that things were not always what they appeared. "Truth as told by a liar is not truth at all." She heard him say it a million times.

The baby's name would be Reid. She was adamant. But the last name would be Coleman, for it was the only chance she had, in the event that Isaac never came for them. She was far too scared to leave by herself. So Reid it was, Reid of the Sea of Reeds that Israel passed through on their flight from Egypt, on their way to freedom. There was no middle name, just Reid. Reid Coleman.

Elise stayed hidden for as long as she could, safely tucked away, way down Anneville Road. The early days were easy. She spent them with Reid. She worked the farm. Her mother and father left every morning to work at the store. Some days Elise would pack Reid up and take her down the road to Nana's. Some days she would just take her all over the farm with her. She fashioned a sling and tied the baby around her, took her on horseback wherever she went. They were simple days. They were happy days. She threw herself into the child. It wasn't long before she stopped thinking of Isaac. She forced him from her thoughts. There was so much else to contend with.

She made very few trips into town, and when she did go it was only with Nana. Nana was the only one that she trusted to keep her safe. Of course, she would never escape the comments, or the looks. They would be there for the rest of her days. But no one dared anything more menacing with Ellen Adams, the matriarch, by her side. Ellen's mere presence commanded them, forbade them, whether they liked it or not.

And so the child grew in the light of Elise's love. With her blazing red curls and her haunting grey eyes, she wrapped each and every one of them around her chubby little finger. But none any tighter than Bob Coleman himself, for he fell completely in love with his little granddaughter. She took a little bit more of his heart each and every time she fell asleep on his chest, and she never, ever gave it back. There was something about her that made everyone love her.

"It's the way she looks at you," Ellen said, "like she knows something."

Elise didn't know what it was. But there was one thing that she knew for sure. Reid was loved. Deeply, beyond measure, the child was loved. It warmed her heart. It made her happy. She forgot about herself entirely. For them to love her baby the way that they did was more than she could ever have hoped for. At merely sixteen, Elise's life was over. Everything revolved around Reid. The sun rose and set on the top of her red curls, and Elise Coleman's hopes and dreams for herself were gone. She threw herself into securing a place in the world for her daughter. She never had a chance.

# Isaac

JULY 1978...

He had no idea what he would find. The Texas landscape flew by him as he sat in the back of the black limousine, with thoughts of her and his child running through his mind. His mind's eye tried, but could not focus on them. He hadn't seen Elise in so long, and he had never seen the child. He knew it was a girl. It had gotten back to him somehow. Someone had told his parents before they moved back to California. He hadn't had any contact with Elise since the night she left him standing there at Onyx. He had relived that night over and over in his mind since then.

He told the driver that the turn was coming up. It would be a right onto Anneville Road, and then all the way down to the end. Satisfied that his driver understood, he waited, and wondered what he would find.

He told the driver to pull into the driveway. The imposing car came to a stop in front of the farmhouse. All was quiet. Isaac got out of the limousine and walked up the steps to the front door. He was already sweating. His t-shirt was sticking to him. The Texas heat was unbearable.

He stood on the steps of the old farmhouse. He looked back at the limo. It was striking sitting there in the driveway. He had chosen it for one reason and one reason only. He may still seem like a kid, but he was a kid that had traveled all over the world with the most famous band in the country, and he wanted everyone to have no question over what had become of him. He had made it. "The best guitar player on the planet," they had said about him. Now he was coming back for Elise, and the child.

He knocked on the front door. There was no answer. He listened hard. There was no sound. He looked around and saw a pickup parked at the barn. He walked around to the back side of the farmhouse and saw no one. He was thinking of leaving and coming back later when something caught his eye. It was her. The bright red of her curls was blazing in the sunlight. She was with Bob, out in the garden. This was not what Isaac hoped to find. He wanted to find Elise first.

He began to walk past the big barn, down to the garden. Bob had seen the car. He stopped what he was doing and watched the stranger walking toward him. He looked a bit familiar, although he couldn't place him at first. Then it struck him. It was Isaac Ingram. He picked the toddler up from where she stood in the watermelon patch and held her. She wriggled to get down.

"What do you want?" Bob Coleman asked.

Isaac stood before him and looked him right in the eye. "What do you think?"

Bob's hold tightened on the child and she began to protest. "Put her down, I'm not going to take her." Isaac spat the words. But Bob Coleman did not budge.

"I said put her down!" He yelled in the man's face.

Bob released his hold on the little girl and she toddled over to her spot in the dirt where she had been playing with her toys.

"You have no business here," Bob told him.

"Of course, I do."

Bob's heart began to race. He had to get rid of him. He had to get him out of there before Elise got back. He knew why he had come, and Elise was eighteen, she could do whatever she wanted now. He couldn't bear it. They weren't going anywhere. He just couldn't bear it. His fear overtook him. His fear of losing his girls, and his fear of what might become of them, took hold. Before he even realized what he was doing, he found himself telling the biggest lie his imagination could dream up.

"You're too late."

Isaac tore his eyes away from the child. "What are you talking about?"

"Elise, she's married."

"I know. She married me, remember?"

"No. That was illegal. She was underage and didn't have our consent."

"It was legal Bob, and you know it."

"No, it wasn't. But it is now. She got married and her husband adopted the baby, so you're out of the picture."

Isaac felt sick. "You're pathetic and you're a liar." He studied Bob's face for anything that gave the lie away. There was nothing. Surely, it wasn't true.

Bob saw the look on his face and knew he had him. He decided to finish him off once and for all. "She saw you that night, with that woman. She knew you were no good then. She met a good guy, found her a husband and a father for the baby."

Isaac looked at the child. She studied all that was going on between the men from her spot in the dirt. He felt sick. Surely, it wasn't true.

"I want to see Elise. I want to hear it from her."

"You really gonna' do that to her? Bring all that back up?" Bob clenched his fists. He hated Isaac. What this boy had done to his daughter was unforgivable. He had gotten her pregnant, taken her from her family, and left her in a dingy apartment in Los Angeles while he was out drinking and chasing women. The night Bob found Elise in Los Angeles everything he had hated about his own father, everything that he had tried so hard to forget, had come back to him. Bob Coleman had spent his whole life trying to prove that he was not his father. There was no way in the world that he would ever allow Isaac to leave Kilroy with his daughter and grandchild.

"Do you know what she's had to go through? And your coward ass just blew into town today? You're way too late, buddy."

"I'm not leaving here until I see Elise."

Bob was furious. He hated the boy. He didn't act like them. He didn't think like them. He was an outsider. Isaac had no idea that Bob wasn't even seeing him anymore. He saw his own father, based on his own judgement. He saw Clyde standing there threatening to take his happiness away, and he would never let that happen again. The only thing that kept him from blowing Isaac away with his shotgun was Reid. She was sitting there playing in the dirt, cautiously watching them.

"Do you have any idea what Elise has suffered because of you? Do you? She waited for you. We all knew she was waiting for you. All alone she endured it, all alone. She brought this child into the world and you never even showed up. She had to go on. You can't show up here now and start causing problems for them. You know this place. You start stirring things up and they don't have a chance."

"Of course, they do. They can come with me. I don't care if Elise is married."

"After that show you put on with that woman that night, you really think she would leave her life and go with you? You're filthy and she knows it."

Now Isaac was the one who was furious. "That was just some groupie at a bar. It wasn't anything. Nothing happened. I've never been with anyone but Elise."

"You'll never convince anyone of that."

Bob Coleman turned his back on Isaac and picked up his shovel. He went back to what he was doing, digging watermelons with his granddaughter in the watermelon patch. Isaac looked at the child. She had begun digging in the dirt with her grandfather. She was so beautiful. She turned around to look at him, and his heart stopped. What he saw there made him want to turn and run. She was scared of him. He could see it in her eyes, those grey eyes. He was a stranger to her, and she was terrified of him.

Out of the corner of his eye, Bob saw him studying the child. For a moment he felt something stir, regret, compassion, and then it was gone. "They've gone on without you, Isaac. Now you need to go on too. Let them be happy. If you ever really loved Elise you'd just turn around and leave. Don't bring it all back up again. It's too late."

So many thoughts went through Isaac's head, all at the same time, crashing into each other. He remembered seeing Elise's face that night at Onyx. She was crushed. She really thought he was with that woman? She must've. He had never been able to tell her anything different. He had sent letters, but he was sure they were intercepted. He had called and called, but someone changed the number.

And then time had gone by so quickly. He had been discovered one night playing his guitar at a hole in the wall in east LA. Before he knew it, he was skyrocketing to fame with a band that would soon become a legend. He had been touring all over the world since Elise left, and every dime he made he had saved for them. Everything that he had accomplished since that night had all been for her, and the child. He stood there as it all vanished right before his eyes on a Texas farm in the middle of nowhere. None of it mattered. Without them, none of it mattered.

He couldn't take it. The fact that Elise thought he was with that woman the night she left was too much for him. It made him sick. The woman wanted him, sure. But he wasn't interested. He only ever wanted Elise. She was the only one for him. He remembered how she looked that night at Onyx. She was standing there so very pregnant with her blond hair everywhere, in that long pale colored dress. He remembered how much he loved her. She had been so unsure of herself standing there, and there was no need. She was the most real and beautiful thing he had ever seen and everyone else in the room looked ridiculous. Oh, how he wished he could turn back time. He loved her so much it hurt. He wanted to take all of her pain away. The thought that he had been the source of it was something that he could not bear. Maybe Bob was right. Maybe the only thing he could do was walk away and let her be happy. She had been so afraid of L.A. And he had been so young, without a clue, not knowing what to do with her.

He would go. He had to. It tore his heart out to think they were afraid of him, the girl that he loved more than anything else in the world and his own flesh and blood. He took a couple of steps and felt as though his heart had been ripped from his chest. He walked back to the child and kissed the top of her blazing red curls. Then he left Bob Coleman with the words that would torment him every time he looked at his granddaughter.

"You think you can be God? Well, you can't. She's my flesh and blood and you can never change that. You will see me over and over again in her, and there's not a damn thing you can do about it."

Bob never even looked up. He kept digging until he heard the car drive away. He felt sick. He picked Reid up and held her close. She kissed his cheek with a slobbery kiss and he kissed her back. "Papa will keep you safe. Don't you worry," he told her. She giggled and slobber-kissed him some more, far too young and innocent to realize the tragedy that she had just witnessed.

Isaac told the driver to take him back to Dallas, to the hotel. He would leave today. He sat back and began to replay the last two years, how wrong they had gone, how nothing had turned out the way he expected. He never even saw the old Thunderbird pass, with the top down. If he had been paying attention, he would have seen Elise driving with her wild blond mane blowing in the wind, and Nana riding shotgun. He never even thought to ask the child's name. If he had heard her name, he would have known that Bob was lying, and if he had known that Bob was lying, how different things might have been.

Elise pulled the car up to the farmhouse and got out. Her blond curls shone in the hot July sun. She looked so frail in her jeans and boots. She barely ate anything anymore. She and Ellen walked out into the garden to get Reid. They had left her there with Bob to run into town for a few things.

Bob saw his daughter standing there. He felt so sorry for her. She had loved that boy so. Bob thought about his own mother. How much she had loved his father, in the beginning, until he became an alcoholic. He felt no guilt. In his mind, he had saved his daughter from his mother's fate. Even if Elise was the town outcast, at least she would be safe and well cared for.

Elise was worried about her father as soon as she saw him. He looked terrible. She told him that he needed to go inside and get a drink. "The heat must really be getting to you." He told her that he would.

From that day on, life became a terrible lesson in the power of a lie. The victims never even knew it, all except for one. He watched as Elise's youth slipped away, day after day, raising her daughter in her parent's house. He watched Reid develop into a beautiful, lost creature that was more foreign to Kilroy than any of them had ever been. He watched Isaac Ingram's rise to fame and his destructive behavior, knowing full well that he had pushed him over the edge. He watched Abby, Ellen, Maureen, Elise, and Reid, five generations, forge an alliance, share a bond that he would never enjoy, never understand.

As each day of his life passed, Bob became more protective of them and more afraid of losing them. They were his strength, his confidence, his reason for living. He also became more and more aware of the truth in Isaac's last words to him. No matter how they loved Reid, no matter how close they kept her, she was always just out of reach.

Bob's lies slowly devoured him. Isaac stayed on his mind. It wasn't long before everything he did was motivated by fear, the fear of seeing his girls hurt, and the fear of losing them. At the critical point in time when the making of choices was of the utmost importance, when it concerned right or wrong, Bob had chosen wrong. He had chosen the lie. He was afraid, afraid of all that was different, afraid of all that he did not understand.

And so Isaac Ingram spent his days and nights chasing the feeling of fleeing Kilroy with Elise by his side, chasing the high of youth and first love. But no matter where he went, no matter what he did, he would never even come close.

Life went on for them all. Time would find them back together again when the child became a woman...

Isaac turned on the news. He was exhausted from rehearsing his part to all of his old songs. He sat in his pajamas thinking about the concert tomorrow. His girlfriend brought him a glass of wine as he relaxed in his leather chair. He would watch the news and then turn in.

I'm getting too old for this, he thought. At almost fifty, he had long since stopped touring, but he had agreed to play a charity concert in Munich with the original members of Eye. As he sat there relaxing and preparing himself for the grueling travel and concert ahead, all of his travel plans, in fact all of his life for the past twenty six years, came to a screeching halt.

He processed all that the newscaster was saying. It was Texas, a hospital. He saw them, Ellen Adams, Bob Coleman, Maureen. They were on the news. What the hell for? He sat there and watched. He could not believe his eyes. Of course, the cast of characters were obviously older, but they were all there. Every last one of the people that had haunted his thoughts for the last thirty three years of his life were involved in some sort of drama, playing itself out on the news, World News.

He turned the volume up so loud that his girlfriend was annoyed. "Do you know those people?" the pretty blond asked as she watched his reaction.

"Shh." He snapped at her. He could not believe what he was seeing. That beautiful redhead, the one that he watched every night, everywhere he went, over a glass of wine at the end of his evening... Could it be? He studied her picture. She was his daughter. The realization flooded his senses. She was hurt, in a coma, in Texas. She had gone there on vacation.

And then his heart stopped in his chest. Elise stood there in the hospital, with a reporter from World. She had tears in her eyes. She was older, but still so beautiful. She spoke softly. He hung on every word. "Yes. Thank you, Steve. We would like to say thank you all for the kind words and prayers for Reid. We would also like to tell everyone to keep it coming. We will not give up on her, just like she never gives up on anything or anyone. Thank you."

Reid! He saw her name at the bottom of the screen. Her name was Reid Coleman. That's right. He remembered now, but he had never put it together. He had seen her hundreds of times on television and in print, but had never guessed that she was his daughter. How could he? This woman was a reporter for the most prestigious news conglomerate in the world. To him, his daughter was still a child somewhere in Texas. He sat in his chair with a glass of red wine in his hand, processing all that he had seen and heard. She was in a coma. What if there was something that he could do? Medically, what if he could offer something?

"Kelly! Call the guys. I'm not going to be able to make Munich."

"What are you talking about?"

"I said I'm not going to Munich." He challenged her with his eyes.

She was disappointed, to say the least. She loved traveling with him when he played different cities. Those times were few and far between now.

"Why not?" she asked.

"I'm going to Texas."

"Texas? For what ?" She was horrified. She had them both packed for Munich and he was telling her that he was going to Texas.

"You've lost it," she told him.

"Not this time. I've finally found it."

Something in his tone commanded her attention. He had been far too interested in that story about that reporter from World, as if it was personal or something. What if there was something going on?

"You're not going looking for that woman, are you?" she asked him cautiously.

"That woman is my daughter, and that is exactly where I'm going."

Isaac Ingram changed out of his pajamas into an old concert t-shirt, jeans, and boots. He threw some things into a bag, grabbed his leather jacket, and took the elevator down from his Manhattan penthouse to the street below where he hailed his own cab. He hadn't done that in years. He took a deep breath, the exhale clearly visible in the cold New York night. He hopped in the back seat and told the cab driver that he was headed to JFK. Then he prayed nonstop for the child that had grown up without ever having known him. Isaac was on a collision course with his destiny, and for the first time in a long while he felt completely and totally alive.

# Reagan

January 2010...

The phone woke them both. Reagan could see the light coming from Nana's room. He made his presence known by standing in the doorway. Ellen was sitting up in her bed, resting on the mountain of pillows that were propped up against the white wicker headboard. She was lost in a sea of pink and white. Her quilt was pink and white. Her pajamas were pink with white trim. Pink and white pillows were all around her.

She winked at Reagan, letting him know that she knew he was there. He studied her face but couldn't determine the nature of the call. Ellen sat in her bed, holding the receiver to her ear. She began to speak softly, in measured tones, as if she was speaking to a small child. "My darling, it's me. Don't you go anywhere. I'm getting my old bones out of bed and I'm on my way. I'm bringing Reagan. He's here with me. I'm keeping him safe. We've been waiting for you to wake up."

There was a pause, and Ellen spoke again. "Yes, of course. We're on our way."

Ellen looked at Reagan as he stood in the doorway of her bedroom, dressed in a navy and gray striped pair of pajamas. His face was hopeful, but still so very scared. "That was Elise. It appears our girl has opened her eyes."

"Did she say anything?"

"No, not yet. Elise said she's sedated, but let's get dressed and get to the hospital."

Reagan went back to the guest room where he hastily dressed in a warm sweater and jeans. He brushed his teeth, grabbed the keys to the rental car, and went looking for Nana.

Ellen stood in her pink bathroom. The door was open. He watched from the doorway as she carefully applied her makeup. "Got to put my face on."

He wanted to run out the door and get to the hospital as fast as he could. He wanted to get to Reid. But instead of being annoyed, Nana's presence calmed him. There was something about her demeanor that caused him to move through time with ease. She had seen so much. Her age, her wisdom, her manner of speaking, all had a soothing effect on him. He already loved her so very much.

At last she was ready, dressed in a grey wool pantsuit, silver sneakers, and matching handbag. The soft white curls on her head were combed and styled, and she looked so very pretty. "Nana, I don't know how you do it. You look so perfect even though the world is upside down."

Ellen smiled at him. "I've had a lot of practice."

They walked out the front door of her little stone cottage and into the cold January morning. The sun was barely peeking over the horizon. Reagan paused for a moment to consider his surroundings. Yes, it was beautiful. Texas was beautiful. He could see how Reid might love it so. But for him, it wasn't any more beautiful than any other place he had known. He thought of all that Nana had revealed to him last night, all that they had discussed. He thought of all the pictures he had seen, pictures of Reid in various stages of life, Maureen and Bob, Frankie and Bobby, Mama and Papa, Ruth Johnson and the girls, even a picture of Reid's father, with his guitar, on the front porch swing.

He knew that Reid was drawn to Kilroy, to this place, for reasons he would never understand. He longed to take her away and keep her safe from everything that had ever hurt her, so that it never could again.

He opened the car door for Nana and helped her in. Then he got into the driver's seat and started the Ford rental car. They drove down Anneville Road in silence, passing pastures with long horned cows and beautiful horses. There was nothing but land as far as the eye could see. This was Reid's home. He took it all in. This land was part of her and she loved every inch of it. Her entire family had worked it for at least five generations. This place was in her heart.

Reagan thought about his own family, how his parents longed for a land that he had never even seen. His mother and father had been young. Their families had been forced to flee Haiti under the brutal regime of its self-proclaimed President for Life, Francois Duvalier. He had heard the stories over and over since he was a child, but he had never paid them much attention. He thought about his parents now, and about Reid. It was essentially the same. They all loved and longed for a land and a people riddled with conflict, the source of much heartache. He had no such feelings about any place or any people. He had enjoyed a simple childhood, remembered no difficulties. Life had been easy and kind. Their intense feelings were something that he could not identify with. He had no concept of what pulled them in the direction of where they began.

At last they came to the highway. They made a left onto the farm to market road and drove the rest of the way into Kilroy, then on to Fort Worth. Reagan and Ellen said very little to each other, each lost in thought.

When they finally reached the hospital, they were shocked to see reporters there. They were camped out. It was World. Reagan recognized Steve Marshall speaking to the camera man. "What are you guys doing here?" he asked Steve's back.

Steve turned around to see Reagan standing there. "Reagan!" They shared a warm embrace. "Are you kidding? This is a huge story. Everyone is wondering what happened to Reid. We can't keep up. The fan base outcry has been huge. They want to know what happened. We have to be here. They are glued to the set all over the world, trying to find out what happened to their girl." Reagan couldn't help but grin.

Everywhere in the world that she went, people were drawn to her. They loved her, couldn't get enough of her. She had that effect on people. She made them stop and pay attention. She lived to tell a story, to wake people up. It was no wonder that World was there.

"Harvey will be here in an hour," Steve said.

"What?" Reagan was shocked.

"Yeah, said he's taking a leave of absence until she walks out of here. Said he's bringing her back to New York."

"Really?" Reagan had no idea.

"You thought you were the only one, Brother?" He slapped Reagan on the back. "No way. The whole world is in love with Reid Coleman."

Reagan grinned. He told him that he would keep him updated, then he disappeared with Ellen into the hospital to see what they would find.

The elevator seemed to take forever. Finally, it came to a stop. The doors opened. They walked to the nurse's station. "We're here to see Reid Coleman," they told the nurses.

One of the nurses recognized the tall handsome man as Miss Coleman's fiancée and told him she would go and get her mother. "I'll let Doctor Walker know that you are here also. He wanted to talk with you." Reagan began to feel sick. Doctor Walker was the obstetrician that specialized in high risk pregnancies. It must be about the baby. He braced himself for the worst.

The nurse disappeared down the hall and came back with Elise. Elise smiled at Reagan as soon as she saw him. His face was worried. She walked toward him, dressed impeccably in a camel colored blouse and matching pencil skirt, stockings and heels, perfectly accessorized. Her newly-bobbed blond hair was perfect, and her face looked fresh and rested. Where did it all come from, he wondered. How do these women keep it together like that? He had never seen anything like it.

"Good morning, Reagan. She knows you are here. She is speaking now."

"What? What did she say?"

"She cried," Elise told him. "Of course, the minute I told her that you were here, she knew that we all knew. I told her everything is fine. I told her that we had met you and we knew about the baby, and that everything is fine. She's waiting for you now."

Reagan walked down the hall and into the room. Reid's eyes followed him, searching his face as he came to stand over her. The tears began as she whispered to him, "I'm sorry."

He took her hand and kissed it, tears streaming down his own face. He couldn't even look at her. He was so ashamed of himself. He had been so angry with her. He had not understood anything. He had misread everything. Reid was too gentle, far too gentle for this world, and yet she was the toughest, strongest soul he had ever known. It was quite some time before he could speak. They just sat there, both of them crying.

He spoke first. "There's nothing to be sorry about. It's all right now. Everything is all right." He kissed her cheek and stroked her hair. He looked into her grey eyes and knew that he would never grow tired of them. He knew that he would never want anyone else, and if they lived a thousand years it would never be enough time.

He sent up a silent prayer of thankfulness, warring with everything inside of him to keep from breaking down in front of her. He had almost lost her. He would never let her go again.

Doctor Clayton Walker came in and smiled at them both. Young and in a hurry, he did not waste any time. He was on call and had several more patients to see, but he wanted to talk to them both, together, about the baby. "Okay, I know you want to know about the baby, now that the mother is out of the woods. As far as we can tell, everything is fine. There were never any abnormalities for as long as she was out. However, that doesn't always mean everything will come out okay. There could be something that we can't see, something that we missed. But I will tell you honestly, my gut instinct is that this baby will be delivered healthy."

There were a million questions that Reagan wanted to ask. He began his barrage. He felt Reid touch his arm. He looked down at her. Her eyes pleaded with him. "Reagan, don't. Let's just accept that. That is enough."

Reagan turned back to the doctor. "Never mind, I guess we're going to run with the hope that you just gave us."

Doctor Walker nodded, then looked at Reid. "You should be delivering in a couple of months, around the middle of February as far as I can tell. Without your medical records, I can't be exactly sure. And it's a little hard to tell on an ultrasound at this stage of the game. Just follow up with your doctor when you get back to New York. We'll fax all your records up there."

Reagan was concerned. "Are you sure, Doctor Walker? I mean she really isn't showing that much. Most people don't realize that she's pregnant. It just looks like she's gained a few pounds."

Doctor Walker grinned. "She's measuring about thirty-two weeks, which puts her delivery date right around the middle of February. I'm not worried about her size, and you shouldn't be either. She seems healthy, and so does the baby. This is her first baby. That can make a difference as well. Sometimes women don't show very much with their first pregnancy." Reagan felt much better. Doctor Walker shook both of their hands and was gone.

Reagan got into the bed with Reid. She was still weak and sore from the fall, but he gently picked her up and slid her over. He settled into the bed beside her. She relaxed and lay with her head on his chest. Neither one of them spoke. She lay listening to the beating of his heart, while he lay listening to the sound of her breathing. There were no words between them. They didn't need any.

Too soon, they were disturbed by one of the nurses. She came in to tell them that there were people that wanted to visit. "Once she is moved to a regular room she can have everyone she wants with her, but as long as she is in intensive care it's two at a time."

Reid began to protest to Reagan. "I don't want to see anyone else. Just stay with me."

"I'm not leaving. I'll be here. I'm going downstairs to see Steve Marshall. I'm going to throw him a bone."

"Steve Marshall? What are you talking about?" Reid was confused.

"It seems that Sleeping Beauty is all over the news." He couldn't help but laugh. "You are all over the news right now."

Reid's face turned bright red. She was horrified. She would go anywhere, do anything to tell a story, but when the focus was herself, when she was the story, she couldn't take it.

Reagan kissed her and left the room with the nurse. He made his way down the hallway and saw Elise standing there. She was deep in conversation with a man. Something was going on. He moved toward them, to tell them that they could go in now, but they didn't even notice him. They were lost in each other. The man was not Ron, her husband. He had seen Ron in photographs. This man was someone else, but someone familiar for some reason. Reagan felt as if he had seen him somewhere before. He overheard their conversation. He could not believe what he was hearing.

"I came back for you. Your father said you were married, said your husband adopted the baby."

Elise looked away. She could not look at him. "It was a lie, all of it. I waited for you."

"So, all this time you thought I just never came back for you?" the man asked her in disbelief.

"No, just ten years." She could hardly get the words out. "Reid was ten when I overheard my father telling my mother that you had come for us. She insisted that he tell me, but by that time it had been almost ten years. He refused. I never did anything about it. I figured it was too late by then."

"It has never been too late, Elise." The man looked at her. She had to look away.

Reagan struggled to make sense of all that he was hearing. The man was trying to explain something, leaving. Reagan felt as if he should not be standing there. He saw the look on Elise's face. She looked beaten. She looked tired, much different from the way she had appeared just a short while ago.

She looked up at the man. "Isaac, it was all so long ago. It doesn't even matter anymore." But her words were hollow. She didn't believe them any more than he did. "What matters right now is Reid. Go in there and meet your daughter."

Reagan studied the man. Isaac Ingram stood there, still as a stone, holding his leather jacket, dressed in his 1987 Eye Rock Concert Tour t-shirt, faded Italian jeans, and handmade boots. His hair was still a thick sandy mess, despite his age. He looked good. He was still so handsome, but his green eyes were different. They were older.

"I can't just go in there and introduce myself."

Elise couldn't help but smile at his insecurity, even though it was a serious situation. "Well, actually you can. You don't know your daughter, but I can tell you right now she's not like anyone you've ever met, or ever will meet again. She will be glad to see you, no questions asked. Come on."

Elise took Isaac by the hand and led him down the hallway. At some point they had noticed Reagan, but they hadn't even addressed him. The chemistry between the two was electric, almost visible. They were lost in each other at the moment, and Reagan was completely speechless at all that he had just witnessed. Isaac Ingram, THE Isaac Ingram, was the father that Reid had never met. Unbelievable.

Isaac Ingram had been all over the world. He had found himself in a Chinese jail once, had been beaten and left for dead on more than one occasion, had nearly died when he crashed his Ferrari in 1985, and had ultimately lived his life never being afraid of anything. How could he be afraid of anything, after the only thing he ever really cared about was taken from him? He paused outside the door to her room. He took a deep breath. Life was about to come full circle. He was about to come face to face with his daughter, and stand before the part of himself that was always missing.

Reid opened her eyes. She had dozed off after Reagan walked out, waiting for whoever was coming next. Her mother walked in holding the hand of a stranger. It took all the self control that Isaac had to keep from bolting out the door. She was so beautiful lying there in the hospital bed. She had Elise's hair. Isaac remembered Elise's wild blond curls. Only Reid's hair was red. And she had the most arresting eyes he had ever seen.

"Reid, it seems that you are all over the news. When this man saw the story, and me on the news, he realized that he was your father. He got on the first plane from New York to Texas to come and see you." A huge smile spread across Reid's face. Isaac felt it. It traveled across the room and touched his heart.

"I'm going to leave you two alone for a moment." Before he knew what was happening, Isaac was alone with Reid. He didn't know what to say. He just stood there.

"My favorite song of yours is Lost. You know, the one where you have the two minute guitar solo at the end. I played it every day of my life when I was a teenager."

He smiled. He was still amazed that this incredible woman was his daughter. He had followed her stories all over the globe and had never known. He just didn't even know what to say to her.

It was as if she read his mind. "I always knew who you were. Mother never kept it from me. I used to dream of you coming to get me. I would dream that I was far away from Kilroy, that I belonged with you. But what's funny is, when I woke up I was scared to death that you might actually come and take me away. Isn't that strange?"

Isaac said nothing. He just listened. "Everyone in town would talk about you. You know, the kind of talk that they pretend they don't want you to hear, but all the while they are carefully choosing the most hurtful of words to prick your heart and make you bleed." She swallowed hard and then continued. "But mother always told me how much you loved me. She said that truth told by a liar is not truth at all. So I just tuned it all out and went on."

Isaac recognized the words, words he had said to Elise so long ago. Finally, he found the courage to speak to his daughter. "I don't know how much you know, but I came back for you both. Your grandfather convinced me that it was best for you if I left and never came back. He lied to me. And I saw you that day, sitting in the dirt. You had to be about eighteen months old. It broke my heart to see you afraid of me."

Reid smiled at him. "It doesn't matter. I survived it. They didn't get me. It's Mother that had to pay. It's Mother that suffered the most."

Isaac nodded. He looked at his daughter. He couldn't control the words and he didn't plan them either. They just came. "Why did he do it?"

Reid looked at him with old, old eyes. "The way he masters his fear is control." She took a deep breath. "I am preparing to face his wrath. You saw my fiancée?"

"Yes, I did." He smiled at her.

"Did you consider the irony?"

Isaac was puzzled. He did not understand what she meant. She went on. "It hit me, while I was riding, right before I went down. Everything that he is afraid of, every situation that he has tried to control, has manifested in me, and I'm the one that he loves more than anything. My whole life he's been right there. He has been my shadow for as long as I can remember, always watching me with that look in his eye, his intense love for me at war with all that he did not understand about me. It's difficult... " She began to stare through Isaac, looking at something he could not see.

"I always wondered how I could be so incredibly different from my family, how I could be part of them and yet so different. I have come to realize that there is something much larger than myself at work, and that I was given to them for a reason. I don't believe for a moment that mere fate can be that absurd. I just haven't quite figured out what that reason is yet."

Isaac listened to all that she said. "Even after all he's done, after the lives he has destroyed, you still love him don't you?"

"More than you can imagine."

Isaac nodded. She went on. "I have absolutely no hard feelings about growing up without you. There's no time for them. Life is going by way too fast for anything like that. Instead, I hope you will stick around for awhile. I hope that we can go forward. You know you are going to be a grandfather very soon?"

He smiled and nodded. He was amazed at how easy it was talking with her, like they had never been apart. They were interrupted by the nurse. She came in to let them know that there were visitors for Reid, waiting. Isaac got up to leave. He walked over to her, bent down, and kissed her cheek.

"Reid, of the Sea of Reeds, it is so nice to finally make your acquaintance."

"What did you just call me?"

"Did your mother never tell you how you got your name?"

"No, but then again I never asked."

Isaac told her the story. He told her about the night that he and Elise had sat up reading the Tanakh, in the porch swing at the farm house, by the light of a flashlight, and how he had translated Hebrew for her. He told Reid how it had affected Elise to find out that what she always thought was the Red Sea was actually the Sea of Reeds, that the place where Israel crossed to safety upon fleeing Egypt was a different place entirely from what she had been told her whole life.

He told her how they joked about naming her Reed, Queen of the Sea of Reeds, how he had begged Elise to name her Reed. He had even told Elise that if she really loved him she would name her Reed, of the Sea of Reeds.

"What can I say?" he smiled shyly. "We were little more than kids." His eyes began to sting with tears that had been unshed for years.

Reid reached up and touched his face that looked so like her own. "It's perfect. My name, I mean. I have always loved it, even before you told me. Thank you," she told him. "Thank you for telling me that."

Isaac walked to the door. "Don't get too far," she called to him.

"I'm not going anywhere," he called back.

Reid sat in her bed thinking about all that had just happened, wondering who was about to come through the door. Finally Harvey Finn burst into the room with an armload of flowers. Reagan was right behind him.

"What are you doing here?" She yelled out loud and erupted into a fit of giggles. Harvey Finn, her boss and best friend, came to stand over her in her hospital bed. Everything about him screamed New York City, from his finely tailored suit to his thick accent. "I came to find out what the hell was going on down here. I came to kidnap you and take you back to civilization." He bent down and gave her a hug. Then he kissed her cheek and leaned in close, "But I see civilization has come to you. Now what the hell was Isaac Ingram doing in here with you?"

Reid and Reagan looked at each other and smiled. Harvey looked back and forth between them. "Long story," they both said at the same time.

"Harvey, I can't believe you're here." Reid patted her bedside. "Come sit with me." She lowered one side of her bed. Harvey got in the bed with her. She laid her head on his shoulder. He patted her back and pulled her close in a tight embrace. He became very serious. "It scared the hell out of me when I heard," he told her.

"I'm sorry."

"Don't be sorry. Just don't do anything stupid like that again."

"I won't."

Reid sat with Harvey and Reagan in the room, catching up, until the nurse came in to tell them that visiting hours were about to be over and there were still two more that wanted to get in before the day was done. They got up to go. Reagan told Reid that he would see her first thing in the morning. She kissed him and told Harvey goodbye.

Then Reid saw her mother, grandmother, and great-grandmother come through the door. The three of them sat around her. The nurse had been very strict about the two at a time visitor policy, so Reid was pleasantly surprised that all three had been allowed into her room.

"However did you get past the visitor police?" Reid giggled.

"We paid her off." Ellen winked.

All four of them began talking at once, thankful that they were all healthy and back together again.

"Gram, I'm sorry."

Maureen knew exactly what Reid meant. It was there in the room. She was sorry for all that her grandmother had endured so very long ago. She was sorry for all that she had gone through since then. And she was sorry for bringing it front and center, all over again.

"Mother, I'm sorry."

Elise could not even look at her daughter. She did not want to give away how incredibly fragile she felt. Seeing Isaac again, and being confronted with Reid's scandalous pregnancy, had brought back so much, so much that she had tried for so long to forget.

"How's Papa?"

No one said a word.

"It's okay. I can take it," she assured them, but still there was no response.

"That's why I came home, to tell you all. I came to tell you about Reagan and the baby in person, and to tell you that we were getting married. But when I saw Papa, when I saw all of you, I just couldn't seem to get the words out. I never wanted to be the source of pain for any of you, never wanted to cause any embarrassment. If I could have gone through it all, if I could have done any of it without you finding out, I would have, in order to spare you. But I'm a very public figure. Everyone would have found out sooner or later, and I knew it would be far worse for you to hear it from someone else."

The words she heard made Elise physically sick. She knew exactly what her daughter was feeling. She had lived it herself. And as she sat there listening to her, she decided the time had come for it all to end. Maybe it took almost losing her daughter, maybe it was seeing Isaac again, whatever it was, she was feeling courage that she had never felt before. She was so tired of living the way that she had lived for so long. She herself longed to flee, flee that little town that had held her for so long. As long as she stayed, she would always have to hear, "from a family of nigger lovers, father was white trash but married up, got knocked up at sixteen." They couldn't see past their own judgement. And those judgements had ruined lives. Those judgements had taken lives.

Elise looked at her daughter. There was only one good thing that she could think of. They had been blessed with Reid. She didn't know how and she didn't know why. All she knew is that they didn't deserve her. And Reid, of the Sea of Reeds, since the moment she had come, had been teaching them about life, beautiful lessons that they had been unable to learn on their own, over and over again.

Maureen could not stand to see her granddaughter upset, especially after all she had been through, and all of it because of them. "Darling, don't worry about him. He'll be all right in time. He is just angry right now. You have caused him to think about a lot of things, things from the past, things that he has tried to forget, and he just doesn't know what to do with himself right now. I think he knows that we're tired of his ways. And he knows that when it comes to you he'll have to go up against us all. He's fighting with his pride right now. The best thing anybody can do is stay away. Let him be."

The four of them sat together, talking about the baby, talking about Reagan. Reid told them all about his family, how wonderful they were. She talked on and on about the plans that they had made together. She talked about work, about the stories that she couldn't wait to begin working on. They talked until the visitor police came through the door and announced that they had to go. One by one, they kissed Reid goodbye and left the hospital, telling her they would see her in the morning when she was moved to her regular room. She hoped she would be going home tomorrow.

Reid fell asleep that night after a ridiculous good night message came to her by way of a nurse, from none other than Harvey Finn. She was feeling lighter than she had ever felt. There were no more secrets. She could move on with life, and move on with love. She was sorry that her grandfather was hurting. She knew there was some good inside of him because she had seen it so many times over the years. She remembered how he had fed half the town for free, out of the store's stock, because they couldn't afford decent food. She remembered the running tabs, credit that they could never possibly repay, how he would set their balances back to zero. He told her that he remembered being hungry and couldn't stand to see people suffer when he had the means to help them. She also remembered how those same people would turn around and call him white trash, and say terrible things about his wife, daughter, and granddaughter. It had hurt him so very much.

Reid knew that his hatred for black people had come from something way before her. She knew that it flowed from somewhere she couldn't even begin to understand. Her grandfather bore many scars from his childhood, and he had made Gram miserable for a long time for something from her past that he could not forget. Reid had heard bits and pieces of the stories her whole life, but had never been able to make complete sense of it all. And even though the four generations of women were so very close, there were some things that remained off limits. They were just too painful.

Reagan stopped off at a gas station in Fort Worth and bought a six pack of Heineken. He felt like celebrating. He and Harvey were headed to Nana's house in the rental car. Ellen told him that she would ride home with Elise and Maureen in case he and Harvey wanted to go and do something, sightsee. She offered her house and told them to make themselves at home if they got there before she did.

"The door is unlocked," she told them.

"Of course, it is." Harvey chuckled.

Reagan was tired from not sleeping the night before, so he decided that he and Harvey would just have a couple of beers at Nana's house, eat something, and go to bed. They would have to get up and do the whole thing again tomorrow. The doctor had ordered one more test for Reid, and depending on the results, she might be released.

When they got to Kilroy, Reagan drove Harvey around the town. He showed him where Reid had gone to school, all thirteen grades. He showed him the grocery store that the family had owned. He showed him her mother's house. He even drove him out to the colored cemetery, and told him what had happened to the Johnsons and to Reid's grandmother so long ago. Harvey studied the tiny Texas town. Reagan told him that there were no blacks in the town, even today. Nothing was lost on Harvey. It was his nature, not to mention his job as Creative Director at World, to pay close attention. He found it interesting that such a place had turned out such a soul as Reid.

There was a hole in the wall that appeared to be a café, next to the bank. It was open. With a mischievous grin, Harvey looked at Reagan. "What do you say we go in there and have a beer?"

"We can't. It's dry, no beer in the county.

Harvey threw up his hands. "Of course, it is."

Then Reagan remembered. "But we have a six pack of Heineken in the back."

Harvey laughed out loud when he saw the BYOB sign in the window. "You feeling up to it?"

Reagan could not help himself. He began to laugh too. "Let's do it."

So they parked the rental car in tiny downtown Kilroy and went into Cactus Moe's.

"Check out the vehicles." Harvey said.

Reagan looked at the trucks that lined the street in front of the little establishment. There was nothing but big four wheel drive pickup trucks parked there, dusty work trucks. There was absolutely nothing but trucks except for the little Ford rental car and a tractor. They both erupted when they spotted the tractor in a parking place. They were feeling good.

"If this is any indication of what's inside, you're in trouble, Brother." Harvey slapped Reagan's back and they opened the front door.

It was dim inside. The place had no windows. Harvey carried the beer to a little table in the back. Reagan followed him. A waitress came over immediately. She had on absolutely the shortest cut off shorts either one of them had ever seen, with the most horrible bleached blond dye job to match. She was probably about fifty years old and reeked of cigarette smoke and cheap perfume. The acrylic nails on her hands were long and red, matching her lipstick. She looked, to Harvey and Reagan, like a character right out of a movie, but she was completely real standing right there in front of them.

"Can I git you boys some fried jalapenas er a basket uh onion rangs, er somethin'?" she asked them in some kind of dialect that was right on the verge of being a foreign language.

Harvey felt like playing. "What do you recommend? We'll have whatever you recommend," he answered in his most charming uptown accent.

"Well, I always tell everbody tuh have the onion rangs. They're the best."

"Onion rings, it is," Harvey replied.

She noticed the six pack of Heineken and asked them if they needed a bottle opener. They told her they did. She disappeared behind the bar then through some swinging doors, into what must have been a kitchen. Harvey took out his cellular phone.

"What are you doing?" Reagan asked him.

"I'm calling Reid."

"Don't, let her rest. I don't think she can get calls anymore anyway. Visiting hours are over."

But Harvey wasn't listening. "Yes, this is Harvey Finn. Creative Director. World News. Listen… What is your name?" There was a slight pause.

"Yes, that's right I remember you. Donna. I need you to get a message to Reid Coleman, in her room. It's very important. I want you to tell her that I am in a place called Cactus Moe's, having a beer that I brought myself, and that I will never forgive her for dragging me to Assbackwards, Texas. If you can get her that message, in those exact words, there will be five hundred dollars at the nurse's station with your name on it tomorrow. Thank you very much. Bye now."

He laughed out loud, so loud that every good-ole-boy in the place turned to stare. Reagan couldn't help it, he cracked up too. "What do you think she's going to say?" Reagan asked him.

"Say? I don't know what she'll say. But I know she is going to wish like hell that she was here with us."

Reagan grinned from ear to ear thinking of her. "You're right about that."

The waitress appeared with their onion rings and disappeared again. Reagan took one and was about to taste it when Harvey slapped his hand, causing the deep fried concoction to fall back into the basket. "You barbarian. Don't you know that the natives smother them in ketchup?" He promptly poured ketchup all over the fried onion rings. Together, they ate the entire basket without speaking. They were both starving.

They were each opening their last beer when Harvey turned serious. "Now that Reid is okay, I've got to tell her something."

"What is it?" Reagan was worried. Harvey was hardly ever serious.

"I just got a green light from the producers for the restavek project in Haiti. It's her story. She talked them into it. She fought for it, but it's going to Chandler Scott. She's seven months pregnant and in the hospital. It's one of the hardest things I've ever had to do. She's going to be so upset. This story is hers. She knows it backward and forward, and it's going to drive her insane to see that pompous ass take her story."

Reagan nodded. "That's too bad, but there'll be other stories. This is just not the time for her. This is just not the one."

Harvey shook his head in agreement. They downed their last beer, and left a one hundred dollar bill on the table for the waitress, for shock effect. They were on their way out the door when the small television on the bar caught their attention. The local news was reporting on Reid. It was a brief report, nothing compared to the story that World was putting together. There wasn't much love for Reid in the local news. Reagan overheard the men sitting at the bar, talking.

"Well, that's what Reid gets. She deserved it," one said.

"Haven't seen Bob around," another one said.

"Hell no ya' ain't seen 'im. He's too damn embarrassed to show 'is face. Wouldn't you be if ya' had a nigger lovin' wife, and a Jew lovin' daughter that got herself knocked up with a nigger lovin' granddaughter?" The response touched something inside of Reagan that he didn't know was there. He had never felt it before.

Harvey and Reagan stood frozen behind them for a moment. The men did not care that a black man was listening. At the same time, they hadn't said it for his benefit. Instead, what was worse was that his presence meant less than nothing to them. He did not exist.

After the disgusting exchange settled around them like a thick dark cloud, Harvey grabbed Reagan's arm and tried to steer him out the door. He really wanted to pummel the idiots, but he knew it just wasn't worth it. Reagan jerked away.

He addressed the men with every bit of composure that he had within himself. "You have no idea what she is, what she represents. You never deserved her, and it makes me sick to hear her name in your filthy mouths." He walked out the door with Harvey right behind him. Neither spoke until Reagan started the car and drove away.

"Bravo, Brother. Bravo," Harvey finally said.

They drove the rest of the way out to Nana's house, in silence. Reagan made the turn onto Anneville Road. He drove all the way down to the end to show Harvey the place where Reid had grown up, then they turned around and drove back to Nana's.

Harvey took his bag inside and put it in the unoccupied guestroom. The two men made some sandwiches and sat down on Nana's tapestry sofa. Reagan got the remote and turned on World News. They watched the news while they ate. They waited for Steve Marshall to come on and give his evening report about Reid. In the mean time, World was airing clips of an old story that she had covered in Australia, on the last of the aborigines. After it was over, they turned off the television and got ready for bed. While Reagan was in the shower, Ellen came through the front door visibly exhausted. Harvey met her at the door.

She had been introduced to Harvey for the first time at the hospital, and insisted that he stay with Reagan at her house. She had liked him immediately, even though he was a little abrasive. His loud voice and manner of speaking was incredibly foreign to her. But it didn't take long for him to steal her heart. It was the way that he looked when he spoke of her granddaughter that endeared her to him immediately. She could tell he cared deeply for Reid. She also learned that he was happily married. He was a good guy, the real thing.

Ellen was so exhausted. After she greeted Harvey, she went straight to her bedroom, dressed in her pale pink pajamas, and fell fast asleep in her white wicker bed, in the middle of her prayer of thankfulness.

Reagan was next. He slipped out of his robe and slid beneath the pale blue quilt. The big iron bed felt so good. But he hauled his exhausted body out of it, put his robe back on, and bowed himself on the rag rug beside his bed. It was dark except for the moonlight that lit the room through the lone window, casting a silvery glow. He humbly bowed himself before the Creator and thanked Him for sparing his love and his child. He begged forgiveness for anything he had done wrong, and he begged for strength to be a better man. He prayed for the men at the little bar, and he wondered, there on his knees, how those same men could go to church on Sunday and pray with those mouths that had uttered such disgusting things. It had been only moments before that they were expostulating over their preacher's most recent sermon. He remembered something he had read in the Scriptures. "This people honoureth me with their lips, but their heart is far from me." He thought about it for a moment. There truly was nothing new under the sun.

Harvey lay in bed that night, wide awake. He too sent up a prayer, which was highly unusual. But for some reason he was remembering a discussion he had with Reid about prayer. They were in Amsterdam at the time, shooting a documentary on prostitution. He asked Reid a question about the lighting outside on the street. She had her eyes closed and whispered, "Shhhh."

He thought she was listening to something.

After a few seconds she said, "Okay, now what were you saying?"

"I was asking you about the lighting, but what were you doing?"

"I was praying," she replied, then proceeded to tell him that the lighting was fine and launched into an explanation about why she thought it would show up brighter on camera.

He wasn't listening. "What for?" he asked her, hoping he wasn't going to be stuck with what he referred to as a "holy roller" while he was in Amsterdam.

He had not been altogether sure that he had made the best decision when he hired Reid. She was fresh out of college, just graduated from NYU with her degree in journalism, and had gone straight to the New York office of World to apply for a job. She had made it all the way up the interview ladder when someone put a note on his desk requesting that he be present for an interview with a new reporter. He called the hiring manager and asked what the meaning of the note was. He was told that they all really thought he should see "this one." And so, even though he was up to his eyeballs in his own work, he took his lunch downstairs to the broadcast room where World shot the nightly news. He watched the screen test for the attractive red head and knew that he was witnessing something huge. There were no nerves, just poise, grace, and a command of the English language that Harvey had never seen before. The camera loved her.

The minute Harvey saw her, he began formulating ideas for possible stories for her. He walked over to where she sat. He did not even introduce himself. In his most obnoxious New York accent, he addressed her, "Why should we hire you for World? There are thousands of kids, just like you, that would sell their soul to work for the biggest news network on the planet. So why you? What makes you different?"

He didn't scare her. She found him interesting. She studied him for a moment, then smiled at the man that was about to become her boss and would eventually become her best friend. In the most humble, sweetest voice he believed he had ever heard, she answered him with a touch of the Texas accent that she would never fully shake. "Well, sir, being different is something I've struggled with my whole life. If you're looking for different, then you have found it. But as far as why you should hire me for the best news network in the world, that's a different matter altogether. The first reason is because I'm not afraid of anything. The second, and undoubtedly the most important, is that unlike the thousands of applicants that you are referring to, I will never sell my soul."

She had won Harvey Finn with the grace and confidence that belied her 22 years. She got the job and began her illustrious career at World. She quickly became their golden girl. She had begun by wrapping the Creative Director around her little finger, and eventually stole the heart of the Editor-in-Chief of the magazine division. Everyone there from the janitors to the producers loved her and respected her, but it was the people that watched her and followed her stories all over the world that kept her at the top. She had a fan base like World had never seen before. She had a gift for telling the story, whatever the story, that left them wanting more, more of what she had to say.

Harvey turned over on his side and began dozing. The last thought that he had before he drifted off to sleep was the answer that Reid had given him to the question he had asked. In Amsterdam that day he had asked her, "What for?" He wanted to know what she prayed for, and why, right there on the street with prostitutes all around them. Her answer had blown him away. It was something he would never forget.

"I pray that I tell the truth, not my version of things, but the truth. Their story. There is light in truth. There is freedom in truth. Everyone, everywhere, is trying desperately to reconcile where they come from with where they are going, so that they can be who they were born to be. The only way that we can get there is truth. There is only darkness in a lie, and bondage in deceit."

Harvey listened, and tried to make sense of what she said. At last she had smiled at him and patted him. "I hate the dark, and being told what to do. Always have. I even sleep with the light on." Then she was gone, preparing for her story.

That was her prayer each and every time she told a story, each and every place that she traveled to, that she would tell the truth, in a desperate attempt to shed light on whatever she could find, in her restless quest to chase away the darkness.

It was a peaceful night's sleep at the next to last house down Anneville Road. The night before had been long. But Reid was safe and sound, now. They were finally able to rest.

The telephone rang early, while Reagan and Harvey sat with Ellen, enjoying their morning coffee. Ellen got up to answer it.

"We were just about to leave," she said into the receiver.

"Yes, I understand. Goodbye, darling."

Ellen replaced the receiver.

"That was Reid. She has been moved to a regular room and is being released this afternoon. She said that she wants me to stay put, to have you boys come and rescue her."

Reagan and Harvey both laughed. They finished their coffee, had some breakfast with Ellen, and left the house. They got to the hospital, spoke to Steve Marshall a bit on camera, and went inside to find Reid. The information desk gave them her new room number. They went to find it. They walked into her room and were glad to see her dressed, looking much more like herself than the day before. Reagan noticed her growing belly. Most people had not even realized it. She was not showing much at all, and she had gone to great lengths to conceal it. But he noticed, because he knew every inch of her body.

She was dressed in an ivory corduroy dress, with her cowboy boots. She was putting her denim jacket on when they entered the room. Her wild red hair was restrained in a pony tail. She looked so good to the both of them. The three of them sat and talked, passing the time until Doctor Walker came in.

While the doctor went over all the test results, Harvey Finn made his way to the nurse's station with five hundred dollars in hand. The nurse had kept her word. She had delivered the message last night, just how he had instructed. Now, he was keeping his. He learned that Reid had erupted into fits of giggles upon hearing the persnickety nurse utter the words, Assbackwards, Texas. And to Harvey that was worth every penny.

Reid was finally released and walked out of the hospital into the cold Texas morning. She gave Steve Marshall a brief interview and thanked everyone for all of their support. Then Reid, Reagan, and Harvey piled into the little Ford rental car and headed to Kilroy. Reid talked nonstop the whole way. It wasn't until they got into Kilroy that she stopped. She got quiet. They drove out of town and turned onto Anneville Road. She relaxed. She even smiled, a quiet contented smile. She was almost home.

They parked the car in front of Nana's house and went inside. Ellen was waiting for them. She had made their lunch, with Janie's help. She had been busy since the men left. She fried a chicken, made mashed potatoes with cream gravy, cooked some green beans, and had even made a pound cake. "Your mother and Ron are on their way out. Gram said she is coming too. I called Frankie and Bobby. They both said to tell you that they love you and they will be out later this evening."

Reid entertained them with stories of the previous night in the hospital until the others arrived. Ron gave her a hug and told her he was glad to see her. He was pleasant to Reagan. She hadn't been sure how he would take it. She wasn't always so sure about him. He was her mother's husband, but she didn't really know him very well, and he and her grandfather had always been so close. She had been concerned that if Ron did not approve of her and Reagan, he would take it out on her mother. Reid did not want to be the source of any problems between them. Then there was Gram. Reid was still so worried about her. She could tell that her grandmother had been crying.

Everyone enjoyed the meal that Ellen had prepared. Ron was the first to leave. He hugged Reid and told her how glad he was that she was okay. Elise stayed behind to spend as much time as she could with her daughter. She knew she would be going soon.

Reid noticed Gram getting ready to leave. She looked so worn out, so beaten. She went to her. "I want to come and talk to Papa."

"Honey, now is not a good time. He is in a dark, dark place right now." Maureen could not hold back her tears.

Reid followed her out and got in the front seat of the car with her grandmother. "Gram, I have to get it over with." Elise ran to the car and got in the back seat. She would not let her daughter face this one alone.

Reagan watched from the window, as Reid got into the car with her grandmother. He watched as Elise jumped into the backseat. He started to go after her, but Ellen grabbed his arm. Her strong old hand held him.

"Let her go. He won't harm her," she told Reagan.

"Won't he?" He wasn't so sure.

"No, Reagan, he can't. He loves her too much."

Reagan looked like he was still unsure.

"You have to let her go. She has to face him. She has to be free."

Reid watched the dust trail behind them from the passenger mirror. She looked back over her shoulder at her mother. Elise stared out the window. She was lost in her own thoughts.

Maureen parked the car and went in through the back door. Bob Coleman sat in his recliner with the blinds drawn. The room was dark and quiet. Maureen went to her bedroom. She thought it would be best if they were alone. Elise stood just inside the doorway. She would be there if Reid needed her, otherwise, she would say nothing.

Reid opened one of the blinds and he saw her standing there. Rage ripped through him and he wanted to strike her. But as he saw the way the light bounced off of her, and the way it played on the top of her red hair, he softened just enough to sit still.

"Papa, I'm sorry," she told him. He said nothing.

"I'm sorry for hurting you and I'm sorry for the way that I have done things." Still, there was nothing.

"I haven't made the best decisions, but I have chosen the best man."

Bob felt the anger rise up inside of him. "How can you say that? You chose a nigger."

The words cut Reid. They hurt. "Papa, Reagan is a good man. The only thing that I regret is not doing things the way that I should have. I should have told you from the start. But there is no sense in going back. It's too late. I can only go forward."

"You will go forward without this family," he told her. He threatened her.

Elise winced. She remembered. "Oh, how I remember," she whispered to herself. But this was Reid's battle. She must say nothing.

"No, Papa. I won't," she answered.

"Oh, yes, you will, and you are not welcome here anymore. When you leave, don't ever come back. I don't ever want to see you again. You make me sick."

Reid could not believe he could treat her this way. Of course, she always knew that it was a possibility, but she thought somehow, someway, that his love for her would win out over the darkness that was in his heart.

"Papa, I'll go and I'll never come back if that's what you really want, but before I do I'm going to speak my mind." She did not falter. Her voice did not shake. It was steady, strong.

"I know you feel the way that you do because of things that are beyond my ability to understand, things that happened long before me. I also know that you have loved me and protected me, as best you could, for as long as I can remember. And regardless of what you may think, I am grateful for that. I know that I love you and that you have a good heart, and no matter what you say or do, I will hold on to that."

She stopped for a moment, then went on, "But don't you dare take it out on Gram, or Mother. It's not their fault. They both love you so. And besides, I think we both know that you have put them through way too much already."

Bob acted as if he didn't even hear her. "Get out of here," he told her.

She went to her bedroom and gathered her things. She found Gram and kissed her goodbye, then she headed for the front door with the keys to her car in hand. She turned and spoke to his back, one last time before she left.

"I met my father yesterday, and I know that you lied to him so that you could keep us here. He told me that he came for us." She had reached him. She could tell.

"The damage that you have done to us all is tremendous, irreparable, and in spite of it all, we still love you."

There was one last thing, a warning. "But I don't know how much longer we can keep it up. Everyone has a point, Papa, where they can't take anymore, where they won't take anymore. And I think I've come to mine, Papa. In fact, I know that I have come to mine."

Those were the last words he heard before the slam of the front door. Reid ran down the steps of the old farmhouse with her mother right behind her. They jumped into her car and she started it. Reid took one last look at what she had always considered home, and for the first time she was truly ready to begin her life with Reagan. She smiled through her tears, thinking of him waiting for her at Nana's. She pulled out of the driveway and saw Pandora drinking from the tank. The horse did not look up. There were so many things she would miss about the farm, but she hoped one day that she would be able to come back. She hoped that she could bring her children. For now, it was time to say goodbye. Life was calling her once again. She sped down Anneville Road in a cloud of dust, in answer.

Reagan sat at the kitchen table with Ellen and Harvey. He was getting worried about Reid. He should have gone with her. The minutes were creeping by as he sat there pretending he was listening to the conversation going on around him. Finally, he heard a car. He got up and looked out the front window. She came bounding up the steps and into his arms. He could tell that she had been crying. She smiled up at him and he gathered her closer to him.

"Are you okay?" he asked her.

"I'm fine. Everyone else is a wreck, but I'm fine." They walked into Nana's house, hand in hand.

Harvey heard Reid. He went to her. There was something he just had to know. "I don't get it. Why do they care? You left here years ago. What is this fascination with what goes on in your life, after so damn long."

"You mean the town?" she asked him.

"Of course, I mean the town."

"It's strange, Harvey, and extremely complicated. If you were from here you would understand it. It's difficult to explain to anyone who didn't come from here, but I'll try. All they know is Kilroy. They don't know anything else. They believe everything that their parents told them, and for most of them it has never occurred to ask or think otherwise. For the few that might question the way things are, their curiosity is choked out by fear, because to be different in a place like this can be very dangerous."

Reagan interrupted her. "I had no idea that this level of prejudice actually still exists today. I mean the President is black. Do they even know that?" he joked.

"Oh, they know it, but it doesn't affect them. That is all so far from here, on so many different levels. That means nothing to them," Reid explained. Harvey shook his head. He just couldn't wrap his mind around it.

Ellen began to speak. Harvey and Reagan could hardly believe the words that came out of her mouth. "The crazy thing is, all of them claim to be Democrats. But they don't even know what that means. They are opposed to everything that the party stands for, and yet they still mindlessly vote for whoever their Daddy would've voted for. Ironically, they helped elect the first black President, but they were so sure that he would be assassinated and that the Vice President would take his place. If I heard it once, I heard it a million times. That's all they could talk about around here. They were sure he would never be sworn in."

Reagan shuddered. "I had no idea. I really didn't."

"That's just because you've never seen it." Reid told him. "Of course, everyone has read about it, heard about it happening in other places, happening at other times. But until you've seen it, until you've actually lived it, it doesn't mean anything. Just like my stories. Most people can't relate to what's going on in the world unless it's happened to them. I guess that's why I go after them, chase them, because I've seen it all in this tiny little town. I've lived it all. I can relate to anybody, anywhere, that has ever been misunderstood, mistreated, hurt, despised. I want to expose it all, everywhere, so that people can feel it and learn from it. It's what makes me feel alive."

The men nodded. Nana listened to her great granddaughter, so happy that she had found her place in the world, that she had learned to soar with her broken wings, far away from Kilroy.

"I can't wait to get back to New York. I'm going straight to the office. I want to know where they are with the restavek project. I'm ready to go to Haiti. It's getting worse. I've been in touch with a friend of mine from the Associated Press that just got back from there."

Reagan shifted in his seat. He couldn't stand it for her. He knew how much the story meant to her. "What's wrong?" she asked.

Reagan looked at her, but she wasn't speaking to him. She was speaking to Harvey and studying his face.

"Don't blow up on me. Just listen to me," he told her.

All confidence faded, he just knew she was going to lose it on him. "The good news is that the producers gave the story a green light, full funding, full crew, everything you asked for, so the story is going to be told."

He took a deep breath. "The bad news is that they gave it to Chandler. They said it's too dangerous for you."

Reid sat there in disbelief. Harvey expected her to raise her voice. He expected anger. He got the complete opposite. She calmly crossed the room to sit at Ellen's feet. Ellen reached down and touched the stray red curl that had escaped from her ponytail. Then she tucked it behind her ear. Reid sat there for a moment, thinking. No one knew what to say. She finally looked at Harvey, and with all of the defiance that she had in her body, she told him no.

"I'm going to Haiti to tell that story if I have to fund it, film it, and tell it all by myself."

Reagan saw the fire in her pale grey eyes. He saw the tilt of her chin in defiance, the straightening of her spine in resolve, and he knew that no matter what he said or did, she would go to Haiti. He also knew that he would not try to stop her. He had learned so much about her over the last few days. He understood a little more about where she came from, about what had shaped her and made her the woman that he loved. He also knew that she would never be happy if he tried to stop her from doing what she loved, what she lived for. Despite his promise to himself, that once he was with her he would never let her go again, he knew that he would have to. He would have to let her go.

Reagan, Harvey, Ellen, and Elise watched as Reid took control of the situation. Within minutes she was on a conference call with the producers of World, and within the hour she was making her flight arrangements. She wasn't even going back to New York. She would leave from Dallas. She would be traveling with an obstetric nurse that specialized in high risk pregnancies, as a precaution. She had arranged that for Reagan. She knew that would make him feel better. She felt ridiculous about it. She rationalized that women all over the world had babies every day, in far worse circumstances than hers. Those babies and those women were fine. She would be just fine and her baby would too.

She would only be gone for a couple of weeks, back in plenty of time to sit and kick her feet up for the last month of her pregnancy. She felt the baby move. It was a feeling that she loved, to know that the child was growing inside of her, her child, Reagan's child.

Everything was settled. She would leave in two days. Chandler had already been notified. To Reid's surprise, he called to wish her luck. After chatting with him for a minute or two, she hung up the receiver and laughed out loud. Harvey asked her what was so funny.

"He sounded relieved," she laughed, "he must've been terrified."

She looked at Harvey, still so excited about the prospect of full funding and full crew for the story that she had been fighting for, for so long. None of it was lost on Reagan. Chandler was no cream puff, arrogant yes, but definitely not a cream puff. That did not sit well with him, nor with Harvey, nor Ellen, nor Elise.

Reid would spend the next day showing Reagan the farm. They woke at dawn. It was a cold morning. She dressed in layers. She put on her boots and urged Reagan to dress comfortably. He hadn't packed a lot, but he had a pair of jeans and a sweatshirt. He put them on, then his coat, and grabbed his ball cap. One of the hands brought Pandora and Ellen's thoroughbred, Mamie, over for them to ride at Ellen's insistence. They rode all over the land. Reid never let Pandora so much as trot. She kept her at a slow walk all day long.

Finally, they got hungry and went back to Nana's house to make a picnic lunch. Harvey was awake and moving around, so they urged him to come along. He declined. He wanted to give them some time alone since Reid was leaving the next day.

So Reagan and Reid set out alone, on horseback, for the Trinity River. They found a spot right on the bank, and spread out the blanket that they had brought. Reid was starving. They ate their sandwiches and drank hot cocoa from an insulated thermos. It was cold, but they sat for a long time just listening to the sound of the water, stretched out on the blanket, in each other's arms.

"Aren't you even a little afraid?" Reagan broke the silence.

"Of what?" Reid asked.

"Of going to Haiti, of being there, where there is so much violence, where life is so cheap."

She was always so amazed that both of Reagan's parents were Haitian, had come from Haiti when they were just teenagers, and yet their son had no idea what Haiti was really like.

"Haiti is just like Kilroy," Reid announced.

Reagan realized that Kilroy had issues, but it hardly compared to Haiti.

"Yes, there is violence there. Yes, to some, life is cheap. But there are people just like me there, trapped. There is corruption, and people trying to rule one another for their own ill-gotten gain, just like here. There are people that love their home, people that have a connection to the land, even though they've known little more than misery there, just like here. That's why I want to go, to tell their story. I want to bring light to it, so that they have a chance, a chance to be free."

Reagan took her in his arms and kissed her. The kiss was warm and deep, the intensity of it burned inside both of them. They had been apart for too long. She lost herself in his arms, the love she felt so strong that it rendered her completely powerless.

They spent the afternoon exploring the river. They felt happy and alive. They laughed, and played, and loved, all afternoon. The river was Reid's favorite spot on the farm. She loved the ancient oaks that shaded its banks. In summer, she loved the cold water on her skin. She loved canoeing it, tubing it, loved fishing it. She had loved it since she was a child, and had respected it as a living thing for as long as she could remember. It was her most favorite of creations on the farm, and it had kindled a love of nature inside of her that would last for the rest of her days.

The sun was beginning to set. They climbed onto their horses and began to head back to Nana's house. Reagan watched Reid ahead of him, her silhouette against the beautiful Texas sunset. She turned to look at him. The smile on her face needed no explanation. She was happier than she had ever been in her entire life. She rode the horse she loved, on the land she loved, with the man she loved right behind her. Their child was safe and sound within her, and at that moment all was right with the world. Reagan knew that he would never forget the way she looked. For the rest of his life, he would remember seeing her on her horse that day, against the Texas sky, the sun in her wild red hair. She was the most beautiful thing he had ever seen, and he knew if he spent every day of the rest of his life with her, it still wouldn't be enough time.

The night was spent with friends and family. Elise, with Ellen's help, cooked dinner for everyone at her house in town. Reid's aunt Frankie was there with Clint. Her uncle Bobby was there with Karen and the boys. Aunt Annalyn had come with Gram.

Her father called from Munich to tell her to be careful in Haiti. She had insisted that he make the concert, when she found out that he was skipping it because of her. They made plans to get together when she returned to New York.

Everything was wonderful. Harvey and Reagan watched her interaction with her family. It was obvious how much they all loved her, how much they had missed her. It was a wonderful evening, but Reid couldn't help but feel the loss, for there was no Papa. He would not come. She hadn't seen him since she left him that day. She didn't know if she would ever see him again. And while she was happy with Reagan, and ready to go forward with her life, her heart was still broken for her grandfather, but more for what he was doing to himself, than what he had ever done to her.

She and her mother sat in the porch swing on the wrap around front porch. "You know Reagan wants to go with you, don't you?" Elise asked her.

"Yes, of course, I know, but it's ridiculous. I'll be back in a couple of weeks, three at the most. He has work. He has already been gone for too long."

"Are you sure you'll be all right?" Elise was afraid.

Reid looked at her mother. Normally, she left from New York to cover a story, so no one knew exactly where she was going or what she was doing. This time, she was leaving from Dallas, and they had all heard the details of the story she would be chasing, how dangerous Haiti could be.

"I'll be fine, Mother. I'll have a whole crew there with me. I'll be back soon, and then you will come to New York around the middle of February, to be there when the baby is born."

Elise patted her daughter's leg. She couldn't seem to shake the bad feeling that she had. She wanted to beg Reid not to go, she wanted to make her stay, but she knew she could do neither. Her daughter was just as strong willed now as she was the day she came into the world, and Elise would never be responsible for taking that from her. It was the very thing that had carried them through, time and time again.

Maureen saw her granddaughter and her daughter sitting in the porch swing together. She found her mother in the kitchen, and they joined them on the front porch, claiming a couple of rocking chairs. It wasn't long before the four got lost in each other, like there was no one else around. Abby was missing. She had gone years ago, but the baby was coming. They talked about the baby. Would they come to New York to see the baby? Or would Reid bring the baby Kilroy? What would she name the baby? How long would she take off work? Would she breast feed? How often would she phone while she was in Haiti? Exactly how long was she staying? They talked, and they talked, and they talked...

Bobby saw them through the window. He shook his head and smiled. They had escaped. He had seen it so many times before.

They were stealing their last few moments together before Reid disappeared again. He saw them sitting there, their circle impenetrable. Their flesh and blood bond was a result of all that life had brought, their relationship so complex that no man would ever understand it, four generations of women that had been through so much together. There was nothing any stronger, nothing any braver, than what sat there together, out there on that porch. He knew it, and he was thankful to be sharing this life with them. He felt honored and blessed that their blood ran through his veins.

The evening quickly brought the next morning. Elise drove Reid, Reagan, and Harvey to DFW International Airport. Reid was headed straight for Haiti dressed in her only pair of maternity blue jeans, an old I Love New York t-shirt, and cowboy boots, with nothing else but a small crocheted bag from Guatemala. Reagan was bound for New York, while Harvey announced that he was going on vacation. He would not be returning to New York right away.

Elise and Reid said their goodbyes. She would give Reagan some time alone with her daughter before he had to board.

"You get yourself home safely. Don't take any chances. You hear me?"

Reid nodded. "Mother, I'll be fine. Don't worry, I do this all the time."

"I know you do. Right now, I just wish that you didn't," Elise told her.

They embraced. Reid was shocked at what she saw in her mother's face. Elise was truly terrified. Reid hated to see her mother this way. She was so incredibly fragile. "Mother, it's okay. I'll be back."

Elise kissed her daughter and left. She had to get out of the airport before she broke down. She just couldn't get rid of that nagging feeling.

Reagan sat with Reid, holding her hand, until they called him to board. She gave him a quick kiss, and he whispered how much he loved her in her ear. The warmth of his breath on her ear made her tingle. Her heart leapt as she watched him go.

Finally, alone, she sat there watching all of the people go by. Her mind began to race forward to what she was about to see, what she was about to do. She couldn't wait to get this story. She was going to blow the whole thing wide open. She was going to tell the truth about the restavek system in Haiti. It was slavery at its best, something even darker and more sinister at its worst. She was preparing for battle. She wasn't afraid of anything. She was going to give those children a voice. Together, they would tell the world.

Reagan took a deep breath as the plane ascended. He wished he had gone with her. He couldn't imagine getting through the next few weeks without her. He felt empty. He felt lost. He sent up a silent prayer that no harm would come to either of them and that time would find them back together again. Then he fought like hell to chase her from his mind.

It was no use. The flight seemed to be taking forever. He couldn't stop thinking about her. The way she laughed, the way she cried, all of it, everything about her consumed his thoughts. How wild she was, how different, beyond anything he could comprehend, how complex she was, how amazing and brave. He was glad that he had gone to Texas and experienced where she came from. He felt as if he understood her so much better, this woman that he never expected to find, this woman that would soon be his wife.

He couldn't get her out of his mind. Each second that passed meant that he was getting further and further away from her, and he hated it. He tried to be rational. They would be back together, soon. This is what she does, he told himself. She is a journalist. They do this all the time. But he knew that she was about to be thrust into another dark place, the reality of child slavery, in a country that she loved, a country that he should know.

His mother's country, his father's country, Haiti, it was little more than some other place to him. He had never even been interested in visiting there, so far removed he was from where his people came from. He struggled to remember stories that he had heard so long ago. Instead, all he could remember was how it had embarrassed him to hear his mother speaking French to his father at his little league games. Nobody else's parents spoke French. It was even worse when they spoke Creole. It sounded even stranger than French to him. He thought now how silly that was, what a tragedy. And then, how much did he really know? Who am I really?

He was about to become a husband, and a father. And he was never more unsure of himself than at that very moment. He was the Editor-in-Chief for World Magazine. That, he knew. He had spent so much of his life reaching for it, attaining it, but he asked himself what it really meant. Who am I really?

He realized, in that moment, that despite the insanity that Reid had grown up in, despite the pain that she had endured and the way that she had been treated, she knew exactly who she was. He realized that because of it all, she had found out early. She had to be strong so that they did not break her.

The rhythmic beat of distant music penetrated the corners of his mind. It was coming from the young man that was sitting next to him. Reagan noticed him when they changed planes in Atlanta. The young man had squeezed past him to take the seat next to the window. He was dressed in oversized basketball shorts, oversized jersey, and matching bright colored high tops. He was wearing a sweatband and headphones, bopping to the music on his iPod. Reagan could hear that music now.

He needed a diversion. Something came over him. He tapped the young man on the arm, to get his attention. The stranger removed one of the ear pieces. He did not speak. Instead, his eyebrows went up, questioning Reagan.

"That's got a good beat. What is that?" Reagan asked him.

The young man was obviously surprised. He rattled off the artist and song title so quickly that Reagan did not understand a word he said, then he held out the earpiece. Reagan held it up to his ear, close enough to hear what was coming out of it. The beat was infectious. But then he heard it, what normally would have gone right over his head because it didn't directly affect him. He looked at the young man who was trying to make sense of him.

"Doesn't the use of that word bother you?" Reagan asked.

"What? You mean nigga'?" the young man replied.

"Of course," Reagan returned.

"No, not when it's bein' used by us."

Reagan thought about what he said. He thought about how much Texas had changed him. Just being around Reid's family and hearing their stories, what they had lived through, had made him think about things he had never realized before. He thought about Joe and Jeremiah Johnson, how their lives had been cut short, the suffering that they had endured. He had heard someone say before, that blacks had essentially claimed the word, that it held no power over them anymore. Reagan thought, now, how ridiculous that was. He looked at the young man beside him. He couldn't have been more than nineteen with his whole life ahead of him.

Reagan didn't know what he was doing. It was completely out of character, but he went for it anyway. "I know that you think it doesn't mean anything when it's used between friends. But did you know that, for some, it was the last thing they heard before they were murdered, that they died hearing it on the lips of someone that despised them, someone that was beating them to death, killing them? How can that word be claimed for anything good? Why on earth would it ever be used between friends?"

The young man was surprised, but he thought about what the stranger said. "It ain't like that, man. It's just hood talk."

Reagan saw the young man assessing him, and he could tell that the young man had his own ideas about him. It was obvious that he thought Reagan could not possibly relate to him. Reagan wondered how and where everything had gone so completely wrong. That place in time was not that long ago, and yet young people had no idea. Reagan imagined Jeremiah Johnson sitting there next to the young kid with the iPod. What would he say to him? Finally, Reagan spoke.

"I understand a lot more than you think I do. It's one thing, to not allow a word to have power over you, to define you. I get that. But to use it carelessly, knowing the suffering associated with it, now that is another thing entirely. That word has history, energy, whether we like it or not. You underestimate the power of the spoken word, Brother."

But the young man had stopped listening. He had already passed judgement. He took his earpiece and went back to staring out the window, watching the clouds go by, what he had been doing when Reagan disturbed him.

Reagan considered their exchange. Before Kilroy, he was like that nineteen year old kid, not truly grasping the history and energy associated with that word. How could he? Reagan had been protected, had never known any unpleasantness, had enjoyed a very simple and privileged existence. His parents were successful. They had done all that they set out to do. They had raised their children up safe and sound, but unaware of where they came from.

They had tried, Reagan was sure of it, to tell them about their history. But what had they said? What did he remember? "Who am I, really?" He realized that he said it aloud. The young man could not hear him. He was in his own world again. But the woman sitting to his left was looking at him like he was insane.

He stared out the window of the plane, at the clouds moving beneath him. He thought about Nana, and what he had learned. "Who we are begins long before our first breath…" she had told him. Then he went back, as far as he could remember.

# Margaret

April 1961...

Marguerite stood still and quiet in the Port Au Prince airport, next to her older brother. She had been told not to speak. She was sixteen and beautiful, with dark brown hair that had been streaked with auburn by the Caribbean sun. Today it was styled neatly in a chignon, exposing her delicate shoulders and showing off her striking cheekbones. Her dark eyes scanned the crowd while trying to appear calm.

She took a deep breath. Once they were on the airplane, once the plane took off, they would be safe. Until then, she could not be sure. The young girl was leaving her country, all she had ever known, wondering if she would ever see her mother and grandmother again. But she would not cry; she was too afraid to shed a tear. And besides that, she had promised.

Her brother took her passport and presented it along with his to the official. Fakes, both of them. She prayed the man did not notice. He looked them over, then waved them through, and on to the waiting airplane. Marguerite wondered if he had been waiting for them, strategically placed there by her father. Or had the passport really worked?

Everything was moving so very fast. She held onto Girard's hand as the airplane began to ascend. She watched out the tiny window as Haiti's coastline came into view. Then there was nothing but the beautiful turquoise expanse that was the Caribbean Sea. Her heart was breaking, but still no tears. She would not cry.

They traveled in silence, simply holding hands. She wondered what would happen to her now, what life would be like in New York. Her father and her three older brothers awaited their arrival. She wondered what Girard was thinking. She could not tell. She remembered what her mother had said to her, right before she left.

"Do not be afraid and always, always do what's right..." Then she had touched her daughter's face, "...no matter what the cost."

Marguerite dare not ask when they would see each other again. She dare not bring light to the awful truth. They both knew that they may not live to see one another again. The brutality of Duvalier's regime had threatened them many times already. Soldiers had searched them in the streets. They had even been terrorized by the Tonton Macoutes, Duvalier's bogeymen. They knew full well that it was the adoration of "Madame Rigaud" that kept them all alive. Most families in Port Au Prince had been touched by her kindness and generosity, in one way or another, and their loyalty to her ran deep. But it was last night, when the soldiers of the new army had finally come for them, that Dominique Rigaud had packed her last two remaining children off to America. If they stayed, she knew they would be killed. Instead, they would join their father in the States, if she could get them there. She would stay behind. Her face was too well known. She could not travel with them. It was too late now.

The men had beaten on the big front doors of the mansion, demanding to be let in. The housekeeper had answered and told them that the family had already fled. The soldiers stormed the beautiful house looking for them. Marguerite and Girard hid in their closets. Their mother listened from where she hid in her own closet. She waited, and she listened. She would only reveal herself if they found the children. There hadn't been time to get to them. She hoped they were well hidden. By the time she heard the soldier's voices, they were already on the spiral staircase.

They found her. They ordered her out. She knew she was about to be shot. She stepped out into the lamplight to meet her fate, tying her lavender lace dressing gown more securely around her. Her long dark hair hung like thick ropes down to her waist. She came face to face with the commanding officer of Duvalier's army, whose mission was to exterminate the elite mulattos. His first stop was what was left of the Rigaud family. She held her head high and looked him straight in the eye, the magnitude of her presence in sharp contrast to her tiny four feet eleven inch frame.

The officer yelled in Creole to his men, "This is not Madame Rigaud. This is a servant."

"Where is Madame Rigaud?" he demanded of her.

"She fled with her children," she returned in Creole.

The officer flew into a fit of rage. He grabbed the yellow vase from its place of honor, the center of her mahogany dresser. Her insides churned. She almost made a move to stop him.

He hurled it to the ground. She retained her composure, never batted an eye, even though it broke her heart. It was the only thing she had left from her childhood, the only possession that she had ever cherished. Her father had given her the delicate vase with a single white rose in it when she was just a girl. She had kept it safe ever since.

She eyed the officer with cold defiance. He returned her gaze. He looked at his men with a twisted smile. They returned with a knowing smirk. He ordered one soldier to stay, gun drawn, and on her. The others, he ordered to wait for him outside the house. She was terrified of what would come next. She had heard so much about the torture that had been perpetrated by the dictator's army. She did not move. What was he going to do to her?

He waited. When he was sure they were gone, he signaled the officer to drop his weapon. "I am Roger Jean Baptiste. You employed my mother and educated her until she married my father. Her name was Josephine. Do you remember her?" he asked.

Dominique Rigaud gained control of her voice. "Yes, of course I do. She was a very intelligent girl. She wore a gold bracelet that had been her mother's. She never took it off."

The officer smiled. She remembered. "She told me all about you, and your husband. She told me about your kindness. She told us all, and she said she was never made to feel like a servant. You treated her with dignity and respect, and you advised her and befriended her as if she were your sister. She said your husband sent her to school, educated her as if she were his daughter."

He took a deep breath. "I have come to repay that debt. I have come to warn you. Duvalier will slaughter you all, if you do not flee."

He saw the sorrow in her eyes, as well as realization and confusion all at once. "I do not serve Duvalier. I am a soldier for Haiti, a freedom fighter that has infiltrated his army. I am a rogue," he said, as he ceremoniously bowed.

He stood straight, once again, and met her gaze. "You must flee, Madame." She understood very well. He did not stay. There was nothing more to be said, and he had to hurry, before the others began to suspect. He turned to go.

"Wait, you must kiss your mother and tell her what Madame Rigaud has said..." She searched her heart for the words. "She has raised a fine son, a good man. She has done well. Tell her I said thank you. Tell her that Haiti says thank you." And with that, she reached up on her tip toes, pulled his face down to hers, and gently kissed both of his cheeks. "Au revoir," she told him, and then he was gone.

She ran as fast as her feet could carry her, calling for Marguerite and Girard. They heard her, and came running out of their rooms to meet her in the hallway of the enormous house. The three of them came together. They embraced.

"The officer, he knew me. That is why we were spared," she told them. "Quickly, dress yourselves for travel. You cannot stay here."

Marguerite watched the clouds go by, feeling Haiti slip further and further away. They had left their home, the beautiful house that she had grown up in, the house that she had been born in. Marguerite had said goodbye to her mother in a little shack in Port Au Prince. Soon after, she and Girard were bound for the airport, and then on to the United States. Her mother was probably being smuggled right now, to the mountains with her grandmother, until such time that they could safely flee to America as well.

Marguerite thought about her mother. Dominique Rigaud had never been content as simply a beautiful accessory to her dashing and powerful husband. Her passion for Haiti's people had forced her out of the shadows and into the public eye. She had joined the ranks of her husband to fight for the welfare of all Haitians, and had made quite a name for herself. She had become known as "Madame Rigaud," a force to be reckoned with, known for her own strong opinions and political crusades as well as her quiet dignity.

Marguerite felt a chill, remembering when it all began. It had been a Sunday afternoon. Her mother had refused an invitation to the Presidential Palace. She instructed the servant to turn the messenger away. She had essentially spit in the face of the new "President for Life." Soon after, the Tonton Macoutes began to terrorize them, to hunt them, awaiting the command that called for their lives. Marguerite's father and three older brothers had already been sent, one by one, to the United States, in exile. They had been granted political asylum, while she and Girard had stayed behind with their mother, waiting their turn.

The wait was now over, but despite the excitement and the anticipation, Marguerite Rigaud could not keep her eyes open for another moment. She slept from Miami, Florida to New York City, dreaming of the mountains, dreaming of Haiti, dreams that she would carry with her for the rest of her days.

She would go to school and become a doctor. She would fall in love and get married. She would have the most wonderful children a mother could ever hope for. But no matter how much she achieved, no matter how much happiness she found, there was one thing that would continue to elude her... Closure. It was something that she would long for, something that she would crave.

Marguerite Rigaud had been ripped from her home, her country, when she was just a girl. She had never been able to say goodbye, and after so long it became a wound that would not heal. The pain would never truly go away. She would just learn to live with it.

It was the last time she had seen her mother, the very last time. And she had never gone back, never returned to her homeland. She made her home in the United States. Her children were American, apple pie, from their Jackson Five albums to their Adidas. But it was Haiti that always held her heart. It was Haiti that she dreamed of, and all that she had left behind, in the middle of that April night, in 1961.

# *Reagan*

JANUARY 2010...

Reagan tried to remember more, but it was no use. He had stopped listening a long time ago. And while his mother had tried to tell her children about her country, had tried to keep Haiti alive, it had been no use. The kids did not care. The stories were not important to them. They had never been anything but safe and sound. They could not relate to political unrest, danger in the streets, being hunted by Duvalier's Tonton Macoutes. They had grown up "Americanized."

Of course they learned a little, here and there, about Haiti and Haitian culture. It was the result of the closeness of the family, and the numerous aunts, uncles, and cousins that they had grown up with. They learned how much Haitians love Haiti, the respect that they have for their land and their people. But unfortunately that respect was nontransferable. It was impossible for the younger generation to truly understand. They had never seen it. They had never felt it.

They had never witnessed the strength of the people. They had never seen the grace and beauty of the Haitian women that raise their children amid poverty and hunger, still demanding greatness because they know what their children are capable of. They had never seen the strength and dignity of the Haitian men that struggle to provide for their families in the most oppressive of circumstances, had never seen them openly weep with love for their children. And because they had never seen the sun set on Haiti's glorious beaches, or the moon shine over the majestic mountains, they did not realize the magnitude of their heritage.

"Haiti is not what you see on television," he had heard his mother say. "It is so much more than that, so much more."

Reagan scanned the crowd at JFK International Airport, looking for his mother. At last he saw her. She was smiling. He almost felt as if he were seeing her for the first time. There were questions that he wanted to ask her, things he wanted to know. None of it had been important before, but it was different now. Reid had caused him to consider so much that he had never considered before. Seeing and feeling where she came from had helped him to understand her better. And her stories about Haiti and Haiti's people were something that he had grown up hearing about all his life, but had never really given much thought to.

He decided he would take the opportunity, while Reid was gone from him, to discover himself, to figure out where he came from, where he was going, so that when the two of them came together again, when the baby came, he would be the best husband and father he could possibly be.

There was much to learn, much to understand. And as his mother stood there in the John Fitzgerald Kennedy International Airport, he thought she had never looked more precious to him, or more beautiful. She stood straight and tall, her flawless bone structure so like his, but more delicate because she was a woman. She carried herself with confidence, just like he did. As he approached her, he was met with the quiet grace that he had always known.

"My son, finally you have arrived."

He kissed her cheek and gave her a hug. "Hello, Mother."

"Reid? She is not with you?"

"No, she's flying out of Dallas, on to Haiti, to cover that story in Port Au Prince that I told you about."

A faint smile touched the corners of Margaret's lips, a smile that would have gone unnoticed before, but not today. Reagan watched his mother. The smile was knowing, wistful. Her eyes were sad. There was much that he did not know, so much. He thought about the baby. Up until now he had lived in the moment, for the moment. But the time had come to learn about his history, to figure out where he really came from. He had no idea that he was about to find himself caught up in a living, breathing, beautiful moment in time, that there would be tragedy as well as triumph, that his past and his future were about to crash headlong into each other, and that his life would never, ever be the same.

## Harvey

January 2010...

Reid sat back to rest for a moment. She stretched her legs out in front of her. Reagan should be arriving in New York, soon, if he hadn't already. She let her mind wander, as she relaxed in DFW International Airport. Harvey had left them both, and ran off in the direction of his own flight. He had been very secretive about where he was going. He never told them exactly, only that he was taking a little vacation before he returned to New York. Reid was concerned about her friend. He had not had any contact with Jillian, his wife, the whole time he had been in Texas, or not that Reid had witnessed anyway. She had heard rumors, before she left for Texas, that something was going on with him. She hoped that he and Jillian were not having problems.

She put Harvey out of her mind and began to think about Haiti again. She should arrive in Port Au Prince around 5 pm. She had an extended layover, prior to that, and she was not looking forward to it. She always preferred a nonstop flight.

She began to consider all the possible angles for her story. She was piecing it together, how she wanted it shot. She did not have a lot of time, and she had a lot of ground to cover. She was lost in her own thoughts when she saw him.

It was Harvey. He was walking toward her with his leather carry-on, smiling like a Cheshire cat. He watched, as a huge smile lit up her beautiful face.

"I'm going with you," he told her.

"What?" she asked him, with disbelief all over her face.

"Why?" She was unable to contain her excitement.

"I want to. Quite frankly, I've been feeling old, dumb, and damn near dead. I want to see something again, be a part of a story, do something with myself."

Reid was extremely excited. They had not worked on a story together in years. She was also very suspicious. "You're not doing this for me, are you, Harvey? Because I can handle myself. You should know that by now."

He knew where she was headed and he didn't want to get too deep with her, for fear she might find him out. There was much he did not want her to know. "I am well aware that you are the best reporter on the globe. I just want to be there for this one. I need it. Don't worry, I'll stay out of your way. In the trenches you're the boss, Baby Girl."

She narrowed her eyes at him. She was trying to figure him out. There was something that he wasn't saying. She was sure of it. But she knew, before it was over, she would know all. Laughter escaped them both. They began to talk about the story, about Haiti, their excitement taking over the moment.

It was eleven fifteen when they finally touched down in Port Au Prince, six hours later than they had been scheduled to arrive.

Their flight had been delayed in Miami for several hours due to bad weather. Reid had been so glad that Harvey was there. He kept her entertained while they were stuck at the airport, and she had slept on his shoulder for at least two hours. But finally they had made it. They were in Haiti at last.

It was late. Reid was greeted by the darkness, as she and Harvey walked out of the airport and into the Haitian night. Her heart leapt. She was on a journey, once again. She was, like so many times before, on foreign soil. She looked up into the dark night sky. She closed her eyes. She heard the sound of a car whizzing past. She heard a horn honk. She heard the beautiful sound of Creole, the mix of French and the ancient African tongue. It was music to her ears. She searched the landscape for the children, but they were nowhere to be found. No doubt they were sleeping, exhausted from the day's work. She couldn't wait to see them. It had been so long. But time had not changed the love that she felt for them. She had fallen in love with them the moment she saw them, and they had continued to hold her heart, day after day, year after year.

She had visited Haiti for the first time in 2004. She was working on a short documentary about the devastation that Hurricane Jeanne had brought to Gonaives. It was flooded. There was mud everywhere. Jeanne had destroyed much of the already weak infrastructure of the city. Conditions were terrible, and yet the children with their wise eyes, their strength of spirit and resilience, plodded forward like little soldiers, the way they always had. She had fallen in love with them. Their incomprehensible strength represented Haiti's history, which was something that fascinated her.

Haiti had won its independence in 1804, as a result of the only successful slave revolt in history. The African slaves had been treated brutally by the French. They had been subjected to horrifying treatment that often resulted in their death, which translated to new

347

slaves being brought in from Africa on a regular basis. Upon reading everything she could get her hands on about Haiti, and interviewing the Haitian people, Reid quickly discovered how a group of slaves could revolt and win.

They had heart, and ultimately they had nothing to lose. The French had absolutely no regard for their lives, not even as possessions. Slavery, in her own country, had been so successful because the slaves had been treated as possessions, with intrinsic value. The most successful slave owners had even convinced the slaves that they were being taken care of, that they would never be able to survive on their own. And while it was still a brutal and horrible institution and existence, most American slave owners had a desire to preserve the life of a slave, even if it was for their own personal gain. But for Africans brought to Haiti, it had been different. As far as the French were concerned, the Africans were dispensable. They were merely disposed of and replaced. The stories of their treatment were unimaginable, beyond anything Reid could comprehend. And yet it was the perfect formula for one thing... Freedom.

In the end, the slaves rose up and fought, for they remembered freedom. They fought, and they won.

The very nature of Haiti's history had shaped a dignified, regal people, a people that retained their dignity in spite of poverty and oppression. Reid had seen their standards unmatched anywhere on the planet. Haitian doctors were the most thorough she had ever experienced. Haitian tailors were the most meticulous she had ever come across. Haitian teachers were the most passionate she had ever known. Haitians demanded excellence, had the highest standards that she had ever seen. The poorest Haitian woman could be working as a maid, and yet her standards were never compromised. She could be hungry, not knowing how she would feed her family, and still she would not touch the loose change that lay on the floor of the house that she was cleaning. For every sweep of the broom, for every swish of the mop, she held her head higher and higher, becoming more and more determined that her children would graduate from the most prestigious of universities, and then she would move heaven and earth to make sure that it happened.

Reid recognized Haitians as a deeply devoted people, with an incredible love of life. They were kind to her. They made her feel welcome, had embraced her as if she was one of their own. They had touched her heart like no other people had ever done, and she had been longing to return to them ever since the day she left them struggling to pick up the pieces that Hurricane Jeanne had left behind.

There was to be a driver waiting for them outside the airport. Reid had left a message for the crew, informing them of her late arrival. They heard a horn honk. Reid and Harvey got into the dusty jeep, excited to see Stan.

Stanley Huebner, one of the camera guys, Reid's favorite in fact, gave her a kiss on the cheek. He was so happy to see her. The whole crew had gone crazy with excitement when they heard that Reid was reporting after all. No one had been looking forward to shooting with Chandler Scott. The crew, as a whole, thought he was just another pretty boy on television, without any real substance. Unlike Reid, Chandler treated every assignment like a vacation and delegated most of the tough stuff to the crew. He was known for getting a story and getting out. He never went above and beyond the call of duty.

Reid, on the other hand, would keep digging until she found something else, something new. That was why any crewman or woman at World would do anything Reid Coleman asked of them, because she was right there beside them, in the trenches. She did not ask or expect anything of them that she was not willing to give, and she was always looking for a new angle, something that had been missed. She had earned the respect of every member of every crew at World, and they all wanted to work with her. Any story that she was covering was the one that they wanted to be on.

Stan could not believe that Harvey Finn was with her. It was rare that Mr. Finn was on location with them. For the most part, he stayed at World, and called the shots from there. Stan couldn't wait to walk into the hotel with Reid and Mr. Finn. He couldn't wait to see everyone's face. Mr. Finn was the guy that everyone wanted to impress. He decided who went where and who worked on what. He was the one to know.

Reid rode through the streets of Port Au Prince. With her flaming red hair blowing in the night wind, she held on tight as Stan maneuvered the jeep over the bumpy roads. She asked herself the nagging question that she desperately wanted an answer to. If Haiti was the only place in history where slaves had successfully revolted and won freedom, where those very slaves had sworn to revolt again at any moment were their freedom and liberty ever threatened, then however could it be that three hundred thousand of their very own children had been sold into slavery before their very eyes? Her own grey eyes drifted to a place that no one else could see. She was about to find out.

Stanley drove the jeep into the circle drive of a charming white stucco hotel. It was surrounded by palm trees and presented a pretty little courtyard. Reid watched as a distinguished Haitian man came out. He was dressed in beige linen, and charming, with dancing eyes and a warm smile. He shook Stan's hand and exchanged polite chit chat. Stanley introduced Reid and Harvey to the man. Stanley called him Mr. Henri. Reid understood that Mr. Henri was the owner of the small hotel, and that Jean, who also happened to be the doorman, bell boy, concierge, and front desk attendant, had already gone home. Mr. Henri was doing it all.

"It is very good to meet you," Mr. Henri told Reid. He kissed her cheek in greeting, and told her that he had seen some of her stories.

"I have much respect for you, Miss Coleman," he told her.

Reid blushed. With eyes downcast, she thanked him. She mumbled something about how the crew deserved all the credit, and ducked behind Harvey. She was always uneasy when it came to receiving praise. Even though she was the most famous investigative journalist in the entire world, she had maintained her shy ways and humble responses. That's why her transformation into fearless ferocious reporter, exposing the atrocities of the modern world, was always so amazing to those who knew her. It was as if she became someone else when she needed to.

Stanley showed Harvey and Reid to their rooms. They were upstairs on the second floor, overlooking the little pool in the back courtyard. Reid plopped down on the bed. She wanted to lie down and sleep forever. The trip had been exhausting. Guessing that it was just after midnight, she walked across the room to the little sink on the wall, and splashed some cool water on her face. She left her room again and went to find Stan. He was still talking to Harvey in the hallway.

"Stan, can you rally the troops? I want to have a short, maybe twenty minute meeting, to develop a strategy for tomorrow. We only have two weeks, and I don't want to waste a single moment of it." He told her he would knock on everyone's door.

"Tell them it's no big deal. If they are already dressed for bed, just have them come on down to the little table out there by the pool, in their pajamas. I'm too tired to wait for anyone to change and freshen up." A faint smile touched the corners of her beautiful lips. "Unless, of course, they're naked. In which case, I'll wait for them to throw some clothes on."

She made her way down the iron staircase, with Harvey, through the little lobby area, and out the back door to the table by the pool. They waited for her crew to show up. One by one, they came out. First was Leon. Reid stood up to meet him, so happy to see him.

"I'm so glad to see you," he told her, as he gently touched her belly and laughed. They embraced, sharing a warm hug between old friends.

Leon Fisher was a Columbia graduate, Class of 2005. He was a Brooklyn native, born and raised in one of the toughest neighborhoods in the city. His mother had been a drug addict. She overdosed right before he graduated from high school. He had never known his father. He died at Ryker's when Leon was only seven years old.

Reid first met Leon at World's New York office. It was September, 2004, and he had just begun his internship. Reid was leaving the next day for Gonaives, with an assistant that would be shadowing her while she was in Haiti. Allison Edwards was already packed and ready to go when Leon walked into Reid's office. It was late, and Leon was upset that she had passed on a story about drug warfare in his old neighborhood. She had decided not to cover it. Instead, the studio had cast another reporter that was not nearly as famous as Reid. It had immediately angered the young man. He knew the type of attention that anything with Reid Coleman's name on it could get, and he was upset that she had passed on it in order to go to Haiti to cover Hurricane Jeanne.

"Why do you want to go to another country, to cover the aftermath of a Hurricane, when there is a story right here in this country that needs to be told?"

Reid was shocked. She barely even knew the intern that stood before her. He must be talking about the crack cocaine story that she had turned down. She paused for a moment and studied him. She knew immediately by the look in his eyes, and the tilt of his head, that this was personal. She also knew, by the way that he looked at her, that he had his own assumptions about her and her motives.

"Sir, what is your name? I do not believe we have ever met." She stood up from behind her desk, and put her hand out."

"Leon Fisher." He did not take her hand.

"Well, Mr. Fisher, I assume that you already know who I am. Please, sit down."

He remained standing while Reid settled back into her chair. She spoke to him carefully and compassionately, all the while reading him in his expressions. "Because you are an intern, and because it is obvious that you have a personal attachment to the story in question, I will forgive you for your rudeness."

She paused, watching him. "It is obvious to me that you have misjudged my motives. I can read that in your eyes."

The young man looked away, unable to meet her gaze. She continued, "Mr. Fisher, I have learned many lessons in this business. The lesson that corresponds to this issue is simple. I am not the one to tell that story. I know you think that you know why, but you are wrong. I am simply not the one. The stories that I tell call to me. If I try to forget about them, they won't let me go. That one is just not my story. It's as simple as that. It will be told, but not by me. Not by me."

He sat down in the chair opposite her. He looked so very sad. He had walked into her office heated, defiant. He sat before her now, defeated. She studied his face, his downcast eyes, and his slim build. She saw before her a struggling college student, sleep deprived, and probably on the brink of starvation, desperately fighting for his future while still being held by his past.

"Leon, do you have a passport?"

"Yes, I do. We had to get one in order to work here," he told her.

"Good. Go home right now and pack a bag. You are going to Haiti as my assistant. Be back here no later than ten tomorrow morning."

He looked at her as if she were crazy, but she could see the excitement in his eyes. She picked up the phone and called Harvey on his cell.

"Call Allison and let her know that she's staying. I'm taking an intern with me. I need a ticket in his name."

The decision to walk into Reid Coleman's office had changed Leon Fisher's life. He left the next afternoon with the rest of the World crew, bound for Haiti. He shadowed Reid for the entire assignment and returned home with a completely different perspective about people, about life, about success. His respect for Reid was unprecedented. Before, he thought she was some arrogant white lady with a cushy job. He thought she had turned up her nose at his neighborhood and its hardship for her own personal gain, her own personal glory. When he returned, he knew she was the real deal, unlike anyone he had ever known before. She stood for everything that was good and she was fearless when it came to defending it. She hadn't gone to Haiti to make a name for herself, or to be in the spotlight. She had gone to Haiti because no one else would. No one else cared. And the fact that no one else cared was what endeared Haiti to her, in turn, endearing her to Leon.

On the return flight, twenty minutes from La Guardia, she began to fall asleep. Leon heard her whisper, he himself groggy from the long flight.

"Leon, there were seven reporters in line behind me for that story about your old neighborhood. Do you know how many there were for Haiti?" she asked him, with her eyes still closed.

"No," he whispered.

"Just one, Leon. Just one." She drifted back off to sleep while Leon watched her, so thankful for all that she had taught him.

That was almost six years ago. Since then, Leon Fisher had graduated from Columbia and gone to work for World as a legitimate employee. He had made a name for himself as the man that could get things done, operating behind the scenes, problem solving for the crews on location. It wasn't often that he got to work with Reid anymore. For the most part, she solved her own problems. But Harvey Finn tapped him as soon as the producers gave the green light for Reid to cover Haiti. Harvey was taking no chances with Reid on this story. It was dangerous, and she was pregnant, very pregnant. He wanted the best of the best with her.

She was so excited to see Leon. "Can you believe it?" she asked him.

"Of course, I can. You're the only one crazy enough to do this story the right way."

Reid laughed at his response. She hugged him and sat down at the little table with him, where the others were seated. Reid looked at her crew. There was Stan on camera one, Brigitte on camera two, and Eric for backup. There was Leon, her right hand, Paolo from editing for advisory, an obstetric nurse by the name of Anna, and Harvey for anything else she might need. That was eight, including her.

There was a flurry of questions, but not about the assignment. Instead, everyone wanted to know about Texas, how she was, what had happened. She assured everyone that she was fine.

"I am so glad to see you all. I am so honored and humbled by the opportunity to be here, to be the one to tell this story. It is incredibly close to my heart, above anything else I have done so far. As you all know, I happen to be pregnant. And while that should have no bearing on my ability to get this story, I want you to keep eyes and ears open, as I forget about myself when I am working. I do not want to get this story at the expense of my child."

The crew was silent, waiting for what she would say next. "Has anyone notified the embassy that we're here?"

Leon spoke up. "I made a call just before we left, but I think it would be smart for us to go there and check in, just in case we need anything while we're here. They did tell me that there is currently an advisory. They do not consider travel to Haiti safe, right now."

Reid laughed out loud. "Well, good, I would hate to be wasting my time with someplace that is safe."

She went on. "Okay. Our first stop tomorrow morning will be the embassy, then to the orphanage and the school. We will be out all day, so be prepared. We won't be returning until late night, so pack well and be ready to go."

They all said goodnight and made their way upstairs. When Reid got to her room, she found a tray with fish, rice and peas, and fried plantains. She ate every bite, then showered and slipped into her nightgown. She made a mental note to purchase some appropriate clothes tomorrow. She slid beneath the cool white cotton sheets, and fell right to sleep in the middle of her prayers.

The morning came quickly. Reid woke to a knock at her door. When she opened the door, Harvey stood there in the hallway with a tray of food. He could not help but laugh when he saw her. "What in the hell happened to you last night?" he teased her. Her bright red hair was all over the place, and her eyes had dark puffy circles under them. "You'll have to wear sunglasses today. You look positively terrible."

"Is it that bad?" she asked him. She moved aside so he could bring the tray into the room. He put the tray on the little table and sat down to eat. Reid shut the door. She crossed the room to the windows and pulled back the curtains to expose a beautiful view of the swimming pool and courtyard below. The room filled with the soft light of dawn. She joined Harvey at the bamboo table.

He was already dressed and ready to go in some khaki cargo shorts and a crisp clean white polo. He wore hiking boots at Reid's insistence. She warned him of the garbage that littered the streets in the ghettos of Port Au Prince.

"I can't believe you are up and ready to go this early," she told him.

"And I can't believe that you are not."

Reid sat and ate her breakfast of fruit and Haitian patties, still in her white cotton nightgown. It was the only other garment that she had brought, other than what she had traveled in.

"We have to get me some clothes. This is all I have other than what I wore on the airplane."

Harvey thought about the I Love New York t-shirt and the battered blue jeans she had worn. He laughed at her. "It's nice to see that you are no more high maintenance now than when I hired you. You haven't changed one bit."

"I know." She giggled.

"Do you still love me?" She teased him.

"Love you? I think you are positively the most uncivilized human being I have ever seen in my life. Look at you."

Reid turned to see her reflection in the mirror behind her. Laughter overtook her. She looked a mess. Her hair was everywhere. She popped one last bite of mango into her mouth, and went to tidy up. She brushed her teeth, then coaxed her wild red hair into two braids. She put her I love New York t-shirt on over her nightgown, and proceeded to put on her cowboy boots. Harvey thought she looked somewhere between completely ridiculous and utterly beautiful. She reminded him of the bohemian girls that ran around the village, back in the city, without a care in the world about what they had on. She pulled her bright colored Guatemalan bag over her head and secured it over her shoulder, across her body, across her belly.

"I'm ready," she told him.

"Of course, you are," he replied with a smirk.

Together, they made their way downstairs. Everyone was there. They all piled into two jeeps and headed to the American embassy. Reid was in the first car. She jotted down a few phrases on her notepad while Stan drove. Anna, the nurse, and Harvey were in the back seat. The other four were in the jeep behind them, with Leon driving.

The crew stayed put in the jeeps while Harvey and Leon disappeared into the embassy. Reid looked up for a brief moment. The embassy looked like the buildings that she had seen on Army bases all over the United States. It looked more like an Army fort than a place for diplomats to conduct business. She quickly went back to her notes, recording phrases and information that she wanted to include in her story.

Harvey climbed back into the jeep. "Okay, they know we're here," Reid heard him say. Stan started up the jeep. Reid looked behind her. She saw that Leon was back in the driver's seat and went back to what she had been doing. She put the familiar disc into the compact disc player. She sat back to enjoy the ride. Their next stop was the orphanage. Tracy Chapman played, Revolution...

The jeeps made their way through the streets of Port Au Prince. Stanley drove, while Harvey filmed their journey. Brigitte was behind them on camera two, with Leon driving. The streets of Port Au Prince were full. Haitians were going about their daily business of making some sort of a living. Reid remembered a conversation she had with Reagan. He had brought up the unemployment rate in Haiti.

"Unemployed?" She had been amused by his assessment. "I can assure you that every Haitian that we consider unemployed is indeed employed by the daily business of survival. Each and every one is an entrepreneur on a very basic level, devising some sort of business for the day to stay alive."

She thought of this now as she watched them making their way around Port Au Prince. Most of them were selling something. They will sell anything, Reid thought. The thought caused a chill to come over her, and the hair on her arms to stand on end. That was precisely why she had come.

Harvey had never been to Haiti. His eyes took in all that he saw. There were women in brightly colored dresses that were faded from so much wash and wear. And there were men dressed in tattered clothes, some of it urban American wear. He couldn't help but smile at the site of a man dressed in a Philadelphia Seventy Sixers jersey with a white skull cap on his head. It was seventy-five degrees, factoring in the humidity it felt like a hundred and twenty. But in the spirit of what was considered fashionable, the Haitian was wearing a hot winter skullcap. "Vanity knows no bounds, and its confusion is universal," he chuckled.

Both jeeps stopped along the street in front of a brick house. Despite its obvious disrepair, the house was clean and well cared for. "This is it," Stan shouted to Leon. Everyone clamored out. Reid waited while they got their gear together. Harvey helped carry some of the equipment up the steps.

Reid knocked on the door. They could hear the sounds of small children inside. A Haitian woman came to the front door. She spoke to Reid in English.

"May I help you?" she asked.

"Yes, I'm here to meet with Philippe. My name is Reid Coleman. I am a reporter for World News, and I've brought my crew."

The woman told her to come inside. She told her to wait in the foyer while she went to find Philippe. All eight of them crammed into the small area just inside the door, with their gear, while the woman disappeared. Harvey noticed how bare the place looked. There were no pictures on the walls, no decorations, no trace of happiness, or of children. But it was clean, and based on the presence of the Haitian man that he had seen walking around the place in a t-shirt that simply said "SECURITY," it was safe. He supposed those were the two most important things.

A tall, thin, Haitian man made his way toward them. He was darker than any human being that Harvey had ever seen. He was dressed in navy shorts, a red and navy striped shirt, and wore sandals on his feet. His presence commanded attention. Harvey felt as if he were standing before a king.

"Hello, I am Philippe. Welcome to Hearts and Hands. I am the director here."

He took Reid's hand, then gave her a firm handshake and a kiss on the cheek. He seemed warm and kind, and Reid liked him immediately. He took them on a tour of what he referred to as their "facility." The facility consisted of little more than a house with some homemade bunk beds, a kitchen, and a small play yard that doubled as an outdoor laundry mat.

The smell of bleach hung in the air. Reid could feel it burning her nose. She watched as the woman that met them at the door began the task of washing the hundreds of cloth diapers by hand. It was hard work. Reid watched the woman use her strong dark arms to agitate the diapers in a huge tub of what could only be bleach water. She pointed out, on camera, how something as simple as a washing machine and running water could make such a huge difference for them.

They stayed at the orphanage, known as Hearts and Hands, much longer than they had planned. Reid could not bring herself to leave. She interviewed each and every staff member. It was the same story over and over again. They did not have enough food, they did not have enough space, they did not have enough money, and yet month after month, somehow, they remained operational. Most of the funding came from churches in the United States.

"The people in your country are very generous. Unfortunately, the problem is so grand that there is still never enough," Philippe told her with sadness. "The money comes, the money goes. I learned a long time ago that money is not the answer, but until such a time that there is major change, it is critical to keeping the children alive."

The crew ventured outside the gates of the orphanage to film the neighborhood surrounding it. Everywhere they turned, they saw nothing but shacks and garbage. The orphanage stood right in the middle of what was known as a "bidonville." Literally translated, it meant trash town, and that is just what it appeared to be. A little village of makeshift lean-tos, constructed out of whatever materials could be found, surrounded by garbage in the streets.

"As you can see, there are many more children that need assistance, but it is just not available. There are many that want to give their children to an orphanage for a better life, for food and shelter. It's heartbreaking. Even though they want their children, even though they love them, they want to give them away because they cannot take care of them."

Reid listened to Philippe. All the while she was thinking of her own child safely inside of her. She could not imagine what these Haitian mothers must feel. She could not imagine bringing her child into the world and not knowing how she would feed it or clothe it. Her child would be born into a loving family, with a mother and a father, both of them with a means to support a family. She thought about all the things that she took for granted on a daily basis, when she saw all that these Haitian mothers did not have.

She toured and filmed the outskirts of the bidonville, careful not to get to close. Usually Haitians were open to sharing their story, open to telling their plight for the cameras. But there had been an instance, in Gonaives, when a man had gone after her and the camera crew, railing and hurling rocks. He yelled to them that he did not want to be filmed. He kept screaming how rude it was to film someone that did not want to be filmed, how they had no right. From then on, Reid never let her crew film anyone that had not given permission. Anyone that did not obey her rules was terminated on the spot.

The screaming Haitian had greatly affected her that day. It was his story to tell, if he wanted it told. She had no right to take it from him. She had violated him. She understood.

A group of children was coming down the street, approaching the camera. They were in some sort of uniform. Reid guessed they were walking home from school. The children saw the cameras and the Americans, and ran to them. Reid touched their hands and passed out the candy that she had in her bag. She raised her voice over their laughter and cheers.

"Can I take your picture?" Philippe translated for her.

The children cheered even louder. Reid was lost in a sea of little dark shining faces. Her joy was almost tangible. She was born for this, Harvey thought, for this very thing. She was born to feel people. She was part of everyone, everywhere. He could see her glow, could see her light. He knew at that moment why Reagan had let her go, why he had said nothing, why he had not tried to stop her from going to Haiti. He also knew why he, himself, loved her so, why he was drawn to her. Her love of life was exhilarating, infectious, and for the first time in a very long while, Harvey Finn, Creative Director of World News, felt alive and present, which was exactly why he had come.

# Yisma

January 2010...

Reid told the crew to relax and just film. She wanted them to get acquainted with Haiti and the children, for now. She wanted to embrace all the goodness that Haiti had to offer. She knew full well that she was about to delve into darkness. The children, in bondage, had called to her with their haunted eyes. And now she had come back for them, to tell the truth. She had answered.

Leon was staying close to Reid. He was taking no chances. She was surrounded by Haitian children, singing to her in Creole. They sang for the camera. Reid watched them, delighted by them. Leon watched Reid, never looking away, not even for an instant. He had a foreboding feeling. He saw the way that some of the Haitians looked at her. They were people of authority, people with power. They were not comfortable with her presence. They must have something to hide. In any case, he was not letting Reid out of his sight.

She chatted with the children through Philippe. They spoke very little English. She wished she were fluent in Creole so that she could understand their every word, but she was not. Still, she could read most of what they said on their faces and in their eyes.

In the midst of the laughter and chatter that she found herself in, Reid's eye was drawn to a figure approaching the crowd in the street. It was a girl carrying a huge jug of water on her head. The girl was thin and frail, dressed in a tattered dress, no shoes. She must be about ten, Reid thought.

Reid wondered how she could sustain the weight of what she carried. The girl did not look up. She stared off in the distance, up the road in front of her, at the familiar journey in her mind that Reid could not see.

Reid watched her go. Something about the girl called to her. The singing stopped, or at least Reid no longer heard it. The children disappeared, or at least Reid no longer saw them. Time seemed to stand still as the girl passed by. Brigitte followed Reid's eyes. She filmed the girl passing. Reid watched the girl disappear over a hill, haunted by her.

Finally, Reid bid the children goodbye. The crew followed her back into Hearts and Hands, where the orphans were returning from school. The little school, just down the street, was funded and taught by missionaries from Ohio. Reid had been planning to film there as well, but it would have to be tomorrow, for school was out now.

The children of Hearts and Hands were eager to share the details of their day with Reid and the cameras. They spoke through Philippe about what life was like before they came to live at Hearts and Hands. Their stories of abuse and neglect left the World crew shocked and horrified.

"Both of my parents were killed. My uncle told me he was sending me to live with my aunt in Port Au Prince and that I would go to school. But when I got there, there was no school. There was nothing but work and hardship," one little boy told Reid.

"I was beaten every day by the woman that said she was my aunt. I woke at dawn every day, and was forced to do whatever she said. At night, I ate off the floor, the scraps from the meal that I had prepared. And then I would fall asleep under the kitchen table, only to get up and do it all again the next day. It was no life. It was hell," he told her.

Reid sat there with the boy. She was still dressed in her I Love New York t-shirt, white cotton nightgown that now doubled as a skirt, her cowboy boots, and Guatemalan bag. She could scarcely hold back her tears. Stan watched the scene through the lens of the camera, moved by her. She had something that no one else did. She moved people. He knew what he was filming was priceless. He also knew that she had gotten up and put absolutely no effort into her appearance, had jumped right into the reason they were there... The children.

The public would never even know that Reid Coleman had brought absolutely nothing but the clothes on her back. There was so much that they could not see, no matter how effective the cameras were. Reid was the best investigative journalist on the face of the earth and there was a reason for that. She cared, really cared. And because she cared so much, she moved people. Stan watched the little boy through the camera's lens. The child was lost in her grey eyes. He had never seen eyes like hers before. He wished she would take him home with her. They all did.

As Reid sat in the baby room and held the little babies, she forgot about the cameras. It was just her and the babies. They were so sweet and so cuddly. She thought about Romania, about how stark and cold the babies' stares had been. Not like these babies. These babies were happy. They were getting love and attention at Hearts and Hands.

She would make sure to leave money with Philippe before she left for home. He was doing an excellent job. He had effectively created a family environment. The older kids, between seven and ten, would hold the babies, play with them, and give them the love and attention that the babies so desperately needed. In return, the babies would look up at the children with their dancing dark eyes, with adoration and love, warming the hearts of the older children.

It was midnight when they returned to the hotel. Mr. Henri was waiting for them. He had set a table for them in the dining area, complete with fresh fruits, Haitian patties, and fried plantains. Reid ate until she thought she would explode. He gave her some phone messages that he had taken. One was from Reagan. She made a mental note to call him back as soon as possible. She did not want him to worry.

The crew sat around the table and began to discuss all that they had seen that day. Anna, the nurse that was hired exclusively for Reid's pregnancy, had been greatly affected. She was normally quiet. In fact, she rarely spoke. But it was obvious that she had much to say, after seeing the children.

"I just can't believe it. After all that they have been through, they still hope, they still laugh, and they still love. It is a testimony of the resilience within the human spirit.

Reid smiled. She placed her hand on Anna's s arm. "Yes, they do still have hope. But those are the ones that have been saved. It's the children that are still out there living as slaves that have lost hope. They never laugh. They don't even know what love looks like anymore, if they ever did. And those children are why we are here."

The crew nodded. They had only been filming for one day and already the story was intensely personal.

"Did anyone see the girl that passed by us when we were filming outside of the bidonville?" Reid asked.

"See her?" Brigitte asked with a hint of amusement. "I broke the rules. I got her."

"What do you mean?" Reid asked.

"I mean, I got her. On camera. When I saw the way you watched her, I followed her. I know that you won't use it, because you didn't have her permission, but I got her anyway."

Reid shot up, grabbed Brigitte where she sat in her chair, and kissed her on the cheek.

"I love you," she shouted. "I have to see it right now. I want to find that girl."

"Uh oh," Leon muttered. He had traveled with Reid enough to know that they were about to deviate from every plan that they had ever made to find that girl. He also knew that this story was about to take on a life of its own. He was up for it. He knew that Reid was too. He just wished she wasn't pregnant.

"You don't sound very excited." Harvey Finn startled Leon out of his preoccupation with Reid.

"Oh," Leon paused, "look at her. She's about to take off on this. It's just that I wish she wasn't pregnant. I don't want anything to happen to her, or to that baby."

Harvey gave him a solid pat on the back. "That's why we're here."

Leon looked at Harvey Finn dressed in his new cargo shorts, new polo shirt, new hiking boots, looking like it was his first day of school. He knew that Mr. Finn hadn't been out in the field for a long time. He also knew that he hadn't the slightest idea of what chasing a story with Reid Coleman was like anymore. She had grown up since the early days, when he traveled with her. She was no longer green. She was a seasoned journalist, tough, tireless, and fearless. Leon held back all that he wanted to say. Instead he nodded, and made the vow once again. Come hell or high water, he would not let her out of his sight.

Reid dismissed everyone with her order to meet in the foyer the following morning at nine. She followed Brigitte to her room, and sat on the bed while she found the footage of the girl. At last, Brigitte excitedly handed her the camera, "Here she is."

Reid took the camera and looked through the lens into the lonely, desolate world of a restavek child. Her dress was little more than a red rag, baring skinny legs. The young girl's feet were rough and calloused from walking barefoot everywhere she went. Of course, she could merely have been a girl from a poor family, on her daily trip to get water from the closest public well, but Reid guessed that she was not, by the slump of her shoulders and her unwillingness to make eye contact with any of them. The girl silently passed the spectacle in the street.

Reid studied her through the lens of the camera. The girl never looked up, so accustomed to life without human contact or conversation, except for abuse and ridicule. Her hair was unkempt, little straggly braids coming out of her head. It was an indication of the absence of loving and capable hands. The girl passed by the crowd, never even looking up, staring at the horizon at something they could not see.

Reid was quiet, watching her on camera. There were thousands of these children everywhere in Haiti. She had only to walk down any street, in any neighborhood in Haiti, to find one. But as she watched the little girl go back to wherever she came from, walking strong under the weight of the jug of water, she knew that she had found her story. She felt it way down in her gut. She would not stop until she found the child. She would not stop until she gave her a chance. She began to wage war in her mind, but she would soon learn that the battle would prove to be more than she could ever conceive of. She was about to learn that in order to help the young girl, she would have to be willing to give more than she ever dreamed of.

Finally, after watching the girl over and over again, she handed the camera back to Brigitte. "We'll film the school tomorrow and wait for her. I'll ask Philippe to translate for us."

"Sounds good, but now you really need to get some sleep. If you don't, you'll be dragging tomorrow. Don't pregnant women need more sleep?" Brigitte teased her.

"Yes, they do," Reid told her. "Good night."

"Good night." Brigitte got up to let her out of the room.

Reid went back downstairs to look for Mr. Henri. He was getting ready to leave. She found him, keys in hand, bidding good night to Jean. "Mr. Henri, may I use the house phone to make a call."

"Yes, dear. Yes, of course. Jean will show you where to find it."

Reid told him good night and thanked him for taking such good care of them while they were in Haiti. He replied with a grin, "I'm honored to be boarding you, my dear, and the World News crew. I am prepared to show you Haitian hospitality, at its finest."

"Thank you so much. I feel almost like I'm at home"

"That is the highest compliment that you could have possibly paid me, my dear. Thank you. Good night," he told her.

"Good night," Reid told him.

Jean took Reid through the kitchen of the little hotel and to a telephone. She called Reagan.

"Hello." He sounded like he had been sleeping. Reid was sure he had been. It was close to two a.m. where she was, and in New York also.

"It's me, Reagan."

"Reid?" She could hear him come around. She imagined him sitting up in bed, fully awake now.

"Yes. Oh Reagan, I miss you so much. But I think I found my story today. We'll see tomorrow what comes of it. But a young girl, certainly a restavek, passed us today when we were filming in the street, and I fell in love with her. She just emulated strength, and resolve, and dignity. I'm going to find her tomorrow..."

She was talking so fast that Reagan could hardly follow her. "Slow down," he told her.

"How are you feeling? Are you taking care of you?" he asked her.

"Yes, I'm eating and sleeping. And Anna the nurse is wonderful. She takes my blood pressure constantly, even though that has never been an issue. I just let her. It makes her feel better."

Reagan let her talk until she wound down. He missed her so much. Just hearing her voice was causing him to feel sick in the pit of his stomach. He wanted to be with her. "You feel safe?" he asked her.

"Completely. There has not been anything about being here that has made me feel otherwise," she told him. "Any word from home?"

"Nothing," he told her.

"Okay, well I'll talk to you again in a couple of days. If you need to reach me, call the hotel. Mr. Henri will get the message to me."

"All right." Reagan paused. He did not want to let her go. He knew that this was what she did. She was a reporter, an investigative journalist for the premier news conglomerate in the world, but right now he wished she wasn't. He wanted her with him, safe and sound.

"Reid, I love you."

"I love you too," she told him.

Then he heard the click. He lay in his bed. She was safe. She was happy. And he fell back to sleep praying that she would be home soon. He had less than two weeks to go now.

Reid replaced the receiver and raced up the stairs as fast as her belly would permit her to go.

The morning came quickly, but Reid did not linger in bed. She prepared to meet the day, dressing in a traditional Haitian dress. She had found it in the market on the way home yesterday. It was turquoise, with yellow flowers. It was the traditional style of dress that Haitians were known for. It was hand sewn, in cool cotton fabric, loose fitting with pockets, perfect for her pregnancy. She braided her hair in two long braids and pulled her cowboy boots on. They were the only shoes she had brought.

She looked at her reflection and simply said, "Why not?" Then she locked her room and went to find the others. They were waiting downstairs, minus Leon.

"Vintage Haiti," she commented on her attire.

Anna gasped as soon as she saw Reid in the Haitian dress. "It is absolutely beautiful on you," she told her.

"Thank you." Reid twirled and proceeded to stomp her boots in a clumsy, awkward pirouette, making a spectacle that had everyone laughing. "Vintage Haiti, with my Texas influence," she told them.

Harvey watched her. "More like a bull in a china closet, if you ask me. Isn't that what they say in Texas?"

It was so good to see her laugh. He was so happy to see her antics again. He thought about Texas, about the bar, about the men that spoke her name as if she were trash, garbage, about what life must have been like for her. He watched her now, twirling and stumbling, giggling. He almost cried. He was so moved by her resilience, at how she just kept right on going. She just moved through life, greeting each new day with wonder and grace.

She was so special that she scared him. He had forgotten. He hadn't traveled with her in so very long. He had forgotten how innocent she was, how fearless she was, how it made her a target. There was too much evil in the world for her. He vowed right then that he would hand deliver her safely back to Reagan, and not a moment too soon. He was starting to feel what Leon had been trying to explain. There was something.

Finally Leon emerged on the stairs and they all set out in the jeeps. Reid jumped in to go with Stanley. "Not today," Leon told her, "I'm driving you."

She began to protest that she needed to ride with camera one. Leon told her to regroup. He was firm. He was driving her. "If you want to find the girl, I'm driving. And I'm shadowing you all day long. It's too dangerous. You are a celebrity, of sorts, whether you choose to admit it or not."

She smiled at him, at his serious tone. She remembered the kid that had stood defiantly in her office and pretty much accused her of being a bigot, with hatred in his eyes. Now he was exercising his authority in an effort to protect her, because he had grown to love her and respect her. She saluted him and got in.

The morning was beautiful. Reid could feel the Caribbean sun warming her exposed arm as she stretched it out of the moving jeep. She sat back and closed her eyes, tilting her face toward the sun. Leon could not see her eyes under the dark lenses of her sunglasses, but he figured they were probably closed. She prayed and meditated on the beginning of the day. She was thankful for the child that she could feel moving within her. She was thankful for the life she was living, and for all that she had been blessed with.

Finally, she drifted back into the present just outside of the Mission School for Children. The crew climbed out of the jeep and made their way toward what appeared to be the front of the school. It was a new building. Reid could tell. It was bare, not very happy looking, but it was sturdy and large enough to serve its purpose. There were hundreds of children that came through the doors daily. The mission was unique in that it held day school and night school.

During the day, the school taught Haitian children from under-privileged families for a minor fee, roughly ten dollars a month. At night, it doubled as a shelter for the homeless children that lived on the streets of Port Au Prince, and served as asylum for the restaveks. Not only did the mission feed them, the staff offered basic reading and writing lessons for them. Reid planned to spend the entire day there, into the night. She had no doubt that they would be quite shaken before they returned to the comfort and safety of their cozy hotel beds.

Frances Dunne met them at the door. She was a short woman with grey hair, piercing dark brown eyes and a short, to the point manner of speaking that caught Reid off guard. She was American, from Ohio, a retired school teacher.

"Follow me. The children are getting ready to say their blessing before they eat their breakfast. You may come and say hello."

Reid kicked into high gear. There were no trivialities, no introductions. It was straight to work. She signaled Stan to shadow her, and instructed Brigitte to fan out from the back of the room. The children curiously watched the strangers enter the room. They began to whisper. Frances led them in blessing their bowl of hot steamy oatmeal, then introduced Reid. They ate their oatmeal and eyed the woman with the flaming red hair and strange grey eyes.

Reid smiled. They were so incredibly cute in their uniforms of light blue seersucker collared shirts and khaki shorts for bottoms. Each one looked a little bit different in the hand sewn garments, but all were wearing the same fabric. The few girls that were there wore jumpers made of the same light blue seersucker material.

Reid addressed them in English, without an interpreter. Frances insisted. "It will be good for them," she said, "We teach them English. This will be good practice."

"Good morning, children," Reid told them. "You look positively beautiful today." They giggled.

"My name is Reid, and I am here to learn about you, so that I can tell the rest of the world how special and amazing the children of Haiti are." She had their undivided attention.

"My friends and I are going to spend the day with you. Each one of your parents already gave permission for you to talk to us, so if you want to talk to us you can." They nodded excitedly.

"Okay, we'll be seeing you around." She signaled to the crew to hang back, to let them digest what she had said.

She spent the rest of the day talking with the children, filming the classrooms, reporting on what a wonderful job the mission was doing with the underprivileged children that they served. The children were poor, but for the most part they were happy. They appeared to come from families that had enough to meet their basic needs, with enough left over to send them to school every day. Some of the children from Hearts and Hands recognized the crew.

They ate lunch with the children, then waved goodbye as they filmed them leaving for the day. There were no parents to pick them up. They all walked home in different directions, children as young as five and six. How different life was for a child in Haiti. Reid took it all in. There may be many things wrong with the country. There may be terrible things going on. But there was still innocence and goodness existing right alongside it all, and she was becoming more and more aware of it. She wanted to bring it to the forefront. She wanted to pull it out of the people, out of the country. She wanted to nurture it, and watch it grow.

Reid led the crew back in the general direction of where they had seen the girl the day before. Philippe met them in the street. They filmed the outskirts of the bidonville and talked, waiting for the girl. But she never came. Reid was disappointed. She was afraid this would happen. She knew there was a huge possibility that she would never find her. She would try again tomorrow. For now, she would go back to the school and wait for the next wave of children to come to the mission, the restaveks.

The crew sat together as Reid educated them on the conditions of the children that they were about to see. But there was nothing, no words powerful enough, to prepare them for what they would see in the next few hours.

The first child to come in was Charles. He limped into the mission, no shoes on his feet, clad only in a torn blue t-shirt, and stained underwear. He sat down on the ground in the courtyard without saying a word.

Next, there was a group of four boys, ranging in age from eight to ten. They sat beside Charles on the ground, without a word. One of the boys had a fresh cut that he attempted to bandage with a torn garment and some twine. Anna could not resist him. She immediately put on latex gloves, retrieved from her medical bag, and led him away to wash the cut. It was clear that he had no idea what she was saying to him, but he knew that she was going to help him because she was talking kindly and pointing at his cut. He went with her.

Over the next half hour, nineteen restaveks appeared out of the shadows. They sat quietly on the ground of the mission's courtyard, patiently waiting for a meal, a short lesson, and a kind word. Reid had never seen anything like it in all her life. Nineteen children sat before her, clad in rags, malnourished and dirty, staring past her at something that she could not see. They did not make a sound, not a single sound. They were too hungry to speak, too exhausted to move. It broke her heart to see them, and she knew that every one of their stories was pretty much the same. They had been sold to a family that promised a better life, school, the basics, in exchange for domestic servitude. Each one had been lied to. There was no better life. There was no school. Childhood was gone forever, replaced with backbreaking work and every kind of abuse imaginable, childlike smiles and innocent eyes snatched by all that they saw and lived through. Reid knew that they would wake again tomorrow to the same fate as today, and it tore her heart out.

She watched as the sharp-tongued, rigid Frances Dunne transformed into an angel of mercy before her very eyes. Gone was the woman that she had seen earlier, shouting orders and running her tight ship. Instead, Reid saw a kind compassionate soul that appeared to live for the night shift. Reid watched her come alive caring for the forgotten children.

Reid helped serve them their dinner of rice and beans. They didn't look at her. They looked through her. They did not trust her, and they were far too exhausted to even care why she had come. Harvey jumped in and so did Leon, doing whatever they could to help. Anna set up a sort of triage for the aches, pains, and minor injuries that plagued the children. They did not trust Anna either. They were not used to having any physical contact, other than beatings. But each one seemed to have something that needed medical attention. Before they even realized it, the World crew was caring for the children and had completely abandoned any other agenda that they had for the evening. Only Stan kept working. He kept the camera rolling.

Reid sat down in the middle of the children and began talking to them, through Philippe. He had agreed to interpret for her for the duration of her visit. Of course, she could have hired an interpreter to travel with them the whole time that they were there, but she had long since learned that so much could be lost in an interpretation. She wanted someone that was familiar to her and to the story, someone that understood what was really going on.

"How is everyone doing tonight?" she began. The children said nothing.

She cut right to the chase. These were no ordinary children she was dealing with. "How many of you are restaveks?"

All nineteen raised their hand. "Well, I am here because I want to tell the rest of the world about you, in hopes that I can help you. I want to build schools for you. I want to build homes for you. I want to help you have a better life." She studied all nineteen faces. They were listening.

"Will you help me?" she asked them.

Then she waited. They could have said no. They could have dismissed her on the basis that they had already heard that same line before. They could have refused to talk and gone back to where they had come from, after their meal of rice and beans. But instead, in spite of all that they had been through, in spite of the lie that snatched their innocence, they stayed. They allowed hope to reign, once again. The silence and stillness of the moment were broken as all nineteen heads shook in unison. "Wi," they said. "Wi." Haitian Creole for yes. Reid felt the magnitude of what she had taken on. The weight of their world was now on her shoulders.

They began to open up to her, one by one, telling her stories of how they came to live with the families that had taken them in. Some of them had become modern day slaves because they had lost their parents and had no one to care for them. They had been sold by some other family member. Some of them had come from the mountains, where the people were poor, uneducated, and had many children that they could not feed. They had given their children to someone in the city who promised education and sustenance, in exchange for domestic servitude. There were still a few that had been sold, having no memory of why or where they came from.

Their stories were gut wrenching. The signs of physical abuse were all over them. One child, by the name of Benson, was now homeless. He had run away after his "aunt" had poured boiling water on top of him for eating off of the floor. The scraps of food were to be eaten by the family dog. Benson got nothing more than a bowl of cornmeal.

"I was so hungry that I was falling asleep, and falling down. I was afraid I would not wake up. That is why I ate the food from the floor. But now I have to live with this." He pointed to the scars on his arms and head. He had raised his arms in an attempt to shield his face from the boiling water, which left them scarred and disfigured.

The boy told Reid of how he lived on the streets, fearing that the family would come for him, to kill him. "Sometimes I wish that I would die, so that I don't have to live this way," he told her.

Her heart was sick. How could someone do something so terrible to this child? And yet it was going on all over Haiti. She spoke to him gently, with tears in her eyes. "Benson, I'm glad that you are still alive. You are brave, and you are strong." The boy looked away. He could not look at the woman. She looked at him with something that tempted him to cry, and he hadn't cried in a long, long time.

Reid touched the top of his head where his scars were. She touched the scars on his arms. He almost recoiled in horror, but something about her commanded him to be still. "Look at me," she told him. As she sat in the circle of children, she looked into his eyes and told him the truth, and he recognized it, even though it had been so long since he had seen it.

"You lived for this moment right here." She motioned to the circle of children around her. "You lived for today."

He didn't know why, he didn't know what it was about her, but he believed her. He believed the stranger with the long red braids, pale grey eyes, Haitian dress, and cowboy boots. He believed her, and he cried.

Reid took her eyes off of the boy for a moment. A girl had come to join the circle with a bowl of rice and beans in her hands. Reid watched as the girl took her place in the circle and began to devour the food. The girl stopped for a moment, as if she could feel Reid staring at her. She looked up, and into Reid's eyes. Reid met her gaze and stopped. Everything ceased for the moment. Time and space were of no consequence.

It was the girl from the street. And as she looked at Reid, eye to eye, Reid knew that this was why she had come to Haiti. It was as if everything in her life had led up to this moment, when she would come face to face with this little girl. Reid was drawn into her gaze.

"Hello, I'm Reid." Philippe translated.

The little girl returned in perfect English, "I have been waiting for you."

Reid watched as the girl went back to finishing what remained in the bowl. She had dismissed Reid for the time being. Reid forced her attention from the girl, back to the group. They were all looking up at her now, wondering what she would say next.

She took some candy from her bag and passed it around. There were wan smiles as the children ate the sweet licorice that she had brought. Those wan smiles were beautiful. To bring any element of joy into their dark and lonely world was more than Reid could have hoped for, because the truth was that she could do nothing else for them tonight. They would all have to go back to where they came from and whatever was waiting for them there. The restavek system had become deeply intertwined in Haitian culture over the last hundred years, and there was no way one reporter was going to change that in a night. Reid realized it and it made her sick inside. She had no power there, and she knew it. There was no one to call to report the abuse. For the most part, the police were more corrupt and dangerous than the people that enslaved them. Most of the police officers would kill a restavek, rather than deal with one.

Reid hugged them all before they made their journey back home. Some of them flinched. Some of them just hung there with her arms around them. They did not know how to respond to affection. She did not care. She hugged them anyway. She knew they felt it.

The girl hung back and waited for the other children to leave. Finally, she told Reid that she wanted to speak with her alone, without the camera. Leon shook his head. The girl saw him with her wise, dark eyes. "I will not harm her. I only want to speak to her, away from your ears. You can watch us if you do not trust me." Her English was flawless, with an accent that was not exactly West Indian. He couldn't put his finger on what it was.

Reid followed the girl to a spot in the courtyard, under Leon's watchful gaze. He wondered what she would say. Maybe she was asking for money and thought she would have a better chance if Reid was alone. Maybe she was telling her a secret. He didn't know. But her demeanor was harmless, or else he never would have let Reid take two steps in her direction.

Reid sat on the bench in the courtyard, with only the light from a little lantern and the moon. The girl sat next to her. Reid was quiet, waiting. The girl eventually spoke. "I was taken from my home by a group of men." Reid listened as the girl went on. "My mother and father were killed when I was very small, so my grandmother took care of me, high up in the mountains, away from all of this. After her death, I was a child living alone. The men found our house one night and discovered me. One of them wanted to rape me, but the others said I would bring a better price if he did not. They took me from my home and brought me to Port Au Prince. I had never seen the city. They sold me to the family that I live with now."

Reid started to speak, but the little girl silenced her. "I have seen you," she told her. "I have seen you in my dreams, your red hair. You have come for me."

Reid did not know what to say. The girl waited for a response. Finally Reid found words. "I saw you in the street yesterday. Did you see me then?" she asked her.

"Yes, I was carrying the water. But it was not for us to meet yesterday. The time for us is today. I have no work now. We have all night. It is the Shabbat."

Reid wasn't sure that she heard her correctly. Had she just referenced the Sabbath, the seventh day? "What do you mean?" she asked her.

"Today is my day of rest, rest from my duties in their house. I do not work for them on this day."

Reid thought things were getting stranger and stranger. She did not even know what to say, what to ask the girl. She studied her. "Where did you learn to speak such perfect English?"

"My father taught me. I speak French, English, Hebrew, and of course, Creole."

"Hebrew?" Reid was confused.

"My grandfather came from Poland to Haiti in 1944. He was Yehudim, fleeing the Holocaust. He settled here in Haiti. My grandmother was Yehudim, from Morocco. Her family settled in Haiti as well."

Holocaust? Had she said Holocaust? And Yehudim, it was Hebrew. It meant Jewish. Reid could not believe her ears. This girl that sat before her looked like any other Haitian girl, like any other restavek. She was obviously neglected, but pretty, of medium hue, with huge dark eyes and the scraggly unkempt braids that Reid had seen the day before.

"My father was their son. My mother was a Haitian girl from the mountains. My father fell in love with her the first time that he saw her, but she refused to leave the mountains. He stayed there with her and they reared me there, until they were killed by a mudslide. I survived and went to live with my grandmother, even higher in the mountains. But then she went to sleep one night and never woke up."

Reid was speechless. She did not know what to say. This story was unlike anything she could have imagined. "The people that bought you, are they Jews as well?" Reid asked her.

"No." The little girl shook her head.

"But they let you observe your Sabbath?"

"When I first came to live with them, they beat me every time I told them that I would not work on this day. Finally, when the woman beat me so bad that she almost killed me, she stopped. She realized that there was nothing that would make me work for her on this day, and if I was dead she would have no help, so she stopped and let me be."

Reid was processing all that she heard. "You said that you dreamed of me. What did you mean?"

"I dreamed that you were on a road somewhere, and you walked, and walked, and walked. You were lost, like me."

Reid gasped. The little girl was describing the nightmare that she had, the night she spent away from Reagan at the Waldorf Astoria hotel. It made her shiver.

"I don't even know what to say."

"You don't have to say anything. I'm going to tell you where to find the men that took me and sold me. They are selling girls all over the place. They are even taking some out of the country."

Reid listened as the girl exposed the tangled web of human trafficking that was going on in Port Au Prince. She had heard it all before, same song second verse. The girl had been taken by a group of men that took children from the mountains. These men sold the children in Port Au Prince, into the restavek system, restavek literally meaning "rest avec," or "stay with." They promised the families of the children a better life, by convincing them that the child would be educated in exchange for light housework. The families, believing that the child would then be able to help the rest of the family by delivering them from poverty, would sell them or give them outright to the traffickers. Because of the remoteness of Haiti's mountains, this went on and on, with no end in sight. But for this girl, it had been different. She had been snatched. No family member had given her over or sold her.

Leon interrupted them to make sure that Reid was okay. She said she was fine and that she needed more time. He went back to where he sat with Harvey, to watch her.

"This sounds like a pretty big operation. How do you know that they are taking the girls out of the country?" Reid asked.

"Because I heard them talking when they took me."

Reid didn't know what to say. She didn't know where to start. She never expected to be confronted with the identity of human traffickers. She could not tell the authorities. She could not call the embassy. It didn't work like that in Haiti and she knew it. It was like the Wild West. She looked at the girl and smiled. "Good thing I wore my boots." The little girl was puzzled. "Never mind," Reid told her. She began to formulate a plan, beginning with them meeting the next night, at the same time.

The little girl told her goodnight, and then clung to her in the moonlight. There was no sound, no movement, no passage of time...

Reid sat on the bench, watching her go, wishing that she could do something. She called out into the night. "Wait! Your name, you never told me your name!"

"Yisma."

Reid heard her say it, right before she disappeared into the darkness.

The crew packed up and left the mission. They would return the following evening. Reid was quiet as they drove the short distance back to the hotel. Over another late night meal, they discussed the events of the day. Reid shared the little girl's story with the crew. She did not mention the part about knowing the identity of the men. She did not want Leon and Harvey to know that part yet.

So while the crew developed the story, and made it ready for the rest of the world, Reid devised her own plan to expose the traffickers and get them off the streets. She contacted a friend of hers at the United Nations to find out her options. If she could prove it, and the Haitian government still chose to look the other way, then the U.N. would get involved. She decided to go for it.

Each and every evening, after filming the story with the rest of the crew, she and Yisma plotted alone in the courtyard of the mission. It was perfect. Reid would pretend that she was looking to buy Haitian girls for a brothel in America. She would wear a wire with sound and camera. She would be able to get them arrested, convicted, and off the streets, making an example of them. She was sure that when her story aired, when the world saw what was really going on in Haiti, the children would be free. That was all that she truly desired.

She had learned so much about them, so much that she had never known, their heritage richer than anything she could have imagined. Haiti, in so many ways, reminded her of her own country. Haiti, like America, had been born of revolution, born of the quest for freedom and the desire for liberty. Haiti, like America, had been born a republic. And over the years, just like America, Haiti had served as asylum, providing a safe haven for people all over the world fleeing evil and injustice. There was so much about Haiti that the rest of the world did not know. Yisma illustrated the magnitude of what Haiti represented, a mere snapshot. Reid finally understood the depths of what compelled her to Haiti, why Haiti's restavek children had called to her, and why she must tell their story.

They were just like her, prisoners. Reid had been a child growing up in Kilroy. She had done nothing wrong. She had simply been born, and because of the evil nature of men, she had paid dearly for the circumstances of her birth. But it did not end there. Because she had been different, because she would not be subjected to their nonsense, and because she failed to bow, she had been punished. Kilroy could not change her, they could not rule her, and so they had tried to destroy her. She could relate to these children on a fundamental level. Of course, it was not exactly the same, for these children were hungry. These children neglected. But just like her, in one way or another, they were being held captive, their childhood stolen, and the ones that would not bow were being destroyed.

She felt something inside of her rise. She would have it no longer. Their freedom and their future had been snatched and she would risk everything to help them get it back. She saw herself in every one of their faces, with absolutely no control over the circumstances of their entry into this world, and she vowed to give everything she had to fight for their freedom. Somewhere in their veins flowed the blood of slaves that had revolted and prevailed. They were the sons and daughters of revolution, of liberty, just like her. And if it took the rest of her life, she would show them what that meant.

Reid walked quietly out the front door of the hotel. It was just after three p.m. on January 12th. She knew everyone was resting. She took great care in not waking them. She was wearing her I Love New York t-shirt, the tattered maternity jeans, and her cowboy boots, yet again. The jeans were much tighter than when she had arrived in them. With about a month to go, she was beginning to look very pregnant. She spoke to her belly, "Let's go get some bad guys."

She was already wired with sound and camera. She prayed as she drove herself, alone, through the streets of Port Au Prince. She wished that she could tell the crew what she was doing, but she knew that she could not. Harvey and Leon would never let her go through with it. So there she was, in broad daylight, wired and ready to sit down with ruthless modern day slave traders. She hoped she could pull it off.

She stopped the jeep outside the mission. Then she saw Yisma, coming from the direction of the courtyard. Yisma got in and smiled at her. Reid smiled back.

"Are you sure?" she asked Reid.

"Absolutely, but let's pray first."

Yisma nodded. She took Reid's hand and began to whisper. Reid tuned out the pounding of her heart and listened. The little girl spoke in Hebrew. Reid could not understand her, but the words were so soothing. Yisma met her gaze. "That was from the 31st Psalm."

Reid bowed her head and whispered her own prayer, simple, sweet, and from the bottom of her heart. "It's me, and I humbly bow myself before you, The Creator of Heaven and Earth. I pray that you guide, guard, and direct me. Please don't give up on me tonight, or ever. And please don't let your grace and mercy depart from me. In Jesus' name, I pray."

She started the jeep and began to move. Yisma directed her through the city, into a neighborhood that was comprised of a bunch of shacks nestled together. It was just a slight step up from a bidonville.

She tapped on what appeared to be a sort of door on one of the shacks, and a woman answered. Yisma asked for Eddie. The woman disappeared.

After what seemed like an eternity, a man came to the door. He was disgusting. Yisma spoke to him in Creole. Reid understood enough to know what the two were saying. Yisma told him that the American wanted to do business, that she was looking for children, girls. He eyed Reid. He said he didn't know what she was talking about, and turned to shut the hammered together boards that served as a door. He told them to get out of there, before he killed them.

Reid saw their opportunity disappearing and called out to him. With absolutely no regard for herself, forgetting everything she had ever learned, she flung herself into the dark twisted world of human trafficking. She was not herself, not at the top of her game by a long shot, still so shaken by all that she had been through in Texas. The way that her grandfather had spoken to her, the way that he had treated her, it was all still there, just beyond consciousness. It angered her, agitated her, and slowly began to gnaw at her until she had no regard for herself anymore, for her life. She was reckless at the memory of his treatment, quickly spinning out of control.

"I will pay American dollars for little girls, more for virgins."

The man stopped. She meant business. She spoke in terms he could understand, filthy terms that reached him.

Reid hated the taste left in her mouth by the foul words that she spoke. She still could not believe they had come out of her. But she had come for a reason. And as he looked her up and down like a piece of meat, she whispered under her breath, "I'm gonna' nail your balls to the wall." She met his gaze with grey fire in her eyes.

He motioned for her to come in, but said no when Yisma tried to enter. Yisma spoke to him in Creole. She told him that Reid needed her to interpret. He relented.

They entered the shack. There was no sign of the woman that had answered the door. He asked Reid what she was looking for. She spoke in English and Yisma translated. "I want some girls, young, to take them to work in America. I will pay more for virgins." She still couldn't believe that she was speaking the filthy language.

He paused for a moment and studied her face. Then he said, "How many?"

"Four."

He told her that would cost her two thousand American dollars. She told him that she was prepared to pay, but that she wanted to see them, to see if they were healthy, to make sure they would return a profit. He told her that he would let her choose from what he had. They were hidden just outside of town.

Jackpot... She was going to blow the whole scene wide open. He leaned in close and Reid almost choked on the scent of him. He was a filthy specimen. She saw him massaging his crotch whenever she spoke. Just watching him breathe and occupy space made her sick to her stomach. She despised him, and as she watched him she could not shake the feeling that she was looking evil in the eye.

He told her to come back tomorrow at the same time. He would have four girls for her that he was sure she would like. She told him that she could not wait. She convinced him that she was leaving town tomorrow and must make the deal today. He agreed, but was hesitant. He told her to stay there with Yisma while he went to get the girls.

Reid and Yisma sat close together in the shack, not saying a word. Each passing moment seemed to go on forever. Finally, after they had been sitting there for at least thirty minutes, they heard the rattling of the makeshift door, and saw him ushering four girls in. He had a gun. The sight of it made Reid feel fluttery. Her eye kept drifting toward it. What was she doing?

All at once she came back to her senses. She was exposing these girls to more danger. She was subjecting these little children to the barrel of a madman's gun. She started to feel sick. She looked at the little girls, one by one. They looked to be between six and ten. Reid could not believe her eyes, or what she was doing. The little girls were terrified of him. She wanted to grab them and tell them that everything was going to be okay, but she had to use her head.

She told him that she would take them. She told him that she had to make arrangements for their travel, and that she would return with the money. She explained that if the girls were all there, ready and waiting, tomorrow at the same time, she would pay him extra. He smiled. She smiled back ruefully, thinking how surprised he would be when he was arrested. She motioned Yisma to come.

They were just about to leave the house when the woman returned. She was talking fast and loud, in Creole, and pointing at Reid. The man looked at her. Reid had no idea what was going on, but she could see the rage in his cloudy, yellowed eyes. He grabbed her by her beautiful red hair and struck her. Yisma caught her as she fell. He struck Yisma with a blow to her head that knocked her out. He dragged Reid across the floor of the shack and cut the fly to her pants open. She was pregnant. He hadn't even noticed it before. He fumbled with his own pants while Reid tried to scream and fight, but she was in so much pain she could barely speak or move. She could feel her own warm blood soaking her hair. Her struggle ceased. She looked at him. She looked him in the eye. She looked at him with all the courage that she could muster.

The monster looked back into the pale grey depths. What he saw there paralyzed him. She was not afraid. She was not afraid of him. He was about to rape and kill her, and she was not even afraid. Something about her made him stop. He hated her. He knew as he looked into her eyes that he would never reach her, that he would never get to her. And it was in that moment that she got to him, her courage and her goodness spoke to him, told him what he had become, truth that he did not want to hear.

He took his knife and cried out in rage as he sliced her beautiful face open. She kept her eyes on him until she could no longer see. He kicked her, beat her, and dragged her out of the shack and into the streets. Then he fled.

Reid lay in the streets of Port Au Prince, feeling her life drain out of her. She thought about Reagan, saw his beautiful face. She loved him so. But she knew he would be okay. She would see him again. Somewhere... She thought about the child within her. She was sorry. She made a mistake. She had not thought it through. She had been reckless. They would meet somewhere. Someday... She thought about

Papa, how she loved him, how she wished things had been different. And Gram, how devastated she would be. Then Nana, her Nana. She missed her so. And Isaac, her father. She never got to tell him...

But as Reid lay somewhere between this world and what was next, it was the thought of leaving her mother that ripped her heart out. It was the look in her mother's eye when she left her at the airport, that Reid could not stop seeing. It was Elise that she hated to leave behind, the fragile, complicated, wounded soul that was her mother.

Reid knew that Elise would not survive this, and yet she couldn't stay. She just couldn't. She began to hallucinate, found herself on Anneville Road, walking. She felt the sun on her face, the wind in her hair. It was springtime. Wild flowers were all around. She walked toward the farmhouse, looking for someone. And then she was gone. She was gone.

Yisma woke to the cries of the little girls. She told them to hush. She rattled off the directions to the mission and told them to hurry. She told them to run. Then she picked up the gun that was left on the table. Right then the woman came in and saw her. Yisma pointed the gun at her and told her to get back. Then she ran, as fast as her skinny little legs could carry her. She ran out into the streets for Reid. The ten year old child pulled the woman's body into the jeep and took off. She drove as fast as she could. She hoped she could remember the way.

The jeep tore through the night, out of Port Au Prince, through the country, and finally up into the mountains. The child prayed that she had enough gas to get there. When she finally found the house, barely recognizable from the outside, relief flooded her being. She drove the jeep around to the side, and camouflaged it in the trees. She began to cry as she looked at the woman that had come to save her, to save the children. Reid's beautiful face was covered in blood.

She had been cut. The back of her head continued to bleed. She had been struck by the butt of the gun that Yisma now held in her hand.

Yisma dropped the gun on the ground and began to wail. She prayed over Reid and sobbed. There were no signs of life. She cried out into the desolate night, high up in the mountains of Haiti. She cried for Reid. She cried for herself. And she cried because evil was a force to be reckoned with, over and over again. The beautiful one with the flaming red hair, the gentle soul that had come to save her, was dead. And it wasn't over. It was far from over.

## Reagan

JANUARY 12TH, 2010...

Reid had exactly three nights left in Haiti when Reagan got the call.

"Have you seen the news?" It was his mother. She sounded frantic.

"No. What's going on?" he asked her.

"It's only just happened..." she began. Margaret Rigaud chose her words very carefully, knowing the magnitude of what she was about to say. "It's Haiti. There has been an earthquake. It's all over the news."

Reagan crossed the living room in his apartment and turned on the television. He was confronted with rough cell phone photos and videos of the earth shaking. Utter devastation had occurred in Haiti just moments ago. He could not believe it.

"Where exactly is Reid staying?"

"Port Au Prince. Mom, I have to go."

Margaret Rigaud sat in her favorite chair, alone in her private sitting room, with a dead receiver in her hand. She watched the footage of the toppled buildings and heard the people screaming. It was intensely personal, destruction for her country yet again. It was even more distressing because Reid was there, and she was in Port Au Prince, exactly where the footage was coming from. Margaret could not move. She was paralyzed, watching her television screen.

Reagan called Le Maison. The phone rang and rang and rang. He tried again. Nothing. No answer. He began to panic. He tried the office. He was put straight through to Jim Gates, one of the producers. "What the hell is going on?" he asked him.

"Reagan, I don't know. We aren't getting anything out of Haiti right now. There's been nothing from the crew, and you know as well as I do, if they were able, they'd be all over this."

Reagan's heart sank. "Jim, you've got to get me there. I know you have to be sending a crew."

"Of course, they fly in two hours."

"From where?"

"JFK."

"I'll be there."

"Of course."

Reagan tore himself away from the television and packed a bag, just the basics, change of clothes, toothbrush. There wasn't time to think too far ahead. He had to get to Haiti. That was all that mattered, and by the look of things, his window of opportunity was very small, very small indeed.

The plane circled the Port Au Prince airport for forty-five minutes awaiting clearance to land. Reagan's anxiety was growing. He felt like he might climb out of his skin. He knew that they could easily be turned away, sent back to Miami without permission to land.

But finally the plane landed, and they were greeted with pandemonium. People were running around everywhere. Many of them were Americans. They had come to the airport to try and get out of Haiti, but there were no flights going out at this time. They looked like refugees, lost, with no idea what to do, where to go. Some of them were injured, bleeding. All of them were shocked, and all of them were frightened. There was a military truck waiting for the World crew. It had been arranged by what was left of the Haitian government, in haste, to bring their story to the global audience. They needed help and they needed it quickly.

Chaos ensued. Reagan piled into the back of the open military truck with the rest of the World crew, and they were on their way. The camera guys filmed, while Chandler Scott reported. Reagan almost laughed out loud despite the seriousness of the situation. Chandler was in Haiti after all, and he was terrified. Reid was right. Reagan thought about her and was overwhelmed with fear for her. He put it out of his head. She had to be all right. She just had to.

The scene was surreal. Reagan could not believe it. It was night in Port Au Prince and there was no electricity. Only the light from the truck's high beams illuminated the scene. There was debris everywhere, bricks and mortar, even household items. There were homes, buildings, markets, just toppled everywhere. It was difficult to maneuver the truck through the streets. People were walking, in shock, unable to comprehend all that they were living, the nightmare that they were witnessing. Some wailed and screamed into the night for help, but there was no help. There was only death and destruction. Reagan saw a young child. She couldn't have been more than four. She was walking, alone, like she was in the middle of a warzone. It was as if no one even saw her, so caught up in their own despair. She was crying. She was terrified.

"Stop the truck!" he yelled.

Reagan took control of the situation as best he could. All the while, the camera never stopped rolling. They were live, all over the world. The driver came to a stop and Reagan hopped out of the back of the truck. He went to the little girl. She was covered in a fine white powder. She cried inconsolably, her tears making dark rivers down her cheeks. He took her hand and began to speak to her. "It's okay. Don't cry. Are you hurt?"

He wanted to tell the child that she was going to be fine. He wanted to tell her that they would help her, that they would make everything better, anything to stop her bone chilling cries. But he could not say those words. He knew better. He was not able to fix anything for her. He could not turn back time. There was no telling what she had witnessed, and no one could undo what had been done to her. Whatever had happened was right here, right now, and it wasn't going anywhere.

In her eyes, he witnessed fear, the like of which he had never seen before, and gut wrenching grief. The loss was incomprehensible and there wasn't a damn thing he could do about any of it. He picked up the little girl and carried her to the truck. He called out for water and gave her a drink. Then he reached way down, and harnessed the part of himself that had always been there, but had never been appreciated or even understood.

"Don't be afraid. It's all over. You're safe now. I'll keep you safe," he told her in Creole.

The words rolled off his tongue in the language that he had heard all around him, all his life. The words were spoken in the terror of the night, coming from deep down in his soul. They had been born of sadness, but the sound of them coming out of him in the Haitian tongue made his heart sing, gave him wings. And while Port Au Prince lay in ruins at his feet, Reagan began to find himself, a Haitian prince born on foreign soil, home at last.

He knew that he was exactly where he was supposed to be, and everything that ever happened in his life led him to the spot where he was standing. He wondered where Reid was at that very moment, and he knew that his decision to come to Haiti was so much bigger than he ever anticipated. In an instant, it became about so much more than finding her.

He closed his eyes and held the little girl in his arms. She wrapped her arms around his neck and sobbed softly against his chest. She didn't know why she trusted him; she just did. He climbed into the front of the truck, still holding her. He didn't even know her name, where she had come from, or if someone was searching for her right now. It didn't matter. There was nothing that could be done. It was chaos and confusion everywhere, and he was not about to leave her behind.

The representative for the United States Embassy drove the truck. Reagan asked about the area of Le Maison hotel. "What is the condition of that area? World has a crew staying there. We have to get to them. They were covering a story on the restaveks."

The young man's eyes told him all that he needed to know. "It's not good, sir. It's not good at all. We can try to get there, but it will be difficult."

"Please, we have to get there. My fiancée is staying there."

The man nodded and began to strategically maneuver them around the city, in an effort to get as close to Le Maison as possible. If he could get in the general vicinity, they could walk the rest of the way.

After what seemed like an eternity, the man parked the truck. Reagan had no idea where they were. He was not familiar with Port Au Prince, but even if he had been, he would have never recognized it anyway. What he saw was a hellish jigsaw puzzle all around him. He had no idea what he was even looking at.

The driver pointed and told him that it was straight ahead. Reagan instructed two of the crew members to stay and guard the truck from looters. Everyone else followed the embassy employee to the site of Le Maison. Reagan could not believe his eyes. It was nothing more than a pile of rubble. There were bricks and mortar, little bits of stucco, broken tiles from the roof. Whole floors had collapsed on top of each other.

Secure in Reagan's arms, the little girl buried her face in his neck, hiding from the destruction. He made sure the camera guy was still filming. Then he addressed the world.

"This is Reagan Jacques, reporting live from Port Au Prince. We are at the site of Le Maison, a hotel here in Port Au Prince, and we need help. As you can see, it has been completely demolished. There was a World crew staying right here, including investigative journalist Reid Coleman. They are all currently unaccounted for, and could possibly be buried underneath the rubble. We need help, equipment, search and rescue teams. We need it now. There are people buried all over the city. And until we know otherwise, we must err on the side of hope and humanity and assume that they are still alive. There is only a small window of opportunity to save them. We have to get them out now." He pleaded with the camera, knowing that the broadcast was being seen all over the globe. "And now, Chandler Scott…"

He began to walk around the rubble, leaving Chandler Scott there floundering in front of the camera. The child's arms wound tighter around his neck. He began to survey the damage. He spotted a Haitian man wandering around, looking like he had lost his mind. Reagan approached him. "Hello. I'm with the World crew. We had some people staying at the hotel here. I'm trying to get some information. Do you know of anyone that would be able to help me?

I need to know if any of them got out, or if they were inside. I need someone to help me look for them."

The man looked at him with a blank look. He was clearly in shock. "This was my hotel. My beautiful hotel is gone. I was at home. I made it out of my house just before the roof came down."

Reagan was impatient. Reid could be buried somewhere. She could be hurt, or dying. He spoke harshly to the man, "Did anyone make it out, I said!"

"I don't know," was all the man could tell him. Reagan began to call her name. He began to call Harvey, Brigitte, Leon, Eric, and Paolo, but there was no answer. The rubble was silent.

Still holding on to the little girl, he began to sift through the rubble as best he could by the light of the trucks high beams. There were only a handful of men. He thought he would go crazy. It was impossible to pick up the cement blocks. Impossible. He screamed out at the night, his cries lost in the sea of darkness. Finally, he sat down in the street, exhausted. He surveyed the destruction that was faintly lit. He bent down, picked up a brick from the base of the pile, and hurled it beyond the light, deep into the darkness. He wanted to throw a fit. He wanted to break down. But the little one watched his every move, and he knew it. And for some strange reason, her presence was giving him strength. Her spirit was giving him courage.

Daylight broke, and with it reality. All that had been concealed in darkness was now visible. The horror was unbelievable. If the World crew had been inside Le Maison, they could not possibly have survived. Bodies were everywhere. A group of local Haitians including Louis, the brother of Jean, began to sift through the rubble, looking for survivors. They dragged the bodies of the dead into the street, in hopes that someone would come for them, that someone would bury them.

The Haitians kept digging, with Reagan right alongside them. He had been able to gather, from Mr. Henri, the general vicinity of Reid's room. He stopped for a moment and took a step back, studying the mountain of debris before him. The little girl watched his every move. She came to stand beside him. Reagan took her by the hand. She said nothing. She still had not spoken to him. Instead, she looked up at him with wide eyes, sensing his sadness, feeling his pain. He did not see her. He was intent on something else. He thought he heard something.

There it was again. He made his way closer, careful not to disturb the debris. If someone were buried alive, any shift of the debris could be fatal. He listened. He heard it again. It was a tapping sound. He grabbed a small rock and tapped four times on a piece of roof. Then he waited.

The sound came to him, four taps, just like his own, faint, muffled, but still there. Four taps... He waited a moment. He tapped the roof again, two taps this time. Again, he waited. This time the sound came to him, sweeter than any sound he had ever heard, for it was the sound of life, against all odds, hanging by a thread. Two taps...

Reagan called out for help. Then he led the little girl to the edge of the scene and told her to wait there. She settled herself cross-legged on the ground and watched while he, the World crew, and the handful of Haitian men sifted bit by backbreaking bit through the overwhelming rubble, looking for life.

Finally, they unearthed an arm. The cry of pain that came with it was music to their ears. Reagan's heart began to pump harder and harder at the prospect of saving someone's life. His hope that it was Reid was gone the moment he saw the arm. Even with the fine dust that covered it, he could tell that it was too dark to be Reid. But still his heart surged with excitement. They had found someone, and that someone was alive. There was hope at last, all around them. There were survivors.

After hours of intense lifting, digging, and intermittent differences of opinion resulting in frustration and ultimately even rage, the last of the roof was lifted off of the dark skinned man. The makeshift search and rescue effort unearthed him, and cried out in victory against the backdrop of despair. Reagan thought for a moment. The man looked familiar, faintly. He thought hard, and then it came to him. A huge grin spread across his face, for he knew that he was looking at Leon Fisher.

"Leon!"

Realization slowly found him, and the corners of his mouth turned up into the hint of a smile, but the pain that pulsed through his broken body kept him from any real celebration. "Reagan," Leon uttered. Then with some difficulty, through parched lips and with a dry mouth, "I am so glad to see you."

The two men sat together, talking of all that led up to the quake. Leon learned that he was the first to be rescued. Everyone else was still missing. Over the next three hours, they would find Brigitte and Paolo, dead. Stanley had survived, but he was in terrible shape. The truck had gone immediately, attempting to get him to a hospital, with instructions to hurry back in case they found more survivors that needed transport.

Reagan was beginning to get desperate. It was getting dark again, and still no Reid. The precious life clock was ticking, and with it, any chance of finding her alive. Without food and water, she only had a few days. The first day had come to a close. It had been about twenty- four hours since the quake struck. He thought about the fact that she was pregnant. He figured that gave him less time to find her. She was sustaining two, maybe. In any case, she was bound to have less time.

He searched and searched through the rubble, in the area believed to be close to her room. He was searching for Harvey as well. They still had not found him. He was beginning to wonder if the two of them could have been gone from the hotel. He asked Leon as much.

Leon shook his head. "I don't think so. I think I would have known. We were all resting in our rooms. We got up early and pretty much wrapped our story. Everyone was exhausted, said they wanted some downtime. I was dozing on my bed when I felt it move. The roof came down in seconds."

Reagan shuddered, listening to his account. Leon got up and walked around the debris in the general vicinity where Reid and Harvey would have been. His arm was broken, but it would have to wait a little while longer. He hoped there would be more doctors arriving in the next few days. For now a broken limb was not considered life threatening, so he would have to make do. With Reagan's help, he had crafted a sort of makeshift splint with a board and some strips of cloth. He tried to forget about the pain, and think.

"Reagan, you know, the more I think about it, the more I have a feeling that Reid was gone when the quake happened."

"What makes you say that?"

"Well, I'm starting to remember some things, and I know that Harvey had come to my room looking for her." Reagan was listening to Leon, hanging on every word.

Leon continued, "He said that he couldn't find her and was wondering if I had seen her. I told him that I left her by the pool, reading, and that she was about to go to her room and take a nap. He told me that he had just come from her room and she wasn't there. I was going to go and help him look, but he said that she probably went to get something to eat and he would look for her in the kitchen."

Reagan and Leon looked at each other. The implications were huge. It was possible that Harvey and Reid were buried at the bottom of the pile of rubble, where the kitchen would have been, but it was also possible that they weren't there at all.

Reagan began to shout orders. Mr. Henri led them to the general vicinity of the kitchen. They began to dig like madmen, even Leon with his broken arm, but it was absolutely no use. They would never get to the bottom of the pile. Reagan felt his frustration mount.

He stood there, in the inky dark night of Port Au Prince, staring at the monstrous heap of debris. Then he prayed his heart out. He prayed for Reid, that she would be safe until he could find her. He prayed for the child, that he would be able to find her family. There was just so much to do, and things did not look good. The massive aftershocks were interfering with the search and rescue effort. Even so, he prayed. He prayed for all of the people, buried all over the city, that were waiting for help. He prayed for a miracle.

Reagan lay down on a cot in the little camp that they had set up. It was close to morning, the 14th of January. He must try to rest for a moment. He hadn't slept in two days. And while he was sure that he would be unable to fall asleep, he knew that he must force himself to rest for a moment so that he would be able to keep going.

The little girl sat down on the cot beside him. She watched him with her big, dark eyes. She stroked his face, softly. He drifted off to sleep but Reid was there, all of Haiti was there, the little girl was still there. While his body got the rest that it needed to keep going, his mind was caught up in a maze of questions and answers, trying to figure out what to do next. He awoke to someone calling his name. The voice sounded remotely familiar. That accent…

# Ruth

Ruth Johnson sat next to Ellen on the lovely floral sofa, at the last house down Anneville Road. The farmhouse was warm and familiar. She was content beside her old friend.

The two had set out early, bundled up in their warm coats, for it was a cold day. They had driven out to the cemetery around eight o'clock that morning, tended graves until around noon, then headed back to Ellen's house to clean themselves up. They finally showed up at the farmhouse around three o'clock, for a late lunch with Maureen.

Maureen joined Ellen and Ruth in the living room. They planned to enjoy a hot cup of coffee and watch the news. But then they got to talking, and decided to stretch their legs first. And so, the news was forgotten.

They made their way to the creek. Ellen remembered how, as a child, she had run with all the energy in the world down to its banks, and into the cool water. Today she walked, carefully choosing her steps so as not to lose her footing. She was ninety-nine years old, and she knew it.

Ruth picked her path carefully, as well. She wasn't too far behind Ellen, at ninety-five. Even so, the two old women were still in excellent health. But they were not fools. They knew that each day was a gift, and they intended to make the most of every moment.

The ancient live oaks spread their branches all around them. There were no flowers, no green grass, for it was January. But the warm sun was there, in the bright blue sky, peeking here and there from behind the clouds. Ruth walked, enjoying the day and the company of old friends. She asked Maureen how she was doing. She wanted to know how things were going with Bob since Reid left.

"Oh, he just wanders around, doesn't say much. Just answers me here and there." She stopped for a moment, unsure of what else to say. "It's like she died or something."

Ruth thought for a moment. "Well, to him, I suppose she did."

They walked a little further to where the old rocking chairs waited, underneath the king of the oaks, close to the bank. It was beautiful even in January, serene, peaceful, unchanging, just the sound of the water running. Maureen settled herself into the hammock, leaving her mother and Ruth to rest in the rockers. The walk was a lot for the two old women. They were quiet for a moment, each woman lost in her own thoughts.

"Do you think he'll ever come around?" Ellen asked her daughter.

"I don't really know." Maureen hated to admit that she did not know what her husband would do. She thought she knew him most of the time, but there was a dark place, deep inside, that try as she might she had never been able to penetrate.

"Oh, he'll come 'round." Ruth interrupted. "He loves that girl too much. And he doesn't really hate colored folks, just hates himself. Look at me, all these years and he's never been anything but good to me. And my girls, he's always been kind to 'em. I've seen hate. It's not in him. He's got a good heart. Problem is his daddy, what he came from. He can't forget it."

"It's deeper than that," Maureen whispered.

"If you mean about Jeremiah, I suspected as much. Figured that kinda' complicated things. Been jealous of a dead boy all these years, has he?"

Maureen was speechless. Years had gone by without them ever having spoken of him, without ever having uttered his name. He had lived in their hearts and memories, but never on their tongues, not together, not the two of them. But Ruth had finally done it, and now it was time. She had spoken his name out loud, and the peaceful sound of the running creek flooded Maureen's consciousness, taking her back to that night, to the sound of the Trinity River.

She began to speak. The truth that she had hidden away for so long came out of her. She told Ruth about driving out to the house that night, about how she had knocked on the window. She told her about the two of them swimming in the river. She hid nothing. She told her about the kisses, and then finally about the Smiths.

The three women sat there in silence, listening to the creek run, unable to find words. Overwhelming loss enveloped them. They longed for the past. Joe had been among them, and Lloyd, Mama and Papa, and of course, Jeremiah...

Those living, breathing, beautiful moments in time...

But it only lasted for a moment. Ruth was the first to speak. She looked at Maureen with tears in her eyes. "Thank you."

Maureen had finally freed her. What Ruth had always known had been confirmed. Her son had been everything that she ever believed him to be, right up until his very last breath. He had been strong and brave, beautiful and honorable, truthful, kind, and loving. He had been a gift from the Creator, and once again she was confronted with the realization that she had been blessed beyond all that she could imagine to have been the one to bring him into the world and watch him take his first breath.

"I have never forgotten him, Ruth. Never. I'm so sorry," Maureen spoke with difficulty.

Ruth had much to say. "Oh darlin', I have watched you for over fifty years. Over fifty years of feeling guilty because you lived! I watched you go from sunshine and moonbeams, to thunder and lightnin'. But my pain was so great, I couldn't offer you anything, anything at all, wouldn't offer you anything. It took all I had to get from one day to the next. And in a way, I blamed you, even though I knew better, even though I knew none of it was your fault."

The words that Ruth spoke next would free Maureen, after so, so long. "I forgive you Maureen, for whatever you think you need forgiveness for. But truth be told, there is nothin' that requires for-giveness. You didn't do anything wrong."

Maureen left the hammock. She walked to Ruth and sat at her feet. Then she cried her heart out, a seventy year old child, with her head in the old woman's lap.

Ruth spoke to her softly. "Sometimes, I think we blame ourselves because the truth hurts us so much. That's how women do. The truth is, we had absolutely no control over any of it. Oh, sure, I could have refused to let him go to that school. And you could have steered clear of him. Would things have been different? Maybe. But maybe they would have been worse. Maybe the Smiths would have killed us all, every one of us, and the girls would never have lived, would never have become the women that they are today."

Ruth stopped for a moment. Then with fresh tears, she contin-ued. "Maybe Jeremiah would have been killed without ever having lived." She took a deep breath, overcome with emotion. Then she picked Maureen's face up in her hands. "That would have been the tragedy, Maureen. That would have been the real tragedy." They got lost in each other's gaze.

Ruth went on. "There is one thing that I know for sure. He would have never been happy just accepting things as they were, as his lot. He would have never been content just being safe. And I know now that it woulda' tore my heart out to see him broken. Creatures like Jeremiah weren't meant to be broken. They were meant to be wild, free. They're made of different stuff. You know? It's like they come into this world already knowing what it takes us a lifetime to figure out. Like they've danced with angels..."

Ellen thought about what Ruth said, and she watched her, watched her with Maureen. She could not help but think about the day that Reid had come to see her, the day she told her about Reagan and the baby. She thought about how Reid had cried, just like that, her head in Ellen's lap. She shuddered, and she thought about Bob, how he had learned nothing after all these years.

He had spent his entire life being judged by circumstances that he could not control. He had spent his whole life trying to prove that he was more than white trash. He didn't even realize what he was doing, that he was doing the same thing that had been done to him, over and over again. And Elise, he had ruined her life, made her dependent on her parent's approval. She was afraid of her own shadow. Even Ellen herself, he had tried to make her do things over the years that she disagreed with. Sometimes she had indulged him, but most of the time, when the stakes were high, she had not.

It was only Reid that he had been unable to break, that he had been unable to control. She was just like Ruth had said. Like she came into the world knowing what they all had to learn on their own, like she had danced with angels.

Ellen thought back. She and Lloyd had given Bob a chance so long ago, looked past the fact that he was Clyde Coleman's son. He had seized it and never looked back. But he hadn't done the same for anyone else. He never gave anyone a chance. And everyone that loved him, he had bullied them, changing them slowly into who he wanted them to be. But not Reid, never Reid, for she had danced with angels... She watched him with knowing eyes her entire life, and in the end, everything he hated, everything he tried to control, had culminated into the here and now, with her, a sort of moment of truth.

The words escaped Ellen. She spoke them out loud, "Forgiveness... Forgiveness is the key... Forgiving each other... Forgiving ourselves... Reid knows it. She always has."

Maureen could have stayed at the creek forever, listening to the water run, away from the pain, away from the look in her husband's eye. But she knew she had to face him. As she made her way back to the farmhouse, resolve strengthened every step. The magnitude of all that she had just learned was upon her. Ruth watched her, just ahead, wondering what can of worms had been opened.

Maureen marched up the steps and opened the front door to find Bob, but he wasn't there. She went through the living room, the dining room, the kitchen, looking for him along the way, then out the back door. She saw him in the pasture. He had the plow for some reason. She walked out to him, across the field. Ruth followed her, worried, wondering what she was about to do.

He saw her coming and stopped the tractor. He got down and waited for her. He wondered what was going on. It wasn't like her to come out so far. He watched her walk toward him. There was something about the sureness of her step that he did not recognize. As she came closer, he was flooded with love for her. He had been so distant with her. They hadn't spoken in weeks. He hated what was between them right now, and even so, could not even begin to bridge it. He was still too angry, still too lost.

He saw that she was carrying something. He couldn't tell what it was until she was right up on him. "Bob, I've come to tell you something. It's been between us for too long. It's about Jeremiah."

Bob Coleman turned his back on his wife and began to climb up into the tractor. She took the shotgun that she had been carrying, cocked it, and fired it into the air. She barely even flinched. It was Bob that taught her to shoot a shot gun, and he had taught her well.

He stopped, and considered her. She's bluffing, he thought. But as he looked into her eyes he saw something he had never seen before. He knew, right then and there, that he had lost her.

"I loved him. I loved him more than I had ever loved anything or anybody," she began. "I have thought about him all my life. Not a day has gone by that I don't miss him."

Bob Coleman thought he would not live through all that she spoke. Everything that he ever imagined, ever suspected, was true. He could not bear it. He wished she would shoot him, kill him, so that he did not have to hear anymore.

"And you have made me pay over and over again, every day of my life, because you knew it." And then it came, the truth, penetrating his soul with the force of all that she said. "But he was killed. Gone. And then there you were, and it was you that I fell in love with, you that became my future, you that I wanted to spend the rest of my days with." She wouldn't quit. She wouldn't let up. All that had been on her heart for so long was upon them.

"It was you that I pledged my love and loyalty too. And oh, how I have loved you in spite of yourself. I have been a good wife. I have been a good mother. My parents treated you like their very own son. They trusted you, with me, with my future. But it has never been enough, because I cannot erase him, and you can't forget. He lived, Bob. He lived, and I loved him."

Bob Coleman couldn't stand it. He could not even look at his wife. Ruth stood just beyond her. He couldn't face her either.

"I forgive you, Bob. Right here. Right now. I forgive you for all the hell that you put me through, all these years, because I had the audacity to love someone before you. I forgive you for the hell you put us all through, because of your own insecurities and your past. But I'm telling you if it doesn't stop today, I'm gone. And if you try to do to Reid what you did to everyone else, I'll never forgive you. I'll be filled with hate right down into my grave. She doesn't deserve it, and if you try to make her suffer, I'll never forgive you. All she ever did was love you, Bob. And she knows. She knows all of it. She knows all the damage that you have done and she still loves you, forgives you even. She's the best thing that ever happened to us. She's the best thing that ever happened to you."

And with that, Maureen Coleman tossed her head, squared her shoulders, took her shotgun, and walked back to the house. Bob stood there in the pasture, the cold January breeze blowing about him. He watched her go, with Ruth Johnson right behind her.

Ellen watched the whole scene from the top of the hill. It had taken a long time, too long, but Maureen had learned to fight like hell for herself, after all. Ellen knew that her example had been enough. In the end, it had been enough. She just hoped it was not too late.

"It's after ten o'clock," Ellen announced. She and Ruth had spent the evening trying to take Maureen's mind off of all that was bothering her. They had gotten out the sewing basket, then worked the hours away on quilt squares. The three of them were making a quilt for the baby, Reid's baby.

"Don't go," Maureen told them.

The old farmhouse was cold. She got up to make some coffee. On her way, she turned the television set on. They would just be able to catch World's nightly news.

Maureen sat there staring at the television screen in horror. There was silence as they watched the destruction going on in Haiti. It was Reagan. He was live, in Port Au Prince. Ellen gasped.

Ruth immediately began to pray. She didn't need to see more. She disappeared into a world that Maureen and Ellen had never known. She prayed to the Creator of Heaven and Earth that they would never know her pain, that they would never have to bury a child. She begged for Reid's life. She begged for more time.

Maureen called for Bob to come inside. He had been just outside the back door, banging his boots to try and dislodge some of the caked on mud. From the sound of her voice, he could tell something was wrong, very wrong. He hurried to see what the commotion was about, and was not prepared for what he saw. It was an earthquake, Haiti.

The four of them sat, glued to the television set, not moving, not speaking. The implications of the devastation drove all that had occurred moments earlier far from their minds. Of course, it was not forgotten, just put aside for the moment.

The sound of the telephone rang in the distance. It disturbed Ruth. The others acted as if they did not hear it. It was persistent, frantic. She went to answer it.

"Farmhouse."

"Ruth, is that you?" It was Elise.

"Yes, it's me."

"There has been a terrible earthquake in Haiti, Port Au Prince, where Reid is."

"Yes, I know. We are all watching the news right now."

# Bob

JANUARY 12, 2010...

Bob Coleman could not believe what he was seeing. He fell back into his chair in front of the television set. Ellen, Ruth, and Maureen gathered coats and handbags. Ruth announced that Elise was coming for them. She would drive them to Ellen's, where they would wait for word on Reid.

Bob nodded in answer. He heard her, and he knew that they were leaving because of him. No one wanted to be around him. They were done with him, and they did not want him to see their pain, their concern for Reid. He was the enemy. He knew that he should care, that he should be concerned. But as he watched the island of Haiti on the news, watched Reagan appeal to the global audience for help, he could think of nothing else but his beloved granddaughter, his Reid.

He tore himself away from the front of the television set. He went to the telephone in the kitchen. He picked up the receiver. Then he hesitated. He put the receiver down.

Thoughts of his girls flooded his senses, Maureen, Frankie, Elise, Reid, even Ellen. Over the years he had taken care of them all, loved them all, protected them all. Even Ruth, he had grown to love her, and her girls, and their families. He had told himself that they were different, and so they had become family. But when it had come to Reid, he had been unable to let it all go.

"Pride cometh before a fall," he muttered.

He watched Reagan. The news played his appeal over and over again. Each time Bob watched it, he became more and more afraid for Reid. He knew what he had to do. He needed someone to pull some strings. He picked up the receiver again, but this time he dialed the number. The familiar voice answered the phone.

"Yeah, Don. It's me, Bob." He hesitated. "I'm calling in that favor now. Looks like there is something that you can do for me after all."

It only took him a few minutes to pack a bag and leave a note for Maureen. He turned off the television and all the lights in the farmhouse. He went out the back door, and walked to the barn. He got in his pickup and started it up. He pulled out of the driveway and onto Anneville Road. He passed Ellen's little house, and saw Elise's car by the light of the moon.

It had been a long, long time, but he began to think about Lloyd. He remembered what Maureen told him only a few hours earlier, out in the pasture. She had said, "My parents treated you like their very own son. They trusted you, with me, with my future."

Sorrow flooded his being, and profound guilt. He had failed. He thought about Lloyd. He thought about all that Lloyd had tried to teach him. It was in that moment that Bob realized that what Lloyd Adams had tried to teach him was so much bigger and so much greater than how to run a business, and how to make a living. And it was with the memory of Lloyd that he drove all the way to Oklahoma City and boarded a single engine private relief plane bound for the island of Haiti. It was his first time on an airplane, his first time out of the state of Texas, the first time he had ever been out of the United States. It was the memory of Lloyd that gave him the courage to look for Reid, but it was the fire in Maureen's eyes that compelled him to go all the way to Haiti to find her.

# Leon

JANUARY 14, 2010...

Leon Fisher sat on a cinder block, surveying the devastation
by the light of dawn. There was a panic in the air that was almost
tangible. There were people still buried underneath the quake rubble, while aftershocks continued to shake the earth all around them.
Everyone knew that the chances of finding survivors grew slimmer
and slimmer with each passing moment. Corpses were stacking up
all over the place, and the threat of disease from decay was a concern.
To make matters worse, there was no water and no food to be found.

Reagan and most of the World crew were sleeping, or trying
to at least, leaving Leon alone with his thoughts for the moment.
He sat there thinking about what he had just survived. He had been
buried for about eighteen hours. His arm was broken. It had been
unimaginable. He was terrified, but somehow he believed that he
was not going to die. He wondered if the others that were buried
right now, right this very second, felt the same way.

He looked at the site where he had almost lost his life. He thought about Reid. Was she buried there? And Reagan... Leon could tell that he was about to go crazy. He tried to remember again what had happened. Where was she? Was she down there? He was almost certain that she wasn't in the kitchen because she had been eating something out by the pool not too long before the quake. But then where could she be? And what about Harvey Finn? Had he left the hotel, or was he still inside? And how would they ever sift through all that rubble? They needed machinery. They had to get some equipment.

He heard something. The sound made his head spin around. It was a truck. It was carrying a group of search and rescue personnel. They were moving toward him. Closer. Closer. Leon did not know where they had come from. He did not care. He smiled as they drove up to the site of what had been Le Maison. They were coming to help them.

Leon tried to figure out where they were from. There was an older man looking positively beautiful because he was obviously American and had brought help. At the same time, he looked completely ridiculous. He was dressed in jeans, boots, and resplendent in a ten gallon hat. They were definitely American, all of them. Leon moved closer. They were from Oklahoma, but not the man. The accent...

# Bob

◇◇◇◇

January 14, 2010...

Bob Coleman could not believe his eyes. It only took a moment to comprehend the magnitude and complexity of what they were dealing with. There were mountains of rubble as far as his eye could see. Le Maison had toppled, reduced to a heap on the ground, and somewhere within was his precious granddaughter.

The young man that introduced himself as Leon Fisher was escorting him to the makeshift campsite that the World crew had constructed. He found Reagan resting on a cot.

"Reagan... Reagan..."

Reagan opened his eyes to see Reid's grandfather standing before him. For a split second, he thought he must be dreaming. He had to be. The man in the dream had on a hat. He had on jeans and boots.

The realization that this was no dream became clear in an instant when he saw Leon beside the man, and the ruins of Le Maison just beyond. Then there she was, the little girl, winding her tiny arms around his neck, once again.

"I've brought a search and rescue team out of Oklahoma. They brought equipment, and dogs. They've already started digging."

Reagan was never so glad to see any living soul in his entire life. He threw his arms around Bob Coleman.

Bob stood there, taken aback. He was not exactly sure how he would be received. The little Haitian girl was squashed between them. She held on to Reagan for dear life. Bob saw the way she looked at him. She searched the stranger's face for some kind of clue, what he represented. She wasn't sure about him yet.

Bob turned around to make his way back to the site of the digging, to speak to the team. Instead, he bumped right smack into his nightmare for the past thirty years, his fear in the flesh, the one person that he never wished to see, ever again in his life. Damn it, Reid! She had brought them all together, one way or another. Bob Coleman's head was spinning with the realization that he had much to be sorry for, much to be ashamed of, and much to answer for.

As he looked into the other man's tortured eyes, knowing that he was the source of all that he saw there, he realized how much he hated himself and all that he had done. The women that he loved so much, held so dear, flashed before his eyes. He wondered how on earth they had been able to continue loving him, after all that he had done. He wondered if they still did, if they still could.

He had tried to play God, and it had been a disaster. He had played with lives, manipulated futures, destroyed what they could have been. Ultimately, he had tried to stomp out everything that made him love them so much in the first place. And now, here he was, standing in the aftermath of the greatest earthquake his generation had ever known, searching for the only thing that could help him put everything back together again, Reid.

"Guess you didn't expect to find me here," Isaac spat sarcastically at him.

Bob could never have prepared himself for coming face to face with Isaac Ingram. He almost fell over. "Hello, Isaac. It's been a long time."

Reagan and Isaac shared a hug. Isaac gave him a pat on the back. He could tell, by all that he saw on Reagan's face, the hell that he was going through. But there was no time for small talk. They got right to the reason why they had come. The three of them, along with Leon, surveyed the pile of rubble once again. Reagan explained that there was the remote possibility that Reid was not in the hotel when the quake struck.

"Doesn't matter. Can't leave a single stone unturned. She could be anywhere," Isaac said.

Reagan and Isaac watched as Bob went over to speak to the Haitians that were still digging. They spoke very little English, just enough to communicate with him.

"Who are you looking for?" he asked them.

"I am looking for my brother, Jean. He was employed by the hotel," Louis told him.

There were four more Haitian men standing there. They told Bob that they were not looking for any one person; they were looking for life, any life. He nodded. Then he got to work right beside them.

Bit by bit, they dug through what they could of the rubble. After several hours, the Oklahoma search and rescue team told Bob that they would have to move on. They were certain that there was no life there. Their dogs had not hit on anything since they arrived. His heart stopped. He looked around him. How would they ever find Reid without the search and rescue team, without the equipment?

"You can't just leave. My granddaughter is here somewhere. We have to find her," he pleaded.

Isaac and Reagan watched him crumple. They had watched the old man work alongside the rest of them, desperately looking for life within the ruins of Le Maison, trying to find Reid. What they could not see was the battle that he had just fought, the very one that he had won. He had left Kilroy, had left Texas, had left the United States. He had gotten himself to the island of Haiti to look for Reid.

They did not have a moment to spare, did not have a second to waste. They were in a race against time. The moment he knew that the team was leaving anyway, Bob began to work even harder. He resigned himself to finding her, no matter what. He was going to find her and bring her home, if it was the last thing he ever did.

He picked up cinder blocks, pieces of roof, headboards, chairs, bit by bit, in an effort to find her. He had only Reagan, Isaac, Leon, and the five Haitian men working along with him. The World crew had gone. They had followed the search and rescue team to another site where there were believed to be survivors, a market. They would return later. They were doing everything they could to get help to Haiti.

Bob was tired, and he was hot. His hat sat at an awkward angle on his head. He was filthy. He was hungrier and thirstier than he ever remembered being in his entire life, but he couldn't do anything about it. They had to be careful with food and water. There wasn't much to go around.

One of the men saw Bob stumble. He could see that the old man was getting tired. The Haitian disappeared beyond the rubble, and was gone for some time. Everyone just supposed he had moved on. But then he reappeared with a bowl of rice and beans.

He made his way over to Bob and held it out. He spoke in Creole. "He says you must eat this, if you want to continue," Reagan translated.

Bob looked at the Haitian man. He was slim, dark, with muscles that rippled beneath his torn shirt and pants, his sandals barely hanging on to his feet. Bob looked at the simple bowl of rice and beans in astonishment. Wherever had it come from? The city had been destroyed. There was no food or water anywhere, no electricity, and yet he was being offered a bowl of hot cooked rice and beans.

The Haitian saw the questions in his eyes. "Eat," he said simply.

Bob took the bowl of rice and beans, sat down on a huge cinder block, and ate. It was the best thing he had ever tasted. As the warm food slid down his throat and into his stomach, he realized the magnitude of what had just occurred. Just like Reid had always said, Haitians were employed by the daily business of survival. They were accustomed to hard times, disasters, even death and destruction, but hard times did nothing to alter their character, to dull the brilliance of their humanity. And someone, somewhere, in the heart of this disaster, was cooking rice and beans over an open fire. They were strong, and they were survivors.

The Haitian man that sat beside him making sure that he ate every bite had not gone in search of food for himself. Instead, he had gone in search of sustenance for an old man that he had never seen before, and would probably never see again, an old man that was desperately searching for his granddaughter. Bob had no doubt that the man had not eaten long before he, himself, had his last bite to eat. And even so, the stranger had given him the food. That gift would never be forgotten, nor the spirit in which it was given. It was something that Bob would remember for the rest of his life. It changed him.

The two men went back to work, joining the others in the rubble. They kept on digging and lifting the debris, as best they could. Bob picked up a huge cinder block and began to carry it away. Then out of the corner of his eye, he saw it. It was mangled, crushed, and covered in dust, almost unrecognizable, but it was definitely what he thought it was. It was a foot.

He began to yell, "Over here! I've found someone."

Everyone stopped what they were doing and began to work together to unearth the body. It was obviously not Reid, but it didn't matter. It was someone, and Bob worked to free whomever it was that he had found.

"Jean! Jean!" The man's brother began to sob the moment he recognized him, but Jean was not responsive. He was dead.

"Oh, Jean! Oh, Jean!" The man sobbed. He cradled his brother in his arms, and began to speak softly in Creole. Bob didn't understand a word that he said. It didn't matter. The language of love and loss was universal. Bob wept just the same, right along with him. All that work, looking for life, willing to give anything, everything, to bring it back again, but unable, unable to give life. Jean was gone, and how many others? How many others were losing their lives all over Haiti at this very moment because there were not enough hands, because there wasn't anyone to save them? Bob Coleman wept. He wept for the love that this man had for his brother, the anguish that he felt because he was gone, the overwhelming sadness to have to say goodbye, and the inability to do a single thing about it.

Bob saw the tears running down Reagan's face as well. He saw the little Haitian girl hanging on to Reagan's leg. He heard him whispering something to her in that strange language, and watched as he picked her up in his arms. There was something in his eyes. Bob recognized it as soon as he saw it. It was the same thing he had seen in his own mother's eyes, the same thing he had seen in Lloyd's eyes, the same thing he had seen in the Haitian stranger's eyes when he brought him something to eat. It was goodness, humanity, decency. It was love.

Bob saw the tears in Isaac's jaded eyes, felt the compassion that came out of his soul, and it was in that moment that he realized how very wrong he had been. It took an earthquake to reach him. It took nine men, from different parts of the world, with different backgrounds, diverse religions, standing there together in that living, breathing, beautiful moment in time, bound by the common thread of humanity, weeping, trying to find their way.

# Maureen

◇◇◇◇

January 14, 2010...

Maureen sat with her mother, her daughter, and Ruth, glued to the television set. The farmhouse was cold and quiet, except for the sound of weeping, weeping that was coming from the television, weeping that was coming from the four of them. Maureen still could not believe that Bob was really there, in the middle of it all.

They watched the devastation for signs of Reid. Each time the World news camera followed another story, they held their breath until it returned to the rubble of Le Maison. The stories coming out of Haiti were beyond comprehension. People were being rescued from the rubble, some of them even walking away, but scores and scores had lost their lives, as evidenced by the corpses that were everywhere in the streets. It was incomprehensible. They could not believe their eyes. Not one of them spoke, as they watched. It was too devastating, entirely too devastating. Women cried, screamed, clutched their hearts. Men wandered around, lost, openly weeping. Maureen could not believe what she was seeing.

Bob was front and center, standing there in his cowboy hat. She watched him working alongside Reagan and Isaac, watched him working alongside the Haitians. Her heart cried. Why did it take something so terrible to reach people? Why did they have to wait until it was too late?

# Reagan

January 26, 2010...

Time had run out. Any chance of finding Reid alive in the rubble was gone. It had been two weeks, two weeks of searching for her. Reagan was drained, spent. He was out of his head. He didn't know what to do next.

Reid... He began to think for the first time that he may never see her again. He had not allowed himself to even consider that possibility before now. He watched Bob wander around, lost, not knowing what to do with himself. It was heartbreaking. He watched Isaac help the old man up off the ground, watched him offer a bottle of water. Could it be possible that she was teaching them something with her death? Is this how it was meant to be? After all, the three of them had learned to get along. They had been through much together. Reagan knew that he never would have tolerated Bob, had it not been for the circumstances.

He had no tolerance for what he considered ignorance and stupidity, and he believed that racism fell into both categories. He never had any desire to try to change the mind of a racist. He believed that they were too stupid to waste time on. How in the world, then, did he end up actually feeling compassion for one? He considered Bob. The old man was broken. Reagan felt sorry for him. He actually felt sorry for him. He couldn't help but be tragically amused by the fact that, in the end, they had been bound together by their love for Reid, rather than torn apart. He only wished that she could see it.

"Reagan, we have a feed to New York. They have your mother there. You won't be able to see her, but she can see you." It was Chandler Scott. Reagan didn't even know he was anywhere around, so lost in thought he had been.

He followed Chandler to where the camera was set up. He could not see her, but as her voice reached his ear across the miles that separated them, he felt something that he had not felt since he was a child. He wanted his mother.

"Reagan?"

There was a pause. "I'm here."

"Are you all right?"

"Yes, I'm fine."

But Margaret could see that her son was not fine. She could see the tears in his eyes at the sound of her voice. She could see how filthy his clothes were, how hollow his cheeks were, how much darker he was from being out in the sun, digging through the debris. He was not fine, and she was afraid that he never would be again.

"Reagan, I have been in touch with my cousin. He is coming to get you, and he will take you to his house for awhile. You can rest, get yourself together, decide what to do next." There was no response. Margaret could see her son, but he was not responding. "Reagan?"

432

"I'm still here," he said. She waited. "I can't leave the others," he finally told her.

"Of course, they are welcome. Frederic is sending transportation for you. I don't know what, and I don't know how, but he says he will send for you. You must go. You cannot stay out there in those conditions forever. Do you hear me?"

"Yes. Yes, I hear you."

"Good."

She saw the little Haitian girl settle herself into his lap. She had seen the story on television, how Reagan had picked her up off the streets the night the quake struck. Margaret figured everyone on the globe that owned a television set had seen it. World played it over and over again.

She watched the child and could tell immediately what was going on. It wasn't Reagan that had saved the little girl. It was the little girl that was saving Reagan. Each and every time that she looked up at him with her big dark eyes, she kept him from cashing it in, from giving up. She had given him a reason to keep going, someone to be strong for. Margaret watched the little Haitian girl on the screen, from where she sat in the darkened studio. "My gratitude knows no bounds," she whispered. She hoped that one day she would be able to thank her properly, and she was reminded once again of the strength within Haiti's people.

Reagan would not remember leaving the ruins of Le Maison. He would not remember the ride out of the destruction of Port Au Prince, the drive through the Haitian countryside, or the steep climb up into the mountains. He had disappeared into a place where there was only pain and unspeakable loss, and every great once in awhile there was the little girl.

Frederic Rigaud, his mother's cousin, came for them. He took them from Port Au Prince to his home in the mountains, where he fled after the earthquake. He and his wife had been in Port Au Prince, at their home, when the quake struck, but they had not been harmed. Their house was still standing. They fled to their home in the mountains, as soon as they realized the degree of the destruction. There was no food, no water, no medical supplies, and dead bodies were everywhere. They knew that they must go.

It was just the two of them. They had no children left in Haiti. Their three sons had gone years ago. When he got the call from Marguerite that her son was in Port Au Prince, he did not hesitate. He went to get him.

And so, Reagan sat in the mountain retreat of a distant Haitian cousin, while his entire world came crashing down. The love of his life was gone. She was gone and there wasn't a damn thing he could do about it.

Life looked different. He didn't want to get up in the morning. What for? The world just wasn't as bright without her in it. He thought about her, and how silly she was. He thought about how she annoyed the hell out of him, how she would zone out and disappear into a world that only she could see. He thought about how emotional she could be, how irrational. He was completely rational, absolutely all of the time. Her emotions got in the way. It drove him crazy. But now that she was gone, now that he would be facing every single day of the rest of his life without her, he realized that those emotions were what had set her apart.

He thought he knew peace, until the first time he woke up in her arms. He thought he knew compassion, until he saw the way she treated people. He thought he knew life, until she showed up. And love... Reagan had never known love, until he had been loved by Reid.

He hauled himself out of the chair that he was sitting in. He walked outside to the deck, where he could watch the sun set from the cliff. Frederic saw him and went to join him.

"You may stay as long as you like. You are welcome here. This is your home, a family retreat, you know? It belongs to the Rigauds. Your grandmother is buried here. This is where she hid, until she was tracked by the Tonton Macoutes. She even left a journal."

Reagan listened to his cousin. The pieces of the puzzle began to come together. His family had been hunted and ultimately forced to leave Haiti because of the class cleansing that Duvalier had perpetrated. "Papa Doc" had systematically set out to destroy the wealthy and upper middle class during his reign of terror. He had tweaked the not so fortunate and convinced them that he would raise them up. He had called for the lives of the social elite, mulattoes, doctors, lawyers, artists, poets, and all of the critically thinking citizens that opposed his rule. He had enslaved Haitians under their very noses, with a corrupt government that they still, to this day, had been unable to get out from under.

Reagan began to wonder about the nature of men, their desire to rule one another, and to be ruled. It was poisonous. He thought, once again, how there was truly nothing new under the sun. The Scriptures said so, and he had seen it time and time again. Freedom is worth fighting for, freedom is worth dying for. His grandmother had known it, for she had refused to bow. Reid had known it. Freedom motivated everything she did, for true love could never really exist without it.

Frederic reached him for a moment, gave him something to think about. Then Reagan was gone again. There was nothing left for him. There was no Reid.

# Frederic

JANUARY 31, 2010...

Frederic Rigaud woke even earlier than usual. He dressed himself and prepared to meet the day, thankful for life, thankful for another day. The sun was peeking up over the horizon, just beyond the beautiful turquoise expanse that was the Caribbean Sea. He paused for a moment to take it all in, from his deck built high on the cliff. The smell of something cooking was coming from the kitchen, bouillon. Bouillon for breakfast, bouillon for lunch, and bouillon for dinner, the hearty Haitian stew had done well to sustain and fortify the household in the days since the quake.

He made his way into the small kitchen and saw Bob standing there stirring the pot of stew. "Good morning," he told him.

Bob heard the strong friendly sound of Frederic's voice. It startled him. "Good morning," he returned.

The two men sat in the little kitchen with a bowl of bouillon and a cup of coffee.

"I never thought soup with bananas in it could taste so good," Bob told him.

"Plantains. They are not bananas. They are plantains." The familiar joke passed between the two.

Frederic had grown to like Bob very much. Together, they had spent many hours discussing life and all that they had seen.

"There's something I just have to say," Bob began. Frederic was listening. "I like to think that if the tables were turned, I would offer you the same kindness that you have shown me. But the truth is, I know that before all of this, I would have never invited you into my home."

Frederic nodded. "Life will teach us much if we allow it to," he said. "I would not have cared for you either."

Bob's look was questioning. "Because I'm white?"

Frederic erupted with his hearty laugh. "No. Because you are not Haitian, and your manners are atrocious."

Bob grinned at him, but then his mood turned dark, brooding. "I don't even care what happens to me anymore. Without Reid, life just doesn't even seem worth living." Frederic sat there nodding, listening as the man gave life to all that was in his heart.

Reagan and Isaac walked into the kitchen, then Leon. The room was too small to hold them all, so they made their way out onto the deck. From where they sat, on the side of the mountain, they could see the sea.

"It is time for you to earn your keep," Frederic told them. "As soon as you finish your breakfast, you are going to make rounds with me, all of you."

He looked at Reagan. "The child will stay with Sophia." Reagan whispered to her in Creole. The little girl went and took Sophia's hand. Sophia Rigaud kissed her husband goodbye, and took the child to a nearby stream to bathe and play.

And so Reagan, Bob, Isaac, and Leon hiked up the steep mountainside to the tiny village of Carita, with Doctor Frederic Rigaud. Frederic's car was unable to make the journey. Only an all terrain vehicle or burro could make the journey on the primitive roads.

They spent the day visiting the sick and wounded in the little community. Frederic had no medicine, no supplies, only his vast knowledge and willpower to sustain them. "It is the most frustrating thing a physician can see," he told them, "to know that there is something that can help them, but that you do not have access to it."

They saw the many that were sick and wounded, that still did not have access to proper medical care almost a month after the quake. And while Carita had not been as affected as areas like Port Au Prince, Leogane, and Jacqmel, they were still suffering. The effects were being felt all over Haiti.

Outside in the warm sunshine, a group of children gathered around Reagan. They began to sing in Creole. Reagan recognized the song. His mouth began to form the words as the melody entered his heart. In spite of all that he had lost, Reagan sang loud and strong.

Isaac couldn't help himself. He laughed out loud. In spite of everything, these children were singing and they were smiling, living a simple but peaceful existence, high up in the mountains. Reagan, Isaac, Bob, and Leon had the exact same thought at the exact same time. Reid... They felt her. Somewhere out there, just beyond consciousness. This was what she had come to Haiti for. This was what she had died for.

Frederic watched the four men smile through their tears. He knew that they had come a long way. He also knew that there was still far to go. They would be returning to the States soon, without what they had come for, and he grieved for them way down deep in his heart, and prayed that they would find peace.

# Zyga

Reagan had no idea where he was, what part of Haiti. The past few days had gone by while he simply went through the motions of living. But now he slowly made his way down the mountainside, through the foliage, back the way he had come, toward his cousin's house. Frederic took his hand and led him to the most beautiful spot on earth that he had ever known, perched on the side of the majestic mountains. Bob, Leon, and Isaac watched from just a few feet away.

"This is Haiti, Reagan."

The view took his breath away. From the cliff where he stood, he looked out at the horizon, past the lush green valleys, across to the brilliant greens and blues of the Caribbean Sea. Reagan thought about the people beyond, with their spirits that refused to be crushed. They had survived days in the rubble, weeks even. Their strength and courage were unmatched anywhere on the globe. He felt the tears burn his eyes. He felt so much for the land that stretched out before him. He had gained an appreciation for it, along with an intense love and respect for the people, his people.

Of course, he had heard the suppositions of the superstitious, and no doubt there was evil in Haiti just like any other place in the world. But there was also something else, something far greater that stirred his consciousness. Matthew 22:36-40... He had seen no better evidence of it than right here. He had watched a starving Haitian man give his meal to a stranger, a racist, a bigot. He offered it with compassion, without even a thought for his own life. Reagan had witnessed the gentleness and peacefulness of the Haitian people, their love and respect for the Creator far greater than anything he had ever seen in his own country. They did not desire material things. They were thankful for each day, thankful for life and limb, and always willing to give whatever they had to someone with greater need. The people had reached him and made him proud to be of Haitian descent, proud to come from a nation of slaves that had risen up against the mighty French and had taken their freedom back.

Deal with the devil... he had heard the self-righteous say. As if the only way that a group of African slaves could take France, that a man could secure his freedom, was by making a deal with the devil. What about the danger in that accusation, professing to know the hearts of men, passing judgement without wisdom? How many people make a deal with the devil every single day and don't even realize it? Every man that tries to rule his brother, enslave his brother for his own self-gratification, without recognition of the sovereign, free state of his soul, his being? Every man that tries to be God? For isn't that where the original deal took place?

Oh, how he missed Reid. He wanted to talk to her. He wanted to share with her all that he had learned. He wanted to see her face, look into her grey eyes. He wanted her to see who he was, the man that he had become.

442

Isaac recognized what he saw on Reagan's face. He was missing her too. Just like Reagan, he was heartbroken. But he was also furious. He had lost his daughter all over again. He was so close, so close to sharing life with her, and now she was gone again. Isaac turned on Bob and confronted him with everything that he had ever held back, his handsome face contorted with a rage so great that no one there could bear to look at him.

"You stole everything that ever mattered to me. How could you? How could you do it? What did I ever do? What did I do to you? I tried to make it right for Elise and Reid. I tried. I came back for them. But you lied. You took them!" he screamed.

Bob faced the man that stood before him, and he was sorry, so very sorry. He was sorry for all that he had done, all the pain that he had caused. He saw a man that had been robbed of the only woman that he ever loved, of his own child, and all because of Bob's hatred, his pride, all because Bob had been too stubborn to forgive him, to stubborn to move forward. Of course, it was wrong for Isaac and Elise to be sneaking around behind his back. Of course, it had been wrong for her to get pregnant and run away. But how much of that had he caused? He had been a self-righteous tyrant, and he had tried to control them all. And that was where everything had gone so terribly wrong. That was what brought him to right here, right now, to life without Reid. The stoic Bob Coleman crumpled before them.

He cried, and he wailed, and he let out all that he had held within him for so very long. Reagan grabbed him and held him, tried to support him. "I'm sorry," Bob cried. "Oh, God, I'm so sorry." He clutched Reagan as he cried, like he would never let him go. Reagan let him cry. Reagan stood there and held him up as he let it all out.

Then finally, high up in the mountains of the Republic of Haiti, the men began to talk. Bob confessed all that had made him the way that he was. He spoke of his own difficult upbringing, about what it had been like growing up with his father, how he had only ever wanted to protect those that he loved from what he had lived through. Reagan and Isaac listened. For the first time, Reagan saw the man through Reid's eyes. This was a man whose actions were born of fear, and Reagan actually felt sorry for him.

Isaac saw the remorse in Bob's old eyes. He felt his own pain leaving his body as he watched the old man cry. Bob told him how sorry he was, and asked for his forgiveness. Isaac was tired. He had been carrying the pain and the regret around for too long. Before he even realized what was happening, he had forgiven him.

Reagan was startled by a sound. "Shhhh," he told them.

He heard it again. It sounded like some kind of wild animal. The hair on the back of his neck stood on end. Isaac was thinking that they should keep heading in the direction of the house, but Reagan was moving toward the sound.

"What in the hell are you doing?" he asked him.

"Shhhhhhh." Reagan shushed him.

The sound reached Reagan and compelled him to come closer. He began to feel his way through the foliage and bushes. Bob and Isaac followed him. As soon as he recognized what it was, he began to fight his way through, like a madman, with Bob and Isaac right beside him. Leon and Frederic were not far behind.

There was a house. It was falling down, with trees and vines and bushes growing all around it, even inside of it. But it was a house, and the sound was coming from inside. They fought their way through the thick foliage, and inside. They came face to face with a young Haitian girl that stared through them. She held a gun. She pointed it right at them.

Reagan felt something that he could not comprehend way down deep in his gut. Then he heard the sound again. It was a baby's cry.

She stood between him and the infant. There was something terribly wrong. And the cry, the baby's cry, it haunted him.

"Please, don't shoot us. We have come to help you," he told her in Creole.

Still, she did not move. Isaac looked around. There was a distinct odor floating on the breeze. He saw two decomposing bodies in the distance. Bob saw them as well. Frederic and Leon did not move. Reagan addressed the girl in Creole again. "We are not going to hurt you. We want to help you. Is the baby okay?"

It was as if she did not even hear him. She shook all over. Then something caught her attention. It was the boots, the cowboy boots. She dropped the gun and fell at Bob Coleman's feet. She grabbed his cowboy boots and held on for her life. She began to sob. She spoke in perfect English. "She told me you would come."

Reagan made his way through the decaying house with Isaac right behind him and Bob carrying the girl. Bob held her and comforted her as she clung to him. Reagan followed the baby's cry. He walked right up to the miracle that he had begged for.

Reid lay in an iron bed, partially concealed by the foliage that permeated the house, trying to quiet the child. He went to her, unable to believe his eyes. She cried out as he took her in his arms. She was still so very fragile. He looked at her beautiful face and saw the deep gruesome scar that went from her left temple, down the side of her precious cheek, and ended just above her jaw. It had been roughly stitched together, at the hands of the small girl no doubt. She clutched him and held onto him like she would never let him go. She buried her head in his chest and smelled him. She couldn't believe it. She had prayed for nothing but to see him again, and for the baby to live. She had gotten both.

"Yisma. Yisma..." she called. "Where is Yisma? Is she okay?" she asked Reagan.

He barely even heard her. He was assessing her and the baby, looking at every inch of them. The baby was a girl.

"Is that the girl's name?" he asked.

Reid nodded.

"She's fine." he told her.

"Yisma! Yisma! Where are you?"

Bob carried the little girl closer. He sat her gently on the iron bed with Reid. The child had done her best to make Reid comfortable. She had even found clean linens, still stored in an old blanket box. They held each other and sobbed. The power of all that they had lived through was an undeniable force that permeated the room.

"I told you they would come. I told you my family would come."

The woman, the girl, and the infant were lost in a surreal embrace. The men were like props in a play that was their reality. The females before them were something that they could not comprehend, would never understand, no matter how hard they tried. Their strength and spirit such that they would never know, existing simultaneously with a tenderness and fragility that was truly something to behold.

Yisma had killed the two men that had come for them. They were child traffickers, associates of Eddie, and they wanted to protect their interests. Their rotting corpses lay just outside, a symbol for all evil to beware.

Bob watched his granddaughter and the child that had guarded her, protected her. He saw the love, compassion, and trust between them. He felt it all around him. Reid called to him. He went to her. He began to cry gut wrenching sobs that wracked his entire body.

Bob had every opportunity to make things right in Texas, but his pride held him back. And so the fall had truly come, like no one could have imagined. He sobbed uncontrollably, leaning over the side of the bed, realizing that he had been narrowly delivered from the unimaginable, from a world without her in it.

Fear, hatred, and every other dark thought left his body as the sobs wracked him. And Reid saw the truth, just as she had always known it. Bob Coleman wasn't inherently evil. He had been deceived. Deceived... Reid saw the truth filling the spaces where the lies had dwelt. He buried his face in her hair, so thankful that she was alive, so thankful that she was still breathing and still sharing this world with him. He recognized her for the first time, in the spirit that she had been given, the beautiful creature that had been dragging him, dragging them all, kicking and screaming to the light, since the day she entered the atmosphere.

They made their way back down the mountain to Frederic's little house. Reagan carried Reid. Isaac carried the baby girl. Bob held onto Yisma and helped her make the trek. She was weak from all that she had survived. He carried her for the last part of the journey, down the mountain, gently in his arms. He cradled her. He could hardly believe that the little skinny girl was capable of all that Reid had told them. He could not forget how she had collapsed at his feet when she saw his boots. He was ashamed of that scene, for he had the wisdom to know that it was him that should be at her feet, kneeling before her. It was Bob that owed her more than he would ever be able to repay. And if it took the rest of his life, he would prove to her that he was worthy, worthy of her trust, worthy of her love. He would do everything he could, to be the man that she believed him to be.

It was a matter of days before Reid found herself in a hospital with the baby. Yisma would not leave her side. There was no sign of the family that she had lived with. Their house had been destroyed in the quake. Reid and Reagan were working with the American embassy and the Haitian government to adopt her.

The little Haitian girl that Reagan found on his first night in Port Au Prince had a name. It was Marie-Anise. Her photo had been plastered all over Haiti, as well as every other country in the world, in a desperate attempt to find her family. At last, a neighbor had come forward. Marie-Anise was the lone survivor of a huge family. She was three years old. Her father had owned a grocery store. Her mother had been a teacher. She was the only one left out of their six children, out of a family of eight. Their house had fallen the night of the quake, and she had walked out of the rubble. There were no other known survivors, no grandparents, no aunts, no uncles, cousins, nothing. Reagan refused to leave her in the hands of an orphanage. She had become something of a celebrity, her notoriety making her a target. He and Reid were fighting to adopt her along with Yisma. The Haitian government had agreed to work with them.

Reid waited for Reagan to bring the World jeep around to the front of the building. She was finally leaving the hospital after receiving a clean bill of health. The baby appeared to be fine, but of course, only time would tell. Reid looked down at her baby's sleeping face. She made sure that the girls were close by. Then an overwhelming feeling of sadness came over her. Something was missing. Harvey…

Still, he had not been found. Reid would not leave Haiti without an answer. She must know what happened to him. She even hoped, against all odds, that he was out there somewhere, alive and well.

Reagan parked the jeep in front of Frederic and Sophia's home in Port Au Prince. After getting everyone settled inside the house, he took the baby and laid her on the bed. He changed her diaper. He kissed her little feet. He rubbed his face on the top of her soft, sweet little head, still unable to believe all that she had survived.

It had been four weeks since the quake struck, and still there was no sign of Harvey. They had posted his picture everywhere. World was appealing to the global audience for any trace of him. Reagan hoped for the best, but prepared himself for the worst. Reid had already told him that she would not leave until she found out what happened to him, but Reagan was worried that they may never know. As usual, Reid would not give up. "He would never leave without me, Reagan. Never."

Everyone else had returned to the States. Anna had been found, and Eric. They were out shopping for souvenirs when the quake struck. They ended up at the same hospital as Stanley, and eventually the three of them flew home together. Bob and Isaac had gone with Leon a few days before. She and Reagan would stay behind indefinitely. There was still much business to tend to...

Reid was still searching. She had no idea what she would find. She parked the jeep in front of the huge tent, looking for answers. It was obvious that Hearts and Hands had been destroyed, reduced to a pile of rubble just beyond the big blue tent. But what about the children? Had any of them survived? And Philippe? Was he still alive? The baby was crying her little heart out. Reid picked her up and swaddled her in the light cotton blanket. Then she gathered her in her arms, climbed out of the jeep, and slammed the door.

Philippe could see her bright red hair glowing in the morning sun. He could see something in her arms. A baby. Was it her baby? He ran to meet her, so happy to see her alive. He immediately noticed the scar. She felt him staring at it. Then their eyes met. "It does nothing to diminish your beauty," he told her. He kissed her cheek, softly, gently. Tears stung her eyes in answer.

"Were you buried under the rubble?"

"No," she said with a grin. "But if I told you the truth, you'd never believe it."

"Try me." His smile matched her own.

Philippe motioned for her to follow him beneath the shelter of the big blue tent, where she found the survivors of Hearts and Hands, broken, battered, but thankful to be alive. They sat there on the ground, together. She held her sleeping baby in her arms, and told him the story of all that had occurred in the moments before and after the quake struck. She told him all about the child traffickers, and about Yisma saving her life. He listened to her, amazed at how the story ended.

"So how much longer will you be here? Or are you staying for good? Has Haiti stolen your heart?" he teased.

"We'll be here for as long as it takes," she said. Then she told him all about the girls. First Yisma, then Marie-Anise. She and Reagan would not leave Haiti without them. "And then there's Harvey. I have to find out what happened to him."

Philippe looked at her. He was shocked. "Don't you know?"

"What?"

"He was here. When the quake struck, he was here. He was looking for you."

"What!"

"Yes. He had just come inside and asked if you were here, when we saw the room beginning to shake. We escaped as the roof was coming down. He helped me to dig every child out of the rubble, dead or alive. Then we went to the mission, together, to see if there was anything that we could do."

Reid could not believe what she was hearing. The baby began to stir. She was hungry. Reid began to nurse her under the cover of the soft pink blanket.

"The mission was completely destroyed, but we could hear the children crying within. So we began digging, pulling out everyone that we could find. While Harvey was working to free little Benson, there was an aftershock. He hurled the boy to safety, just as the walls came down."

Philippe could see the sorrow in Reid's cold hard stare. He could see her struggling to come to terms with all that he had revealed. Philippe felt his own tears begin to fall, remembering... "There was no suffering, Reid. It was instant."

Then he whispered the words that would both comfort and destroy her, "It was a good death..."

Reid's heart stopped. She looked at the sleeping child at her breast. Some had been saved, but so many had been lost. Harvey was gone. He was gone...

But whether she wanted it to or not, the world continued to turn. Reid stroked her infant daughter's face. Her tears fell onto the child as she waited for Jillian's plane to arrive. Harvey had been gone for almost a month, and yet she had only found out yesterday. She called Jillian as soon as she heard the news.

Reid watched, as Jillian Finn came walking toward her. She shed no tears. Reid could not help but smile. Harvey would be laughing hysterically if he could see his wife right now. She was dressed impeccably in a black Chanel suit, so sophisticated, so New York, and so totally out of place. She kissed Reid and looked at the beautiful baby girl. Reid was the first to speak.

"How was your flight?"

"Impossible. How are you doing?" she asked Reid.

"I'm a wreck."

"Well, the baby is absolutely beautiful."

Jillian put her hand on Reid's back and maneuvered her out of the crowd of passengers that had just arrived. They walked to the waiting jeep and drove straight to the mountain where Reid had spent her days after the quake. Jillian was shocked by Haiti's beauty. She never expected it. They came to a stop. Then together they hiked, with the baby in a sling, to the spot where Harvey had been buried.

It was the same spot where Reagan had been standing when he heard the infant cry.

The view was breathtaking. Jillian could see all the way to the Caribbean Sea. "Oh, Reid, this is perfect."

Reid held the baby tight and said a silent prayer of thankfulness for Harvey. She would miss him so very much. Life would never be the same without him. Jillian paused, then silently said her own goodbyes, made her own peace.

Reid was taken aback by the matter-of-fact way that she was handling the death of her husband. Jillian looked out at the land below, the place where her beloved husband had lost his life. "Reid, you have got to let it go. You should not be grieving like this. It's just not healthy."

Reid was shocked. She could not believe what she was hearing. "Jill, I loved him so much. You know that. And even worse, I feel responsible. Harvey was looking for me when the quake struck. I was out trying to catch some bad guys on my own, and he was trying to save me."

Jillian shook her head. "Oh, Reid, don't you see? He was alive again, fearless, not wasting a single moment, up until his very last breath."

"I just keep thinking that if I had stayed at Le Maison, if I was with him, then things might have been different."

"And then what? He would have slowly wasted away in some hospital, with everyone coming in and blubbering over him, been buried in some perpetual care cemetery upstate?" Jillian shook her head, "Not Harvey. That would never do. This is exactly the way he would have wanted it."

Reid was confused. "What?"

Jillian answered the blank look on Reid's face. "Oh, my gosh. You don't know, do you?" She gasped. It was clear to her that Reid had no idea.

"Right before you left for Texas, Harvey was diagnosed with a tumor on his brain stem, inoperable. They only gave him a couple of months to live, told him that he would probably go blind first, then become paralyzed, if he survived the seizures. He said it would never get him. He was going to fight it all the way."

Reid could not believe what she was hearing. She thought about her best friend, and all the times that he had right there beside her. She remembered him walking into her hospital room, in Texas, with an armload of flowers, how tightly he had held her, so thankful and relieved to find her in one piece. She remembered the look on his face as he walked toward her that day at the airport, the same day that they had left for Haiti. He knew. He knew then that life was no longer a certainty, and realized that it never really had been. She thought about how he had fallen in love with Haiti's children, and how he had given his life to save them.

Thankfulness filled the depths of her soul for the man that had been her very best friend. To love him and to be loved by him had been such a beautiful thing.

"I didn't know. He never told me," Reid whispered. "Oh, Jill, I just can't imagine my world without him in it."

Jillian Finn smiled at her. "Yeah, I know. The world won't be nearly as exciting, and the light won't be nearly as bright."

The two of them took one last look at the magnificent view, and then walked away. Reid handed the sleeping infant to Jillian, who held her all the way back to Port Au Prince.

The world continued to turn. Reid bought a small building that was already on its way to becoming a school and dormitory for The Light, a rescue operation for orphans and restaveks. Little Benson was to be the face of the school. He was the first student, the first occupant. He smiled when he saw himself in his uniform. Reid would not leave Haiti until the operation was off the ground and running.

She and Benson were going to make a change in the world, one child at a time.

Jillian donated the entire sum of Harvey's life insurance policy to get it going. Even so, Reid recognized that it would not be easy. Until The Light became self sufficient, it would take extensive resources to keep it running. It didn't matter though. She was in it for the long haul. Reid was not building a charity organization. She was building a future. She would teach the children how to support and sustain themselves. They would get through it, one day at a time. For Reid learned a long, long time ago that there wasn't enough money in the world that could bring true reform and freedom. She had learned that true reform and freedom exists in the hearts and minds of a select few that can conceive of it, and it is up to those precious few to exhaust every possibility in the hope of making a change for good, for light. She and Benson would do just that, or at the very least never give up trying.

The black Range Rover turned onto the narrow dirt road. Wild flowers bloomed on all sides, as far as the eye could see. Bluebonnets, Indian Blanket, Texas Paintbrush, Black-eyed Susan... The dust began to trail out behind them. Reid watched it in the rear view mirror. Yisma smiled at her from the back seat. The little girl looked beautiful in her new pink dress with the satin collar. Her hair was neatly braided in a style that complimented the high forehead and perfect cheekbones that Reid never grew tired of looking at. Her pretty lips were parted in a grin, exposing her perfect white teeth. Her dark eyes danced as Reid whispered that they were almost there. She was the most beautiful little girl that Reid had ever seen. In spite of all that she had lived through and all that she had witnessed, she was still so much a little girl. She was a little girl with hopes and dreams, a little girl with a past, and a little girl that finally had a future...

Marie-Anise clutched Yisma's hand. She smiled in anticipation. Her ivory lace dress had been a gift from Margaret, and she looked absolutely beautiful in it. She grinned at the back of Reagan's head. She knew he was watching her from the visor mirror.

The baby was asleep in her car seat. Reid saw the sunlight playing on the top of her tawny curls.

Reid reached for Reagan's hand as he rode quietly in the passenger seat. She had insisted on driving the last leg of the journey. She just couldn't sit still.

She pushed the button to release the Rover's windows. The wind rushed in and rustled her wild red hair. She pulled Texas deep down into her lungs. Tracy played in the background, If Not Now...

She turned into the driveway of the old farmhouse and smiled at the oaks that lined the drive in welcome. She parked the vehicle and paused to consider the sweetness of the moment. Then she got her family out of the car, and together they walked up the steps to the front door. Yisma turned to see the creek behind her. She couldn't wait to investigate it.

The front door opened. Bob and Isaac grabbed Reagan, and the three embraced. It was an embrace that said, "I am more than glad to see you." It was an embrace that said, "We have done something together that no one will ever understand."

All of Reid's family was there. Nana, Gram, Papa, her mother, Ron, her father, Aunt Frankie, Uncle Clint, Karen, Uncle Bobby, the boys, Aunt Annalyn, her girls, Ruth, even Pauline and Cora Bell...

She smiled through her tears as the women converged and freed Zyga from the locks of her car seat. The baby began to cry. They had awakened her from the serenity of her dreams and grabbed her into their loving arms. Crazy women in all their flawed glory... Reid was happy just watching them. Life would be different for Zyga. For all that they had been through, she would be free. She would be free...

Reid's eye was drawn to the front door. Someone had left it open. She moved to close it, but then stopped for a moment and looked down the length of the driveway at Anneville Road. It called to her, but she wasn't lost anymore. She knew exactly where she was going, because she knew exactly where she had been. She had learned so much. She had learned that everyone has an Anneville Road.

She stepped onto the front porch of the old farmhouse. She touched her cheek and felt the deep scar that would be with her for the rest of her days. Her mother came to stand beside her, holding Zyga in her arms. Gram saw them and followed with Marie-Anise, then Nana holding Yisma's hand. The seven of them stood there together on the front porch, strong and steady, looking out at Anneville Road. Ruth came to join them. She bent and kissed Zyga's little forehead, then took Yisma's other hand. They stood there in peaceful solidarity, women joined together by a force that can never be explained. A force that just is...

Each one of them had been shaped and molded by the living, breathing, beautiful moments in time that testify of the living. They had been through so much, each one in their own right. No doubt there was still more to come. But as they looked down the road that led out into the world, they felt peace. For each one of them knew, deep within that special part of them that was female, that in spite of all the bad, there was still some good. And no matter how dark the world might seem sometimes, the faint light that shines through the darkness is worth chasing. The light is worth fighting for. The light is worth dying for. And they knew that they would never grow tired of chasing it, of finding it. So they bid goodbye to Anneville Road that day, and sought the shelter of the old farmhouse. They would spend some time together, gaining strength from one another, laughing, crying, and loving, in this beautiful place we call life.

39950340R00275

Made in the USA
Middletown, DE
29 January 2017